Certainly Will Die

by

Amey Zeigler

Certainly Will Die

Cover Art by *Jennifer Greeff*

The Wild Rose Press, Inc.
PO Box 708
Adams Basin, NY 14410-0708
Visit us at www.thewildrosepress.com

Publishing History
First Edition, 2022
Trade Paperback ISBN 978-1-5092-4414-0
Digital ISBN 978-1-5092-4415-7

Published in the United States of America

Dedication

To my sister Merilee, the real-life Andy Baker

Chapter 1

Andy Miller lied. A thrill of excitement trilled up her spine. Hiding behind a food truck dressed as a biker chick and directing an operation wasn't exactly keeping her promise to her maybe-boyfriend Christiaan Johannson to stop investigating. A slow grin rose to her lips. Andy missed the anticipation of bringing in bad guys.

With thundering heartbeat, she tightened her do-rag on her forehead and scratched under the long blonde wig of her biker persona. Scents of slow-cooked lamb floated on the warm Texas breeze in the gravel lot in south Austin.

Even though Nikki's only opened a month ago, the two Greek brothers who owned the business, Nikki and Gaspar, hosted a lengthy line spreading clear across the food court and down South Congress.

Nikki's food was good, but it wasn't *that* good. All her senses were on alert. Distrust, more than hunger, roiled in her stomach.

Three and a half years ago, after her father mysteriously disappeared, Andy took up his mantle, and his pen name—Andrew Baker—as an undercover investigative journalist busting crime in St. Louis. After she ratted out the Mafia, she changed her identity, became a food blogger, and promised to stop investigating. Yet when her friend, Paco De La Cruz, ate at this food truck earlier this week and wound up so sick he had to be hospitalized, she trusted her instincts to investigate. Was the illness food poisoning or something more sinister?

"You in place?" she asked Hin Cho through her comms unit. Holding her breath, Andy squeezed between two trucks parked near the wooden fence separating the gravel food court lot from the brick-and-mortar business next door.

"I'm about to order." Hin Cho's voice crackled. "You know, I'm going to miss American food while I'm in Europe."

Andy grinned. "Liar. Although after you eat Scottish haggis, you'll be begging for a hamburger." The small space between the rows of parked food trucks had plenty of hiding spots.

"I really miss me some good phoenix talons."

"Ugh, aren't those chicken feet?" Breathing steadily with anticipation, Andy leaned her back against a cupcake food truck. The scent of vanilla wafted on the wind. She dug into her backpack for a small bottle of olive oil.

"They're tasty and good for your skin."

"No, thank you." Andy peeked from behind the cupcake truck's AC unit and thumbed the container of oil. "Just remember…don't actually eat the gyro. You don't want to wind up in the hospital like Paco."

"Indeed."

The door to Nikki's shut. Footsteps crunched away on the gravel.

Tensing, Andy nodded. "Nikki just left for his break." He always took a fifteen-minute break at two.

"And Gaspar is finishing with the other order. I'm

almost up."

"While he's distracted with your order, I'm going in." She swallowed hard. The timing had to be perfect.

"I'm up."

"All right. It's show time." Outside, Andy lubed the hinges with the oil and dropped the bottle in her bag. Without so much as a squeak, she cracked open the back door to a sliver. Calming her nerves with a silent breath, Andy eased her head through the door. Intense aroma hit her with full force—onions, ripe tomatoes, and feta cheese. A burble came from her stomach. Using a mirror from her pocket, she peeked around the countertop.

With head bent, the hulking Greek hunched over the toppings next to the cash register and spread *tzatziki* across a pita. A gold necklace slipped from his shirt. He ran a wrist across his sweating brow. Then he faced the rotating lamb on a vertical spit on the far side of the truck. With a large knife, he cut strips which fell onto a fluffy pita. After distributing onions, tomatoes and sauce, he wrapped up the gyro in paper and handed it to the waiting customer. He faced the cash register.

Hin Cho stepped closer to the window. "Ooh, everything looks so good. You don't mind if I take a minute to decide."

With an exhalation, Gaspar leaned against the cash register and glanced at the long line behind her. "Sure."

Crouching, Andy pocketed the mirror and snaked through as far as her shoulders. Maneuvering in a leather jacket, biker chaps, and boots was no easy feat. She might have to rethink this disguise in the future.

The truck was as clean as she expected. Warehouse-size containers of condiments lined one shelf under the cashier's desk. To her right, another was filled with plasticware and napkins.

Paco showed signs of botulism, but the bacterial test results weren't back yet. What else could cause respiratory distress? Listeriosis from unrefrigerated feta? She needed a sample to process in a lab.

All the way inside, Andy breathed shallowly. Nervous tremors rankled her. If she found evidence of mishandling food, she could report them to the health department. This news would create a stir on her food blog.

"All right." Hin Cho nodded. "I want the number one with all the fixings."

"Five seventy-four." When finished with the gyro, Gaspar shook his dark locks.

"Oh." Hin Cho huffed.

Good, good. Andy needed Hin Cho to stall so Andy could peek in tubs behind Gaspar.

"Can I also get a bottled water?" Hin Cho mumbled.

Andy froze. The bottled water was behind him—right around the corner from where Andy knelt. What was Hin Cho doing?

"Uh, sure." Gaspar nodded.

With heartbeat thundering in her ears, Andy ducked and tucked herself into the doorway behind the counter. Did he see her? With every muscle in her body tensed, she waited with her head tucked into her drawn-in knees. One breath…two breaths. She was safe. She exhaled a wavering breath.

Why did Hin Cho order something else? With shaking hands, she raised her head.

Hin Cho counted changed through the comms unit.

Andy only had seconds left to inspect and grab something. While still on the floor, she nabbed a container of feta and tucked it into her backpack. Andy heard the crunch of the gravel of the next person stepping up to the counter.

"Number seventeen." At the window, a man coughed.

A start sparked through her. No menu item number seventeen existed. She tucked herself into the doorway behind the counter and peeked out with the mirror.

Instead of pivoting to the line with lettuce, tomatoes, and cheese waiting in clear plastic tubs, Gaspar bent and grabbed a white brick sitting under the cash drawer and placed it solidly in a paper bag. He didn't grab a brick of vacuum-sealed white paper napkins, either.

The block was heroin. She recognized the drug packed in plastic hundred-gram bricks. She'd heard about secret menus, but this item topped them all!

The customer stuffed a wad of cash into Gaspar's fist, and the till overflowed with bills.

Dropping the feta, Andy inhaled. Sweat prickled her armpits. Paco didn't have bacteria. He experienced an accidental drug overdose. She'd better leave fast. Last year, she and Christiaan had a nasty run-in with a Mexican drug cartel, and she didn't want to repeat the experience. With her hand on the door, Andy retreated and closed the door quietly.

Outside, someone tapped her shoulder.

Andy spun.

Nikki's dark brows furrowed. "What are you doing here?"

With adrenaline rushing, Andy blurted out the first

thing that popped into her food-blogger head. "Your *tzatziki* sauce is amazing."

He glanced between the door and Andy. "It's not that good."

"I just want the recipe."

His dark eyes narrowed to slits. "Did you see inside?"

"Me? No, I uh, just got here and—" Blast! She lost her ability to lie with any kind of credibility.

He swung a clenched fist.

Andy easily side-stepped his clumsy haymaker, but the truck and propane tank trapped her within his reach.

Then he flicked a knife from his pocket.

As if a knife threatened her. Andy grinned and arched her brow. Though, she didn't have much room to maneuver between the fence, the tank, and the truck. She swung a leg forward in a downward heel kick and caught Nikki's knife with a heavy biking boot.

The knife fell to the gravel.

He stumbled back.

With feet crunching in the rocks, Andy circled to the front of the truck and busted through the line of waiting customers. Ignoring the cries of protest, Andy briefly wondered how many people in line knew about the "secret menu." "Call the police!" Holding her wig in place, Andy ran toward Hin Cho. The biker chaps weighed on her thighs and slowed her down.

Hin Cho got on her phone.

Looking over her shoulder, she saw Nikki and Gaspar rounding the corner behind her. Her biking chaps weighed on her legs. Running away would be impossible. She stopped and stood her ground.

Nikki recovered his blade and slashed it in front of

him near Andy's face.

Andy jumped aside, narrowly avoiding his slice. Snatching his wrist, she twisted his arm in a joint-lock and knocked the knife free. She dropped him and ground his face into the gravel.

Gaspar snagged her wig.

Cool air breezed across her head. Oh no! Her disguise was compromised. With strands of blonde hair caught under the backpack shoulder straps, the wig cap hit her shoulder. She snatched it and plopped it back on. Her identity meant everything right now.

Hin Cho hit Gaspar with a superman punch.

Staggering, he doubled over.

This! This kind of a fight was what Andy missed— the thrill of matching with a foe and discovering truth. She searched for her next hit.

Usually chill Hin Cho jumped on Nikki's back and grabbed his neck as he attempted to stand.

Gagging, Nikki swung her around until her feet hit a waiting customer in the jaw.

The man, who stood about six-four and weighed about two-fifty, stumbled into an unwitting elderly lady behind him. Shoving and yelling ensued.

Andy reattached her wig with both hands.

Throwing off Hin Cho, Nikki threw an uppercut into Andy's middle.

Hot pokers shattered through her ribs. She doubled over from both pain and shame. Heat flamed her cheeks. Too much time had passed since she'd been in a good fight. She was a better fighter than this. She curled her fists. Once Andy could breathe, she surveyed the scene.

Chaos had spread. Customers fought one another.

Nikki broke through the line, running away.

Hin Cho gave chase and landed a flying kick in Nikki's thigh.

He collapsed.

"She might be small," Andy said to no one in particular. "But man, she can fight." Jogging to catch up, Andy kicked Nikki in the ribs while he was down. "That's for Paco." She hoped he would make it out of the hospital. At least, she had an answer to his illness.

Police swooped in on bicycles. A squad car arrived with sirens blaring.

Customers scattered like cockroaches in the light.

Well, that answered that question. A lot of people knew about the heroin.

"She started it!" A teenage girl with a phone pointed toward Andy. "I videoed the whole thing."

Scowling, Andy approached police officer talking to the girl. "Come with me." Holding her aching rib, she waved to the police and opened the back of the truck. "Heroin."

"We can take it from here." The officer picked up the pained Nikki and cuffed him.

Andy leaned against the truck to catch her breath. The officer had no idea she had put dozens of bad guys behind bars. "The brother escaped."

"Yeah, we'll find him. Haroldsen, search the truck." The officer turned toward the food truck. "Thanks. You can go back to your life now."

She unhitched herself from the truck. Heat broiled in her gut. Busting criminals *was* her life. But she couldn't go back. She could only go forward. "But I think we can—"

"Thanks. Let the *professionals* do their job."

Puffing out his chest, he thrust up his chin.

"I can help. I'm a—" She stopped herself.

"What?" His eyes narrowed.

With the Mafia still after her, she couldn't go back home, couldn't use her real name, do any investigating, or even be seen as herself in public anywhere in America. If she did, the Mafia would find and kill her— or worse. Then she'd never earn her university degree and work for the CIA to find her father. Andy gulped. "Nothing." Shaking her head, she slapped her thigh.

"That's what I thought." He joined other officers writing down witnesses' testimonies.

Hin Cho touched her elbow. "You did great."

Andy blew out a whoosh of breath. Pain racked her ribs. She rubbed them. "Thanks for your help. We found out what made Paco sick, busted a heroin ring, and started a riot. I'd say we've had a productive day." She elbowed her friend. Working with someone had perks. "And I failed. I put you in harm's way. I'm sorry. I promised your sister I'd take care of you."

Hin Cho batted the air. "Ah, she's all the way over in Kowloon. She couldn't have kept me safer."

"She's a better fighter than I am, for sure." Andy sucked her teeth and pulled an exaggerated frown. Although Andy was so proud of her sixth-degree black belt, she knew when someone's skills outmatched her own. "Now you're going to Europe without me. When do you leave?"

Hin Cho jabbed a thumb over her shoulder. "I have my clubs in the car. I'm heading to the airport right now."

Despite the pain in her side, Andy huffed. "You always have your clubs."

"Just trying to make a name for myself in amateur golf." Hin Cho swung her long hair over a shoulder.

Andy arched a brow. "You're already well-respected for your restoration of beryl minerals. I still need an undergrad degree." The sooner Andy applied to the CIA, the faster she'd find out what happened to her dad.

Across the lot, Nikki, who had been bloodied and bruised by petite Hin Cho, covered his head with his shirt to escape the news cameras and cell phones.

Andy nodded toward the crowd. "Let's check out the arrest." She followed the police.

Lowering his shirt, Nikki spat words in Greek as one of the officers stuffed him in the squad car. His eyes blazed. "I'll get you for this. This is not the end." He shouted over his shoulder. As he left the lot, Nikki glared out the window.

Gulping, Andy froze on the gravel. Terror raked through her. The mobsters said the same thing after the conviction hearing.

"Hey, you okay?" Hin Cho asked.

"Yeah. Just remembering something," she murmured. The echo of Nikki's threat replaced any thought. She trembled. They would come after her. Just like the St. Louis mobsters. This conflict was not over.

****

"I'm here to see Fabian. Caspian sent me." Christiaan stood on the limestone stoop and waited for someone to read the message he slipped through the mail slot in the tall oak door of a mansion in the Eighth arrondissement in Paris. Down the street were the hottest name brand shops. Darkness fell hours ago. These kinds of criminals worked in the night.

Two armed men opened the door.

He stepped into the mansion's cut marble entryway. The tall ceilings echoed every footstep.

Christiaan held his hands over his head, while his legs and chest got the pat-down. Velvet curtains blackened the front, street-side windows and dampened the sound and the light. Christiaan smelled money—lots of money.

The second guard with reddish hair extracted a jangling ring from Christiaan's left pocket. "Keys?"

"To my apartment."

The guard returned them. He searched Christiaan's right pocket. "Twine?" He pulled a spool from another pocket.

"I was out of laundry cord." Since his last case in the States, he had been in the habit of carrying around more stuff. Not in a red weekender tote as Andy did, of course, which would've been way too conspicuous, but he pocketed useful things—just in case.

The first man grabbed the twine and placed it in his own suit breast pocket. "I'll keep that." Then the man flicked a metal bracelet around Christiaan's wrist. "What's this?" He pointed the tip of his semi-automatic to Christiaan's chest.

Christiaan shrugged. "Jewelry."

The man arched a brow and narrowed his eyes.

"What? A man can't wear jewelry? Equality, remember?"

Finished frisking Christiaan's legs, the other guard stood. "He's only carrying cash. He's clean."

"*Allons-y.*"

The curious one escorted him upstairs. Paintings, impossible to discern between imposters or masters without professional training, hung above wainscoted walls. Thick, gilded crown moldings encircled the ceilings, and decorative cornices finished the corners.

The escort knocked on tall double doors and waited.

A woman dusted what appeared to be a Ming vase on a massive pedestal. Christiaan waved hello.

Seeing them, she backed into another doorway.

"*Entre*," a voice called from inside.

The wooden door creaked open. Another armed man welcomed them inside with a nod of an unshaven chin.

"You might want to oil those hinges." Christiaan hoped for a smile, but no dice.

The armed man stared with dark, bulging eyes.

Behind a desk sat a dark-haired, and rather skinny, Frenchman. A European-cut suit hugged his small frame. Dark circles under his eyes and his unshaven face bespoke an utter lack of attention to his health. Not to mention he held a cigar between his lips.

Fabian snuffed out the cigar in a crystal dish on his wide mahogany desk.

The taint of smoke lingered in the air. Everything in the room dampened the sound—from the padded walls to the carpet. No windows, either, he noticed. Fabian filled the shelves behind his desk with a smoothed rock sculpture, one golden, Imperial Fabergé egg, a marble bust, and several decorative books. Counterfeit or not, it was an impressive collection. "Nice pad you've got here." Christiaan's feet sank into a Persian carpet.

The two guards flanked Christiaan, guns still at the ready.

Fabian blew out the last of his smoke. "I enjoy keeping up with my neighbors."

Fabian's neighbors were some of the wealthiest in the world. His French accent punctuated his words. Christiaan coughed. "Indeed."

"And what can I do for you?" Fabian squinted.

Remaining calm, Christiaan raised his chin. "Caspian told me where to find you. I have a question about something you've recently acquired."

Fabian arched an eyebrow and tugged at his cufflinks. "Caspian sent you, eh?"

"We're old friends." Christiaan used the term friends loosely. Last time he spoke with Caspian, Christiaan left him with two broken legs.

"I don't have friends. I have allies. Keeps me out of the Bastille. What have you come for?" Fabian leaned back in his chair.

"Emeralds."

Fabian pressed his hands against the leather armrests. "I am fresh out of emeralds at the moment, but I'll put you on my waiting list. Now, if you'll excuse me…"

Christiaan stepped forward. "I'm searching for two matching emeralds. Stolen from a museum in Cairo and ended up in your hands. Caspian says you have friends who don't ask questions about specialty goods and rare finds. Who bought these emeralds?"

"My client list is one of my closest guarded secrets." Fabian's gaze flicked away. "Mara?" He raised his voice.

Christiaan turned.

A young woman stood behind Christiaan. Her dirty blonde hair covered her face. With a nod, she slipped through the double doors at the back.

"My tea, Mara."

How had Christiaan missed the young woman with slumped shoulders in the shadows? He mentally kicked himself. He was losing his touch. In his line of work, being aware of everyone in the room meant life or death. Anyone could be an assassin. Facing Fabian, Christiaan dislodged stacks of euros from his pockets and laid them on Fabian's desk. "I'm sure with enough persuasion, you can forget your loyalty."

Fabian eyed the growing mound of cash. "How much?"

"Enough to make it worth your while."

Mara entered again. She placed the tray before Fabian and opened the napkin over his lap. She whipped back her hair. Pink scars marred her face.

Although striking, the scars didn't distract from her simple beauty.

Fabian leaned forward. "Time for my afternoon tea."

The young woman poured the tea then glanced toward Christiaan. Her eyes widened. She dropped her jaw. She over-poured, spilling hot tea on Fabian's lap.

Swearing, he jumped up from his seat. The dark stain on the front of his pants steamed. "*Imbécile!*" A rash of foul French tumbled from his puckered lips. He blasted the woman across the ear with his forearm.

Her whole body moved with the force. Scowling, Mara grasped the scarred side of her face. She mopped up the excess, then bowed and backed out of the room, clutching her ear.

Christiaan clenched his fist, ready to take action, yet stopped himself. If he removed Fabian now, he'd never find the emeralds. The emeralds were key to his revenge.

"Prepare a fresh pair of pants." Fabian straightened his tie and sat again. "Where were we?"

"You were telling me about the Cairo emeralds."

Fabian scowled and poured his own tea into his cup. "I do not ask where they find the jewels. I reset them and sell them to clients who care more about quality and discretion than origin."

Christiaan stepped forward. "Where are the emeralds Caspian sold you in December?"

The two guards stopped him with the tips of the guns.

Fabian sneered. "I. Won't. Expose. My. Client. List." He dropped a lump of sugar in his tea with each word.

Raising his brows, Christiaan mentally turned up his nose at the overly sweetened tea. "Then tell me where the emeralds could be, and I'll find them." Perhaps Fabian would respond to softness.

Stirring his tea, Fabian huffed. He tapped the spoon on the edge of the cup and placed it on the saucer. "You going to steal stolen emeralds?" A hint of a smile touched his lips.

"Who will report them stolen?" Christiaan shrugged.

Raising his eyebrows for a split second, Fabian sipped his tea. "You have a point." His eyes flitted to the ornate metal bracelet encircling Christiaan's left wrist.

Christiaan moved his hands behind his back. "If they are in a setting, the rest might fall back into your lap."

Fabian returned his teacup to his saucer. "You can't cut them, you know. They are too fragile and have too many fissures. They will break." He lifted his cup again.

"I don't want to cut them."

Fabian's eyes glittered over the top of his teacup, steam distorting his face. "Have you heard of one who can heal emeralds?"

"No." Stepping closer, Christiaan inclined his head. "What do you mean?"

"The Chinese government is searching for the scientist who can heal the emeralds with a formula of oil, emerald dust, and heat to fill the identifying fissures of the gem. I, too, search for this person. I will be first. You see, stealing emeralds is a tricky business. Fissures are well-known—some even recorded. But imagine if they could be returned to a flawless state. They would be disguised and sold on the open market. And they'd fetch quite a price."

Christiaan's brow dripped with sweat. The French didn't believe in air conditioning. "I have no interest in healing the emeralds." In fact, healing these emeralds was the last thing he wanted.

"Too bad." He shrugged and set aside the tea.

This conversation was getting him nowhere. "The Cairo emeralds?" Christiaan slid the stack of euros closer, tempting his greed.

With both arms, the Frenchman gathered the notes toward him on the desk, like a dragon collecting jewels. A thin, wide smile appeared on his lips. "No. I do not think I will tell." He nodded toward the two men.

Dread clenched Christiaan's stomach, but he remained calm. "Thank you." He turned to leave.

The two men held his upper arms.

A colossal mistake. Busting the thin plastic case around his disk-shaped chakram, Christiaan slammed the lethal razor blade encircling his wrist into the right captor's nose.

The thug screamed and clutched his bloodied face.

The other still held firm and lifted his semi-automatic.

After disabling him with a joint lock to his arm and a slam to his head from his knee, Christiaan disarmed his gun, then tossed it away.

"You fools." Fabian stood, his pinched voice rising. "I told you to search him thoroughly." He picked up his phone.

In one swift movement, Christiaan grasped the shoulders of the second man and kneed him in the face, then side-kicked the other in his chest. Then with a jump spin-kick, he knocked him unconscious with a blow to the head.

The first man returned.

Christiaan sliced him again, deeper, diagonally across the bridge of his nose with the chakram.

He stumbled back, his hands protecting the cut.

Searching the downed man's breast pocket, Christiaan retrieved his twine before knocking him unconscious with a severe blow to his neck. From the corner of his eye, he noticed Fabian on his cell phone. Releasing the chakram from his wrist, he spun it on his finger while backing toward the door.

The Frenchman's eyes grew wider as the chakram gained momentum with a whirring sound.

With a flick of his wrist, Christiaan sent the circular chakram across the room where it sliced both the fingers and the phone in Fabian's hand—the hand that slapped Mara—and embedded into the leather chair behind him.

The broken phone fell to the ground.

Fabian bellowed, but the sound would stay in the soundproof room.

Christiaan slid out the doors. He searched for something to block the outward swinging doors. He could tie the doorknobs together with twine. But with enough force, the twine would easily be broken.

The massive pedestal.

Grunting, he shoved the Ming vase with pedestal, scraping it along the parquet floors in front of the doors. Now to disarm the men at the front door and exit quietly.

"Help me."

Christiaan spun.

Mara ducked into the shadowed doorway of another hall. Blood dribbled from her ear canal onto her neck. A few drops of blood dotted her white shirt. The shadows exaggerated her rippled scars.

She was older than she appeared, in her twenties, maybe. Christiaan stepped toward her. "What do you need?"

"Help me get out of the house."

He checked the office door. The Ming would buy him time. But not a lot. "Are you running away?"

Her large brown eyes gleamed. Her eyebrows peaked and rippled her forehead. "I need to get out of here."

Urgency laced her voice. He hesitated for a moment. Fabian gave her quite a beating. She was Fabian's girl, and his goons would be on him like gum to the bottom of a shoe on a hot summer day if he left with her. "Sorry. I can't take you."

"I know where the emeralds are."

He arched an eyebrow. "Still, it would be kidnapping."

"We are already kidnapped."

"We?" His eyes widened. Mara wasn't his girlfriend or his daughter. She was enslaved. And there were others. "How many of you are there?"

"Seven."

Christiaan let out a low whistle. Saving one girl would be tricky. Seven would be a circus, not to mention riskier for all of them.

Mara's eyes widened. "Some of us, Fabian's men stole from their homes as children and traded and collected us like objects. Like his art."

If he would risk freeing one girl, he might as well free them all. Below them in the vast lobby, two men guarded the door, blocking the exit. He took her shoulders with a gentle touch. "Gather them up. Quickly and quietly." He didn't know how long before the men upstairs would regain consciousness and help Fabian recover from the shock of losing his fingers and escape the room.

"Is there a back door?" Christiaan needed more options.

"Twenty-five men patrol the garden and the side entrances."

He chewed his lip. "We'll go out the front. Tell the others to escape through the lobby." He paced and tapped his chin.

A man stepped from the shadows with a gun.

Since he was only an arm's length away, Christiaan

disarmed him silently, then trapped the goon's neck, rendering him unconscious. Hiding in the shadows, he bit his lip. How could he rescue all these people? He was a man of action, not a planner.

Closing his eyes, he channeled Andy. What would she do with keys and twine? She proved herself quite clever when they worked together in St. Louis.

Sliding down the darkened stairs, he disarmed the first guard with a surprised joint lock and Russian Sambo move. He blocked the second attack, knocking the gun from the thug's hands with a kick then threw him down with a judo move. He tied them with the twine and gagged them with their own neckties. The front lobby was now secure. He could just leave right now, and he'd be free. Yet he had to rescue seven lost souls. Energy coursed through him. They didn't have much time.

Inspiration or stupidity gave him an idea. With haste, he slipped out his keys from his ring, one by one. Upstairs, the doorknobs started wiggling.

From the shadows at the back of the house, the first prisoner braved the lobby—the hunched older lady who dusted the Ming.

"Meet at the café on the corner of..." Mara whispered then dove back into the shadows.

The elderly lady hobbled across the lobby toward the front door. With widened eyes, she glanced all around. "Are you the rescuer?" she asked Christiaan in Russian.

Christiaan didn't nod. "Hurry," he said in Russian.

"Aren't you coming, too?"

"When everyone else is safe."

She patted his cheek and passed the threshold into

the night.

Thinking of Andy, he quickly tied twine onto each of the holes in the keys with a square knot. Then at the top of the massive staircase, he dug four keys into the grout between the marble stairs and the mahogany woodwork. He looped twine through the holes at the top of the keys and circled the wooden balustrade spindles opposite the wall. Four trip-lines crossed the dimly lit stairs. He grinned. He'd have to tell Andy about this trick someday. He stood and opened the door. He swept the room with his gaze.

A second person entered, a tall, gangly young girl about sixteen with raw and red hands. Her eyes shone with tears.

The third and fourth came together.

Christiaan patrolled the hallways for any other perpetrators. He knocked out a man with a gun and tied him up as the others. He paced and breathed deeply to keep himself calm.

Hovering in the corner, Mara waited for the fifth one, a boy about fourteen to cross the foyer. His cast-down gaze focused on the ground.

Above Christiaan, the Ming vase shattered on the marble floor, and the pedestal fell with a crash.

The doors flew open, and Fabian, fingers wrapped and bleeding, stood at the top of the stairs. "Get them!"

Christiaan inhaled sharply. Now what?

Chapter 2

Standing in the doorway, Christiaan wiped sweat prickling on his brow. He still had one more rescue to go.

When the teenage boy slipped out, Fabian cursed. He grasped the railing with his good hand.

The last person huddled near Mara—a young girl about twelve.

No time for hesitation. Tilting up his chin, Christiaan coaxed them out into the marble-floored lobby.

"What do you think you're doing?" Fabian roared from the top of the staircase in French. His pale face and bandaged hand remained from the failed negotiations.

The dark-headed man with the diagonal slash across his face, and with more than a few bulging muscles, followed Fabian.

The slimmer man with a broken nose straggled behind them.

"Ignore them." Christiaan motioned to cross the lobby.

The girl stared with wide eyes as she ducked under his arm.

Her clothes hung off her gaunt frame. "You can trust me." His heart ached. Such neglect. He clenched his jaw.

Fingering a gun clumsily with his left hand, Fabian thundered down the stairs. "Shoot them. Shoot them all." His poorly aimed shots exploded in the wooden doors.

Christiaan held the door until Mara ducked under his arm and disappeared into the street. He faced Fabian over his shoulder. "They're safe now. Take this meeting as a warning. Never enslave people again."

Fabian and his men never reached the bottom. The three men tumbled downstairs following distinct pings. Keys ricocheted off the marble.

Christiaan slammed the door on the scene of broken arms and twisted ankles.

Fabian deserved a far worse punishment.

After fifteen minutes of evasion techniques, Christiaan slowed, assured he wasn't followed. The reality of his actions settled upon him when he entered the café.

The group of half-starved, beaten, and worn people huddled around Mara.

Mara lowered her gaze to the cobblestones. "Thank you for saving us."

"What shall we do with your friends?" He nodded toward his small band.

The older woman touched the collar of his shirt, kissed his cheeks, and thanked him again in Russian.

Many in the small crowd thanked him in different tongues. Even the young had lined faces. Sadness hollowed their eyes. Yet he was their hero—not a role he felt entirely comfortable with.

The café owner frowned and wiped his hands on the white apron around his waist. "Who will pay for these ragtags?"

"They are not ragtags, and I'll pay for whatever they want to eat." He always carried "mugger" money in his socks if he got frisked, or in this case, if someone stole the whole of his cash.

As the sun rose, he left the clamor of the café to call the police to care for these lost souls. He might have failed in his mission, but he could at least do something noble today. He leaned on the seating host's stand outside and watched the sun rays brighten the darkened city. No doubt Fabian and his outfit would be long gone by now. Those who dealt with illegal trade were slippery to pin down or find.

Christiaan stuffed his hands into his pockets and wandered to the outdoor seating. What a night! And he'd lost his favorite chakram—a worthy trade for seven souls.

But he didn't have the emeralds. Back to square one.

Mara approached, carrying a warm cup of *tissane*. "You should drink." Pulling the chair across the cobblestones, she settled on the metal seat. She handed him the cup of tea.

"Thank you." He grasped the cup. The scent of chamomile tingled his nose as he sipped. Warmth filtered through his hands.

She dropped long, slender sugar packets.

He shook his head.

"What's next?" She propped her head on her hand beside him.

He finished his sip. "You're free now. Do you need help finding your family?" The chamomile soothed and relaxed him.

"I don't have a family." She grabbed his forearm.

"I want to come with you."

Mara's blue eyes sparkled in the midst of her pink face. She was attractive, even with the scarring. Settling the cup, he smiled without pleasure. "I'm flattered. But my life is too complicated to take care of another person." He didn't have time for stragglers. Or for another woman in his life. Already he had one woman who warmed his thoughts and a fake girlfriend. Two women was one woman too many. He needed to get rid of one.

"Then how can I show my gratitude?"

Christiaan patted her hand. "Send me a greeting card every year." He didn't rescue her for the gratitude. Saving her and the others was the right thing to do. Scum like Fabian didn't deserve to live. If he had known about the girl and the others, he would've sent his chakram into Fabian's chest. Tightening he jaw, he sipped again. The warmth spread through him with the curl of steam.

Her gaze dropped. Her eyes swelled with tears. "You don't want me because of my face?"

Choking on the hot liquid, Christiaan nearly spilled his cup. "No. Why would you say that?"

"People say I'm ugly."

"You're not ugly." Christiaan softened his tone. In fact, she reminded him of someone he once knew—a long time ago. A flash of memory flittered before his eyes, but it escaped before he could capture it.

She bowed her head. Her dishwater blonde hair fell over her face. "You want to know where the emeralds are."

He froze. In the chaos of the rescue, he forgot her declaration and dismissed it as a desperate lie. As

Fabian's personal assistant, she could have some knowledge of them. He leaned toward her. "Who has them?"

Mara raised her head. "Fabian didn't say who bought them, but I know where they will be."

"Where?" Christiaan faced her.

She poked the plump sugar packets. "The client specifically requested the emeralds for a charity event at *El Real* in Madrid. Next week."

"Does Fabian know this?"

"Yes, of course. He stressed over the deadlines and yelled at his craftsmen to please his important client and to finish on time. That's why I remember so clearly."

He swore under his breath. If Fabian suspected he would be there, recovery of the emeralds might be a bit more complicated. He needed a disguise.

She picked up a sugar packet. "You couldn't get in anyway. The event at the Opera House will have heightened security. The invitation list is elusive and exclusive. Alejandra Garcia will be sponsoring the charity event."

Christiaan arched an eyebrow. "Who?"

She prodded him with a glance. "The Prime Minister of Spain."

"I have resources." He sucked down the tea.

Mara nodded. "I'm sure you do, but the ETA has been threatening violence against the Prime Minister."

"I'm well acquainted with the Basque Nationalist extremist group." They were another foe to deal with.

She grabbed his elbow. "Take me with you."

"You should return home."

Her gaze trained on him, pleading and desperate.

Christiaan dropped his gaze.

"I have no one. You saved my life. I want to go with you."

Placing the cup on the table, he grasped her hands. "You have your life back. You are young. Go, be free. If you come with me, your life will be in danger again. In more ways than one." Fabian would not easily forget this day. Christiaan stood. His metal chair scraped against the cobblestones. He pointed toward the cup. "Again, thank you."

She grabbed his forearm. "You can't toss me away that easily."

He patted her hand and gently removed it. "I'm not tossing you away. Do what you want. If I were free, I wouldn't follow me. The police are coming to help you. Isn't that wonderful?"

Sirens sounded in the distance.

Her gaze lifted to the direction of their screams. "Can I text you? I don't have a phone now, but…"

A number was easy enough to give. "All right. Here's my number. You can call or text me. The police will help you return to your life."

She folded the napkin with the number and placed it in her pocket. "I will tell the others." She disappeared into the café.

One by one, the lost, now found, souls waited at the curb as the police exited their cars.

Eliminating himself from unwanted attention and questions, Christiaan crossed the street, jumped to a low-hanging fire escape ladder, and hauled himself up to observe the crowd. Each tired and rugged face turned from fright to relief. He searched for Mara. She wasn't in the crowd. Where did she go? Why didn't she stay to be aided by police?

****

Andy climbed the stairs to her apartment. If the video of the brawl made it to the Internet, she'd have to move as soon as possible. Did the remnants of the St. Louis mobsters comb the Internet for videos containing her? She didn't want to be a sitting duck to find out. She'd have to transfer school transcripts. Again. She sighed. This move would be the second time in two months.

Maybe she should give up. Andy shook her head. What was she thinking? She could never go back to being Andrew Baker—the investigative journalist. Her dreams of joining the CIA and becoming a Master of Disguise grew more elusive every time she switched schools.

Andy halted by her door. A scent of unfamiliar cologne lingered in the hall. The hair rose on her arms. All the muscles in her body tensed. She held her breath. Her door creaked ajar with the movement of air. She backed down the stairs until she bumped into someone. Andy yelled.

The guy yelled.

Heart pounding, Andy turned.

Will, the concierge from her building, blinked. His glasses slid down his nose. Wide eyed, he pushed them up. "I didn't mean to scare you." He stared at his worn tennis shoes. "I mean, you scared me. I wasn't expecting you to back up."

"My door is open." Andy panted and grasped the banister. Tremors shook up and down her legs from the adrenaline rush. "Someone's been in there." Since moving in, Will tried engaging her in conversation.

Andy was out of excuses. Will was a nice guy, as nice as they come—a perfect ten for someone else. Andy hoped for someone different—someone far away. Did Christiaan still care? Six months was a long time.

"Oh, I went inside." He motioned to her door. "An express letter came so I placed it in your apartment."

Fully recovered, she stepped backward. "Entering my apartment without my permission is against the law."

Red spread over his face until it pinked the tips of his ears. "I know. I worried your letter might get stolen. Although it is addressed to Andy Baker."

Andy Baker? Andy's heartbeat quickened. Only Christiaan called her that. He mashed her investigative journalist pen name with her nickname. She stepped backward up more stairs. "I'd better see what it is. Thank you." She hoped to cut off any more conversation.

"Hey, I was thinking, did you want to go out tonight? I read about this really popular food truck named Nikki's Gyros. Maybe we can grab dinner there sometime."

"That's awfully nice of you, Will." Andy landed on the top stair. "But Nikki's is no longer in business. And I have to…" She couldn't think of anything final enough to get through his thick skull she wasn't interested. "Move."

That was the truth.

He pushed up his glasses. "Move?"

But Andy already bounded down the hall and cautiously entered her apartment. She kept it tidier since Christiaan mocked her mess last year.

Their investigation together in St. Louis, their

chemistry, and their kisses tingled her belly. Had it been six months since his brawny arms held her? Had it been half a year since he teased her with an offer to work for the super-secret, UN-sanctioned OverSight and yet didn't text her? Not. One. Text. When she saw him again, she'd blacken one of his perceptive blue eyes. Or worse.

The letter was worn and crinkled. Express stickers covered the outside.

How did Christiaan know her apartment address? Not even her mother knew. Andy tore at the tape encircling the envelope. Inside, she found an envelope with flight vouchers. Within the envelope was a letter. With trembling fingers, Andy slid it from the sheath.

I need your help. Pack your bags for Madrid and bring a sexy dress.

Andy glanced at the postmark. Two days ago.

You are the only one I trust.

The letter was signed simply with a drawing of a seraph—like the tattoo on his lower middle back.

Andy ran a thumb over it. Then she noticed the post script.

P.S. Don't tell anyone where you are going and what you are doing. And Andy, don't trust anyone.

Andy dropped the paper on the table and paced. "You don't call or text for six months, and I was just about over you. Then you do this! I don't know. Maybe I won't go. Maybe I'll just ignore your letter because you've ignored me." She pounded the table.

The last six months had been horrible. Every day she waited for him to text. She woke and checked the phone, hoping today might be the day she'd hear from him. After a few months of radio silence, she gave up.

She kicked a chair. She didn't want to have to forget him again. Ripping him from her heart was too hard the first time.

If he did need her help, why didn't he call Sabrina Guiterrelli? She would love to bail him out with all her access to OverSight.

Sabrina had a thing for him for sure. And he probably couldn't resist her long Italian legs, full lips, and emerald-green eyes. Why not contact *her*? He trusted Sabrina enough to enlist her aid to be his fake girlfriend. Surely, joining him in Madrid to wear a sexy dress was slightly below that.

But Christiaan had a few advantages of being employed by a super-secret spy organization. If she helped him, maybe he would help her track down her father.

Sighing, Andy picked up the phone and dialed the number on the airline vouchers. She resented being so attached to someone. She gave her whole heart to him and offered so many sacrifices for him. Perhaps she could gain something in return.

And she wasn't thinking of their last kiss, either.

She bit her lip and stared out the window at the University of Texas campus. She wanted information on her dad—why he left, where he went, and why hadn't he come home. Nearly four years had passed since he failed to return. With the phone tucked under her chin, she grabbed her red, wheeled carry-on bag.

Christiaan needed to explain why he was in Europe and dragging her into his problems. If nothing else, she wanted to slap his face and demand to know why he hadn't texted in six months.

Chapter 3

Andy's head whirled from fifteen hours of travel. Her sense of time and direction were all messed up. And Spanish was spoken everywhere. She heard phrases in Heathrow when she boarded the plane bound for Madrid, as well as at baggage claim once she landed. She hauled her little, but heavy, carry-on through customs and immigration. A bit of panic rose in her throat. She didn't speak Spanish. She'd studied a semester in Austin, but she was nowhere near fluent.

Christiaan, in khaki cargo shorts and a white T-shirt, waited on the other side of customs. His tanned and toned twenty-inch biceps slid from his short sleeves.

His piercing blue eyes shone with amusement. Just the sight of his broad shoulders and sandy-blond hair weakened her knees.

Forget butterflies—full grown condors flapped in her stomach.

He spread his arms to his sides. "*Bievenitas à Madrid.*"

Impressive perfect Castilian accent. But his charming welcome couldn't erase six months of radio silence. She slapped him hard across the face. Her hand stung.

Lowering his brow, he widened his eyes. "What was the slap for?"

She placed her fists on her hips and thrust out her chin. "For not texting for six months."

"I have my reasons." He rubbed his stubbled cheek. "That hurt."

She cast him a sideways glance. "If I really wanted to hurt you, I would've landed a jump kick in your chest. This was just a friendly hello."

"I'd hate to see an unfriendly hello." He scowled and grabbed her luggage. "I'm not surprised this weighs more than a hippo. Gah, what's in there? This bag has to be carrying more than a few wigs."

She snatched the handle. "You didn't tell me what we would be doing, so I brought everything I might need. But I will have to shop for a dress."

Crossing his arms, he stood next to a wall-sized billboard of a perfume ad and motioned toward the parking lot. "You didn't bring any clothes?"

"Nope." She barely packed underwear and a toothbrush.

He furrowed his brow. "I specifically told you to bring a sexy dress."

"I can buy a dress anywhere."

He entered the parking lot near the airport. "Then what's in the suitcase?"

"Stuff I couldn't have overnighted or obtained legally here in Europe." Tiny, brightly colored foreign cars crowded the lot.

He arched a brow. "Which would be?"

"Liquid latex, powder, makeup, etc. I packed hair strands, too. That suitcase holds an abbreviation of my old closet. I made it more portable." She raised her chin and waited for his smile.

Christiaan grinned and shook his head. "You'll

need all of those things for this." He disarmed the alarm on his car.

The hot summer sun reflected off the paint.

Andy paused before loading her bag into the trunk. "Which brings me to a great question: what are we doing?"

He tossed on his sunglasses. "Get in the car, and I'll tell you."

Andy opened her door and slid in the sun-drenched car.

Driving in the city was noisy. Cars honked, and pedestrians yelled at each other and at other cars. Street bands played.

With the convertible top down, Andy closed her eyes and breathed in the sunshine and the different smells. Perfume, exhaust from cars, and the slight scent of cigarette smoke—bitter European cigarettes, not American—greeted her nose.

When she opened her eyes, she needed her sunglasses. But she didn't want to search in her bag. Instead, she squinted in the sun to see the cathedrals and the limestone buildings with red-tiled roofs. The city seemed designed from a castle. She noticed only a few modern things—the yellow arms of the construction cranes moving around the tops of the red brick buildings. "So what are we doing?"

Christiaan kept his gaze glued to the windshield. His jaw tightened. "I worried you wouldn't help me, which is why I couldn't tell you earlier."

She huffed. He had good reason to worry. "You were afraid I wouldn't come?"

He nodded.

"A good supposition since I haven't heard from

you in half a year." She didn't ask it, but the question hung there: where did you go?

"I was busy."

Six months ago, Andy gave him her heart. In the whole world, only Christiaan understood her. She wished she could understand him. He still hid things. If only she could unwrap all of Christiaan and peel back his layers.

Behind sunglasses, his blue eyes focused on the road. A white scar split his left eyebrow in two.

He remained silent—infuriatingly quiet. She wanted an explanation. But the answers wouldn't come now. Andy sighed. "Whatever it is, I will help you, but only if you help me with something in return."

"What is that?"

"You have connections at OverSight. Help me find my father."

Christiaan bit his lip and kept his gaze on the road.

A little old lady with a cane hobbled in the crosswalk.

He stomped on his brakes and clutch, then shoved the gear shift into Neutral. After the woman passed, he shifted into gear.

"When my dad disappeared four years ago, he discovered something big. I want to know where he went. He bought tickets to Dallas, but from there, he could've gone anywhere."

"And what do you want me to do?" He checked his mirror before switching lanes.

Swallowing hard, Andy leaned closer. The whole reason she came to Europe hung on this hope. "Leverage OverSight resources to help me find him."

He frowned, crinkling his stubbled cheek.

"Americans don't appreciate us snooping around their country."

Batting at her fly-away hair, she snorted. "A lot of countries don't appreciate your snooping around." She crossed her arms and sat back into the seat. "If you don't agree, I've scheduled a return trip for tomorrow." She might have lied. Well, she slightly bluffed. But if he really needed her, he would say yes.

"I'll do what I can." Finally, he glanced her way. "I can't promise anything concrete."

"Try." She sat straighter and leaned toward him. "What did you need me for?"

"Emeralds." The muscles in his jaw twitched. He stopped at a light near an old building with a dome crowning the top.

"Huh?" Andy craned her neck to catch a view of a golden-winged statue on top.

"I need to find some emeralds."

Andy rolled her eyes. "I should've known it would've been important. Jewelry shopping?"

A smiled parted his lips. "Oh, no, we have to do more than that. Way more."

What could be so important about jewelry?

****

Andy rested in her suite for a few hours before knocking on his room in a hotel in downtown Madrid. Thankfully her sunny windows hung with heavy damask curtains to block the light. Although the fixtures were dated, as if still stuck in the 1980s gold-obsessed era, her room possessed thick carpet, real wood dressers, and artwork that didn't seem painted by a first grader.

Once in the hall, she smelled the scent of fresh

flowers. A bouquet sat on a marble-topped bureau under another ornately framed oil-painting. At the last door of the hallway, she knocked.

The door opened. Christiaan filled the doorway. "Ready?" He lifted his chin.

Christiaan's master suite consisted of several rooms. Gold curtains draped from the high ceilings to the floor, and excess folded fabric revealed afternoon light. Instead of modern art, massive paintings of women in black-and-gold Elizabethan costumes hovered on the wall behind the bed, in the sitting room, and in another room with a table beyond Andy's view.

More refreshed and alert, she had more questions. "So, who contracted you to find the emeralds? Some rich Russian princess? A millionaire in South Africa?" Christiaan pinched his perfect lips together. He never gave away anything.

He squinted and circled an entry table filled with silk flowers. "Remember last year when I told you I was in China?"

Andy rolled her eyes. She'd never forget Christiaan's lies. Last year, when Andy formulated her disguise as a debutante to break into a building to find a secret message hidden in an office, she texted him. When she never got a response, she figured Christiaan just lied about being in China. "The night of the T-Building heist?"

"Of course."

"The week before, I chased the emerald smugglers," Christiaan whispered. "I got a tip. I followed the lead. Sadly, I lost them again. But this time, we got them. The emeralds will be at the *Teatro Real*—or as the locals call it—*El Real*." He pointed to pages of schematics spread on the gold, patterned bedspread.

"*El Real*?" Andy glanced over the drawings, then pointed to a section of chairs. "An auditorium? The seats in this section don't even face the stage."

Christiaan tilted his head toward the window. "The Opera House is around the corner. It isn't known for great seats, but they will be hosting a charity exhibition tomorrow night."

Andy furrowed her brow and studied the schematics. "The emeralds are on display there?" She checked to confirm with Christiaan.

He shook his head. "They'll be worn by a guest."

"We're stealing emeralds off a woman?" Her heart burned. Every feeling in her repulsed this idea. This plan could go wrong in a dozen ways. "Won't she alert police?"

"We are stealing *stolen* emeralds. She bought them illegally from a fence. Besides"—he braced her shoulders with both hands—"this is why we brought you aboard."

Shaking free from his grip, Andy stepped back. "I am no thief."

"You're cute. I didn't invite you here to steal them." He grinned. "I asked you here to create a disguise, so I can steal them."

She crossed her arms over her chest. Was she insulted he didn't think she could be dishonest, or was she pleased he thought so highly of her disguise skills? A burst of pride burst through her. "It's still stealing."

With his hands like in prayer, he pointed outward. "We're *returning* them to their rightful owners."

"Who are…?" Andy didn't expect him to answer.

Christiaan always avoided sharing his shady past, no matter how many times she asked.

Pinching together his lips, Christiaan crossed his muscular arms and shook his head.

Andy placed a hand on her hip. "How do you know they'll be there?"

He tensed his muscles. "Sources."

Christiaan was still tight-lipped. Andy sighed. When would he open up? "Why don't we find out who owns them and then follow her home and break into her house? Stealing in a public place creates so many hazards."

He shook his head. "Too much time. Breaking into a private residence can take months. We'd need schematics of the private building and the location of any security cameras. Planning would be a pain and take too long. Easier to pinch in public where we can get schematics, we can blend in, and once it's over, she'll never know exactly when they were stolen."

"Fine." Defeated, Andy bent over the schematics of *El Real*. Christiaan grinned with a hint of triumph in his eyes. Andy smoldered. "What's your plan?"

He pointed toward the front lobby on the schematics. "The charity hired extra security. They'll be set up in the lobby. The Prime Minister of Spain will be there."

The Prime Minister? This job just got a lot tougher. No wonder Christiaan didn't tell her any details. Andy arched her eyebrow. "We'll be stealing emeralds under the nose of the Prime Minister?"

Christiaan cocked his head. "If we can get in, yeah."

Narrowing her eyes, Andy stepped forward. "Why

do you want these emeralds so much? I'm guessing this isn't an OverSight mission."

He stiffened. "No, I—"

She prodded his chest. "Let me guess, you can't tell me because this heist has something to do with a secret Order?"

Christiaan shushed her then nodded toward the open door of the next room.

Arching her brow, Andy moved to see into the room.

At a large table, hidden behind two large screens, was a man with dark eyes and sun-touched, brown hair. He tilted up his head to reveal a smile.

Andy lifted her chin in a greeting then faced Christiaan.

"Please stop asking questions." His tone changed to a whisper. His eyebrows peaked.

He was almost begging her. Yet Andy had little patience. "I'm an investigative journalist. I want to know everything."

With a hand on each of her shoulders, he bent over and kissed her nose. "I will tell you someday. I'm new at this trusting thing. I have to get used to it. Much of what I believe isn't believable."

Andy flushed at his kiss and wished he'd missed her nose by about a thumb's width south. What wouldn't she believe? She knew better than to ask now. His secrets were locked tighter than her underwear drawer. "Down to business then. How do we get in to *El Real*?"

Christiaan headed toward the other room. "That's where Hector comes in."

"Who?"

"Me." Emerging from behind the two large computer monitors set up on the corner of the table, Hector met them at the threshold and slung forward his hand. He wiped crumbs from his blue T-shirt of a white explosion hovered over the words, *Never split an infinitive.*

"Hector lives here in Madrid. He works for OverSight and has—shall we say?—special talents. He works for the RECON department and gathers and processes intelligence. I've contracted him for the week."

"And the money's already gone."

He lisped his words in a distinct Castilian accent. "Oh?" Andy glanced at the unassuming Spaniard. Nice. At least they had a native helping them.

Christiaan rolled his eyes. "I don't want to know how you blow your cash."

"Blow? Interesting choice of words." He smirked and led them back to his desk. "Follow me. Let's see what we can find."

Andy shot her gaze to Christiaan.

Huffing, Christiaan rolled his eyes. "He's into explosives. He worked in DES OPs before RECON."

Andy shrugged. "Say what?"

Arching a single scarred brow, Christiaan smirked. "DES OPs destroys things and creates diversions—that sort of thing."

Shaking her head, Andy leaned closer to the computer screens. Different apps ran on each sectioned-off screen and one black and green coding app. A half a dozen videos surveyed streets where names of plazas and streets were all in Spanish.

Christiaan stepped closer to the screens. "Think we

can get invites?"

Hector's fingers flew around the keyboard. "I can either forge something or find someone who has a copy. I've got eyes on everyone on the list."

The screens flickered through scores of passing images in the blink of an eye. Nothing escaped his technical observation. Andy raised her eyebrows. "Wow! What can't you do?"

Hector spun his chair to face her. "Get a date for Saturday night. And sometimes good take-away pizza. Both are hard to find." He spun again and clacked on the keyboard. A fuzzy picture of someone's email on their phone flashed across the screen. "Surely someone has opened one near a camera. Ah-ha!" The image paused then filled in with pixels until it was readable. He found an invite to the charity event. "I knew at least one person wouldn't be cautious." He punched more keystrokes enlarging the invitation. "I'll recreate that. And now you've got invitations to the event."

"Okay, we're in." Christiaan clapped his hands. His eyes widened. "You're amazing, Hector."

Brushing away imaginary lint, Hector sat back and blushed. "I know."

"How are we running this op?" Andy asked. "What do you need me for?" She crossed her fingers. Maybe she didn't have to do anything in this op.

Christiaan pointed toward his friend. "Hector on ears and eyes. You and me on the floor. You'll help me search for our mark."

So he did want her for more than just skills with hair and the sexy dress he required. He also wanted her keen eyesight.

"Christiaan needs a disguise." Hector coughed into

his fist, nearly obliterating the words.

Andy faced Christiaan. "Why do you need a disguise? Looking over the op, you could easily slip in and out without detection. Why all the trouble?"

He shrugged and stared up at the ceiling. "I rescued a girl." He then leaned over and studied the computer screen, then clicked a few things with the mouse. "Her former captor might not have appreciated it very much. He could show up."

Hector glared at him, then retrieved the mouse.

Andy threw up her hands. "Great. So we have to avoid boogies."

Flexing his biceps, Christiaan tossed her a flashing grin. "You can change my appearance."

"Only to a certain extent." Andy pushed on his shoulder. "Adding to a person's appearance is easy. Need to add height? Put lifts in the shoes. Need to add hair? Wear a wig? Facial hair, weight, glasses—all easy to add. Taking away something is nearly impossible."

"You mean you can't disguise my broad shoulders and winning smile." Christiaan winked.

Shaking her head, Andy flashed a half smile. "Hard to disguise a big ego."

Smirking, Christiaan challenged her with his eyes.

Drawing breath, Andy continued. "But we can change hair color. And I brought latex. We can give you a rounder face or higher cheek bones."

"More muscles?" He puffed out his chest.

That would be nearly impossible because he was so ripped. But saying that out loud would only encourage him. "I can give you a hunchback." She flashed him a tight-lipped smile.

Christiaan curled his lip. "No thanks. You work on

a design." He signaled between him and Hector. "We'll work together on a plan." Clapping his hands, Christiaan rubbed them together. "So objectives once inside *El Real*: locate the emeralds, isolate the woman, distract her, and retrieve them. If we have to, reclaim them by force."

Did everything Christiaan did involve his fists? She shook her head. "I've got an idea. Stop thinking with your fists and start thinking strategy. Make friends instead of enemies. You could butter her up and slip them off her neck."

He stared with widened eyes and opened mouth. "What do you mean?"

Obviously, this was a new, strange concept for Christiaan. "Use finesse instead of force." She crossed her arms and tapped her fingers against her biceps.

"You use finesse, and I'll use force." He jabbed a thumb at his chest. "We'll make a great team." Christiaan smirked and leaned back. "We should go shopping and get you something sexy. I just have to figure out what to wear to a black tie event."

His sparkling blue eyes taunted her. "Yes, *I'll* go shopping." Andy slapped him on his back with finality. "Without you." She thrust up her chin. But her confidence shrank. Their plan had so many holes in it. How could they possibly succeed?

Chapter 4

Parts of Madrid reminded Andy of a fairy tale. Buildings with stunning architecture crowded the wide boulevards. Decorative cornices adorned older buildings, and sunny balconies laced the apartment complexes. Cypress trees cropped up in gardens alongside the broad-leafed trees and over-sized elms. The capitol of Spain held a charm unlike any other city Andy had seen.

Lights flared around buildings, and hotels illuminated the sky. Cathedrals loomed large and impressive. High-end customers trotted in designer heels along the sidewalks. The tourists spoke in snippets of strange languages.

When Andy entered the *El Real* Opera house, she sensed Christiaan, unseen, observing her in his disguise. She stood tall, empowered, and attractive—dangerous in her dress, which held her tight and let her loose. Letting out a wavering breath, Andy handed her clutch to the security detail.

He searched the contents—a few bobby pins, sewing kit, superglue—just the normal purse filler.

With heart pounding out of her chest, she was sure he would detect her on her elevated heart rate alone.

The security officer slid the pocket purse through the portable x-ray.

Security for the opera house event was tighter than

at the airport and riskier, too—definitely more dangerous. Sweat pricked at her body. Breathing deeply, she focused on keeping her body loose and natural.

Wands beeped at metal near her. Security yelled at a man to remove his belt.

Cowering, the man bowed and drew out the leather from his loops.

The security continued to yell in Spanish and motioned for him to step aside while another guard detained him.

Despite not knowing the language, reading their non-verbal communication worked pretty well. She gulped. Now she stepped forward for her turn. She held her breath when a scruffy guard with facial hair waved the wand over her head. It didn't pick up anything—not her hairpins, not her earrings dangling to her shoulders, not her weapon. Her pulse thundered in her ears through the ordeal.

A guard examined her hair, patting it with gloved hands and motioned to her to remove her hair sticks.

Although she didn't understand Spanish, she understood his meaning by his force and direction. With trembling hands, Andy slipped the sticks free of her huge tangle of hair to show they were only for decoration. She clenched her jaw.

A guard pressed his fingers into the mass still on her head. He nodded an all clear.

Almost there. She reinserted her hair sticks, keeping an eye on the security detail. Next came the pat down. Personal space meant nothing to the security. To protect the Prime Minister, nothing was untouched.

Gritting her teeth, Andy held her breath. The

airport security in America held nothing to these guys. A heavily mustached man stuck his hands up her dress and patted her legs. The violation lit a fire within her. She'd never forgive Christiaan for subjecting her to this sort of behavior. Many years had passed since some of this skin had been touched. She scowled and set her jaw. Thankfully, she wore her pretty panties because they were nearly seen by everyone in the room.

At last, she was free to go. With her sheath evening gown hugging her trembling figure, she retrieved her clutch and nearly stumbled across the threshold. "*Gracias.*" She entered the lobby of the *El Real* Opera House. Relief filtered through her. She made it through.

Behind her, others said "*gracias*" with the Madrid lisp, a mark of upper-class Spanish. The lobby for the *El Real* surrounded her. Large, Spanish-red pillars supported the second floor. Marble gleamed beneath her feet. Staircases rose to the next floors.

Lights glinted off the jewelry encircling women's necks. How would they find one necklace among so many? Smells of foreign perfume found her nose as she wove between the sumptuously dressed patrons. Where was Christiaan?

****

A slender red gown attracted Christiaan's attention. Clothing didn't usually distract him, but amidst the well-dressed, well-groomed upper-class, this dress stood out. What the dress revealed, not concealed, intrigued him. From his vantage point on the stairs, Andy's creamy shoulders glowed under the lights of the *Teatro Real* Opera House. He wished he could flip up his eye patch to get the full effect of her dress.

With a hand on the carved railing, Christiaan

watched, as Andy propped up a leg on a stool. The slit of her dress fell open and revealed a toned thigh. His heartbeat kicked up a notch.

The security guard patted up one leg and down another.

Christiaan narrowed his eyes. The man who slid his hands up her shiny legs then used the backside of his hands to assess her chest had no idea she was a fighting machine. With a heavy breath, Christiaan faced away. Then he glanced back.

The man didn't care what or who he touched.

Christiaan gritted his teeth for his violation.

Now finished, Andy moved with grace and with perfect posture. As much as she protested these events, her bearing proved her as regal as the other guests. Despite her reproduced invitation, Andy belonged here.

The security guard returned her clutch.

She strode into the room, shifted her weight to one heeled shoe, and searched the crowd in the foyer.

Christiaan couldn't help it. She looked ravishing— even through one eye. Her soft neck and her toned and bare shoulders enticed him. That dress would get him killed. It hugged her curves perfectly. He couldn't get it out of his mind.

When he came into her view, her eyes lit up.

Relief washed over him. She still cared. After her slap at the airport, he wasn't sure.

"Colonel Favier." Andy swept up her fingers to meet his.

He bowed. He wasn't the only one wearing a military dress uniform and metals hanging from his chest. As far as he could tell from his limited vision, he was the only one with fake graying hair and age-progression makeup. "Whatever scent you are wearing is positively breathtaking." He kissed her on the cheek. "You are absolutely stunning."

"Thank you." She flashed a smile.

As much as he wanted to linger in her company, he had a mission. One he could not fail. "Search the crowd for any woman wearing an emerald necklace. They should be rather large. The Cairo emeralds are the size of an American quarter or a single euro."

Andy's gaze roved about the room. "I've already started searching the crowd. This will take forever."

He shook his head. "*Dā hâi lāo zhēn.*"

Andy elbowed him. "Chinese?" She hated it when he spoke foreign languages. She so needed to brush up her skills.

"The phrase roughly translates to 'fishing a needle from the sea.' Or in English, the idiomatic expression is finding a needle in a haystack." He tapped his mic the size of a pencil eraser in his collar. "Hector, can you see anything from your position?"

"Hard to see with such petty resources. With OverSight equipment, I could read the date on a coin."

Inwardly, Christiaan rolled his eyes. With his limited personal resources, he could only purchase a certain quality. Nearly his whole paycheck went to recovering these emeralds. If they somehow found these, only one more remained.

"A necklace shouldn't be too hard to spot." In the reception area, Andy paced around each cocktail table draped with red, floor-length tablecloths.

Crowds of four to five gathered at each table, sipping from glass flutes.

He scanned woman nearby, then worked outward

in a circle. "I scanned the lobby. I don't see anyone with an emerald necklace." Hundreds of people gathered here. This plan was a long shot. But they didn't have any other options. "Maybe she's late. Maybe she changed her mind. Maybe, maybe, maybe…"

Andy passed a woman wearing a bracelet studded with jewels. Her gaze met Christiaan's. She leaned into him. "What if we assumed it was a necklace, and the setting is a bracelet instead?"

Hope replaced despair. Energy bounded through him. "Andy, you're brilliant. Scan all the women's wrists."

"Still not seeing anything green come up."

Hector spilled Spanish in his ear as the "eye in the sky" from a security room. Earlier, he set up his security cameras throughout the building. Christiaan split from Andy and searched through well-dressed guests with greater urgency. "The performance is going to start. If we don't find them in the pre-show cocktails, we'll have to wait until intermission."

A women held a drink with her hand. A bracelet draped over her wrist. She then touched her ear with the other hand.

"Or earrings," he addressed Andy in the comms unit.

"What kind of setting are they in? Did your sources say?" she asked.

"I have no idea." Adrenaline raced through him. He quickened his steps in an attempt to cover more ground and study more people. "But we are running out of time. We can't check everyone's ears."

Across the room, Andy quickened her pace. "No

emerald earrings."

"If it's an ankle bracelet, we are dead." Christiaan threw up his hands.

A man passed Andy on the far side of the room.

People funneled into the auditorium.

"Women aren't the only ones who wear jewelry. The setting could be in a watch or a necktie pin or..." Her voice crackled in his ear.

"Again, you never cease to amaze!" He loved how she always thought out of the box.

"Cufflinks." Her voice came again on the comms unit. "I found them, Christiaan. A man is wearing two emerald cufflinks. Watch out, he looks like a mean one."

A thrill shot energy through him. His heartbeat quickened. He hastened across the room to where she stood. "Where is he?"

Crowds at the table disbursed and entered the main hall to filter into the auditorium.

Andy nodded toward the man with dark hair and an even darker mustache.

Two emeralds glowed in his sleeves. He leaned over a table. One cocktail too many gave him sway. He was short and scrawny. Christiaan could take him. "He won't be too tough."

Hector clicked the keyboard in Christiaan's ear. "Bad news. Our target is the extremely rich, extremely powerful, and not very moral Spaniard, Philipe Montoya. He's made millions with his information brokerage, and he is not a soft cookie."

"Information brokerage?" Andy furrowed her brows.

Hector laughed. "He's a professional

blackmailer—a bottom dweller of the dark Internet. He trades secrets and all sorts of nasty stuff. He always travels with his bodyguard detail."

When Philipe moved, several men stayed within at least two feet of him. He escorted a woman by her elbow toward the auditorium.

Christiaan was too late. With his hands behind his back, he paced the foyer. He tapped a nail on his finger. If only he had his *chakram*. He could've stopped Philipe and taken the emeralds. Now he would have to wait for intermission. "Stealing them will be more difficult than I imagined."

A pair of security guards monitored the halls and gathered in the foyer.

Christiaan kept a conscious watch over them with his good eye. He had to wait a half hour. What could he do to kill the time?

Andy hauled him upstairs to the carpet-covered halls.

Red curtains covered the windows, blocking sound and light. The whole aura was quieter.

"I smuggled in a weapon," Andy whispered.

Christiaan spun. Beautiful *and* clever? These were two reasons he would always call on her.

He clearly missed the weapon. She certainly didn't hide it in that dress. The dress didn't have a centimeter of give anywhere. But just to be sure, Christiaan did another visual inspection with the good eye. No gun strap on her inner thigh. He could see most of her leg, up to half her thigh. The other side hugged her so tight that a gun or knife outline would be impossible to miss. Her chest was perky but her own. "You clever vixen." Andy smuggling in a weapon changed everything. New possibilities formed in his mind. "What is it?"

Andy swept back her hair with the palm of her hand. "You know me, I couldn't come in here without something to protect myself."

The guards eyed him.

He wished he could melt into the tapestries hanging on the walls. Tugging her elbow, he moved her away. "Where is it?"

Andy followed. "Wouldn't you like to know?"

With a haughty expression in her eye, Andy tossed her head.

How she made his blood rush! Challenge accepted! Now what should he do with this new information?

He escorted Andy to a couple in Sudanese dress. A shawl draped over the woman's head. A plan formed in his mind.

****

Andy studied Christiaan. He grew distant all of a sudden. His conversation with their new Sudanese friends was all but non-existent. In between listening and responding, his gaze, usually attentive and alert, focused on something in the distance. She continued her small-talk with their new friends, who thankfully spoke English.

"Change of plans," he whispered to Andy. "Meet me by the washrooms."

To the others, he excused himself.

Andy admired his new identity. He didn't look half bad as the forty-five-ish statesman with graying hair and a missing eye. His fitted military dress uniform gave him a distinguished air. She continued to converse.

Christiaan slipped out of the circle. The light blue

sash crossed his navy jacket. The medals were Andy's idea. The gold epaulets dangled from his broad shoulders as he walked away.

Once finished with the conversation, Andy crossed the carpeted floor to the restroom door. Where was Christiaan? Did he mean another restroom? Andy turned her back to the door. It squeaked open.

Grabbing her hand, Christiaan tugged her inside and bolted the door behind them. A plush bench sat underneath a faux window draped with curtains. He held her against the door and pressed his lips and body against hers. "I'm sorry. I had just to kiss you," he said between breaths. He flipped up his eye patch. A red ring circled his eye. "You are just so amazing in that dress."

Andy, who was by no means rejecting his tender caresses, paused. All her alarm bells rang. "We're in the middle of an op."

His lips fluttered across hers. "I know, but we can't get to him until intermission." He lowered his chin into her neck and kissed up to her ear. "Let's take advantage of these few minutes."

And take advantage he did. His hands brushed the tops of her shoulders and down her arms, leaving a wake of goose bumps. Heat poured out of her. Her lips ached for his touch. Andy flushed at his caresses. Her breathing and heart rate exploded. She barely noticed the rich furnishings—the curtains hung solely for decoration, the polished stone, the painted tile, or the gilt mirror.

Andy's brain died. Logical thought flew— prudence and caution fled. Passion ruled. She wanted to give free expression to what beat in her heart—pent up for so long. She couldn't believe this dress brought it out.

His lips found her jaw line, her chin, and her neck. His fingers grasped at the bust line of her dress before sliding down to her hip, then down around her outer thigh.

Stepping backward, he sat on the bench and drew her onto him. His hands grasped around her legs as she slid on top of him. Christiaan fell to his back and hitched Andy on top. He stroked up and down her back and pressed her into him.

When his hands touched her backside, Andy stopped kissing. She buried her hands into the cushion beneath him and pushed herself up, staring at him dead in the eyes.

"What?" His lips were swollen. His flushed face glowed red. The eye patch was still flipped up on his forehead.

Andy narrowed her eyes. "You're searching for something."

He cracked a smile. "Can't I make out with the prettiest girl in the room?"

Removing herself from the embrace, Andy knelt on the bench and checked her hair with a hand. Most of it was still neatly held in a bun—a near miracle with all that action. "Admit it. You were frisking me."

He propped himself on his elbow and raised a smug chin. "I gave you the most enjoyable frisking you've ever had, I'm sure."

Andy's flush deepened, but she didn't confirm. "You want the weapon I brought, don't you?"

"How did you know?" A crooked grin graced his lips.

She punched his chest and slid to the floor. The coldness of the tile killed her heat. "You're kissing with your body not with your heart."

Christiaan coughed a coarse laugh.

Andy propped her hands on her waist. "You could've just asked me."

"All right, now that you've got me. Where is your weapon?" He sat up.

Andy smiled. "I smuggled it past security. Aren't you impressed?" She savored the moment as if she had chocolate on the tip of the tongue. Being better than Christiaan at smuggling in a weapon tasted so good.

"Exceedingly. Now give it to me." He held out a hand.

"You want to know what it is?" Andy wanted to drag out his begging longer than the kisses.

"Of course."

"Beg me."

He thrust up his chin. "Absolutely not." Shaking his head, he huffed.

Andy retrieved her hair sticks from a snarl of hair.

"Chopsticks?" He scoffed. "You think chopsticks are a weapon? What will you do? Poke out Philipe's eye? I've done more damage with a fork."

Blowing out a bit of breath, Andy held up a hand. "Wait." She released her bun hairpiece. Inside the little cavity were two thin, doubled-edged razors. Christiaan didn't show his awe, but she knew he was impressed by the slight gleam in his eyes.

Andy slid the razors into little slits in the hair sticks, creating a double-edged blade. "They're not much." She spun the makeshift weapon in her fingers, then held one out for him. "This blade was all I could think of on such short notice."

"No, it's perfect." He pinched one and inspected it. "But I'm afraid you won't use them."

With that, he reached up with his leg and held her while he grabbed the curtain tie from the wall, wrapped it around her, wrestled her to the bench, and within the blink of an eye, everything went black.

Andy awoke on the bench. The scent of dust made her sneeze. The curtains, once on the wall, were draped over her like a coverlet. As she recalled her last memory, heat of a different sort filtered through her. "The rat," she said out loud, sitting up. All sorts of swear words flooded her mind. Christiaan knocked her out and left her here.

She patted the cushion around her. And he pinched her weapon as well. She punched the wall with the back of her fist. He was so dead. So, so dead. Gritting her teeth, she swung her legs off the bench and threw off the heavy damask and then quickly threw it back on.

Damn. Her little red dress was gone, and all she had on was her strapless shapewear bodysuit. Letting out a roar, she tore off the curtain.

To squelch the fire stoked within her, she drew a breath. What torture could she inflict upon him? Visions of all the things she could do with the curtain cord flew through her mind. But even those things seemed too good for this level of betrayal.

"Andy, Andy where are you?" Hector hissed in her ear. "I've lost you."

At least he hadn't stripped her of the communication device. "Is Christiaan still on this line?" Trust? Christiaan was always talking about his trust issues, but nothing could compare with this breach of trust.

"No. He asked me to cut off the two of you. You have to communicate through me now."

She jumped to her feet. "Because he knew I'd give him an earful right about now."

"What happened? Where are you?"

"Boy, he is so dead." Andy kicked the carved wooden door. He locked it so no one else could come in. Voices sounded outside the door. "How long have I been out?"

"Intermission barely started. You must be in the restroom. It's the only place I can't see you. Come out."

"I can't. He stole my dress." Pacing the black-and-white tiles of the bathroom, she stared at her knee-length body shapeware smoothing her midsection. No way would she wear a tight dress without it. Now, it was her only covering. "He is so, so dead." She wasn't sure if she was talking to herself or to Hector. "I need a new dress."

Hector chuckled a little. "Dressmaking is way out of my area of expertise."

Andy wrapped the curtain around herself under her armpits and thought. At least he left her shoes and her bag. "What was he thinking?" Stealing her weapons! She alone risked much to smuggle them in. Then he changed the plans.

Hector laughed. "I know exactly what he was thinking. Who wouldn't want to see you without your dress?"

"Hector." Andy was impatient with all men right now.

"What will you do?"

Christiaan wouldn't get away with locking her up,

taking her weapon, and stealing the emeralds without her. "Improvise." She needed another dress. Biting her lip, she faced the gilt mirror over the sink and smiled at the material draped over her body.

The damask would do nicely. What else could she use? On the wall hung the rest of the curtains, two sheer voile panels, a handful of clips, and a sconce. She yanked them all down. A rolled cushion filled the length of the bench. She could make something with all of that.

A knock sounded at the door.

"Occupied."

Intermission only lasted fifteen minutes.

Christiaan was probably approaching Philipe and his men now.

From her purse, Andy removed a pair of tiny plastic scissors and her sewing kit. Then she removed all the clips from the curtain rod and went to work.

With nimble fingers, she unpicked the seams of the decorative ends of the neck roll right around the piping. When she had two circles, she stitched them together to form the top of a bodice; one circle covered each breast. She folded a length of fabric for shoulder straps, then another for a waistband. Clips and huge basting stitches on the interior of the seam held everything together.

"What are you doing? I can't hear anything other than rustling."

Hector interrupted her concentration. "Hush. I'm creating." Anything left flapping, she glued. This dress wasn't the only one she'd sewn on herself. The first time was when she investigated a director who skimmed money from the actors at the local theater in St. Louis. She needed to blend with the Venetian

Carnivale costumes from the musical *Count of Monte Cristo*. It probably wouldn't be the last time she'd use hand-stitched couture either.

Next, she needed a skirt. Bunching and tucking, pleating and clipping, Andy wrapped the damask and the voile around her waist in a fashionable pomp. Holding it together with a combination of safety pins and curtain clips, she tacked the ends with a needle and thread. The burnt maroon and emerald green were two colors she never would wear together or apart, but she had a dress. And it wouldn't draw as much attention as being in her shapewear.

For just a few seconds, she admired herself in the mirror. "Christiaan thought he was so clever to leave me here without something to wear. Won't he be surprised?" With a sly grin, she nodded approval to her reflection. Now to find a weapon. If he was armed, she would be, too.

Few options remained in the restroom. A glass vase held silk flowers. She could break it and use a shard of glass. Or remove the screws holding the mirror in place and use those in something.

Then she spied the sadly naked and humble curtain rod. Andy hefted it. It was about the same weight as a *bō* staff. She tucked it into the folds of her skirt and opened the door.

An explosion echoed in her ears. Smoke billowed out of the foyer. Everyone in the line ducked and covered their heads.

In the chaos, Andy slid past the queue and raced for the rendezvous point. She didn't have time to wonder what the explosion was. "Hector, where is he? I want him."

Dark, gray plumes of smoke filled the foyer. Charity attendees stood frozen in open-mouthed confusion.

"Who? Christiaan?" Hector chuckled.

"I ain't talking about Santa Claus." She gathered the skirts of her impromptu dress as she dodged shoulders, elbowed men in black ties, and excused herself in Spanish.

"He's heading for the main lobby."

Scads of people ran away from the smoke. Women clutched their faces with handkerchiefs.

Holding a hand over her nose, Andy inhaled the burning stench. "I'll kill him if he's not already dead!"

"What happened to your grand idea for social finesse?" He chuckled.

"Not today, Hector." Andy gritted her teeth and maneuvered around a security guard.

He yelled at the crowd in Spanish, pushing them back with his outstretched arms.

Andy couldn't understand anything they said, so she ignored them, focusing instead on finding Christiaan.

"Aren't you curious about the explosion outside?"

"No time, Hector." She half-wondered if Christiaan pre-planned the explosion without telling her. "Right now, all I care about is finding Christiaan." And hope the explosion didn't get him first.

Chapter 5

Christiaan wanted a relationship with Andy. Trust wasn't developed over dinner or after an introduction or even solving one case together. Trust must be forged in trials and time. Trust wasn't something he was good at giving or taking.

Her ideas of using finesse were all well and good. But with a deadline, force was much easier to use.

Old habits were hard to kick.

Andy would forgive him—eventually.

Armed with Andy's makeshift blades tucked up his sleeve, he crept along the lush carpet to where his target stood and conversed with the red-headed woman around the cocktail tables. Christiaan counted four men surrounding Philipe. He could take that many.

But what he needed was a distraction.

An explosion shook the building.

"Hector, what was that?"

He imagined Hector clicking on a keyboard, controlling the access to hundreds of cameras.

"I found the source. Your man Fabian has caught up with you."

"Give me the surrounding scene." He kept his gaze on his mark. Hector's voice lilted in his ear.

"Surrounding is a good word. From what I can see from the security cameras, Fabian has a few guys at each exit. What did you do to piss him off so bad?"

"I stole something."

"What?"

"His slave-master title."

"Wait." The sounds of clicking keyboard sounded. "I don't think Fabian is exploding things."

"I don't care who it is. I'm using the distraction."

With the explosion, patrons ran everywhere. Alarms blared. Smoke obscured the ceiling. Philipe, his men, and the red-headed woman in a green dress headed away from the crowds.

Philipe's entourage went upstairs.

Grabbing the banister, Christiaan swung himself up the stairs, keeping close on their heels. Angling through patrons at a slalom pace, Christian caught up to the five men. "Halt." He held out the blades, which seemed laughable now, but they were better than nothing. "You have something I need."

Philipe's guards rushed forward.

Two grabbed Christiaan's arms and dislodged the weapons.

A third man raised his arm, cocking back for a punch.

Christiaan dodged to the left and pulled at the man on his right.

The man clobbered his associate instead.

While contending with the other three, Christiaan felt a slash across his left ribs. Pain tore through him. He glanced up.

The fourth held a four-inch blade.

How he smuggled it through security, Christiaan didn't have time to contemplate. Using the two men still holding his arms as stabilizers, he launched his legs around the neck of the third.

The two men didn't loosen their grip.

The third dropped to the ground.

The two men let go of Christiaan.

Big mistake. Christiaan landed on his feet.

The knife-wielding man slashed Christiaan's right fingers with the blade.

With a joint lock and a kick to his arm, the man went down with a broken arm.

Christiaan kicked away the knife. Utilizing a Russian Sambo move, he stepped on the knee of the second, using his weight to tumble him into the first man. He stood and knocked out the last two.

Only Philipe and his girlfriend remained. Tying up her fiery red hair, she waved her hand. "Go. Go."

Christiaan stepped toward them.

Philipe didn't even hesitate and ran through an arched doorway.

What a chicken.

The woman faced Christiaan. Her stance widened, and she held her wrists high.

The slits of her emerald green dress exposed large portions of her toned thighs. A dangerous gleam flashed in her green eyes. She was no ordinary escort. She meant to fight. Christiaan sighed. He wasn't done for the night.

She began with her hands out in front of her, not even near her face. "Familiar with the London Prize Ring rules, are ye?"

His training had prepared him for any type of fighting, but Christiaan nearly laughed at her stance. He'd never seen anything like it. "Boxer, are you?"

She thrust up her chin. "Care for a bout?"

He wasn't sure he was up to a pugilistic round. *All*

right. He inhaled through his pained lungs.

The woman tilted her head. "Don't knock it." She launched a punch at his face.

She was so quick, he didn't have time to block the jab. Christiaan stepped back, head rattling.

After a quick smirk, she launched forward again. This time she grabbed his collar and elbow and forced him into a stone planter.

Pain ripped through his body as he used his stomach muscles to catch himself. The woman held the slight edge only because of his injury. He could've easily bested her otherwise. He glanced down for a fraction of a second. Blood oozed from his side wound. He clapped a hand over the red. How could he fight?

Movement caught his eye. Andy leaped into his view with hideous fabric flying. She immediately jumped to his aid, beating back the woman with a *bō* staff...of sorts. What did she have in her hands? A curtain rod?

Stepping away from the immediate conflict, Christiaan leaned against the railing to stanch the flow of blood from his side.

By attacking with the staff, Andy forced the woman into retreat.

The woman snarled and bared her teeth. "If only I had my *shillelagh.* You'd be whistlin' another tune." She gathered her light eyebrows, returning the attack to Andy in full force, kicking and jabbing.

His heart warmed at how well Andy fended off her attacks. "You're amazing, Andy."

"I've got her." Andy nodded in the direction of Philipe. "Go get the emeralds."

Holding his sliced side, Christiaan picked up the

chopstick knives and tore through the halls, ignoring the throbbing in his torso. Philipe ran, but he hadn't gotten far. He was just up ahead. Christiaan grabbed his lapel. Tackling Philipe to the carpet, Christiaan flipped over his target.

Philipe's eyes widened. His tuxedo scrunched around his neck. He crossed his wrists in front of his face. "What do you want?"

"Those cufflinks."

He thrust out his wrists. "You want these? Take them. Just don't kill me."

With Andy's makeshift knives, he cut loose the cuffs and pocketed the emeralds. "Thank you." Maybe social finesse would be something he'd have to try again. Out of breath and faint from losing blood, he returned to the interior lobby.

Andy and the woman still struggled. Half of Andy's dress had fallen to the ground. A gleaming shoulder shone in the lobby's artificial light. A leg poked through sagging fabric. But she continued to block the woman's advances with the staff.

Christiaan jumped to Andy's aid with a kick to the woman's kneecaps.

She jumped out of the way. With two on one, the woman couldn't keep up. After one leap off the upholstered bench, she headed in Philipe's direction.

"Should I follow her?" Andy panted, her face red and sweaty.

Christiaan shook his head. "No. I got what we wanted." Flashing the emeralds still in the cuffs, he slipped them into a red pouch and tucked them into his shirt.

"Where do we go?" Andy held out her hands.

"Up." Christiaan didn't stop running until they reached the top floor of *El Real*. Time to execute their escape plan. He found the rope ladder.

She pulled a pair of shorts and a shirt from her bag.

Her bag was endless. Christiaan never knew what she would pull out of there. When he worked with her before, she used the contents of her bag to save their lives multiple times.

She punched him with the clothing in her fist. "I think you owe me—"

He blocked and tossed away her hand. "An explanation? I told you I can't tell you anything."

"…an apology. Did you think I would ask for an explanation?" Andy guffawed, tossing up her hands. "I learned a long time ago that you're not Mr. Free and Open." She tossed him a vacuum-sealed packet of hemostatic Stop-a-Clot.

"An apology for what?" He bandaged his side with a blood-absorbing material. He trembled with aching pain.

"For what happened in the restroom."

He gave her a once-over, staring at the fabric slipping from her shoulders. Stitches stretched to unforgiving limits. The whole thing wasn't holding up from Andy's fight and the run upstairs. Where she used to look ravishing, now she looked ravished. "What are you wearing?"

Andy shrugged. "Curtains from the restroom."

Christiaan nodded. Burnt smell still clung to his clothes. Blood made his hands sticky. Wiping them on alcohol pads, he finally could change before dropping down into the gardens below. "I knew you would find something."

"Did you?" Glaring, Andy unwrapped her hair from her bun and removed her fake hair piece. She peeled off her eyelashes and wiped her face with a moist towel to remove the heavy eye makeup. "You owe me an apology." The curtains melted off.

She stood once again in her body suit he'd left her in. And it left little to the imagination. He winked. "An apology for not kissing you longer?"

Holding eye contact, she arched an eyebrow, slid her hand up his arm, and drew him closer. "Perhaps I do regret not kissing you longer."

Her lips parted his and imparted the sweetest sensation. He grabbed her hungrily and touched the soft flesh on her back. This time he meant it. His heartbeat thundered in his chest. "We can't continue."

"Hmm?" Andy kissed his neck. She tugged at his belt, his pants, and his pockets.

Christiaan closed his eyes and tried to tamp down the sensory details. "We can't sit in a parked car and rev the engine. Not good for the engine." He tumbled to a padded bench, bringing Andy with him.

Andy explored with her hands.

Every hair follicle stood on end.

Then suddenly she stopped and stood. "Got it."

"What?" To see Andy more clearly, he braced himself up on his elbows and licked his swollen lips.

She stood a few feet away holding…his wallet?

Slipping a handful of euros from the pouch, she tossed back the black leather bifold. "Thank you for the cash. I shall use it to replace the dress you stole."

He sat up, ignoring the pain tearing through his midsection, and snatched at the cash. "My reflexes are faster than yours."

Andy turned away and slid the bills down her bra. "Ha!" She brandished a winning smirk.

Christiaan sat back, defeated. He couldn't go *there*. His oaths were awfully specific about boundaries. "All right. We're even. Now let's get out of here." He would've gladly paid the hundreds of euros for a kiss like that again.

For a fast getaway, Andy designed his break-away suit. The bottom half of the pant legs were baste-stitched on. He tore at the basting seams and at similar seams of his white sleeves. He tossed his navy military coat, the bottom of his pants, half his sleeves, and his tie into Andy's bag. He unbuttoned his shirt.

Andy traded his shoes for flip flops from her bag.

He mussed his hair to lose some of its gray sheen. A quick wipe of his face removed the aging makeup. He lost the eyepatch ages ago, somewhere between the goons and the woman. He was in full tourist mode and also pretty full of himself.

To leave no trace, Andy stuffed everything back into her bag. No DNA. "Your idea worked." She sprayed protein killer anywhere she found blood.

"When will you realize all my ideas are good?"

She threw the bag around her shoulder and arched a brow. "Um, knocking me out in the bathroom and taking my stuff wasn't a good idea."

"Won't you forgive me?" He only wanted to keep her safe.

Andy crossed her arms over her chest. "Won't you say you're sorry?"

Christiaan thrust out his chin. "Never. Because I'm not."

She huffed and picked up her bag. "Just don't be

surprised if I return the favor."

He grinned at the challenge. "I'll anticipate you tying me up someday."

Andy raised a hand to strike at shoulder height.

He caught it mid-air. "My reflexes are still faster than yours, Andy Baker." He drew her close.

Andy kissed him.

Christiaan broke from her. He placed a hand over his wallet. "What was the kiss for?"

Arching a brow, she lingered near his face. "Just so you know I'm not only affectionate when I steal something."

Grunting, he dropped her arm.

Andy twisted her hair in a quick side braid. "Now tell me why I risked my life for some emeralds."

Christiaan forced a coarse laugh. That was not happening.

Gunshots and screams came from below. His heart plunged.

"Hector, what is going on?" Raising her eyebrows, Andy spoke into her comms unit.

Christiaan flew to the railing. In his own triumph, he'd forgotten about the explosion and Hector. Smoke still billowed up, blocking his view of downstairs. Patrons' screams reached his ears. "I can't see. Let's get a better look." Christiaan sneaked down a flight of stairs to where the smoke thinned, and he could see into the main oval lobby.

A man in black dragged a woman hobbling in broken high heels.

Christiaan already removed his comms unit. "Tell Hector to clear out. If the police discover we're OverSight, we'll lose our credentials and destroy the already shaky relationship of OverSight and the EU."

Andy touched his sleeve. "No reply from Hector."

Christiaan swiveled and opened his hand toward Andy for the comms unit. He slipped it into his ear. "Hector. Can you hear me? Dammit! Where are you?"

Nothing but static echoed in his ears.

"Where was he?" Andy twisted her hair.

"He hid in the security room. With the cameras."

Below, men in black poured into the building. Each carried a semi-automatic poised to shoot.

Christiaan ducked behind the curtains when a few black-clad soldiers trampled up the stairs a few flights down.

Thousands of fast, tense heartbeats thundered in his chest. Sweat prickled his body.

Christiaan held his breath and forced Andy into the shadows. "I'm going down."

"What?" Andy hissed, batting away his hand.

"I don't think those are Fabian's men."

"What do you mean?"

A voice crackled in his ear. Christiaan paused and listened to the lower tones.

"In here."

Then farther away he heard, "Take him."

Christiaan removed his earpiece. "They've got Hector." The smoke cleared the oval atrium. He coughed. Blood and debris covered the marble flooring.

A man clad in black fatigues stormed in. A balaclava concealed his identity. A black beret topped his head. An AK-47 hung across his chest.

Well-dressed women and men cowered in the corners of the room and behind pillars, squatting to avoid notice. Someone had stopped the fire alarms, and whimpers and cries from men and women floated upward.

Other men fanned out throughout the room. They tore fobs from women's ears and ripped their necks free of jewels.

From the side door, Christiaan squinted in the remaining debris of the explosion. Dust grated his lungs. "These aren't Fabian's men. Judging from their uniforms and their organization, these guys are professional. See how they move in patterns, in practiced precision? Where's Hector?" He leaned closer to the rail to observe. Who were these guys? They could be terrorists, but they hadn't searched for the Prime Minister anywhere or announced their goals or intentions. Though men pocketed jewelry. This level of distraction couldn't be for a robbery.

They blew up a huge chunk of the wall—a bit excessive for a jewelry heist. Why create such an entrance? Usual tactics were to get in and out with the least bit of disturbance, the least destruction or distraction. Why the show of force? The whole op didn't make sense.

The search didn't seem random. In fact, the men seemed to be searching for something specific. Christiaan gripped the railing. "Got a gun in your bag?"

Flattening her lips, Andy cocked a hip. "This is Europe. Bringing a gun in here is illegal. We can only fight at close range."

If only he hadn't lost his *chakram*—*his* best long-distance weapon. Christiaan eyed the curtain rod. "Maybe we can. Can I borrow a hair pin? Or a nail would be better."

Andy opened her bag and ducked in her head. "I

have a nail in my bag. Also paperclips, clamps, suction cups, hooks, phones—"

Christiaan held up a hand to stop her. "The nail will do. And can I have the fake pearls from your necklace?"

With an arched eyebrow, Andy removed the necklace and set it in his hand.

Snapping the necklace, Christiaan crouched on the ground, fitting together the pieces. "I bet you have Super Glue."

"Fast drying."

Her eyebrows gathered adorably as she rummaged in her bag. Gah, he missed her.

She tossed him the bottle. "What are you making?"

He cracked open the bottle. With the sharp scent of the adhesive in the air, he bent and gathered the pearls, the nail, and the Super Glue on the carpet. "I believe I have stumped you, Andy Baker. You're not the only one who can make things." Actually, a thrill tickled his spine. Now he understood why Andy loved doing this—making things from nothing. He stacked the beads on the head of the nail and glued them in place. Then he tore in two a receipt from a soda he purchased. He wrapped the first half around the beads while the glue oozed. Then he made a conical shape for the end.

Andy tapped her foot. "But I'm the only one who can make them successfully."

"Have you so little faith in me?" He shot up his head. Then he focused again on his project.

"I see what you're doing."

Andy sounded a little impressed. Good. She couldn't be the only one who had all the cool tricks.

"You're making a dart."

"I've been watching videos. Your curtain rod, my lady?" Standing, he held open his hand.

With a grimace, Andy handed over the curtain rod.

Christiaan loaded the newly appointed blowgun and leveled it at the man in black terrorizing the crowd.

Andy stood near his shoulder. "You won't get enough air. You'll need something more conical at the end to focus the air stream."

"Bah." He waved a hand to dismiss her. "What will you give me if this works?"

"How about a back rub?" Andy arched a brow and shook her head. "You should leave the impromptu weapon making to me."

He raised the rod to his lips. Hand still on the outstretched blowgun, he nodded toward her. "Why don't you go?"

She folded her arms across her chest. "I want to stay and see it splatter."

"Good thing you're a fast runner. When I shoot, run. They will retaliate. Machine gun fire will spray all over up here once I kill their leader. This dart is going right into his neck." He rolled his ears to his shoulders.

She huffed but didn't move.

With tense shoulders, he fit the piece into his mouth. He drew a large breath and blew into the tube.

The dart flew through the air and dropped. It skidded to the floor near the boot of the masked man in the black beret.

He stepped on it completely unaware how close he'd come to death. Christiaan lowered the rod and swore.

Andy let out a chuckle. "You might have wounded his sole."

Christiaan sighed. "The glue wasn't dry and stuck to the inside of the shaft."

Andy tugged at his sleeve. "Let's split up so we can find Hector. He needs us."

Behind the concealed masked man in black, a host of other raiders swarmed the room and checked the faces of those cowering. Then they tossed them aside. They shot those who resisted.

"Go left." Christiaan pointed down the hall but still squinted at the man in black. He was tall and almost familiar. "I'll—" Christiaan froze.

Two men entered the lobby below them. Hector hung between the two. His eyes were nearly swollen shut. A trickle of red fell from his lip. They dragged Hector across the marble floor.

The men threw him before the man in black.

Cold sweat prickled Christiaan's body. With rod still in his hand, he headed for the stairs.

Standing in his path, Andy blocked him. "They'd kill you before you got halfway there."

Jaw set, he stepped around her. "I have to help him."

She held his arm. "Don't be the hero. At this distance, we can do nothing. All his men are armed and dangerous."

Christiaan shook off the hold. "But I hired Hector. I'm responsible for his life. He's my man." His heart thundered. Hector trusted him. Facing the scene below, Christiaan gripped the railing again.

Hector's tie hung loose around his neck. Wincing, he touched his swollen eye.

Andy leaned closer. "So far, they haven't killed any compliant prisoners and have only robbed jewelry and stuff. He might be okay."

The two men whispered something to the man in black.

His gaze flashed upwards and scanned the levels above him. Then he whispered something back to the men.

"Who are you? Who do you work for?" a man asked Hector in Spanish.

Squinting his eyes, Hector spat blood on the man's shoe. "I will never tell you."

The other bent and slapped him across his bruised face.

Cries from the women and even a few men echoed in the hall.

Christiaan had to do something. His neck ached from the tension. He gripped the rod. If only he had a weapon.

Hector raised his head. His eyes burned. "Why are you doing this?"

Christiaan inhaled sharply. Could he take all of these men? With his muscles as tense as a bow string, he leaned into Andy but couldn't take his eyes off the scene below.

Andy wrapped her arms around him.

Her embrace restrained him. Her eyes burned with fierce determination. He was torn.

She squinted her eyes closed. "I can't watch this. This is too similar to what happened to Brad."

Her step-brother was brutally murdered in the bathroom at a casino in St. Louis. His death led her to work together with Christiaan and discover who killed him and why. "Then let me go. I'll kill them all." With all the adrenaline in his body, he probably could take out at least half of them. At least, he could kill the man in black.

Opening her eyes, she shook her head. "Remember what you told me? Know when you are outnumbered. Know when to stay safe."

Nodding, Christiaan swiped his hands across his face. When she felt guilty for not saving her stepbrother in St. Louis, he told her those words. He was certain his words were true then. Now she used the same logic to keep him safe. But he hated it.

A gunshot rang in the silence.

Beside him, Andy flinched.

Blood seeped from Hector. He sat back, red blossoming on his shirt. Then he fell slack.

Bile rose to Christiaan's throat. Terror raked through him. His stomach turned. Unused adrenaline shook his muscles. Andy wasn't safe here. "Uh-oh." The makeshift blowgun fell from his hands. "We better get out of here."

****

The Commander lowered the rifle to his side. He stepped away. Something stuck to his foot. A stray earring or a broken setting must be under his shoe. He bent and examined the item between his fingers.

Not jewelry. A nail with beads hastily glued together. One of the beads fell to the floor. The glue was still tacky. Movement on the second floor caught his eye.

Someone scurried away in the shadows.

Had someone tried to kill him? He nearly laughed. With a hastily made dart? He touched the tip of the nail with a fingertip. *Not a gun.* He rubbed his chin. He only knew of a few men who didn't use guns.

"Commander?"

Lieutenant Pascal behind him broke his thoughts.

"We didn't find the items or the mark."

And their mark didn't take the bait. "You searched everyone?" He reveled in the chaos surrounding him.

Women screamed and clutched bleeding ears. Men and women who refused to cooperate were beaten with the butts of his men's rifles.

He glanced again to where the would-be assassin escaped. "She said he would be here."

"Yes. But we amassed a large quantity of goods." Lieutenant Pascal smiled. Uneven teeth crammed his mouth. He held out a handful of jewels. "These gems should fund us for a while." He paused. "We did find one man. His cuffs were cut from his shirt. And four of his men were already down."

"Gunshots?" The Commander lifted his chin.

"No, sir. Hand-to-hand combat. And the man's cuffs were slashed though with razorblades. He refused to speak, so Künsli put a bullet in his head."

"Our target escaped through the hallway there." The Commander pointed his head in the direction where the shadowy figures escaped.

"Shall we send an assassin after our mark?"

The Commander fingered the dart again. "I don't want him dead. Lìjì will contact him. She will bring him to me."

Lieutenant Pascal stepped closer and whispered. "Forgive me, sir. I am not questioning your orders, but do you really think she is capable of bringing in such a formidable opponent?"

Under his mask, the Commander arched an eyebrow and examined the lieutenant. "I trained her myself on how to manipulate and to tug at one's emotions. Her acting skills are unsurpassed. She is a master tracker. As she failed to bring me the emeralds and let them slip through her fingers, she must make amends for her complacency."

Lieutenant Pascal bowed.

Sirens called in the distance. "Clear out," the Commander whispered. "We've drawn enough attention."

Lieutenant Pascal signaled to his men. "Commence exit strategy."

Men immediately obeyed. Jumping over corpses and debris, they retreated through their hole.

Then the Commander stalked to the Prime Minister who cowered near her dead bodyguards. He drew up his rifle. Raising her chin, the Prime Minister quivered before him, but a touch of defiance burned in her eyes. He must cure her of it.

"You are not political terrorists." She stood, with head and shoulders erect. "You were searching for something else. You didn't even care for me. Nor are you common jewelry thieves. May I at least know who is attacking us?"

The Commander smirked. "We are Unction." Then he lifted his rifle and shot her between the eyes, tucking a manifesto about the Basques in her fallen, lifeless body. "Nothing personal, you see. You're just a red herring."

****

Peeking from behind a cypress tree, Fabian heard the explosion before he saw the men pouring into *El Real*. He couldn't imagine a single man causing such a scene. But no, one man couldn't orchestrate this attack.

A whole organization was behind this operation. Fabian stayed in the garden outside *El Real*. More than one man sought the emeralds—or one man and one organization. He wouldn't try to procure the emeralds or seek revenge tonight.

He narrowed his eyes. Why such an interest in the emeralds? Maybe he missed something. But even if his suspicions were true, he would fetch a greater price for clean emeralds. Unmarked gems were more valuable than marked ones.

Ruens navigated the cypress trees. The wound across the bridge of his nose was still angry and swollen. "I just received word from our contacts in the UK. They captured our target and the solution for the emeralds."

A bead of satisfaction spread through Fabian's chest. After the failure of the night, he needed the good news. "Excellent." He nodded toward his second-in-command. "Move the asset to a secure location. Let's see who will be our highest bidder."

Chapter 6

"Home. For now." Christiaan didn't even glance out the window of the airplane. He palmed the emeralds in a red bag, sometimes used as a gifting envelope by the Chinese. Since he recovered them, he hadn't let them leave his sight. But they came at such a cost.

Hector volunteered. He knew the risk. Since they weren't on official OverSight business, Christiaan filed no bureaucratic paperwork nor requested the organization to pay compensation to his family. Thankfully, Hector wasn't married. His computer was his girlfriend. But Christiaan alerted Hector's parents—a task he didn't relish—and sent them a generous sum from his personal savings. No amount of money made up for the loss of life. Hector's potential was cut short. And his death stained Christiaan's mission. He would have to grieve later.

Hector was loyal, and his loyalty killed him. Everyone around Christiaan died.

Andy had to go home. He couldn't risk her life as well.

From her window seat, Andy sat with her back to the London skyline set against the milky, white sky. "You okay?" She touched his forearm.

Turning away, he deposited the emeralds in his safe-pocket inside his shirt and nodded. "We can talk about it later." He sat back.

Her forehead wrinkled. "Will they come after us?"

"I don't think anyone saw us." No need to alarm her. Or tell her the truth. He glanced past her to the window. The London Eye, Big Ben, Buckingham Palace, the Thames—the landmarks drew closer as the plane descended and ultimately landed.

Andy's features relaxed as they neared the gate. "Where do you live?" She unbuckled her seatbelt at the terminal.

"Here."

"In the airport?" She grinned with a glint in her eye.

He smirked. "In the city."

Andy shook her head and stood. "Do you know how much a London flat costs?"

He shouldered the luggage from the overhead compartment. "I do pay rent here, or OverSight does, so I have a pretty good idea." He bought them tickets and boarded the express train into the city.

Out on the street, Andy opened her mouth at the cars in the opposite lanes. She pointed down. "Thankfully someone painted *Look right* and *Look left* on the crosswalks."

He chuckled. Six months passed since he'd been with an American. Her reaction was priceless. "They call them zebra walks here."

She brought back her neck. "Like the animal?"

"Yes, you know black-and-white stripes." He nodded toward the painted white stripes as they crossed. The air smelled the same—damp and old with a hint of mildew. Even in July, the sky hung heavy with clouds. This apartment wasn't the only one he kept, but it had the most options. He hated being hedged in and constricted. London was the gateway to the rest of the world. He paused at the intersection to check to see if the road was clear.

Andy started into the street.

He held her back.

A car honked. The driver waved as he passed.

The wheels came within inches of her toes.

Panting, Andy placed a hand over her heart. "I was looking the wrong way." Her face was still looking to the left.

He cast her a sideways glance. "Let's call a taxi. Americans are dangerous to take anywhere."

Andy launched a punch at his shoulder.

He caught her hand and drew her close. "You don't want to fight me. I'm a wounded man, but I would still win."

Her eyes burned. "Only if you want to get more wounded." Stepping back, she side-kicked within inches of his wound.

He easily blocked her leg, knocking it down. "Careful."

Once in the taxi, Andy leaned close. "Thank you for letting me stop over before my flight to the States." She tapped him. "It's the least you can do since I saved your life. Twice."

He arched his brow. "Twice?"

"The redhead." Andy raised her chin.

Christiaan rolled his eyes. "Hardly threatening."

She poked him in the chest. "And I kept you from being flattened by the man in black."

True. Had she not kept him back, he would've torn down there and taken on the whole organization. And where would he be? Dead. Like Hector. He grunted again. He stared out the taxi window.

She touched his shoulder. "Are you still thinking about him?"

How could he not? Hector had been a loyal friend. When his life was on the line, he hadn't even ratted out Christiaan. You couldn't buy such loyalty. But why? Hector might've lived had he just said who employed him. But then again, the man in black didn't seem like a man who kept promises, just threats.

His presence unsettled him. The man in black couldn't possibly know he sought the emeralds. And yet...

Back in Spain, Andy said they could find answers on the news. But while he watched TV in the *emergencia* to stitch up his side, he learned the authorities guessed the explosion came from a possible terrorist attack and blamed the ETA.

"Hungry?" Andy asked, rubbing the back of his neck.

Her fingers found all the sore spots. Relaxing a little, he shrugged. The man in black consumed his thoughts. He wanted him dead. But who was he? His men searched for someone and something in particular. All the men they targeted were tall and muscular like Christiaan. How did the man in black know he would be there? Was he another assassin sent to kill Christiaan? If he was there to kill him, he went to a great deal of expense and effort only to fail.

"I've never had British fish and chips."

Andy chirped her words. Christiaan appreciated her attempt to cheer him up.

The taxi stopped at a street lined with shops and buildings.

Christiaan paid the cabbie then stuffed his wallet back into his pocket. "London has better food than fish and chips."

"I know." She raised her shoulders and slumped them again. "I'm just trying to distract you."

She stepped closer and wrapped her arms around him and enveloped him in her heavenly smell. Inhaling deeper, he didn't even feel the pain in his ribs.

"I know how it feels to lose someone. I've already lost so many people. Sometimes I use humor to distract myself because if I fully realized what's inside, I'd fall apart. And I'm not ready to crumble."

Christiaan's eyes burned. He swallowed back tears and pain. He'd think about Hector later. This beauty was his for the next twelve or so hours. Squeezing her in return, he then held her at arm's length and examined all the cleverness and charm before him. He noticed something he hadn't seen before. "You started carrying a backpack instead of a bag?" He unlocked the door to his building. "Toss your stuff in here, and we can go out."

Andy shrugged and wiped a strand of auburn hair caught in her lip gloss. She dropped her suitcase inside a small lobby of his apartment. "A backpack was more practical and less suspicious. I learned my lesson. The red weekender tote was an obvious tell. The uniqueness of the bag helped Tyrone track me down."

Now she sported a sleek black backpack, like every other student in this city. Good...she'd be less obvious. Although he doubted any harm would come to her here in London. Nobody knew she was here.

He sighed. Christiaan only had to entertain her until she caught her flight in twelve hours. But could he say goodbye again?

****

Andy bit her lip. Standing on the corner of a busy street in London, she absorbed the finer details of the busy city. Even the pedestrians walked in the patterns similar to the streets—directly opposite of Americans. Every so often, a red phone booth popped up on the sidewalk and red mailboxes—only they weren't boxes, more like cylinders—appeared. And those red double-decker buses were real. Buildings hugged the street and allowed limited sunlight into the roads. The scent of car exhaust mingled with cigarette smoke.

She loathed not being in control. Even though she spoke English, England was not America. They had different customs, cultural rules, and currency. She didn't have any pounds, just a credit card.

Although she couldn't wait to return home, she treasured these last few moments with Christiaan. Who knew when she would see him again? "No fish and chips, then. How 'bout a pub? Want to deaden your grief with alcohol?" She nodded in the direction of a bar down the street. Christiaan hadn't been himself since they left *El Real*.

Christiaan stuffed his hands into his pants pockets. "No alcohol."

Andy paused. A *whoosh* of air came down between the tall buildings. Come to think of it, she'd never seen him drink. "Not on the job? Or not ever?"

"I can't drink."

His face held so much tension. He was thinking about Madrid and Hector. Her shoulders sagged. "Can't drink? Is this another of your oaths?"

He nodded.

"How many do you have?"

He raised his eyebrows. "Many."

Then his expression eased. There, he was returning to normal.

"I'm sorry. I'm not being a very good host. What would you like to eat?"

"I'm not that hungry." She ate on the plane. And she hadn't exactly heard glowing reviews of British food.

"Then instead of eating, how about I buy you a thank-you-for-saving-my-life gift so you'll stop lording it over me?"

"Deal." She nodded with a grin. She could always add something to her disguise wardrobe. A souvenir of her one and only night's stay in London would be nice.

"Where shall we go?"

Andy perked at the prospect of shopping. "If you're buying, then let's shop at an outrageously expensive department store."

He nodded up the street towering with historical buildings. "How convenient. I live not far from one." Christiaan crossed a few streets to a store encompassing nearly a whole street block.

The huge, lit windows showcased mannequins in bright summer outfits holding paper umbrellas. Adjusting her backpack, she followed him into the department store. Few items were on display and were evenly spaced. So different from American stores where inventory flooded every nook and cranny.

After circling the displays of handbags, she approached a rack of colorful scarves. She ran her fingers over cashmere. The texture reminded her of cat ears. "Quality over quantity." Flipping over a price tag, she dropped the scarf immediately. "Wow, quality indeed."

Christiaan swatted her hand. "Don't look at the price tag. I'll buy whatever you want."

Andy slithered a scarf across her neck. Her gaze never left his. "This isn't my payment for my help. I told you what I wanted."

Christiaan nodded. He fingered leather gloves. "You want to find your father."

His masculine, hulking figure contrasted with the softness of the accessories. Andy nodded. She could never tell him what she really wanted. That wish would never be fulfilled. "I doubt he's still alive. If he were alive, he would contact me, right?"

Christiaan harrumphed. "Unless he couldn't."

"Why wouldn't he be able to?" Andy kept her same number on her personal cell phone and used burner phones for everyone else. "Don't let me hope he's still alive. I've buried him in my heart years ago."

Christiaan winced and shook his head gently. "He might not be in a position where he has access to a phone."

"You mean a prisoner?"

"Or in some kind of low-power position. I'll contact my resources. RECON is very good at their job. We'll find out where he went. I promise." His gaze met hers. "And I never break a promise."

In the fluorescent lights, Andy noticed his white scar splitting his eyebrow in two. "I know." She rubbed the scarf on her cheek. He had never broken a promise. Not like the thousands of men who promised ski trips and birthday presents but never delivered. Of course his loyalty to his oaths kept them apart. Perhaps she wished he were a little less true to his word. But then where would they be? Would he be just like every other cad? What made him different made him attractive. But what made him different also made him unattainable. His oaths bound him to his promises but separated him from Andy. If only they could be together for even one night. What would she wear? Did they even sell those things in this store? She craned her neck to check out the departments.

"Tell me. What do you want?" Christiaan stood in front of her. He grasped her elbow.

Good thing he couldn't read her thoughts. Her face burned. "Hmm?" She gulped. Her mind wandered far from the store. She shook the image free of her mind. "I want one of those fabulous British hats. Like the queen."

"She hires a private millinery." His chin dipped.

"Oh." Of course the queen didn't shop here. "Then I'll settle for a large, floppy hat."

Finally, a grin touched his lips. His blue eyes sparkled. "One fabulously hideous hat coming right up."

In the accessories department, Andy combed through the umbrellas and gloves until she reached the hat rack. After plucking at a few turbans and wraps, she found a white, wide-brimmed, straw hat that spanned the width of her shoulders. She settled it on her head and checked herself in the mirror with a huge grin. "I love it!"

Christiaan smiled.

Andy flipped over the tag hanging from the brim. "Gah! No!"

"Do you fancy it?" He set his jaw.

She clutched it to her chest. "I love it."

He grasped the tag and read it. He rolled his eyes. "Of course you'd find the most expensive hat in the store."

"It's too expensive." She put it back on the stand.

Instead of replying, he removed the hat and headed for the cash desk.

Her one night in London and Christiaan bought her a silly hat. Why couldn't he let down his guard for just one night?

****

On his street, Christiaan thrummed his fingers on his thumb. Seeing Andy again was like sliding into his favorite cargo pants. Being beside her filled him with peace—peace he hadn't felt for a long time. In the setting sun, her hair lit up as if fire ran through her strands. Was it close to her real color? He had no idea. How he wanted to run his fingers through her hair and kiss each lock.

What would life be like if they could be together? Constant fighting? Only to anticipate making up. Not a bad prospect. Maybe she could stay. Could he ask her to give up what she wanted to stay? He offered before. No. After Hector's death, she had to return home. He couldn't endanger another person, especially not Andy.

Outside his flat door on the street, he paused on the limestone stoop.

"When will I hear from you again?" Andy's eyes grew large.

He gulped. How could he tell her everything he needed to do? Was he even worth waiting for? Christiaan didn't know if she'd still accept him if she knew everything. He wrapped an arm around her waist.

An object sailed over her shoulder.

Acting on pure instinct, he shoved her out of the knife's path. A knife? The blade bit into the wood door behind them. "Get down," he shouted and yanked her to the sidewalk. While in a crouch, he spotted a man disappearing onto the crowded sidewalk. Christiaan tore after him until he sensed Andy following him. "Go back!" he shouted over his shoulder.

Christiaan ran past the Knightsbridge tube stop.

The curly-haired man ran toward the next street.

With a single bound, Christiaan leaped and tackled him to the ground.

With wild eyes, the man cuffed Christiaan a few times across his cheeks.

Christiaan pinned him to the cobblestones. With his hands around his collar, he knocked the man's head against the ground. "You want me? You can't throw worth crap."

"I wasn't trying to kill you." He furrowed his dark eyebrows, but he parted his lips in a menacing grin. His gaze flitted behind Christiaan to an empty parked car.

With his senses on alert, Christiaan examined the empty car. The hair on the back of his neck stood on end. Dragging the attacker to standing, Christiaan hauled the man behind him across the street.

The man tried to free himself from Christiaan's grasp.

Just from sheer size and weight, Christiaan held the advantage. When he reached the sidewalk, Christiaan's vision brightened, then darkened, and his ears rang. A force pushed his back. He flew forward and landed on his face. Shrapnel and debris landed beside him.

Fire burned in the empty car behind them. Smoke

billowed upward in dark, voluminous clouds, blacking out the hazy sky above.

Christiaan coughed. The stench of the smoke burned in his lungs. Pain throbbed in his leg. The fool lured him out to the explosion. And Christiaan fell for the bait. Shaken and sore, he sat up.

Because Christiaan held the man behind him, Christian was shielded from the brunt of the explosion. He looked over at the man. Glass and shrapnel were embedded in his face, hands, and legs. But Christiaan wagered his back was worse. Christiaan crawled to his attacker.

The man stared into the sky. His body trembled. Soot and ash covered his face. A chunk of hair was gone.

"Who sent you?" Christiaan leaned over him.

A whimper eased from the man's throat. Blood seeped from a gash on his forehead and leaked in a pool beneath him.

Christiaan tore off his shirt, hoping to stanch the man's wound, but he knew by the quantity and color, a mere shirt would not be enough. "Who are you?" he asked again. "What do you want?" Dozens of organizations wanted Christiaan. Assassins were not uncommon.

"Godfather of the Night. We want revenge."

Through his bleeding and cracked lips, the man whispered in a hoarse and forced voice. Christiaan's blood drained as he searched the face of his attacker. Perhaps he heard wrong. The ringing in his ears muffled the sound except the distant emergency vehicles.

Before he could ask again, the man's eyes fluttered

and relaxed, reflecting the horrid scene of destruction. Christiaan surveyed his muted surroundings. Every action slowed. Paper curled in the wind from blown-out windows. Bystanders tended the wounds of the injured passersby. A mangled bicycle sat in the road. The blackened car, burnt out and smoking, languished on the curb. Heat made him sweat.

Where was Andy?

Through the smoke and haze, Christiaan searched behind him. The glass surrounding the tube stairs was either blown or pockmarked by shrapnel. For once, she listened and stayed back. If she had followed him, she would've been burnt toast.

Debate was over. Andy needed to go home. She wasn't safe here or anywhere near him.

****

"Godfather of the Night?" Andy asked, once the bomb squad had determined the place clear. The sun set. Darkness enveloped the streets of London. Bystanders were scattered around the scene. The news crews and emergency responders continued their work. She folded her shaking hands to act nonchalant. "Who is that?"

Through the tall buildings, Christiaan escorted her to his apartment. He checked over his shoulder between the two buildings. "They're after me. Someone ordered a hit. Assassins, bounty hunters, or anyone who wants an easy kill or capture for ten million euro will search for me."

Gasping, Andy tugged at his shoulder. "Why didn't you tell me you have a hit order?"

At his apartment street door, Christiaan removed his keys. "I worried you'd cash me in yourself."

Andy nodded in mock seriousness. "Ten million euro would be useful about now."

Christiaan smiled with no humor.

"Who has that kind of money to waste?"

"I wish I knew." He stared at the door.

The police took the knife as evidence, but the gash in the wood still remained. "That guy had lousy aim." Andy touched the gash. "He missed you by a wide berth. In fact, he nearly hit me."

"He said he wasn't trying to kill me. He lured me out to the car bomb." Christiaan swung open the door and mounted the stairs.

"Because bombing someone is more accurate?" She shook her head. His tactics didn't make any sense.

"More effective, maybe. More chaos. No doubt he thought I couldn't catch him."

His words echoed in the stairwell. Andy followed him. "No, he expected to get away. Why a bomb?"

Christiaan shrugged on the landing, then hiked up the next set of stairs. "A single attacker can be tracked and found. A bomber, on the other hand, could be seen as a terrorist attack. I would've died as an unhappy coincidence."

"Do you recognize him?" Earlier, Andy stood nearby as police searched and then draped the body. His poor face was nearly unrecognizable

He shook his head and went up again, holding the handrail. "I don't know. Ten million euro is a lot."

"I'd sell you for one million." She cracked a smile.

"Still mad at me?" Raising his brows, he leaned against the rail.

"Who are the Godfather of the Night?" Andy changed the subject.

"European mob." He started up again.

"They know where you live?" Andy inhaled. Why didn't they have an elevator in this building?

Christiaan unlocked his door but didn't open it. He faced her. "If they tracked me here, OverSight will switch my flat." He jabbed a finger at Andy. "But you need to get back to the States as soon as possible."

Andy stood toe to toe with him. His breath tickled her hair. "Did you rig this whole thing just to get rid of me?"

A smile crept on his face. He leaned against the doorframe. "I didn't. I promise." He drew up her chin and kissed her. Then he slid his hand into hers and drew her close. "I wish I got more information from him." He hesitated before pointing over his shoulder. "You want to come in?"

"You okay?" Pulling up his hand, Andy gasped. His palms bled. She searched the rest of him. His calf was torn, and his pants were soaked in blood.

Coming off the wall, Christiaan tugged at his pant leg sticking to his wound. "I was in shock. I have no pain."

"We should take you to the doctor." Andy grasped his elbow.

He stuck a thumb over his shoulder. "I've got a first aid kit inside. Are you coming inside?"

Arching a brow, she crossed her arms over her bag and hugged it to her. "I planned to stay at a hostel."

He swung his forearm against the doorframe and leaned into her.

Andy gulped. She wanted him—all of him. Her heart rate accelerated.

"You can stay here. You have a long day of travel

tomorrow." He stroked her hair and kissed a strand pinched between his fingertips. "I won't charge."

Her pulse thundered in her ears. "Very generous. I'll at least wash your cuts." She leaned in and tilted her face upwards.

"As long as you promise to bathe them gently," he whispered into her lips.

"I have to make sure you're all clean." She inched her face closer, trying to silence her heart. Could he hear the pounding through her chest?

"I can think of other things I'd rather do." His gaze dropped to her lips. He brushed his lips against hers.

Andy leaned forward and breathed him in. Her whole body flushed against his.

Christiaan backed against his door.

The door gave way behind him, and they tumbled to the floor.

Andy landed on top of Christiaan. She stared up into an impressive set of legs.

"What a pleasing surprise."

The woman's green glittering eyes lost some of their shine. Her lips flattened into a forced smile. The tone of her voice told Andy the woman was anything but pleased.

"Amanda Miller. I didn't know you'd be here."

Andy hated being called by her real name and hated it even more coming from Sabrina Guitterelli.

Chapter 7

Christiaan cringed. Sabrina looked anything but pleased to see him with Andy. In his scramble to stand, he placed his hands on Andy's back. Christiaan embraced his Italian superior, kissing both her cheeks, then strolled into the kitchen to tend to his wounds. His plans for the evening were ruined.

"What brings you to London?" Andy wiped her lips. "Jack the Ripper back on the streets? London Bank hacked? Crown jewels stolen?"

Sabrina smirked, giving Andy a sideways glance before following Christiaan into the kitchen. "My business is of a confidential nature. And I'm afraid, for Christiaan's ears only."

Christiaan focused on the blood streaming into his kitchen sink. "So you're here for work?" He glanced up.

She arched an eyebrow at Christiaan. "Did you hope I was here for pleasure?" She then swiveled swiftly, facing Andy. A tight smirk tugged on her face. "This meeting might take a while. You should return to where you're staying tonight."

Christiaan's cheeks flamed as he returned his focus on his hands. "She's actually staying here tonight."

"Oh, I see."

Christiaan glanced up.

Sabrina blinked several times. She shook her head.

Her dark curls hid her expression for a second.

"Besides, anything you need to say to me, you can say in front of Andy."

Sabrina stared, her lips froze in a smile.

Andy stepped forward. "No, it's okay. I can see this is a work thing. I'll walk the streets."

Sabrina waited until Andy slid out to the hall and closed the door. "Am I confused, or did we have an agreement?"

"Andy's different." He finished with his hands and searched the kitchen for a towel.

"When you first came to me, I regarded your proposition extreme. To be your girlfriend so that you wouldn't have to deal with all the women clamoring after you."

He stiffened. Sabrina exaggerated his concerns. "I didn't say that."

"No, you said you needed a cover so you would get assignments which violated your oaths. But you waited a year before you trusted me with that secret. Still, I agreed."

An unspoken question hovered in the air. Did he still need Sabrina? He opened a drawer to find a knife. Christiaan shrugged. After drying his hands on a towel near the sink, he bent and slit his pant leg with the knife. The wound oozed clotted and darkened blood. Shrapnel still lodged in swollen flesh. Torn skin gaped open. He sighed. At least Andy didn't see it. She'd suggest stitches and real medical care.

With the edge of the blade he scraped off the clotted blood and metal bits. Sharp spears of pain stabbed through him. He ground his teeth against it. And at least she wasn't listening to this conversation with Sabrina, too. "I don't need the cover anymore." Pain pinched his voice, but he struggled to appear unharmed. He checked Sabrina's reaction.

"Because of her?" Sabrina tossed her head toward the door.

Christiaan didn't answer. *Maybe. No.* He didn't know.

Sabrina watched him. She moved into the kitchen. Her eyes grew large. "You were attacked?"

"Bomb." His hands were rock steady. Someone nearly killing him should have given him some physical response, trembling, fear—something. His emotions must be dead, or he was still in shock. They nearly killed Andy. They hunted him and yet, he felt nothing. And the nothingness scared him.

Sabrina's painted lips parted. "You were involved with that? The local officials alerted OverSight. We spread word it was a confirmed terrorist attack. What was it?"

"Bounty hunters." He held his breath against the pain. He dug into his flesh to release another shard of glass. "I'll need a new flat." At last, he removed all the shrapnel. Now he could wash it. He wrapped his calf with a dish rag and limped to the bathroom. In the tub, he poured warm water over his throbbing calf. He twisted to see the gaping hole.

Sabrina followed. "Let me do that." She grabbed the soap. "Who was it?"

"Godfather of the Night." Christiaan leaned into her.

She bathed the wound. "Thugs from Santorini?"

"They hold a grudge." He gritted his teeth.

So near her, he inhaled her musky, woodsy

perfume. Her silky complexion shone in the bathroom light. Her coal-black hair undulated over her head as waves of obsidian.

"Was that you in Madrid? Fifty dead? Prime minister murdered?"

His head grew fuzzy at her touch. "We didn't cause a whisper of complaint. We only disarmed four men. You know me, no guns. Our mark practically threw me the emeralds. Someone else came." The memory of the man in black flashed in his mind. "He was also searching for…" He wasn't sure what. "Something."

"You called Andy?"

Christiaan exhaled. Now he understood what this argument was about. Andy. He paused. Too many emotions flooded him. He couldn't process them all. "I should've told you about Andy."

Sabrina scrubbed again.

This time her touch was gentle. He relaxed.

"You said you would tell me if you ever didn't need me anymore."

A long pause opened between them. He didn't know what to say.

"Does she know about all of your past?"

Christiaan remained silent for a few breaths. "No."

Sabrina faced him. Her unflinching gaze moved. "Will you tell her?"

"I hope I don't have to." He paused, breathing deeply to stop the quivering pain. "At first I hoped she could help me. She has skills and talent. But now I see my work is too dangerous for her to be here."

"Dangerous for her or for *you*?"

Ignoring her question, Christiaan shook water from his leg. Blood streamed into the tub. "I'm sending her back to the States so she can be safe."

"Or so you can be safe?" Sabrina slid a towel down from the bar and wrapped his calf. "You're lucky you only received one injury."

Christiaan shrugged. A flesh wound didn't concern him at all. The whole event exploded in his mind. What if Andy followed him out there? He shook the scene from his mind. He found a first aid kit under the bathroom sink and treated his leg with antibiotic ointment. "Surely you came here to discuss something other than my love life."

Sabrina leaned against the pedestal sink. "We need to call you in." She flashed him a tight-lipped smile. "While you were on your—what do you call it?—chase of the wild goose?"

"Wild goose chase in English. *Qū zhī ruò wù* in Chinese. Or to chase a wandering duck."

She smiled, lowering her chin. "Yes. While you were gone chasing birds, new trouble has come at a golf tournament."

"Golf. Now that sounds like a vacation." He wrapped his leg in long, white sterile bandages.

Sabrina frowned and puffed out her plump lips.

"Two days ago, in a Women's Invitational, one of the competitors was reported missing. In addition to a missing person, a series of troubling events have thrown the games—small things, but enough disruption the committee is worried. Since the missing girl is a Chinese citizen, their government called in OverSight—against MI5's knowledge—to investigate. The Security Service doesn't appreciate OverSight sniffing into their affairs. While they have sovereignty, the United Nation Accords give us immunity and jurisdiction over all international affairs, but we are supposed to ask for permission. The Chinese government doesn't want the United Kingdom to know we are there. So the British Secret Service must not discover OverSight is involved. If we are discovered, the breach of trust causes all sorts of diplomatic issues. And paperwork." She began with a burn salve and covered his hands. Kneeling beside him, Sabrina motioned for the gauze and finished wrapping. "Ready for your next investigation?" She lifted her face.

She pled with all her beauty and allure. So beautiful and yet only Andy consumed him. "You know as soon as I find all the emeralds, I'll be leaving OverSight."

After finishing his leg, she wrapped his hand. "The directions are in a packet I left on your table. As well as the victim's file with her information, including a photo. Your cover and instructions should be clear. We have a new identity and phone for communication." She stopped and eyed him as he glanced over his hands. "What will you do with Andy?"

"I'm sending her home on a flight to the States. Tomorrow morning."

Sabrina raised a brow. "Tomorrow *morning*? That will be inconvenient since you're leaving in a few hours."

He sighed. Now he wouldn't even get his one last night with Andy. "I'll change her flight for tonight."

"Sorry to ruin your plans for the evening." Throwing the bandages in the kit, she tossed her head.

Sabrina didn't sound apologetic at all.

She folded the cloth. "Does she know about your vows?"

Closing the kit, Christiaan shrugged. "I've told her some."

"But not all?"

Sighing, he rubbed the bridge of his nose. Telling her everything could jeopardize their relationship—a step he wasn't willing to take right now.

"Just making sure she doesn't have—how do you say?—unmet expectations." Sabrina glanced up. "Is she worth the risk?"

When it came to Andy, he struggled to process all his feelings.

Standing, Sabrina shook her head. "She will always be a temptation."

Christiaan remained silent. He returned the towel. The truth of her words stung him. He studied the scrapes on his right hand. He hadn't bandaged it yet. Though only scratched, the skin was torn and colorless. The wound underneath was deep red. "I have no choice. My mission is clear. No one will stand in my way—not even Andy. Let's discuss details." He opened the bathroom door.

Sabrina led the way to the kitchen where papers lay on the table.

"Why such a hurry?"

Sabrina, in her tight green dress, glided around the table. "The victim wasn't supposed to be invited to this tournament. Her name was not on any lists, but yet she received an invite."

"Who is in charge of the invites?"

"Mr. McGuffin."

Christiaan nodded. Being invited was suspicious. Who would want her out there? Why did they go to all this trouble? "Is Mr. McGuffin one of our suspects?"

She leaned an arm against the edge of the table. "Everyone is a suspect. Also, we discovered the victim received a phone call early Thursday morning through our secret contacts within the MI5. We traced the number to McGuffin's Blakely Manor. He saved the village from economic collapse by building the commerce around his golf course." She held up a print of a satellite screenshot. "This is Dornoch. He claimed no one from his household issued the call."

"All roads lead to Mr. McGuffin." He pored over the papers in front of him. "Tell me about him."

"Philanthropist, humanitarian, billionaire." Sabrina's brilliant green eyes shone. "But here's the tricky part: because of his connections to a UN charity, you'll have to tread lightly. We cannot be caught investigating him or his personal residence."

"Or it will be bad press." He sighed. He hated the delicate dance of diplomacy.

She raised her eyebrows and shook her head. "Not just bad press. He contributes millions of euros to UN-supported charities and programs. We can't have him withdraw his support. Our agency runs on his money. Especially if he does prove to be innocent."

Rubbing a hand down his face, Christiaan bit his lip. "Tact requires more stealth and time."

"Your train leaves tonight. The Men's Amateur Open is this week in Dornoch. The place will be crawling with golfers, sport fans, gamblers, caddies, and newspeople. All of them are in danger."

"And all of them suspects." The more people around, the more difficult it was to investigate. "I have a cover inside the hotel?"

Sabrina nodded. "But you'll need to access his

personal quarters which are heavily guarded." She sighed.

He plucked at his chin. "Objectives. One: find the victim for the Chinese. Two: identify the guilty party for the Chinese. And three: investigate Mr. McGuffin with grace and tact. And four: avoid MI5 agents." He rolled his eyes. "Piece of cake."

"*In bocco al lupo.*" Sabrina slid toward the door. Her jacket hung over her arm.

"*Crepi.*" He pinched his fingers.

"I have to go. And you have to pack for Scotland." She hesitated at the open door. Her gaze flitted to the bedroom. "If it doesn't work out, I'll always be here for you."

He flattened his lips. "I know. You're a great friend." Crossing the room, he helped her into her coat.

Sabrina pecked him on each side of his cheeks.

Her musk hung in the air between them.

She backed out of the door.

What Sabrina said haunted him. Andy tempted him more than any other woman. He had to get rid of her as soon as possible. Or live on the edge.

Within moments, Andy entered the apartment from the hall. "I'm packed and ready to go to Scotland."

He glared. "I knew you'd be listening in. You're not going with me."

She bounded to the table and picked up a paper.

"Nope." Christiaan snatched the document out of her hands. "For my eyes only."

Parting her lips, Andy glanced at a picture paper-clipped to a folder. "Hin Cho? I know her."

"You do?" Christiaan's eyebrows furrowed. "How?"

"She's my friend. Why is she being investigated by OverSight?"

Tilting his head, he gathered the rest of the papers. "Weren't you eavesdropping?"

Andy shrugged. "I didn't hear much." She placed her hands over her heart. "Just Sabrina confessing her undying love."

"What are you talking about?"

Smirking, Andy cocked her hip. "When she says she'll be here for you, she does not mean a friendly shoulder to cry on."

Rolling his eyes, Christiaan shook his head. "We're not talking about Sabrina. We're talking about you going back to the States. Tonight."

She marched forward. "No, we were talking about what happened to Hin Cho. Why does OverSight have a file about her on your table?"

His body tensed. Christiaan closed his eyes.

"Something's happened to her, and you're investigating."

Andy didn't phrase it as a question. The truth hovered in the air. He always hated being the one to tell loved ones. "Missing. I'm so sorry."

Andy slumped to a chair. "Where was she last seen?"

"In Dornoch."

"The golf tournament." Andy stood and grabbed her suitcase. "I'm going with you to Scotland."

"No." He grabbed her shoulders. Andy knocked his arms away in a self-defense move.

"You need me. People are after you. You can't go alone."

He loved her gumption and grinned. "I won't be

alone. Your nagging voice will always be in my head." He poked her forehead. Then he pushed her onto a kitchen barstool.

"I have to go." She tried to stand.

Placing a hand on her shoulder, Christiaan set her back again. He picked up his phone and found the app. "I'm changing your flight to tonight."

"You're wasting your time and money. I'm still going to Scotland." She leaped off the barstool.

"I personally forbid it." He secured a new ticket and sent the boarding pass to her phone. "And OverSight has eyes and ears everywhere. You'll never get past their vast network of espionage and reconnaissance. I will instruct them to tail you and make sure your little keister is on a plane back to the States. Your flight leaves in two hours." With his phone, he dialed a number with great exaggeration, his gaze never leaving hers.

"Eyes and ears everywhere?" Andy arched an eyebrow, crossing her arms. "They can't be everywhere. What a violation of privacy."

Speaking over his phone, Christiaan sighed and shook his head. "You Americans are so cute. Privacy is an illusion. RECON can highjack people's phones or home security systems. If it's electrical, has a microphone or camera, is connected to the Internet, or plugged in, they can see you, hear you, and listen to your heartbeat." He eyed her as the phone connected. "Reconnaissance."

She crossed her arms and scowled.

Hung from RECON answered.

"I need back up." Christiaan clicked a picture from his phone. "I'm sending a detailed facial recognition for

Amanda Miller a.k.a. Andy Baker for your team. Yes, *that* girl." He placed the phone on Speaker and continued talking as he scrolled. "She'll be heading to Heathrow tonight to return to the States. I need a tail on her at all times to ensure she makes her flight. Sent."

"You're bluffing."

"Think so?" With a flip of his phone, he showed her the caller ID. "Thanks, Hung!" He ended the call. "He'll make sure you get home safely. With OverSight technology, he has everything at his fingertips to track your tube card, your credit card, and your passport. Our security cameras can follow you in the tube as well as on any phone camera. He and his team can hack his way anywhere." Christiaan tossed his phone on the counter. "Have a lovely trip home." With a grin, he crossed his arms.

"Fine." Andy grabbed her packed suitcase and her backpack. She slapped her large floppy hat on her head. "Do I look British?"

"No." But she did look feisty.

She stepped forward, her eyebrows peaked. "You need me. I can help disguise you from all the assassins."

Lifting his chin, Christiaan shook his head.

"I can help you search around the Dornoch castle for Hin Cho."

"No." If one more person he cared for died, he couldn't live with himself.

"We'll see about that." Narrowing her eyes, Andy forced a smile and tipped her large, floppy hat. "Well, good luck!" She stomped out the door, luggage in tow.

Great. Now he pissed her off. He followed her to the hall. "At least let me take you to the airport?"

She paused in the hallway and cocked her head. "No, thanks. *OverSight* is following me."

Her voice dripped with sassy indignation. But putting her off was for her own good.

"I'll be safe in their hands." With her huge, floppy British hat waving as a stingray on her head, Andy marched down the stairs.

Christiaan relaxed his muscles. At least she would be safe at home.

****

As Andy stomped down the stairs, she fumed. How dare Christiaan keep her from this case, especially one involving her friend! How could she travel to Dornoch? When Andy stepped out into the street, someone approached from behind and tapped her on her shoulder. Using her martial arts skills, she elbowed him in the chest and joint-locked his arm, knocking his face into the wall. Spinning her opponent, she faced him.

"*Che palle*." Antonio stared with wide eyes. Blood trickled from the side of his mouth. "I'm not a field agent, Andy."

Antonio Gueitterli, the attractive OverSight agent, had only one drawback, being Sabrina's brother. But Andy loved him for rescuing her and Christiaan from the Mexican desert. He always had a smile for Andy. She dropped her hold on him. "You shouldn't sneak up on people."

"Sneak? We were on a street."

Antonio flashed a smile highlighting his dimples and his dark curly hair. Her knees went weak.

He leaned in to give her two kisses on each cheek. "How are you, Andy? Missed me?"

Inhaling his expensive cologne, Andy returned the

kisses on his tanned cheeks. "I have ached for you, Antonio." Andy retrieved a hanky and dabbed his lip.

He swiped the blood with his tongue. "Thank you."

"I'm so sorry." She shrugged. "Reflexes. What are you doing here?"

He swiped the hanky. "In the car." He pointed behind her.

A sleek, black Mercedes hovered near the curb. She found his Italian accent adorable. She would follow him anywhere.

"My sister wants to speak with you."

Andy dropped her smile. Except to see her.

Antonio, flashing teeth, pointed the way with one hand while the other wiped his lip. He held the door.

She ducked her head inside to the backseat.

Sabrina sat alone in the darkened cabin. She crossed her long legs. "We haven't seen you in a while, Andy. I mean before today."

"I've been lying low." At least lying.

"Hop in." Sabrina patted the leather seat next to her.

Andy, biting the side of her lip, glanced out toward the streetlamps cutting yellow triangles in the sidewalks. "Where would you be taking me?"

Sabrina's voice softened. "Paddington Station. Or to the airport, whichever you prefer."

"Thanks, but I don't mind walking." Andy stood to leave.

"I also have another matter we need to discuss. If you'll climb inside…"

Andy glanced up to Christiaan's apartment behind her, mulling over whether to discuss anything with Sabrina. "No thanks." She started to close the door.

"I can help you get to Scotland."

Andy held the door but didn't bend. "What makes you think I want to go to Scotland?"

"Oh, Andy."

Though Andy couldn't see her expression, even Sabrina's musical laugh irritated her.

"Andy, I know you can't stand to be left out. If you climb in now, I'll help you get to Dornoch."

Andy didn't want help—didn't need help. "I'm good. Christiaan already asked OverSight to accompany me home via spy methods." She put air quotes around the last two words.

"Want me to help you get there before him? Undetected?"

Andy cherished the element of surprise. But with Sabrina's help? She'd rather hike all the way to Scotland. But Hin Cho needed her. And time was of the essence. She bit her lip and swallowed her pride. She climbed in and slid across the leather seats.

Antonio threw her bag in the trunk.

"I was surprised to see you here with Christiaan."

When the car moved from the curb, Sabrina broke the awkward silence with an even more awkward statement. Andy didn't want to give anything away. "He asked for help in Madrid. Hector was there, too. I believe he worked for OverSight."

Sabrina nodded. "I heard of Hector's passing. He was trained by one of our best operatives working out of Hong Kong, Hung. A sheer genius with technology. As the head of Reconnaissance team, he knows everything. Absolutely nothing gets by him. Hector would've been a big help to Christiaan."

Andy glanced out the tinted window toward the

sculpted buildings. Perhaps death happened frequently in this business. She sighed, breathing out the mental images of Hector's gunshot to the head. "Why are you helping me?" Andy resented being in a low-power position.

"I will speak without a hair on my tongue." Sabrina's eyes glittered in the dim light. "The perspective of a non-OverSight agent will be helpful in Dornoch. You can be an American tourist. You are a natural investigator. Your talent for disguise and instincts are unique. Help us find Hin Cho. Even a little spice contributes to the soup."

Sabrina didn't know she knew Hin Cho. Regaining a bit of upper hand, Andy thrust her chin upward. "Why should I help you?"

Sabrina broke her stare, heaving in a deep wavering breath. "Christiaan is in danger. He is not worried, but I am."

Ah, the real reason Sabrina wanted her in Dornoch.

"People search for him. He has a price on his head. An anonymous source offered ten million euro for his capture. OverSight is tracking down who. You know Christiaan always takes risks and never thinks about himself. I would feel safer if you were there."

Andy mulled this over. The bomb explosion still rang in her ears and flashed behind her eyes. Even the smell of smoke clung to her clothes.

Sabrina slid a thick envelope across the leather seats.

Andy glanced at the envelope. She knew what it contained. "I don't need your money."

"You can't travel to Dornoch without it. The minute you use your credit card"—she snapped her fingers—"OverSight will know."

Andy scowled, staring at the envelope. "But you are OverSight."

Narrowing her eyes, she shrugged. "Right now, I am a concerned friend." Sabrina sat back, her gaze never leaving Andy. "Also, Christiaan asked me to get information about your father. Sometimes paperwork gets lost. However, if you go to Dornoch and protect Christiaan, I will prioritize his request."

Inhaling sharply, Andy flicked her gaze to Sabrina. Now she was talking.

"Take the money."

Her voice was as silky as her legs. Andy wanted to throw up. "I want to do this on my own."

"I can see why Christiaan admires you. You're bull-headed, just like him." She flashed a tight-lipped smile. "But being bull-headed will not get you to Dornoch."

Their gazes met, locked in competition, or maybe understanding. Andy reluctantly retrieved the envelope.

"This will pay for a ticket and operating costs. I trust you know how to evade OverSight. Christiaan is leaving on the next train. Inside is the last airline ticket for tonight. You will beat him by twelve hours. In that twelve hours, you will need a cover and a place to stay and a plan to stay close to Christiaan."

Andy nodded. She didn't need half the time.

"Inside the envelope are more specific instructions: Get into Mr. McGuffin's private quarters at the manor. Avoid any MI5 agents. And don't tell Christiaan I sent you." Here, she paused. She studied her fingers. "You are not the only one who cares for him."

Leaning forward, Sabrina quickened her speech.

Her Italian accent lilted in a song. Andy swallowed hard. Sabrina's confession felt like a threat.

The car stopped at a zebra walk near Paddington Station. Antonio opened the door.

"Christiaan won't be happy when he sees me there." Actually, she couldn't wait to see his face.

"If I know Christiaan, he won't complain too much." Sabrina met her gaze. "Just keep him safe. For both of us. *In bocco al lupo*."

Exiting the car, Andy stood on the street. "What does that mean?"

Antonio removed her bag from the back. "Good luck."

"Thanks."

Antonio waved a hand in front of him. "No, no, no! You'll bring bad luck to say thank you. Say *crepi il lupo*. Or just say *crepi*."

"*Crepi*. What does the phrase mean?"

"It means, may the wolf die." Antonio stepped closer and kissed her farewell on both cheeks.

Speaking of death might bring the Italians comfort, but it did little for Andy. Hauling the suitcase toward the station, Andy, pocketing the euros, wondered if bad luck had already plagued this whole agreement.

****

Gavis, one of thousands of RECON operatives, had been working for OverSight for twenty years, but he had never received a call from the head office asking him to tail some agent's girlfriend. Such an odd request. And not to make sure she wasn't cheating or anything. Just to make sure she boarded her plane.

Sitting in the observing station in the London office, Gavis ran his fingers over the keyboard. His keystrokes sounded as pelting rain. He glanced up through smudged glasses to the monitors surrounding him.

OverSight had digital eyeballs on every corner of the Paddington station.

Gavis searched for a girl with a wide-brimmed straw hat and a yellow sweater he tailed since she arrived. His stomach growled. Even working sixteen hours at a keyboard, his metabolism was insanely fast. But he received strict instructions not to take his eyes off the woman codenamed Slippery Fish.

Paddington station was one of his favorite places to observe. The Art Deco architecture fascinated him. The lighting from the huge, domed glass ceiling wasn't perfect, but it was sufficient to track a person on a sunny day. Sadly, it was night.

From one screen he saw the yellow sweater and wide-brimmed hat enter the fast-food restaurant. A red carry-on trailed behind her. She was just grabbing a bite to eat. Typical American. With a few careful strokes of a keyboard, he tapped into a kid's cell phone who was eating and playing games, as well as the security camera inside the restaurant.

Sometimes his job was exciting, but today, tailing a woman doing nothing but catching a plane to the United States was a snoozer—no information tracking, no clandestine passing of information or valuables. Gavis needed a little liquid pick-me-up.

The woman ordered at a kiosk, then waited for her order.

Gavis's stomach growled again. If he fetched a cup of coffee, he wouldn't be paying one-hundred percent attention to the woman. And he promised Hung not to take his eyes off her. He sighed. Her flight left at ten. He glanced at the time stamp at the bottom of the screen. Eight-thirty p.m.

Slippery Fish lounged against a table, then straightened and went into the loo behind another woman.

Damn. The one difficult place. Not only laws prohibited them—what did he care about laws?—he hijacked people's personal devices for a living—but most people tucked away phones to do their personal business.

Since she'd be occupied for a few minutes, he might as well nab some brew. With his gaze still on the screen, he turned his head only at the last moment to pour himself a cup from a stack of insulated cups and glanced up between sugar and cream. Then he returned to his rolling chair just as Slippery Fish exited the loo with her wide-brimmed hat.

She grabbed her order and headed to the platform.

A crush of people surrounded her, but Gavis managed to keep her in sight. With the yellow sweater and the wide-brimmed hat, she was easy to spot, as if she purposefully wore something ostentatious. Made his job easier. He relaxed a little when she settled on the train.

The conductor scanned her ticket with a handheld laser reader.

Yup, she was there. Every movement was recorded—every bar scan and blip. Her ticket number came up on the screen, and he dismissed it with a finger swipe. He played around a bit, hacking phones nearby, but the train ride to the airport was uneventful. Gavis relaxed into his joe.

Thousands of offices trailing leads existed in this building. Little rooms where people just watched, scanned, and monitored People of Interest. Sometimes Gavis wondered if anyone from OverSight spied on him. He disabled the microphone and kept a piece of tape over his personal camera phone lens, just to be sure.

The train slowed. Slippery Fish lifted her luggage from the rack above her head and headed to security.

Ho-hum. Gavis finished his first cup. He still had a few hours until he would eat again. Why not another cup?

Slippery Fish stepped in line for security.

She wasn't going anywhere. He rose, his gaze glued to the screen, and compiled another brew—coffee, sugar, creamer.

When Slippery Fish stepped up to the security to check into her flight, they zipped her boarding pass.

He sipped. Then he promptly gulped down burning liquid.

The name across the screen did not match Slippery Fish's identity.

He sat up. Who was he tracking?

The woman continued through security.

Gavis flew his fingers over the keyboard, searching for her all around. His heart pounded furiously. He'd lost her. The woman on the screen was not Slippery Fish. Yet, she was still wearing the hat and the sweater, still carrying a carry-on but perhaps not the same color. How had he missed it?

She was not the same woman. He'd been duped. He would never find Slippery Fish. When had they switched? He slapped his forehead. At the Paddington

Station bathroom.

Cream and sugar roiled in his stomach. Gavis sat back in his rolling chair. He could never tell Hung he lost her.

Chapter 8

Swirling the *chakram*, Fabian cursed the man who stole so much. After some time in recovery, he survived the broken wrist and the broken ankle, but the doctors couldn't reattach the missing digits. Fabian paced the entrance of his Paris mansion and swore in French. "I want him dead. I want him to suffer. I want to know why he wanted the emeralds."

A line of his men stood shoulder to shoulder in the lobby.

The same lobby where the man escaped with *his* people. He stood before his first lieutenant who was also drugged and bandaged and barely upright. But with enough painkillers, he managed to stand. They made him wildly aggressive and monstrous. Fabian, though nearly a head shorter than and half the width of any of the men who worked for him, paced the ranks. He couldn't match Christiaan physically. "Who shall I send?"

The first lieutenant growled, the stitches of his slash started to heal and left the beginning of a nasty pink scar. "I'll go. I want to cut his face as he cut mine."

"Ah, the brave type. Barely off the bed of surgery." He scrutinized his man. "Are you sure you are up to this?"

"I want to drink his blood."

The painkillers must be speaking now. But Fabian grinned. What did he care if the man was nearly invincible with what they had pumped into his body? His lieutenant's anger energized him. "I commend you. And I have a gift for you. Passed to me from the ancients of China." Dropping the abandoned *chakram*, he scurried down the hallway to his gallery.

The men followed at a lumbering pace to the treasure room.

The room held the items he loved the most. Fabian entered the hall filled with glass cases along the walls. Each glass case held an antique armor from each of the ages: bamboo armor of the Japanese Shōgun era; Milanese full suit and leather from the noble lords, their ancestors; wooden shields from Africa; metal bucklers from the Muslim states of Sahel; chainmail made of Chinese coins; Roman breastplate and greaves; and Greek muscle armor each glowed in the darkened hall.

Glowing in an illuminated glass case sat his gauntlets. He opened the door and released them from inactivity. Silver blades curved into hooks in double rows protruded from the black leather, lethal twin shark fins along the forearm.

He strapped them onto his lieutenant. Fabian whispered into his ear as he fumbled to buckle them tight, his missing digits throbbing. "Kill him for what he has done to you. For what he has done to me."

****

Just off the grueling, thirteen-hour train ride, Christiaan arrived at the golf club and hotel where Mr. McGuffin hosted the Men's World Amateur Open. Christiaan swept the room, making his usual assessments of the people there for the Men's Amateur.

Day one of the week-long competition teed off tomorrow. The early birds and other competitors arrived a day early to test the course before the competition. And Christiaan wanted to observe the scene unnoticed first before deciding on his plan of action.

By eight a.m., the sun awakened the Scottish sky for several hours. A solarium built onto the back of the older limestone golf club spilled pools of sunshine on the marble floors. Potted palm trees and table groupings dotted the large room. The scent of a newly mowed lawn reminded him of cut watermelon. The smell of outdoors and freedom invigorated him.

A woman in a backless, full-legged romper passed him and left a wake of designer perfume. Her wide-brimmed hat blocked any view of her face. But the cut of her clothes and her designer handbag spelled money. One of many debutantes here.

Women filled the room with shining lipstick, designer sunglasses, large-brimmed hats, and ears heavy with gemstones. He didn't find their showy beauty attractive or desirable, preferring instead the low maintenance of everyday beauty. One couldn't compare the showy peony with its heady scent to the delicateness of lily of the valley. He envisioned Andy among those women—blending in, observing, and waiting for a chance to allure Mr. McGuffin with her body.

But Andy was on her way across the pond.

She had one advantage over Christiaan. Andy adeptly used her sex appeal to approach any man. He eyed the women more carefully. Was Andy among them?

No, no. He slouched and shook free his paranoia. She returned home. Actually, he should check and make sure she made her flight. The Internet on the Scottish moors between here and London pretty much sucked. He pulled out his phone. She should be home now.

Then another woman unlike any other entered the revolving doors but drew little attention. Her nondescript hair flowed long in natural waves around her long sleeves. Her large, red frames hid most of her eyes. A coarse, wide-brimmed straw hat covered her face except her mouth slightly open.

The young woman stood out from the other women. Perhaps because she wore long sleeves in the summer and a longish, unattractive mid-calf skirt. He glanced away, searching for something more desirable to rest his gaze upon instead of a woman out of her depth. He focused again on his phone and searched for OverSight's communication app.

The gaggle of smiling debutantes—all brilliantly dressed and all with radiant skin—moved as one toward a man, drawing Christiaan's attention. Their hair was slicked back against their heads or shellacked into perfection. Expensive bling dripped from necks and encircled wrists. Christiaan followed their action.

Mr. McGuffin, the man Christiaan had been waiting for, strolled into the lobby. With chin held high, McGuffin scanned them with a cool gaze, but his expression said he received no pleasure at the power of femininity. Christiaan clicked on his reporting app. Then he found his open request. Another request drew his attention—the one on Mr. McGuffin. According to his report, McGuffin reveled in power, fast women, faster cars, fine liquor, and golf. Despite his numerous charitable contributions, he was number one on Christiaan's suspect list.

Though he had his cover, he wanted to observe, unnoticed, how people reacted to Mr. McGuffin and how he reacted to them. The interaction fascinated him. He clicked back to his report on Andy.

The awkward woman drew attention now at the desk. She asked questions—loudly. And her accent…

American.

Figures. They always made a scene.

"I booked a room for tonight on my credit card."

The young woman's voice rose with panic. Christiaan's heart ached a little.

"I don't understand why it's not there."

Unlike other Americans, she didn't have the confidence Christiaan expected. Her voice trembled.

The desk clerk replied out of earshot.

"Could you please make an exception?" The young woman leaned against the desk.

Christiaan rolled his eyes. Americans always expected special treatment. She'd soon find out waving her credit card around wouldn't get her a room. Not during an Open.

"I'm sorry." The receptionist spoke a little louder in a broad Scottish accent. "We cannot find your reservation for tonight."

"I just booked it this week." With a hand, she brushed back her long locks.

The clerk drew his lips to a straight line. "Impossible. These rooms have been booked for months."

Christiaan could only see her distorted face in the

reflection in the gleaming polished brass, acting as a funhouse mirror behind the desk. The young woman betrayed her age as in her late teens or early twenties, obvious by her overly animated and distraught mannerisms. Christiaan expected her to throw a temper tantrum right there. But she did not.

Focus. Christiaan returned his attention to his mark and the circle of fawning debutants and to the app.

Mr. McGuffin dismissed himself from the group of debutantes wishing him a quick return.

Lowering his phone, Christiaan eyed the interaction most carefully, sizing up the man who owned the manor where Hin Cho received a call the day she went missing. How would this shrewd man respond to the immaturity of the unprepared American traveler? Would he brush her off with disdain? Or explain clearly, but firmly? This conversation could give him clues as to his character and support Christiaan's suspicions.

The young woman was on the verge of tears. "Could I maybe speak to the manager?"

Mr. McGuffin approached. "I am the owner. What seems to be the trouble?" He tugged at his cuff links.

"She accuses us of misplacing her booking." The receptionist spoke first.

Mr. McGuffin faced the woman. "I apologize completely."

Ah, he's a chivalrous man.

"Oh, I think I have a printed copy of the reservation in here." The girl reached for her bag, knocking off her gray handbag from the countertop. The contents spilled over the gleaming marble floor. The sound drew stares from the others in the lobby. She turned.

Christiaan got a good look at her. The young woman's eyes widened in her sweet young face. With the openness of a child, she knelt on the marble and scooped up each piece.

Mr. McGuffin's steely eyes softened, and with a kindly smile, he crouched to pick up a few papers, a card, and a glasses case.

As the young woman stuffed miscellany into her purse, obviously distracted and embarrassed, she kept her chin down until she finally stood. Christiaan narrowed his gaze.

"I would be so disappointed if I couldn't stay here. I came all the way from Akron, Ohio, to see my cousin golf. You know where Akron is? It's kind of near the lakes?" She flapped the piece of paper as she spoke.

Her voice was breathy and weak. Christiaan doubted the Scot knew where Ohio was let alone Akron.

"Ah, you're an American?" Smiling, Mr. McGuffin blinked in succession.

"Oh, yes, I flew all the way over the Atlantic."

She giggled and spoke with animation. Christiaan rolled his eyes.

"What an incredibly large body of water!"

McGuffin's kind smile remained. *Impressive.* Christiaan would've lost his patience long ago.

"May I see your reservation?" Mr. McGuffin held out his hand and examined it. "Hmm, your reservation is for August seventh."

"What? No." The young woman shook her head. "I made it for July eighth."

Mr. McGuffin chuckled and returned her paper. "I

see what went wrong. You entered the date backward. Did you not notice we use the order 'day, month, year' in Europe instead of 'month, day, year?' "

Sighing, the young woman grasped the paper. Her eyebrows peaked, and she scanned the reservation with large eyes. "Oh, how can I be so dense? I guess I'll have to find another hotel."

"You'll be hard pressed to find anything in town, Miss—?"

She bowed her head and blushed. She fanned herself with the paper. "Ariana Gertz."

He clasped his hand in front of his designer suit. "Well, Miss Gertz, unfortunately for you, every hotel in town is booked until the end of the tournament."

The young woman's lips trembled, and she nodded. "I came so far and now to miss it. Charles Stern will be very disappointed. All for my own stupidity." She stamped a foot on the marble floor then lifted her chin. "At least I have you to thank for your kindness."

Mr. McGuffin adjusted his cuff links. "Stern is your cousin?"

"Yes. We were close as children, but we don't get to see each other often anymore. I spent my life savings on this trip." Her shoulders sagged. "I don't suppose I can get a refund for my room in August since I won't be here, can I?"

Mr. McGuffin smiled. "Of course."

"You are so good." The girl patted him on his cuff. "I'll try to find a hotel in the small villages surrounding here."

Mr. McGuffin laughed and took her in with a kind gaze. Christiaan couldn't believe this could be a potential perpetrator.

"You'll not find anything for several hundred kilometers."

"Kilometers? Is that more or less than a mile?" Tears welled up in her eyes. Her chin trembled. Shaking, she caught her sleeve with her fingers and held it up to her mouth.

Even a bead of pity welled in Christiaan's heart.

The well-heeled women in the corner looked down their noses at the interaction. Some even glared and shook their heads.

"I can't go home."

Her voice breathed in a whisper in the midst of tears. Christiaan barely heard her.

"I'm sure you can do something. You seem so kind and nice."

The girl tilted her chin down but lifted her hopeful gaze to meet his. Her face filled with a tentative smile. She placed a hand on his cuff again, supplicating him. Christiaan anticipated his reaction. She was a lost, weak American kitten.

Mr. McGuffin smiled wide and clasped a hand over the top of hers. "I'll tell you what, though Blakely Manor is usually reserved for special guests and competitors, I'd be honored to have you as my guest."

At this, the girl dropped open her mouth. "Oh, I couldn't impose."

"I insist. Yours was a silly mistake, and any relative of Charles Stern is a friend of ours. Please." He nodded to the young man at the desk.

"I don't know what to say." She paused. "Thank you," she gushed.

"There are plenty of young women who have come to watch the game." He faced the gaggle of women in the lobby.

They all cast her stares of deep disdain. Clearly they would all be friends. Christiaan huffed. *Yeah right.* The kitten didn't see them but gushed and breathed, still dazed by his dashing charm and her good fortune from the escape of living on the streets for a week. Her eyes shone with rapture and gratitude.

"Thank you."

"I'll send around my driver to pick you up."

"I cannot thank you enough, Mr.— Gosh, I don't even know your name."

"Allister McGuffin, at your service." He bowed slightly.

"You are really too kind. I will never forget your generosity."

He bowed his head in a nod. "If you'll excuse me, I have to return to my guests, but after you rest and are washed and cleaned up, dinner at Blakely Manor is at eight, after the links are cleared."

"Wonderful." She scooped up her bag as the driver fetched her suitcases.

She neared Christiaan, and he scrutinized the ditzy girl—Mr. McGuffin's new guest. As she passed, Christiaan met her gaze.

He dropped his jaw. The weak, wet kitten of a woman was none other than Andy Baker.

In a flash, she winked in passing—a mere squint of an eye.

She betrayed no other signs of being a well-trained fighting machine. Christiaan sat up. *How, how, how?* He flicked to her open report. *Did not make destination.* Heat plumed behind his collar. She was in big trouble for coming here.

Chapter 9

Andy smiled to herself in the back of a sleek, black limo with a cool leather interior. Her plan worked perfectly. She felt a twinge of regret of giving her favorite yellow sweater and the new hat to a complete stranger along with several hundred euros. But to see Christiaan's expression was so, so worth any expense.

The driver passed through the little town filled with stone structures and up a hill along a shaded drive covered with a tree tunnel.

Andy continued her Ariana voice and impression while asking the driver about the place. Old Tudor-style buildings hugged the sides of the skinny lanes. She passed men on bicycles with tufts of white fluff poking from under their caps and tickling the collars of their sweaters. The whole village was out of a storybook— musty, rusty, and filled with character. Dabs of color from hanging flower baskets graced the doorways of small, stone shops. Dollops of whipped-cream clouds hung in the sky. Their shadows dotted the green.

They rose up a small drive, a little higher than the rest of the town and through a break in the trees. The town faded behind them. Green links spread over the hills—a verdant patchwork quilt.

When she saw the pinkish stone castle rise from out of the trees, she gasped. Red, hewn stones stacked on top of each other. They passed a gate of the same stonework with an addition of wrought iron scrollwork with a family crest blazed in front of a lion ferociously opening his mouth clawing at birds at his right.

At the security gate, a uniformed man waved the driver through.

Security was tight. Andy was lucky her scheme worked. Her backup plan wasn't nearly as polished.

The tires crunched on the brick driveway to the mansion of Blakely Manor. Andy threw back a strand of long hair for a better view. She didn't have to act in awe for this part. The manor was impressive. Three stories of Tudor-style, leaded windows rose above arches cut of stone. The windows stretched far across the green and beyond where the trees clogged her view.

Perhaps she was closer to Hin Cho. At least she was in a place where she would start searching.

****

Done with watching McGuffin, Christiaan retreated from the golf club lobby. He sensed someone close behind him. He spun. A woman with sleek, red hair and green eyes stood before him. Small freckles dotted the white skin across her nose. Her olive-green pantsuit hugged her slim and fit figure. Her raglan sleeves split open at the seams, exposing her shoulders. Recognition floated beyond reach.

They'd met before. Then her face floated into his memory. Philipe's bodyguard.

She stepped forward and raised an arm.

He stepped back, in a defensive stance, nearly treading upon a woman in high heels and a black pantsuit. He knew what damage the redhead's hands could do.

But she swept her fiery hair behind her ear. "I bet

ye're surprised to see me here."

Her accent was...Irish? "I am." Did she track him down, or was this a wild coincidence?

"Sorry, I didn't mean to..." Her green eyes darted around the room to all the debutants, golfers, and spectators. "I followed you from Madrid. Can we chat somewhere in private?"

With the cacophony of small talk, no one would overhear them. "I'm not going anywhere alone with you." He wasn't born yesterday—or the day before. And in their last encounter, he'd nearly lost his fingers.

She moistened her lips. Her soft, blonde eyebrows peaked.

On closer inspection, purple wells circled her eyes. Grief lined her brow. This couldn't be the same woman who nearly bested him and Andy two days ago. Something haunted those eyes.

"I need yer help."

Always cautious, he didn't relax or drop his defensive stance. "What kind of help?"

She stepped and leaned closer.

Christiaan tensed.

"I'd prefer to discuss our business in private," she whispered.

She touched him gently on the arm where a bruise from their fight still throbbed. "Are you here for the emeralds?"

"No."

Her corona of golden hair shook around her shoulders. If she was acting, she was convincing. "Then what do you want?"

She set her jaw. "Revenge."

"On me?" Christiaan gulped.

"On the man who killed Philipe."

Christiaan stepped back. He searched her eyes for truth. "He's dead?"

She arched a reddish-blonde brow. "I wouldn't be here otherwise."

He waited to feel something. Pity never came. "I didn't kill him."

"I know. Stealin' stolen jewelry is one thing, takin' a life is another. I have an offer." Her gaze flitted to the door. "Do you have a private room where we can discuss some propositions?"

Christiaan nodded. "Come with me." He kept his gaze on her the whole time. Would she try anything in private?

****

Andy now had access to the clues, witnesses, and, hopefully, answers.

When they stopped, the driver opened the door.

Another uniformed man greeted her and relieved her baggage—a mismatched set she bought at a store on the way to town—to a bellhop to haul up the stone steps to the interior.

First things first. She most certainly wouldn't rest as recommended, nor did she want to wash up. She waited until the driver left her alone in her own renovated room with an ensuite bathroom. She tried to make a mental map of the place. Mr. McGuffin's private quarters were somewhere in this castle. *Might as well explore.*

Opening the door to the hallway, she found her bearings, tucking her lock pick case up her sleeve. The wood paneling ran up and down each side of the hall. The main stairs fell off to her left, and in front of her room, a bit of a foyer opened. To the right, the hall narrowed and darkened farther from the giant leaded windows over the stairs. She tiptoed out of the room and closed the door quietly.

Along the paneled hall, suits of armor stood guard between each door frame, and facing each one, a potted palm sat on the opposite wall. But nothing stood against the wall cutting a right angle in the hall. The carpet running down the hall had a thick, soft pile and was the same rust-red shade as the castle's limestone exterior walls—wool definitely—Persian most likely. And it had probably been there since the days of Adam.

Where should she start? Curiosity led her to the door next to hers. A thrill surged through her. This was her destiny. Even with her ear pressed to the solid oak door, she heard footsteps behind her. She straightened immediately. Tucking her lock pick case into her long sleeve, she hoped her behavior went unnoticed to the person behind her. An amused chuckle sounded behind her.

"Eavesdropping, are we?"

Andy spun.

A young man in his mid- to late-twenties watched her with careful, perceptive, and amazingly gray eyes. His darkish hair was slicked back with precision and order. His European-cut silver suit tapered at the ends and his accent sounded British. A thin, black tie ran down his white shirt like a dark stain. His lashes were thick and minky. Andy grew flustered under his scrutinizing gaze and frantically pieced together a good lie. Her armpits pricked with sweat.

He laughed, exposing white teeth.

The young man was everything a proper British

man should be—tall, slender, well dressed, and well-poised. He was very imposing and hot. "I, uh, I was just searching for the bathroom." She didn't have to try hard for her breathy Ariana voice. His good looks literally stole her breath.

The man arched an eyebrow. "Oh, American, are you?"

"Yes, I am. How could you tell?" Then she shook her head and pointed to herself. "Oh, right. The accent."

He rolled something around on his tongue and grinned. "That and a *bathroom* here means a room to bathe, not the loo or the lav. And I believe you have a room with an ensuite. My name is Peter Spencer."

The tips of Andy's ears burned. A man had never made her blush so hot. Why couldn't she control her physiological response? Six months of attending school instead of investigating had weakened her skills. "Ariana Gertz."

"I know."

His hypnotic gaze penetrated through hers. Intelligence flashed in them. How did he know her name? She opened her mouth to ask.

"What brings you to Dornoch?" he asked.

Though lost in the brilliant slim-cut of his silver-gray suit and the depth of his eyes, Andy remembered her cover. "I've come to watch someone compete in the amateurs. And you?" Andy couldn't give up an opportunity to find out more about her tall, slim new friend.

He flashed a grin that lit up his eyes. "I follow all the professionals…and amateurs."

At his choice of words, Andy paused. Was he teasing her? He couldn't possibly know who she was.

But he couldn't be flirting. Impossible with her unattractive and overly modest outfit and taciturn persona. She had planned her cover to arouse Mr. McGuffin's sympathy, knowing his great philanthropy endeavors. She hoped he would see her as a sorry case. She wasn't expecting to run into an exciting, sexy Brit.

She tugged at the long sleeves of her sweater and kicked at the calf-length hem of her skirt. Her long hair extensions made her head sweat under the man's direct gaze. *Was the outfit pitiable? Yes. Attractive? No.* Throwing caution to the Moorish wind, Andy hoped her smile would outshine her Little-House-on-the-Prairie modesty. When conversing with a hot, British guy one must flirt back. "A player, are you?"

"Yes, of sorts. But I play a different sort of game."

He tossed his head, showing off his high cheekbones and defined jaw. Part of her wanted him to leave. The other part of her wished to bask in his attention.

"And who are you watching?"

Watching? Oh, yes, her cover. Panic rose in her throat. She discovered a name online. Andy refocused, finding his name on her tongue. "Charlie Stern."

"Charlie, eh?"

He batted his minky lashes. Andy nearly melted.

"And you flew all this way to watch him?"

His accent enthralled her. Andy forced Ariana back in full force, hating every breathy, timid word. "This trip is a once-in-a-lifetime chance for me. I can't leave work very often so when this opportunity came up—"

"Where do you work?" He stepped forward slightly and inclined his head.

Why didn't all these questions sound like an

interrogation? Was it his genuineness? Or his incredibly sexy accent? Andy found herself transfixed. She could listen to him talk all day. But she needed to respond eventually. The pregnant pause grew awkward. She wanted to say something to impress him, to make his eyes dance with intrigue—to tell him the truth. But instead she had to stick to her cover. "I work in housekeeping." She winced inwardly.

"Ah." The sparkle in his eye drained. And breaking eye contact, he dropped his head.

He was disappointed she wasn't more interesting. Andy cursed herself for having such a boring cover. What could she do to resurrect it?

"I should've known," he said.

Andy leaned forward. "I'm sorry?"

Raising his head, he arched an eyebrow, his eyes flashing. "Snooping at doors…isn't that what maids do best?"

Andy couldn't tell if he was serious or not. Then his lips broke into a beguiling smile. A small dimple near his eye creased his skin. She returned his smile but flushed to the modest tips of her extremities.

"This happens to be my room." He nodded toward the adjacent door.

With a yelp, Andy scooted out of the way. "Sorry," she murmured under her breath.

Extracting his hand from his suit pocket, he placed it on the doorknob. "Just remind me not to hide secrets from you." He slid in his key. As he passed her, he cast a sideways glance before entering into his room and closing the door.

Andy nearly melted into the plush rust carpet. She fell back against the paneled wall. Still in a daze, Andy spun and nearly bumped into a solid chest of a man over six feet tall.

"Excuse me," he said.

Andy stepped back, regaining her balance before recognizing Christiaan's thick accent. "Hey, want to meet—" But then noticing a tall, sleek ginger behind him, she lowered her head, speaking in the breathless timidity of Ariana. "I'm sorry. How clumsy of me. I should've been watching where I was going."

Christiaan just nodded and proceeded down the hall. He stopped at the door on the other side of Spencer's. His hand slid up the redhead's delicate skin above her backless pantsuit, ushering her inside the room. As he closed the door, he winked at Andy behind the redhead's back.

A weird pit opened in her stomach. Who was the woman? She reminded Andy of the woman they fought in Madrid. But why would Christian invite her into his room? Biting her lip, Andy pivoted and continued down the hall. Her emotions jumbled. Head down, she bonked into the wall jutted into the hall.

With closer inspection, she noticed the cut in the paneling and the small wedge cut out of the paneling as a way to pry open the door. She pressed on the panel. It sprang open to reveal a well-lit staircase tumbling to the right. With such a mystery, Andy forgot Christiaan and the woman. "I love old castles," she said to herself, sliding in. "All sorts of hidden things." Holding the small handle, she closed the door and thundered down the stairs only to smack into someone.

"Are you all right?" Grasping both of Andy's hands, an older woman spoke.

The woman's soft British accent was calming. "I'm

so sorry. Yes, I'm all right," she said in her breathy Ariana voice. Her elbow hurt from knocking the wood paneling when she collided with the older woman. "I wasn't expecting anyone else to be here."

"I dare say not. Not at the speed you were going." After searching Andy for injury, the older woman nodded.

Not a single hair moved in her stiff blonde coif. A pink pantsuit clad her small frame. Her rosy complexion was weathered from the sun and years. Judging by the wrinkles, she had easily passed seventy summers. Weighing in at under a hundred pounds and less than five feet, the woman was a featherweight.

"No one was hurt. My name is Margret Prim."

Andy, with her medium athletic build, could've plowed right over her. "Ariana Gertz."

"Nice to meet you." Margret leaned close. "We could've avoided an accident on the servants' stairs if you'd stepped down gently."

"Is that what these are?" Andy didn't have to fake being surprised.

"In the old days, when people employed servants, the lady and master of the house, usually someone titled, desired the servants to move about discretely, practically unseen."

Margret smiled, showing perfectly sculpted and most definitely fake teeth.

"Everything done without disturbing the guests."

The idea sparked warmth in Andy's mind. "Like a magic castle."

Margret nodded with a twinkle in her eye.

"Access without detection." She jabbed her pointer finger in the air.

"And the servants lived in those small rooms upstairs?" Andy's room left hardly any space around her double bed.

Margret chuckled. "Not on those floors. Another secret door leads to a story with smaller bedrooms above."

Even smaller bedrooms? Andy couldn't keep down her eyebrows. "So the twenty-five bedrooms or so the manor claims doesn't count the servants rooms?"

"Heavens, no." She leaned back. "They're probably used for storage these days. Not many people even know about them. If you'll excuse me, I need to be going." Margret patted Andy on her hand. "Nice to meet you. We'll meet again."

"I'm sure."

Pinching her slacks at her thighs, Margret puffed up the stairs with help from the banister.

Andy waited on the stairs until Margret reached the top and clicked shut the door. Andy then crept up and peeked out. Although no more than a few seconds passed, Margret wasn't anywhere in the hall.

But Spencer's door closed.

Andy returned downstairs, promising herself to find the secret staircase leading to the servants' rooms.

Chapter 10

"Who are you?" Christiaan closed the hotel door behind the redheaded woman. His room was one of the larger in the castle with a casement window in a small seating area across from his bed and ensuite washroom. Large tapestries hung from the lathe and plaster walls.

Nearly treading on Andy distracted him. He wanted to demand how she got to Scotland, and to scold her for being here. His questions must wait. Other business had priority.

The redheaded fighting machine sat on the small sofa under the leaded-glass casemate window and pulled out a cigarette. "Aiofa O'Donnell."

He nearly fainted. Aiofa sounded like she said Ava—a name that haunted his dreams. He leaned against a small writing desk near the door. "And a skilled fighter."

"Thanks to the Irish Republican Army. My father trained me to fight. When he passed a decade ago, I had to make me own way in the world. Fighting was the only thing he taught me how to do properly."

Her lips parted in a brilliant smile. Christiaan could see why Philipe dated her.

"That and make potato bread. Mind if I smoke?" She placed the cigarette to her bright red lips.

"They asked us not to smoke in here." He pointed toward the tapestries.

She shrugged and slipped the cigarette back into the pack.

Christiaan could never completely let down his guard. Assassins still hunted him, as London reminded him. She might have recognized him and wanted the bounty. But somehow, he believed her. Perhaps the deep circles under her eyes spoke the truth. "Tell me about Philipe." Her eyes misted at Philipe's name, and her lips trembled. If she were an assassin, she was also an incredible actress.

"I met Philipe five years ago." She glanced at her empty two fingers, rubbing them. "Even from the start, I knew of his business dealin's."

Christiaan gave a short nod. "I am familiar with his line of work."

"He hired me as his bodyguard. No one would suspect a woman being capable of killin'."

Christiaan had seen this before. "You ended up spending a lot of time together, and you fell in love."

She nodded and bit her trembling lip. After a few seconds, she continued. "Who would have imagined a smooth-talkin' Spaniard and a tough Irish brat could love each other? We worked the information circuit together. Philipe really was tender."

Probably the most tenderness she'd seen her whole life. Of course, she'd fall for him.

"I didn't kill him for the emeralds."

She glanced at him, horror flashing in her eyes. Yet Christiaan waited to give his trust.

"I saw who killed him. After our little tussle, I returned to Philipe, to see him mercilessly shot in the head."

"By the men in black."

She nodded. Her thin shoulders shook. "They examined his cuffs and asked him where the emeralds were. When he said they were gone, they shot him." She stared somewhere beyond the walls.

Though he understood her pain, he didn't approach her. Perhaps she hoped to lure him in for a close kill. She might hold him responsible for his death since he stole the emeralds. And yet he did not regret it.

"Why would anyone kill for gems?" she asked.

Christiaan didn't respond at first. Would he have killed for them? He breathed deeply. "Are you sure they asked for the emeralds?"

"Yea."

Christiaan chewed on the piece of intel. "What do you want me to do?"

She stood and approached him. "I want to contract ye."

"Me?" He gulped. He hadn't contracted in years.

"As information brokers, I sent out me feelers to discover the identity of the men in black. He is known only as the Commander—a deadly and brutal man responsible for unconnected attacks and leader of a terrorist group named Unction. Although he frames other organizations at each encounter, he makes no requests from their own organization. Ye are capable. Ye and yer girl. I'll hire ye to find the Commander, and kill him."

Christiaan's stomach turned. He stood. "You're mistaken about what we do."

She arched a red-blonde eyebrow. "Yer not hired contractors?"

"Far from it." Christiaan remembered those days—murdering for hire, never knowing who or why. He didn't want to know the names of his marks. Names would give life to the faces—give them lives and families. He tucked them far into his memory. In multiple ways, he wasn't the same person anymore.

"What do ye do?" She tilted her head, narrowing her green eyes.

Ah, the question. Interrogations always led to this question. Too many things he couldn't answer. "Right now, I'm enjoying the sport of golf." He smiled a mirthless smile.

"Though I can hold me own in a hand-to-hand combat, I canno' tackle an organization. I am willin' to pay for help."

"I'm not for hire." Christiaan lifted his chin.

She glanced at the red-and-green wall tapestry depicting a hunting scene. "Everyone has a price. I know what ye can do. Ye are trained, and ye get around. I've been diggin' around."

Oh, yes. Philipe, the information broker. He moved away from her to behind the desk. "Don't dig too deep."

She huffed. "Too late." She paced the carpet. "I didn't find yer current employer or if they'd be interested in knowin' yer past life. I found interestin' accusations about an explosion in Abu Dhabi."

"They know." The best way to keep from being blackmailed was to tell everyone his secrets. While what he said wasn't entirely true—Sabrina knew almost everything—sometimes a bluff could keep him safe.

She faced him abruptly. Her glance flitted to the door. "But does yer wee girlfriend know? That was her, just now, in the hall, wasn't it? Cleverly disguised, she was. I almost missed her, but she blushed when she saw ye. She has an obvious infatuation."

Christiaan's stomach dropped. His breath stilled. Andy was the last person he'd want to know about his past.

Aiofa leaned across the desk. "With me information and yer skills, we can bring them down together."

The offer tempted him. After Hector's death, Christiaan had his own score to settle with the Commander. "I can investigate and bring him to you, but I won't kill him."

She grinned. "Nothing would please me more than to give him justice meself." She unwrapped the green silk scarf from around her neck. "I'll be in touch with more information." She draped the silk around Christiaan. "Keep this scarf on ye. A tracker is woven into the threads. Come with me to the golf club."

She slithered out the door.

Christiaan unwrapped the heavily perfumed green scarf from his neck and stuffed it in his pocket then followed her out the door. He didn't do trackers. Especially not ones smelling of perfume.

****

Once Andy landed on the main level, the stairway opened in the main lobby reception area with rows of alternating black-and-white marble tile.

A guard stood at the hall to the left.

Two guests, a tall, curly-haired woman, and a beet-shaped woman with a bun at the top of her head, conversed at the foot of the stairs. Andy held up her hand. "Excuse me, I'm terribly lost. Do you know where the dining room is?"

The beet-shaped women eyed her and pointed in

the opposite direction of the armed guard.

Andy nodded toward the armed guard. "Thank you. What's that down there?"

"Those are Mr. McGuffin's private quarters, they are."

The tall, curly-headed woman spoke in a broad Scottish accent. "Can we go in there?" Andy asked.

She shook her curls. "Heavily guarded, and he employs all sorts of electronic equipment to keep out us guests—lasers across the hallway and video surveillance and such."

The beet-woman with graying hair pulled tight into a knot bobbed her head.

"He appreciates his privacy."

"I see." What was he hiding?

"He only stays here during the tournament." The woman continued their conversation.

The tournament. Andy needed to find Charles Stern and make a connection fast if they were supposed to be cousins. She thanked the ladies and headed out the door. Andy caught a cab back to the golf club hotel where she first met Mr. McGuffin. According to their website, the whole golf club was a string of medieval buildings of three stories. A solarium addition to the back provided the needed space for congregating and light. The bottom floor was renovated to a nice 1960s theme. Small glass tables with brightly colored plastic chairs under the solarium with potted palms on white floors gave the room an airy feel.

She spotted Charles Stern crossing the sixties-modern lobby of the golf club with a drink in hand. She recognized him from his online picture she picked on a website as one of the qualifiers. Through the glass revolving doors, she waved.

Tilting his head, he paused and arched a brow.

Judging by his dress—puffy pants, pink polo shirt, and a small hat—he'd just come from the links. "Hello! I have a proposition for you," she whispered. "I'm an American, and I need help. Will you pretend to be my cousin?"

"I like this kind of game." He winked. "Will you tell me why when we're all done?"

Andy nodded. "Possibly. Just remember, I'm your cousin Ariana Gertz visiting from Ohio."

"Dear *cousin*."

Charles gave Andy a far-friendlier hug than any of her real cousins. Andy cringed under the embrace.

"So nice to see you again."

He acted better than she hoped. Americans formed a connection in a foreign country.

"I hit my handicap in my practice round," he said. "I'm so glad they moved the T-box and added another hole."

After listening to the slight slurring of his words, Andy wondered how many drinks he knocked back.

"I might actually win."

"Congratulations." Andy had no idea what a handicap was or how that would help him win.

"No thanks to that guy." He pointed toward a stout man.

He was dressed in the unique uniform of golf in a brown tweed jacket and a hat as if he were a potato with legs. Andy squinted. "Who's he?"

"My caddy. He nearly gave me the wrong iron today. My regular caddy got sick. There's been a lot of weirdness going on."

Andy eyed the caddy, but his only misdemeanor was the matching brown tweed jacket and pants. His mustache clung to his upper lip like a small pelt. "You think maybe your caddy is in on some conspiracy?" She leaned to whisper.

"No, he's just an idiot. All the good caddies are taken, you see. Anyone who is anyone is here. My man, Ben, is recuperating. He should be back tomorrow. But still it's enough to rattle my concentration."

"Recuperating?" Alarm spread through her. She always searched for anomalies.

Charles sipped again. "Stomach flu."

"Or poisoned." Andy bit her lip.

"You're the suspicious type." Arching a brow, he eyed her. He lowered his drink. "So dear *cousin*, when can I treat you to lunch?"

Peter Spencer stalked across the lobby of the golf club.

Who was Peter Spencer? A competitor? Certainly didn't dress like one. Not in his sensible, tapered suit.

At a paneled wall, he glanced around, then entered a hidden paneled door.

"I'll catch up to you later, okay?" Leaving Charles, Andy hid behind a palm. She would've missed the well-hidden entrance if it hadn't been marked *Security Only.* After a few heartbeats of hesitation, she crossed the lobby. Andy opened the camouflaged paneled entry and slipped inside.

A room with rows of TV monitors glowed at the end of the darkened hallway.

Spencer's dark silhouette contrasted against the dim light of the screens. He scribbled notes in a little notebook.

Curiouser and curiouser. Andy turned to leave undetected, but she stumbled on a broom.

The long, wooden staff slapped across the floor.

Peter swiveled. His widened eyes transformed into a wide grin. "You again."

"I stumbled into the wrong room." Andy used her breathy Ariana voice and lowered her chin to appear fragile.

"We seem to be bumping into each other often." Peter drew near. "Or are you following me?"

His soft gray eyes sparkled with amusement and accusation. Lifting her head, Andy didn't contradict him but just smiled sweetly.

He studied her for a moment, both in her eyes and her full body. "You know exactly what you're doing, don't you?" He narrowed his eyes to slits.

Before she could ask what he meant, the door behind her opened, cracking the silence.

Spencer slid his arm around her waist and drew her close, their breaths mingling. He searched her gaze. Lowering his head, he slid his lips onto hers.

Andy, too surprised to respond, allowed the kiss.

His soft lips gently parted hers.

Her legs turned to melted crayons on a hot summer day.

"Oy! You can't be in 'ere." The guard thrust out his chest and pointed to the door. "Can't you read? Se-cu-ri-ty on-ly."

Spencer broke his embrace, jumping away. "My dear man, can't you see we wanted to be alone?"

While still holding Andy close, he spoke in his most piquant and proper Queen's English.

The guard's bushy eyebrows swallowed his eyes.

His body was as round as a barrel.

"You can't be in 'ere."

Spencer stood erect and puffed out his chest. "You cannot tell me where I can and cannot be."

"Is that so?" The security guard unlatched his radio from his hip.

Spencer gave a quick nod and slipped his hand into Andy's. "But now that you mention it, we do have to be going. Cherri-o!"

With marked grace, he slid past the guard tugging Andy by the hand. Andy stifled a grin. Heat rose to her face. Laughter threatened to bubble up inside her.

Spencer didn't stop until they were outside on the green, where competitors and spectators milled about.

Andy blinked in the sun in such a quick retreat. She hadn't had this much fun in ages. "We almost got caught." But caught doing what, she wasn't sure. Her cheeks still burned from her flush.

Spencer chuckled. He pinched a handkerchief from his breast pocket and wiped his brow. "That was a close one."

"He was going to throw us out."

"Yes, indeed. He just might have." He glanced over his shoulder to the doorway where they exited. "Thank you for playing along with the kiss in there. Let's hope he believed he interrupted a romantic interlude."

Their kiss had hardly been romantic, but the embrace came too naturally for Spencer. He was too comfortable kissing a total stranger. Of course, Andy had kissed more than her fair share of unsavory men for a cover. Was she a cover for Spencer? Either he found Andy attractive, or something else was at work here.

Both ideas were worth exploring. "So, what did he interrupt in there?" She struggled to stay in the Arianna character. Curiosity wouldn't let her pass up this opportunity to learn more about the mysterious player.

Spencer tucked his handkerchief back in his breast suit pocket and eyed her, "I've been hired"—he hesitated, his gaze bounced around the golfers and spectators nearby—"as personal security for one of the competitors. With the kidnapping and what not, my client felt safer if I investigate and hang around a little closer to the action."

"Ah, a bodyguard." *Perhaps.* But the unsettling feeling he was not completely forthcoming niggled in her brain. His story would do for now. "So, Peter—"

"Spencer." He raised a hand. "Please, call me Spencer. I find Americans' rush to use given names odd. It's too intimate for my taste. First names are for lovers and pets."

Too intimate? The man kissed her not two minutes ago. British men were a conundrum. And having two first names was confusing. "Spencer, then." Why did he even tell her his first name if he didn't want her using it?

Christiaan passed the large windows facing the green with the woman in an olive-green pantsuit.

Philipe's woman. Andy was certain. Her stomach roiled.

Christiaan returned alone.

"Excuse me," she said, suddenly somber. "I see someone I must speak to."

Spencer bowed.

Andy retreated to find Christiaan. She discovered him poking his head into an abandoned office. "What are you doing?" She crossed her arms across her chest.

"What are *you* doing? I sent you back to the States." He arched an eyebrow.

Andy breathed a bit of relief. He wasn't angry. "Why were you talking to Philipe's bodyguard?"

He thrust out his chin and raised his scarred eyebrow.

Andy loved his power stance—feet wider than hip distance, chest puffed out. He always did it when he tried to exert control.

"Oh, no. I'm not answering any questions of yours. I want to know how you got here." He tugged her behind a corner just out of sight of the lobby and crossed his arms.

"I'm not telling my secrets." She huffed.

He almost smiled. "Who helped you?"

"Who said I needed help?" Half of Andy wanted to tell him everything, but then she remembered Sabrina forbade her. Besides, she enjoyed maintaining the illusion she was powerful by herself. "I want to find Hin Cho. And I have skills."

Christiaan loosened his arms and softened a bit. "I don't need help."

"Oh, I wasn't offering you help. I'll figure this out before you." She crossed her arms, matching his stance. "I want to know who profited the most from Hin Cho not competing."

A smile crossed his lips. "Why don't you go back to the States, and let me handle this?"

He drew closer, challenging her. "Hin Cho is my friend." Andy stepped forward, facing him.

He grabbed her shoulders. "You are out of your depth."

"Don't patronize me." Andy thrust her arms upward between his and knocked his grip off her shoulders with her elbows. "I'm staying."

"*Duì niú tán qín.*" He stepped closer and caught her wrist.

Persistence flashed in his eyes. Andy twisted out of his wrist and faced him. "What did you just say?"

"In Chinese, the phrase means something close to talking to a brick wall." Again, he went in for a guillotine choke hold by folding his elbow behind her neck.

But Andy easily dislodged his hand under her chin, stepped into him, and thrust him against the wall. She won the upper hand. They were lip to lip and breathing hard. "I've kicked through brick." He pushed against her, testing her strength.

"You are acting childish. Want me to spank you for your obstinacy?"

Andy smirked. "You'd enjoy spanking me way too much."

Christiaan broke her hold. He spun her against the wall. "I don't make empty threats."

"You better deliver." Andy's heart pounded. "Or stop talking." Christiaan's lips were so near. His breath mixed with hers.

"I'm not the one always talking."

Andy arched an eyebrow. "To keep me quiet, you have to be creative."

Toe to toe and nose to nose, Christiaan swept his gaze all over her face. His focus lingered on her lips.

Andy had never wanted him to kiss her more. She had bested him—for now.

He closed his eyes.

His measured breath wavered on her face. Andy sensed another smell on him—one she didn't recognize. He opened his eyes—blue and brilliant.

"If you stay, you are on your own."

"Fine by me. I prefer to work alone." He was close. The heat of his body warmed her. His breaths entwined with hers. Andy silently willed him to kiss her. Whatever kind of super-human self-discipline this man possessed was maddening. She couldn't imagine a power strong enough to restrain him, and yet here he was.

He leaned forward.

Andy closed her eyes. A smile of victory rose on her lips—the winning kiss was hers. She waited for his lips to press tenderly against hers and to match him breath for breath.

Nothing.

His warmth disappeared leaving a whoosh of cold air. She opened her eyes.

He was gone.

And she recognized the smell. He reeked of another woman's perfume. But whose?

****

Heart still racing, Christiaan kicked a trash can in the hallway. What was Andy thinking coming here? She wasn't safe. He couldn't guarantee her safety. Although if anyone was capable of handling herself, it was Andy.

Aiofa's offer echoed in his head. He agreed to help her find the Commander for Hector's sake, and Andy couldn't learn of his past—at least, not from Aiofa. He could work on finding the Commander if Andy searched for Hin Cho.

Earlier, Aiofa said she'd research more information and meet with them soon. Just him, he corrected her. As he crossed the lobby of the golf club, an African proverb popped into his head: if you want to go fast, go alone. If you want to go far, go together.

Well, they only had a limited amount of time and they—no, *he* needed to find the information as soon as possible. Hin Cho was in danger. He was torn. Time was of the essence. On his own, he could go faster.

Damn Andy and her stubbornness. He kicked a retro sixties chair in the lobby.

On his own, he would go faster.

Chapter 11

Christiaan spoke with the housekeeper. He wouldn't need his room for two days. He cantered down the stairs.

Earlier, Aiofa contacted him, saying she had some information about the Commander. But she needed to take him to Cork, her hometown in Ireland, for two days—the only safe place in the British Isles to work her operation.

He paced the lobby. Two days away from the golf course and away from Andy would be agonizing. Though, leaving Andy to find Hin Cho for the Chinese government seemed cowardly. But to find out more about the Commander would be worth it. Wouldn't Sabrina want to know about this man—a leader of a group on their watch list?

She'd approve if she knew. *If* she knew. Not contacting Sabrina about leaving his post broke protocol. No one would know.

Should he tell Andy? What would she say? She'd disapprove of him leaving the investigation of her friend but would probably understand if he explained the reason. He must track Hector's killer. But he wanted clear communication with her. He returned upstairs, then knocked at her room.

"Searching for Ariana, are you?"

A voice behind him caught him off guard. A slim

man in a silvery British-cut suit thrust out his hand.

"Peter Spencer. I'm just next door." He leaned against the dark-grained wood paneling. He crossed his arms, eying him.

"Huh?" Christiaan had forgotten her cover. "Yes, of course."

"She left with Charles Stern. Interesting girl, flying all the way out here to watch a cousin's golf tournament."

"Oh, right." He faced the man. Why the interest in Andy? Christiaan kept suspicion off his face as he removed his phone from his pocket. He would ask Aiofa who he was later. "Good day." Christiaan shouldered his backpack and thundered down the stairs. He climbed in the waiting car with Aiofa. "Could you find a man? His name is Peter Spencer. I snapped his picture with my phone."

"I'll do a quick search of my resources." She paused for a minute while she consulted her phone.

Christiaan admired the quaintness of the town of Dornoch.

"Interesting." She frowned. "No tax information at all."

"What does that mean?" Christiaan strummed his seatbelt.

"He doesn't make any money by the government's definition."

Christiaan cursed. "Or he doesn't exist."

"Why are you so suspicious of him?"

Shaking his head, he adopted a carefree air. "Just curious."

"I can do a deeper investigation."

Christiaan studied the countryside. "Good thing

we're headed to your place then."

She pulled out a cigarette. "Mind if I smoke?"

Peter Spencer went on his list of people he didn't like. Christiaan would keep an eye on him—a keen eye.

****

Andy returned to Blakely Manor and caught a glimpse of Christiaan with the redheaded woman again. This time, Christiaan climbed into the back of a car with her—with his backpack. A twinge of pain pinched her heart. Why didn't he tell her he was leaving? She trudged up the stairs to her room. Mr. McGuffin wanted to meet her for dinner, and she planned to be well rested for the occasion.

Later that evening, Mr. McGuffin charmed his guests with wit and grace, and he nearly convinced Andy he had nothing to do with the kidnapping. His affable manner disarmed her, and he had very little to drink. But he guarded his privacy. He held the reception in the formal dining room, not in his closely guarded private suites—a whole wing sectioned off. She would have to wait for a private invitation. The reception tonight was for the immediate guests, some early bird players, and many, many women. Andy frowned.

Mr. McGuffin wasn't as attentive as he had been the first day. Andy was too emotionally drained to be Ariana tonight anyway. Where had Christiaan gone? Stealing away from the crowd, she found the housekeeper in the larder in the back of the kitchen, counting tubs. "A man left today. A tall, muscular man? Did he check out?"

The housekeeper nodded. "He said he won't be needing his room for two days."

Andy could barely understand her thick accent.

The housekeeper rubbed a reddened cheek and winked. "He left the room nice and tidy. And no one will know the wiser."

Andy wasn't sure if the housekeeper knew who she and Christiaan were, but she accepted the hand of providence dealt. "Thank you. I heard there are old servants' quarters upstairs."

"In the attic." She glanced upward.

"How do you get up there?"

The housekeeper furrowed her brows. "Why would you want to go up there? The rooms are filled with dust and cobwebs. Not anything interesting for a young lass."

Again, Andy nodded a thanks and bounded upstairs and picked the lock on Christiaan's room. The air smelled faintly of cigarette smoke and *her* designer perfume. She spun slowly on the carpet. "Christiaan wouldn't be sloppy enough to leave a clue, would he?"

The room had been cleaned already—bed made, trash emptied. She wasn't sure what she expected to learn from breaking into his room. Opening the closet, she found something interesting. A green scarf hung across the hanger bar. Lingering smells of cigarette smoke and perfume clung to the scarf. Why would she leave a scarf here? She stuffed it into her pocket. Perhaps it was a clue. The fact that he left it meant something. She didn't know what.

Where did Christiaan go? And why did he leave without her? Most importantly, why didn't he tell her?

****

Two days later, multiple guests gathered in a lavish antechamber of the dining room for the cocktails before dinner. Mirrors hung over the crackling fireplace reflected the light of the chandeliers, and the plush carpet swallowed Andy's feet. The castle had been built in Queen Anne's time, and the woodwork lining the walls gleamed.

Andy, true to her cover, couldn't wear anything sleek or sexy. She wore something to cover a great deal of skin and kept her hair down and her faux glasses on. She worked her way through the room of high ceilings and dark wood paneling to a buffet table crammed with delectable appetizers.

For the past two days, she'd been searching for the hidden servants' quarters entrance and decided to search closer to the other set of stairs. If only Christiaan had come, they both could have figured it out. Two whole days had passed. Two days wasted.

She scanned the crowd for Mr. McGuffin. Women in backless dresses nursed fluted glasses filled with sparkling beverages. A group of men, competitors, judging by their mismatched attire, huddled together near the fireplace. Spencer, still in his silver suit, conversed with a woman in the corner with blonde shellacked hair and trim dress suit. Ah, Margret Prim. She spoke with him and held a drink in her knotted hand.

Chilled by the damp summer air, Andy stood by the fire and overheard a woman in skimpy evening attire mention to another woman that Mr. McGuffin excused himself for the evening. Not finding her target, Andy surveyed the crowd anew.

"Drink?"

A voice interrupted her thoughts. Andy was about to shake her head when she dropped her jaw.

A member of the wait staff held out a charger.

His white, short-waisted tuxedo accentuated his slim waist and tugged at his massive biceps.

The server smiled.

"Christiaan," she hissed. "Where have you been?"

"I had the devil of a time finding a tuxedo big enough." He flexed his muscles even more.

"What are you doing as a servant?" To be able to move throughout the house was a brilliant move on his part.

"Serving drinks. Have one."

His strong accent was music to Andy's ears. "I don't drink on the job."

He cocked a scarred eyebrow. "I do remember one particularly interesting night when you had a few and fought a whole cantina of men."

Andy flushed at the memory of her prize fighting in a bar in Mexico. "I am not fighting anyone tonight."

"Too bad." And he floated off with his charger and his tuxedo.

Andy followed Christiaan as he wove with grace through the gathered crowds of conversing people. "Did you—?"

"Don't follow me. You're blowing my cover. What would it look like for a guest to be enamored with the help?"

She immediately feigned disinterest and studied the room. "I'm not enamored." She spoke out of the corner of her mouth, hopefully undetected. "Where have you been the last two days? I'm investigating by myself."

"I told you. You're on your own." Without even appearing to talk, he responded, the liquid swaying in the motion of offering drinks to attendees.

"Does that mean I'm the only one investigating?"

"No."

"Were you off with the ginger?"

He moved to offer another couple some drinks. "She has a name."

Andy's stomach flipped. She gulped down rising bile. "You're on a first-name basis with a woman who fought and almost killed us?" Andy followed at a safe distance, speaking to his back. The din of the general conversation hid her words.

"She was a bodyguard, doing her job." He spoke from the side of his mouth. "We were antagonizing her patron."

Andy gulped. A sting pierced through her. "Are you defending her?"

He swept nearby. "No, I'm stating fact."

Frowning, she crossed behind him to pick up an appetizer from another server. On her way back, she passed behind him again. "Have you done any investigating?"

After bowing to the couple who swooped drinks off his charger, he turned slightly toward her and spoke through a half smile. "Something more important came up. You were handling the kidnapping fine on your own. I had duties elsewhere."

Andy circled around the room once before crossing his path again. "Or distractions."

This time, he caught her eye. "Jealous much?"

Andy couldn't discern her feelings. Christiaan leaving with the redhead troubled her. Where was the man who caressed her in the desert six months ago? Was it all an illusion? A mirage? Or an act? A lie? "I don't trust her."

He opened his mouth, then clamped it shut.

Andy followed his gaze.

Spencer approached. Lifting off a drink from Christiaan's tray without acknowledging the bearer, Spencer pressed it to his lips.

Christiaan adopted the air of a disinterested server.

Spencer's eyes shone with a good soaking in alcohol. Andy inhaled, waiting for the worst.

"Ariana, you don't have a glass. Here." He slipped another flute from Christiaan's tray and thrust it into her hands. "How could the most beautiful girl in the room be all alone?"

"I wasn't alone." Andy returned the drink to the tray with a quick glance toward Christiaan.

Spencer nabbed her elbow. "Come with me."

Christiaan glared at Spencer.

Spencer placed his empty glass on Christiaan's charger and removed two full ones. Handing her the second drink, he slipped his hand on Andy's back and guided her through the crowd. "I have people you need to meet."

Andy bumped her way through the crowd and found another server and dropped off her untouched glass.

Spencer stopped near a group of men by the fireplace. "I want you to meet my friends."

A tall, skinny man with brownish hair like a ferret, a broader man with dark hair like a badger, and a redheaded man like a fox.

"Jenkins, Foster, Mayberry." He pointed to the men as he said their names.

Although smiles seemed genuine, Andy noticed an undertone of worry or dread colored their expressions. "Ariana Gertz." She nodded to the men. Spencer leaned too close. The smell of alcohol tainted his breath. Andy backed away.

"What happened to your drink?" Wine slurred his speech.

"Oh, I left it over there." She pointed across the room.

"Let me get you another."

"No, really I—"

"*Garçon!*"

A server swooped in with a tray of filled glasses.

Spencer slipped another drink into her hand. "You won't enjoy the party if you don't drink."

"I don't feel like partying." She faced the other men, hoping to start a conversation, one not involving shoving drinks into her hand. "When I arrived, my cousin, Charlie, told me players experienced accidents. I worry for him."

"Charlie, eh?" Spencer asked.

His eyes seemed sober. His slur gone. Andy arched a brow.

"Charlie Stern? I didn't know he was your cousin."

His drunken slur returned. Andy quickly changed the subject. "Other weird things happened on the links. Are the rumors true?"

"Aye." Jenkins studied the carpet.

The faces of the golfers turned grim. A few of them gulped down their drinks.

"Ah, some people think the pranks are game fixin'." The redheaded man with a waistcoat, Mayberry, slapped at the air.

"And do you think that?" Andy leaned closer.

"It takes more than a missing player and a few sick caddies to fix a game," said a wide middle-aged man.

He possessed a strong Australian accent. Spencer introduced him as Foster.

"But what about all the other accidents," said the soft-spoken, taller, slender man, Jenkins, with his hair parted down the middle of his head.

"What accidents?" Andy asked.

"People are crying sabotage," Jenkins replied.

"Sabotage?" Andy stepped closer. This was what she wanted to hear. "Someone's trying to fix the game?"

"But no clear pattern." Spencer sipped his drink.

Andy turned. "What do you mean?"

He glanced around and swirled the glass in his hand.

"Foster noticed his favorite drivers missing when he played the ninth hole, and Jenkins had a wheel missing from his caddy case for his clubs.

Mayberry nodded toward a badger-faced man with dark hair.

"Just little things to throw off the concentration."

"Did it affect the game?" Andy asked.

"No," Spencer said.

He said it too adamantly. Andy's suspicions were aroused.

Foster puffed out his chest. "My favorite driver goes missing, and I have to wonder why."

"But your score was as awful as it always is on an eighteen-hole course," Spencer said, waving a hand. "Let's talk about something more interesting, Jenkins. Like the missing girl."

Foster's dark eyes blazed briefly. He was obviously affronted by the insult or by the abrupt change in subject while he was airing his complaints.

Andy hoped this conversation would come to Hin Cho.

"If you'll excuse me," he said. "My mate is asking for me."

Even ferrety Jenkins sipped his drink and pivoted to talk to someone nearby. And Mayberry shrugged and sauntered off to talk to someone else. Andy was left alone with Spencer.

Spencer leaned in. "We're on our own," he whispered. "Since the disappearance happened before you arrived here, you probably don't know what occurred. What did you hear about the kidnapping?"

"Nothing."

"Nothing? That's no fun. Ah, I suppose I must tell you. A young woman from China, but most recently she came from a university from across the pond. Perhaps you knew her?"

Andy gulped. He was surprisingly good at sniffing out the truth. "Hundreds, if not thousands, of universities exist in the States."

"Are there really so many? Oh, well. She was studying chemistry as a graduate student at some Uni in Texas."

"I am from Ohio."

"Is that so?" He furrowed his brows. "Oh, yes."

"When was she last seen?"

"Well, that's the thing. Some eyewitnesses said they saw her leave the golf club to practice on the links early morning. She never checked back in. Some say she could've drowned in the ponds or gotten lost in the woods, searching for an errant ball."

"I don't think she'd be that careless." Andy remembered with a sunken feeling in her chest how meticulous she was.

"Indeed?" He arched an eyebrow. "But I heard she came to Blakely Manor because of a phone call."

"Really?" Her gut twisted. This was information she needed. Hopefully, she could milk him for more information. "Was she meeting someone?"

Spencer shrugged.

"Where did you hear that?"

His waved a hand. "Oh, you know, gossip."

"And no other clues or no other information?" Andy spoke quickly.

He shook his head. "The investigations held up the games until after they searched the links. What a terrible tragedy!"

He only thought of the games. Frowning, she tucked her frustration and disgust deep inside to keep her cover intact. "Have they found any clues in her room? No notes? Ransoms? Runaway notes?"

Spencer cast her a sideways glance. "I'm not privy to all the details of the case. Just the bagatelle. The golfing world is a small world. News and rumors travel fast. You seem to be rather curious."

Andy gulped, realizing she was asking too many questions. Rebounding, she gave him a coy smile and shrugged into her shoulder. "Just interested."

"Quite American of you to ask questions." He glanced up.

The competitors moved en masse toward the dining room.

"Ah, dinner is ready."

As she followed Spencer into the dining room, she heard a sound.

Across the room, Christiaan raised his eyebrows. Ever so slightly, he tilted his head to beckon her.

"I'll join you shortly," she said to Spencer. "I need to hit the loo. Save me a seat."

"*Bien sûr!*"

Andy didn't have time to analyze what he said or what the phrase meant and hoped he meant okay. British men were so refined and cultured, speaking in foreign languages and all. Right now she wanted to meet with Christiaan. What was he doing with the redhead for the last few days?

Chapter 12

When Andy entered the hall, she found Christiaan waiting.

He thrust up his chin. "I wouldn't get too close to that guy."

"Who?" Andy crossed her arms.

"Your friend, Peter Spencer." He gestured toward the cleared room with his chin.

She arched a brow. "For your information, he's a private investigator for one of the competitors."

"Unlikely."

Bitterness laced his words. What was his problem?

"Which one?" He squinted his eyes.

"He didn't say."

Christiaan leaned forward. "He couldn't say because he wasn't hired as an investigator."

"How do you know that?" she snapped.

"He's a liar." He stood back, spitting the words.

"You'd know something about that, wouldn't you?" Heat rose to her face. She'd touched a nerve.

He flung an arm toward the dining hall. "The man's a cad. A fake. A phony. I can smell them a mile away."

"Why, because you are one?" She hit below the belt with that comment, but she wanted to make him angry.

"Funny." He huffed and stepped back.

Andy stamped a foot. "Maybe that's just what he wants you to believe. Maybe he's brilliant and clever, and you are just duped."

"Wait a minute." He scoffed. "You think he's an MI5 agent, don't you?"

Andy pinched her lips. She was too transparent.

"He's not the MI5 agent." Christiaan answered his own question.

"Oh? Do you know who the agent is?"

"It's not him." Christiaan shook his head. "I've been around enough of those guys to tell. Trust me. He's not MI5."

She loathed how he always held his experience over her. She arched a brow. "How do you know?

Christiaan scoffed. "Just look at him! He's scrawny."

"He's not the kidnapper. He's more interested in finding the kidnapper than you are." She pointed behind her. "And I'd describe him as lean or wiry."

Christiaan backed up, tugging his tuxedo. "Whatever."

Andy exhaled. Did she dare tell him? "He knew about the call to Blakely Manor." She offered this information as proof.

"How did he find that out?" He thrust up his chin. "And we only found out by spying on our contacts. The fact that he knows proves he's the kidnapper." He pointed in the general direction of the dining room.

She shook her head, regretting telling him. No amount of evidence would acquit Spencer. Christiaan already condemned him. "He's a good man. A little silly, perhaps. Not someone who would wantonly ever hurt someone on purpose." But even as she said it, she wasn't sure it was the truth. What trust had Spencer given her?

"Yeah, good men don't hurt people." Christiaan turned away.

Remembering what he said about his past, Andy winced and touched his massive shoulder. "That's not what I meant or what I said. Good men sometimes have to hurt others for good reason. I just don't think he would kidnap anyone."

"Couldn't do it," he corrected. "That man doesn't have a courageous bone in his body."

She leaned forward and pointed to her chest. "You don't know him like I do."

"Just how well would that be?"

His accent grew thicker. The question hung in the air between them. His accusation stung her. "You think I have a thing for him?" Andy's face flushed.

Christiaan shrugged both shoulders. "You sure defend him like a lover."

A flame burned in Andy. "What about that woman?"

"What woman?" Christiaan shook his head.

"You invited Philipe's bodyguard into your room. And went off with her for two days. I saw you get into her car." Andy's voice turned high pitched, and she trembled despite herself. Emotion overwhelmed her. Her heart pounded a cadence in her ears. She didn't mean to let her voice and emotion lose control. Letting someone know you were angry gave them power over you. But she didn't care. She needed answers. "Sure you haven't bedded her yet?"

Christiaan's gaze bore into hers. He stared, unflinching. Seconds ticked by. He didn't move. "I don't have to tell you anything."

"You never do." Andy huffed. "Why would you start now?" She couldn't keep the bitterness out of her voice.

"You chose to come here."

His accent was heavy. She noticed it always got thicker when he fought her. Heat burned in her chest and flamed her cheeks. Andy spun. She was done with this conversation.

He caught her about the wrist and drew her close.

He searched her face, his gaze lingering on her lips. Would he kiss her? Andy's heart raced for a different reason.

"You let your emotions cloud your judgment."

Andy snaked away her arm and thumped her chest. "My emotions?" Shaking her head, she swiveled to leave. She paused and returned, heartbeat rushing in her ears. "If he kidnapped Hin Cho, then why didn't he flee? Why is he still here?"

"He could have given her to someone else. If he left, he'd be suspected. I don't know, but emotion doesn't impair my suspicions. You should wonder about him, too."

"What motivation could he possibly have?" Andy didn't see any connection, and Christiaan's accusations bothered her.

"I'd be looking for one." He dipped his chin.

A revelation crashed on her. "Being suspicious of everyone doesn't become you, Christiaan Johansson."

Christiaan spun and marched away.

Thrusting up her chin, she inhaled, trying to calm her beating heart. She won the argument. And he wore suspicion as poorly as Margret Prim wore those brightly-colored, double-knit pantsuits. Something else bothered him. What was it?

Left alone in the hall, Andy returned to Spencer at dinner, still flustered. His eyes shone at her return. She placed a hand on her chair under the crisp white tablecloth and leaned toward Spencer. "Are you really interested in investigating more into the kidnapping?"

Spencer hopped to his feet and slid out her chair. "Of course. I love a good intrigue."

Andy seated herself and allowed him to scoot in her chair. "I discovered there are old servants' quarters upstairs. We could search for them tonight." When he was seated, she whispered.

"A capitol idea."

"When all the guests have gone to bed, meet me in the hall. Might want to wear something black. Do you have anything dark?"

"Yes, of course." He bobbed his head.

"And bring a light."

"Brilliant." And Spencer attacked his dinner.

Andy was too upset to eat, still distracted by the fight with Christiaan. Was Christiaan right about Spencer? Could he be the kidnapper? She glanced from the corner of her eye. He wolfed down the breaded lamb chops with such an air of carelessness. She shook her head and focused on her own plate, wishing for something concrete—a clue about Hin Cho, peace with Christiaan, or the truth about Christiaan? Was it too much to ask for all the above?

****

Later that night, after all the guests were in bed, Andy and Spencer poked around their floor, tapping wood paneling and testing every little knot in the wood paneling near the stairwell. Finally, she found an anomaly in the wood, a panel slightly raised along the wall. The molding disguised the knob. She could see why she missed it for so long.

"Eureka." With a click, she pressed the wood paneling. A doorway to a darkened staircase led to an upper level. "This way," she whispered. Spencer, clad only in black, reminded Andy of a lean cat burglar or a mime in his turtleneck sweater and long black pants. When she noticed his shoes, Andy stopped. "What are you wearing?"

He glanced down at his feet covered in black fuzzy slippers. "House shoes."

"Why?"

"First, they are very comfortable, and I have been on my feet all day. Second, they are the only quiet, black shoes I have. The others have a hard heel." He grinned.

Shrugging, Andy retrieved a flashlight from her bag and clicked it on. The boards creaked under their feet. Must and dust tickled her nose. The second level rose above the rest of the manor. Wind whistled around the rafters as she climbed to the unrefined portion. A long, dark hallway veered off to the right. "This place gives me the creeps."

"I found lights. Shall we turn them on?" Spencer led with the flashlight.

Instead of answering, Andy clicked on a round button, illuminating the hall with a pale-yellow light. But even lit, the hall still gave her chills. A crawling sensation snaked up her spine. Peeling paint hung in ribbons down the walls, dust muted the color of mint green baseboards, and large swaths of wood flooring down the length of the hall lost the luster of their polish with the treading of many feet.

Andy opened the first bedroom. Broken chairs, small bedside tables, a few lamps, and bookshelves crammed the room. "Storage." She closed the door.

On the other side of the hall, Spencer opened the next one. "Not very cheery." Sagging beds lined the walls with metal frames and stained mattresses. The pine furniture was simple and serviceable. A small window let in some light, making the dust visible in the stream of moonlight.

"Okay, next." When she opened the third door, Andy's heart leapt.

A chair sat in the middle of the room. Ropes lay coiled around the legs.

Andy stepped in. Goose bumps prickled her arms. A sack of fabric lay on the bed. The attached washroom had an old porcelain toilet from the twenties. No shower or tub. Blood dribbled from the mounted sink. She returned from surveying the washroom. "Someone's been here."

Spencer knelt to pick up one of the ropes. "Recently, too."

Blood drops surrounded the chair, too, but Andy didn't mention that. Long strands of dark hair littered the floor. Andy bent and with tweezers put a few into a paper bag.

Spencer stood and placed his hands on his hips as he continued to survey the room. "I hate to state the obvious, but I think we found where they held her prisoner. Should we alert the authorities?"

Andy glanced up and folded the paper bag. "Can we wait?"

Spencer paused, then squinted. "You are not Charles Stern's cousin, are you?"

His question caught her off guard. "What?"

"You're not Charles Stern's cousin."

She bowed her face to keep Spencer from seeing her face. Heat poured over her. Normally, she kept her emotions in check. "What makes you say that?"

"Charles only goes by Charles. He never lets anyone call him Charlie. Childhood trauma and all."

Finally, she glanced up. "I'm the special exception. He lets me call him that."

He thrummed his fingers against his crossed arms. "Also, I happen to know both his parents are only children."

Andy's heart quickened. "I'm a second cousin."

Spencer arched his eyebrow.

Caught. She stood, dropping her Ariana voice. "All right. You got me."

"If you'd just called him by his last name, you wouldn't have alerted my suspicions." Spencer smiled broadly. "Then if you're not Stern's cousin, the question is, who are you and why are you here?"

Andy was all alone in the creepiest part of the castle with a man who might be a kidnapper. No one else knew they were here. But he didn't have an aura of malice about him. "Promise me you're not the kidnapper?" As if his promise would bring her peace.

Spencer was genuinely taken aback. "Me? Why would I kidnap anyone?"

"You knew she was last sent here."

Spencer winced. "That's common knowledge, wasn't it?"

Andy shook her head.

Biting his lip, Spencer thrust up his chin. "You tell me who you are first. Then I'll tell you."

Andy sat on the stripped mattress. The springs groaned beneath her. "I'm a friend of Hin Cho's from the States. I knew her at university through her sister. When her sister returned to her home country, I promised to take care of her, and now she's missing."

Sitting near her on the bed, Spencer clasped her hands. "I am sorry to hear. I supposed a connection between to the two of you but I... Please take my sincerest regrets."

Andy wiped away a tear. "Thank you." She blew her nose on her sleeve. "Now you have to tell me how you knew she came here."

Spencer scooted closer on the sagging bed. "I suppose I shouldn't sit there. Might be disturbing evidence or something."

She shrugged. "I don't think it matters now. Well?" She lifted her chin.

He picked at something on the bedpost. "I found out through her caddie. He reported her missing and told me she got the phone call from Blakely Manor."

Andy made a mental note to talk to the caddie.

Spencer stood and brushed dust off his black pants. "Let's go downstairs, shall we? We have to tell the local authorities about this room."

"Can I show it to my friend first?" Andy remained seated.

Spencer arched an eyebrow as he flipped off the light. "That brutish server you followed about all tonight?"

The darkness hopefully hid Andy's blush. Nodding, she stood. "How did you know he's helping me?"

"I've noticed you conversing several times. I figured he must be in on your secret."

Oh, if only Spencer knew Christiaan was an OverSight agent. She debated whether to tell him. But still she wasn't completely sure Spencer wasn't involved somehow. Before leaving, Andy crossed the small room to peek out the small window. Green grass, illuminated by the moonlight, covered the back yard. Then she noticed something she'd never seen before. Black outlines of buildings loomed against the horizon. "What are those buildings over there?"

Spencer crossed to her, then looked over her head out the windows. "Those are outhouses. Buildings for tack and saddle, or farrier, or greenhouses."

Andy nodded and retreated from the window and left the room. She'd have to tell Christiaan. Though this discovery didn't lead her closer to Hin Cho, a hint of relief filtered through her. She found where they had held her. At the bottom of the stairs, she closed the door.

Spencer leaned against the door to her room. "Good night." He paused.

Andy stuck out her hand. "Thank you for coming with me."

He held her hand. "This escapade was rather enjoyable. Except for the blood."

Andy sighed. "But I'm still no closer to finding my friend. I shudder to think the kidnapper is wandering around."

With both hands, he held her hand. "Best not to have that kind of rumination before going to bed or you'll never sleep."

Andy smiled.

"You never told me your real name. At least I assume, you have a better name than Ariana Gertz."

"Andy."

"Americans are always so informal. What's your last name?"

Andy paused. She wasn't supposed to reveal her real name at all. In the States, vengeful mobsters still searched for her. Andy Miller was dead. "Andy Baker." A memory of Christiaan flashed in her mind. Now two guys knew her as Andy Baker.

Spencer smiled. "Good night, Miss Baker. I've had a pleasant time sleuthing." He brought her hand to his lips and kissed it. His gaze never left hers, then he backed into the darkness.

A bubble engulfed her. She touched the back of her hand where his soft lips landed. Excitement trilled up her spine. Spencer was the opposite of Christiaan. But Spencer was available.

Chapter 13

The light of the early dawn seeped under Andy's eye mask. She picked up her phone to check the time. "Four a.m.?" She fell back into her pillow. Spencer's kiss across her hand still warmed her thoughts. Sleep wouldn't come if she thought about him. "Might as well go for a jog."

She dressed in her workout clothes, headed out of her room, and crept down the gigantic wood and stone stairs to the side door leading to the gravel-filled driveway. The gravel crunched under her feet until she reached the green surrounding the links.

Fog rose off the ponds and water traps. Feathery trees gathered their heads. The green stretched for miles.

Andy inhaled the brisk air. It smelled of green, of wet, and of moss. What a nice change from the heat. She crested a small hill and stopped to catch her breath. Low-lying, puffy clouds dotted the sky. Their shadows darkened the links in the early morning sun. The green stretched to the horizon in a crazy patchwork quilt. The smell of freshly mowed grass rose to her nose.

Below, a man moved with quick motions. His agile movements were from years of practice.

Someone suspicious. Hin Cho's kidnapping happened in the pre-dawn morning. Who else would be up this early? Then she recognized his broad shoulders and hulking muscles performing a type of *kata*.

Christiaan sliced the air in complicated forms in the wide open space of flat green grass. His shirt draped his broad shoulders as he kicked, punched, and breathed.

Was it only six months ago when they first met? The memory of their kiss on the cruise ship and their adventure in Boston clung the corners of her mind. So many things have changed since then. Andy descended the hill, but she halted when someone else jogged toward Christiaan.

The ginger. Her jogging suit clung to her toned body. Swallowing, Andy ducked behind tall reeds by the rough at the water near the seventh hole. Crouching, she moved closer. Andy only caught a corner of her face.

"Finally, I have more information about the Commander. He's difficult to track."

Her Irish brogue filtered through the reeds.

"He's well funded, well organized. But what does he want?" Christiaan's voice came through the reeds.

Andy inhaled. Was he working with *her*? Andy's face burned. She smoldered in the rough, clenching her teeth.

"Emeralds. He has been at several other places and other jewelry heists. Always, on the list are stolen emeralds. Large ones."

"How many robberies have there been?" Christiaan stood with hands on his hips.

"Other than the one at *El Real*, his men are credited with at least five other heists. Always the same pattern. Take jewelry, and then make some kind of terrorist threat or attack. Last one was on a train in Paris. But among the missin' goods was another emerald."

The man in black. Christiaan searched for him. Andy held her breath.

"How does he know where they were?"

"Insider knowledge? He knew Philipe bought them—sad to think. Who sold them to Philipe?"

Christiaan swiped his face with a hand. "Fabian, a fence, but he bought them from a thief, not understanding what they were." He paused. "How do I find the Commander?"

"To find him, we must understand why he wants the emeralds."

Christiaan remained silent.

"What are the emeralds?"

Her voice turned squeaky and desperate. With a rapidly beating heart, Andy leaned in to hear more.

"Why does he want them so badly? All the enemies Philipe had, and a pair of cuff links killed him?"

Her voice quivered. Peering through the reeds, Andy held her breath waiting for her to speak again.

"Tell me. What is so important about these emeralds that Philipe died?"

Andy bit her lip, anticipating the secret.

"It's classified information."

Andy almost laughed. How many times had he said that to her? At least he didn't share his secrets with the Irish woman, either.

The ginger wiped away a tear. "I want to understand why such a man—a man Philipe didn't even know—would kill him."

Christiaan raised his chin. "You'll get your man, don't worry. We'll track him. If he wants emeralds, we know how to lure him in."

She stepped toward him. "Please, do not underestimate him."

"What security will you give me to ensure you won't share my secrets after I bring him in?"

Behind the waving reeds, Andy held her breath, as if a whisper would give her away.

The ginger raised her eyebrows. "Where is the trust?"

"After years in this biz, I don't trust anyone. What security will you give me in exchange for the Commander?"

She stared long and hard, switching from grieving lover to information broker in those heartbeats. Andy was impressed.

"I will deliver the official documents namin' ye as the perpetrator of the incident in UAE in exchange for the Commander."

Christiaan nodded.

"I'll be in touch with any news." The ginger left.

Andy plopped on the ground. Her heart lunged. She gulped for air. The bottom of her stomach hollowed out. Puking in the bushes might bring relief. He was working with *her*? What was this about the Commander? And what happened in UAE?

Andy hated all the secrets. She needed answers. Gritting her teeth, she crawled back a few yards and then stood and pretended to come down the green.

Christiaan resumed the *kata*. His hands sliced lightning fast through the air. He placed every step with precision and never faltered or hesitated in the grass beneath the brilliant blue sky. He missed nothing.

With thundering heart, she approached Christiaan from behind. His full and rounded shoulders hovered over his deep lunge. "Practicing?"

Turning, he snapped together his feet and bowed. In the last moment, he lifted his perceptive blue eyes before standing to his full height. His shirt clung to his chest while his white linen pants hung loosely from his hips. Beads of sweat glistened on his forehead and matted his sandy-blond hair.

"A diligent student practices every morning." He paused. "You know, you never gave me the promised karate lessons."

In their first meeting in St. Louis, he had asked for lessons. "Oh, yes." She circled him, gritting her teeth. "Should I show you now?" How she wished she could ask him all the questions in her heart.

He bowed. "Yes, *Sensei*." A smile crept on his lips.

With her hands at her side, she bowed then demonstrated a few *katas*. His gaze tracked her, taking in every move. Facing a small patch of trees, dark green at the horizon, Andy finished and stood to his right in resting position—testing him. "You'll have to follow my lead."

Without turning his head, Christiaan smiled. "I'll only let you be senior just this once."

"I'm sorry. I didn't hear you." Narrowing her eyes, she clenched her jaw. She was still angry about the ginger.

"Yes, *Sensei*." He tucked his chin in a brief nod, his smile gone, but his eyes sparkled.

She yelled out the form. She stepped into a forward lunge. He gracefully slid though the patterns in perfect synchronization. Each slice of the hand and each kick of the leg was performed in perfect unity. Two bodies and two minds became one.

The *kata* wasn't a complicated one, but Andy tapped into focus and energy as she kicked and punched the air. She returned to resting position then they bowed to each other. Her gaze locked on his. Without words, she stepped back into attack mode. All she saw in her mind was the ginger and his secrets.

He stepped into her spread legs for an offensive move, his warm body near hers, his chest breathing into hers. He attacked with a forward thrust. His face was inches from hers.

With a high block, Andy moved away his arm. All her frustration and secrets drove her.

Their bodies entwined.

With a reverse punch, she attacked without touching his ribs, then returned to starting position. She initiated the next attack this time with all the force she mustered. Working with that woman? Keeping secrets from her? All the anger from the morning fueled her fire. With the grace of a dancer, he quickly blocked her knife-hand, drawing her close in a hold.

Then he attacked.

Andy blocked, driving her body closer before side stepping, and swept his leg behind him in a split second. She felled him, crying out with a finishing blow to his neck. "Nice. You got me." Christiaan lay on his back.

His blue eyes reflected the brilliant sky.

"Of course, I'm still recovering."

Andy dropped her hands. Balled fists formed at her side. "You don't fight as an invalid. You recover awfully quick."

"Maybe I let you beat me." He tugged her on top. "I'll admit it. You are better than me. At Japanese karate." He pinched the ends of her hair.

"A fine concession." Her lips were nearly on his. His chest rose beneath her with each breath. Andy didn't want to break the peace of the moment, but she couldn't go any longer with doubts between them. Furrowing her brows, she cleared her throat and rolled to her back beside him.

"What is it?" He propped up himself on his elbow facing her. "What's wrong?"

She threaded her hands through the emerald grass. Her heart beat in her throat. She almost couldn't breathe. "I overheard something disturbing." Andy didn't dare glance up to his gaze.

He let out a breath. "Out with it. Let's not have secrets between us."

Andy snapped up her head. Heat grew in her chest. "How can you even say that?" She stamped the grass with her hand. "Everything you've said to me is either a lie or a sidestepped truth."

Christiaan pinched his lips and glanced over his opposite shoulder.

Andy stood. She was so done with him.

In an instant, he hopped to his feet and grabbed her shoulder. "I'm sorry. I have to keep some secrets."

Andy shook off his grip. "I can't have secrets from you, but you can hold secrets from me?"

He placed his hands on his slim hips. "I'll answer one question you want right now."

Andy narrowed her eyes. "Full truth? No dodging?"

He nodded and held up a finger. "Only one question."

"What is the agreement with the ginger?" Andy

waited for him to repeal her fears and say those words she so desperately wanted to hear.

Instead, he hesitated. His gaze flicked to a clump of grass. "What do you mean?"

His broad shoulders loomed over her. "I overheard you talking with the ginger. Philipe's girl."

"Her name is Aiofe."

"What deal did you make with her?" Her heart beat so hard, she couldn't breathe.

Christiaan sighed. "She wants me to track down the Commander. She wants to kill him as revenge for killing Philipe."

"She said she would give you something—a document about UAE?"

With flashing eyes, he placed a finger on her lips. "Oh, no. I told you I would answer only one question." His gaze flitted to her lips. In a flash, he moved his hand and placed a lingering peck on her cheek before swiveling and picking up his shoes.

Andy stamped a foot. She had more questions instead of answers. And he didn't really answer her question in the first place. She touched his shoulder. "What happened in UAE?"

"One question." He snatched up his boots.

"Are you—"

"Only one." He started off the green as more golfers came to claim a pre-tee round of practice.

Andy huffed and kicked her toe into the grass. "Fine. I found where they held Him Cho. Do you want to see it?"

Chapter 14

In the soft morning light, Christiaan paced the storage room. The floorboards creaked under his feet.

"What do you think?" Andy stood nearby in her athletic clothes. In the dim light, she peaked her brows.

He studied a nylon cord then dropped it to inspect the washroom. "What's not here?"

Shaking her head, Andy glanced around.

When she didn't answer, he parted the curtain to the window, then paced toward her. "As an investigator, you have to see what's not there. What's missing?"

"I don't know." Andy glanced around the room.

Christiaan stared, teaching her. She had good instincts; now if he could train her to be better, she would be unstoppable. "If you were holding someone captive for multiple days, what else would you see?"

Andy's eyes lit up. "Food dishes."

Christiaan nodded. Her answer confirmed what he thought. "Bingo. Bowls of water or crumbs from dropped food."

"Mice could've eaten any crumbs."

He nodded, a little impressed. He searched for those, too. "You'd see mouse droppings, and they'd leave trails in the dust, which I don't see."

"Good point. So the captor didn't keep her long."

He placed a finger on his nose. "Or fed her

elsewhere."

"You mean moved locations?"

"This was probably a temporary location."

"How about there?" Andy moved to the window.

Christiaan followed and leaned close. Near Andy, he smelled her hair, scented of strawberries.

"Outhouses."

The buildings sat in the farthest part of the property.

Andy thrust her chin upward. "Another place we should check."

"Good idea." He stepped away from the window. And from her. The temptation was too great. "You did an amazing job. I'll take it from here."

Andy backed toward the door. "No way. I'm making progress on finding Hin Cho. I have help."

"Not from *him*." He couldn't even say his name.

"At least he doesn't step on my toes."

Christiaan rolled his eyes. "Yeah, even if he did, he wouldn't hurt them. You don't want to be with him."

"At least he's open and honest."

Instinctively, Christiaan huffed. "Tell me one thing about him. Other than being a loafer."

She widened her eyes, parting her lips.

Christiaan shook his head and tore his gaze off her lips. Andy was dangerous both to him and to everything he hoped to accomplish. Perhaps he should silence her with his lips and smother her frown with a smile of pleasure. But instead, he opened the door.

"You got me." Andy stood with her hands on her hips. "I don't know anything other than he's willing to help."

"Help? He's hanging on to your shirt tails."

Christiaan filled the doorway. "He follows you around like a puppy ever since you arrived here."

Andy shrugged. "Listen. Let's call a truce and work together."

"You mean you tell me what you know, and I'll tell you what I know?"

Andy laughed and tossed her head. "No deal. I remember a particularly steamy night on a cruise ship. I fell for an empty promise once, and I'm not falling again."

He cracked a smile. This was why he craved her. "Smart girl. All right. Truce. Let's work on Hin Cho and worry about the Commander later." He didn't relish the idea of this Spencer character occupying so much of her time.

Andy passed and headed down the hall. "Where do we start?"

Christiaan trailed behind her. "Find a motive for the kidnapping. The Europeans take throwing the games seriously. Your friend was a favorite."

"Hin Cho was favored to win?"

He hadn't been completely occupied with the Commander. "At least in the top three."

"Perhaps someone rigged the bets." Andy bit her lip. "Why don't you investigate who would stand to profit with her gone? All the bets should be recorded." She folded her arms. "And I'll investigate her hotel room. I'm inviting Spencer." She bounded out the door.

Christiaan folded his arms. This was exactly what he wanted to avoid. Although her idea to check out the winnings was not a bad one, he still didn't want her hanging around Spencer. They didn't even know who he was. He could only use a good South African word from his youth to describe him: a *domkop*—an idiot. And he could be the kidnapper. He trotted downstairs.

"I'll find Spencer." Andy jabbed a thumb behind her. She disappeared down the stairs.

Christiaan headed to the golf club. Mr. McGuffin urged people to bet on the games and even opened a formal house in the golf club. Finding out who won big shouldn't be too difficult of a task. In the back of the foyer, he approached the betting teller. At his turn, he paused in front of an elderly man with white tufts of hair sticking out over each ear. "Can I get a list of previous winners?"

The elderly man brushed the nose the size and color of a strawberry. Christiaan arched his brow.

"The odds give a good indicator of the favorites."

Christiaan didn't mean to confuse the man. "I mean who cashed out on the bets."

The man nodded. "Ah, the house tracks all the winnings. Mr. McGuffin has all the payout records."

Christiaan had yet to talk to Mr. McGuffin. Perhaps now was the time.

****

Andy returned to the golf club after breakfast to search for Spencer. She scanned the links. Time continued to tick, and she had no more information than she did before.

Outside, Margret Prim, wearing a hat of an appalling size, spoke with Mr. McGuffin. The hat overpowered her small frame. Her shoes were all wrong for golf.

Andy rounded the links and spied Peter Spencer with a caddy in a hidden part of the course. Hiding behind a clump of tall grass, she watched the exchange with interest, peeking between the verdant foliage around the green, yet she was not close enough to hear.

Spencer glanced around and ducked farther into the shadowy pines.

The caddy glanced both ways before extracting something from his pocket and stuffing it into Spencer's outstretched hands. He counted it.

Cash. Was he the MI5 agent, rooting out information, or was he a kidnapper? Andy shook her head. Or something in between? Time to blow her cover and find some answers.

At the end of their conversation, Spencer sauntered toward Andy's spot in the grass. When he neared her, Andy stepped out. "Hello, Spencer."

He raised his eyebrows and stuffed the wad into his pockets.

She pinned him with a glare. "And what are you up to?"

"Nothing. Just out for a pleasant stroll before the games commence."

A lie. Andy didn't even blink. She crossed her arms. "Why were you talking to the caddy?"

"You seem forceful all of a sudden." He straightened his spine.

"I want to know who you are."

"I can't tell you." He stepped away.

Another man who averted her question. She shook her head. "Oh? Just from observing, you don't follow golf for the fun of it."

Spencer replied with a tight-lipped smile. "No."

"Nor are you a private investigator."

He winked. "You are a clever lass, aren't you."

Suddenly, his voice deepened to a somber timbre.

"And you're not some simple girl you pretend to be. Oh, I believe Hin Cho is your friend, but you are not simple."

Andy dropped her jaw.

"The real question is: what are *you* doing here?"

Andy winced. She couldn't appear weak. "Who are you, and who do you work for?"

"You are direct." He gave her a short bow and backed away. "If you'll excuse me."

Andy nabbed his elbow. "I know you're no private investigator. I'm curious to know if you're the kidnapper."

Spencer's eyes widened. "I'm not a kidnapper."

"Prove it." Andy thrust out her chin. "Tell me what or who you are."

Glancing around, he tugged at her elbow, taking her aside. "I can't tell you everything."

Planting her feet, Andy resisted going anywhere with him. "You better tell me something, or I call the bobbies."

He winced. "Best not call them."

He sounded quite contrite. Perhaps she would get information from him.

Clearing his throat, he wiggled his tie. Then, his heather-gray eyes stared into hers. "You might say I'm in information."

"Information?" People who were in intelligence often used this as a codeword. A hint of relief filtered through her. Andy never believed he kidnapped Hin Cho. She smiled. "I understand."

"You do?" Raising his brows, he stepped backward, cocking his head.

She nodded. "You're in intelligence."

He tilted his head. "Yes," he said after hesitation.

"I am, too." Andy leaned closer and whispered.

"You are?" He dropped open his mouth.

"Not officially, of course. Back in the States, I was an investigative journalist."

Spencer's eyes shone. "I knew you were not some scrub mistress. But you said *was* not *is*. Are you not an investigative journalist still?"

"I can't go back to it." No matter how much she longed for the thrill of investigating.

"Why can't you?" He furrowed his brows.

Andy sighed. "Long story." She didn't want to bore him with details from her past.

"I'm all ears."

Andy inhaled. "Six months ago, I investigated the mob. Despite going to jail for their crimes, they have long arms, and so I had to change my life around."

"You should be able to choose what you do. Why not continue to investigate. Why should you let those mobsters dictate your choices?" He shook his head.

She'd always thought she chose to stop, but maybe she should continue investigating. "Maybe I will. I always wanted to work for the CIA."

His features fell to relief. "Ah, so you don't work for the CIA or that damnable OverSight."

"No." A nervous laugh rose in her throat, but her heart lunged. Thankfully, she didn't have to lie. "What I want," Andy lowered her voice to a whisper, "is to see Hin Cho's room." British police barred the door.

"Oh?" Spencer bit his lips between his teeth. "I might be able to help, being one of Her Majesty's subjects."

Andy grasped his hand. "Could you get me into her

hotel?"

Spencer slid both his hands around hers. "Shall we meet again later? You'll have to rent a car. Her hotel is a ways from here."

Andy grinned. "You know how to show a girl a good time."

Spencer bowed. "If I assist you, you'll have to do something for me."

"What's that?" Her heart thundered.

"We'll discuss the terms of the contract later."

He lowered his tone to a sexy timbre. Andy held her breath. What could Spencer possibly want?

Chapter 15

At a small corner lot filled with even smaller rental cars in Dornoch, Andy opened the door of a micro car and bit her lip. The steering wheel sat on the wrong side.

"You sure you don't want me to drive?" Spencer asked over the top of the car.

"I'm fine." With a fluttering heart, she slid into the tiny seat on the right side and adjusted the mirrors. The reversed lanes and turning left rather than right threw her. And shifting with her left hand felt awkward. "I'll get the hang of it." After several false starts and only two stalls, she made it out of the parking lot.

Spencer closed his eyes.

Most of the roads in Dornoch were hardly big enough to be double lanes. Most cars were small, and Andy could've passed a car and given high-fives to the other driver out the window. But thankfully, few vehicles were on the road.

Passing grassy fields, she drove along the coast to a smaller village where Hin Cho stayed. On the other side, the ocean spread for miles. The sun tipped bunches of sea grass. Golf courses filled the area beyond the road with green.

Nearing the next town, a truck pulled out in front.

He must not have seen their car. Andy slammed the brakes to keep from hitting him. She crawled the rest of the way along the coastline. She sighed at the ugly view of the flatbed truck.

"No worries," Spencer chirped. "We're in good company. We'll admire the view."

Only Spencer wasn't admiring the ocean. He stared at Andy.

She gulped at his intensity. Why was he staring?

Nearly to the hotel, more cars clogged the roadway, and an engine roared behind her.

Andy glanced in her rearview mirror. Another big truck closed in. The glare of the truck's windshield made it impossible to see the driver's face. "That truck is coming up awfully fast."

Spencer glanced in his sideview mirror. "Speed up."

Andy pointed out the windshield. "I can't. There's this flatbed truck in front of us. And I have no way to pass on this busy road."

"We are sandwiched between what are probably the only two lorries in this area."

Off to her left, a steep drop-off cut into the grass, and to the right, a string of oncoming cars breathed by. Andy glanced in her rearview mirror again. "He's not slowing down. Maybe he's lost control of his car. Brake failure or something."

As the truck drew closer, the sounds of shifting gears grew louder. Then the truck hit the back of her car. The metal on metal jarred her. The impact jerked her in the seat. She temporarily lost her grip on the wheel. Adrenaline coursed through her. Her pulse raced.

Then the driver slowed and revved his engine again and come at them again.

A lump grew in Andy's throat. "He's trying to kill us. He's trying to smash us between the two trucks." Gripping the wheel until her knuckles blanched, she veered to the right to see past the hulking flatbed. A car headed straight for her. She returned into her lane just in time but knocked off the side mirror of the oncoming car. Her heart thundered in her chest.

Spencer gaped over his shoulder. "You hit the man's wing!"

"What are you talking about?" With her whole body trembling, Andy focused on the truck in the rearview mirror.

Spencer pointed. "The man's side mirror. You knocked it clean off. Stay on our side of the road. Who let you drive?" He faced forward.

Andy gritted her teeth. "We can get smashed, or we can get in a head-on."

He held a small handle above the seat. "I don't particularly like either of those options."

Gears ground. The engine roared behind them.

"Here he comes again." Andy relaxed her muscles. She'd read somewhere that relaxing through an impact would be better than bracing herself. Sweat pricked at her armpits.

The truck hit them with full impact, blasting the back bumper and obliterating the back window with a deafening sound of shattering glass.

Andy's neck and back arched when the car rocked, but she kept her trembling hands on the steering wheel. Adrenaline coursed through her.

In the rearview mirror, crunched fiberglass and broken glass littered the road behind them. Debris flew into the car and cracked the rearview mirror.

Andy screamed. They were trying to kill them.

The truck retreated. But his gears still hummed.

"Take the roundabout to your right." Spencer shouted over the wind coming from the shattered back window.

Andy cranked the wheel. "I can't. We're stuck on the back bumper of this truck!" Panic gripped her throat. Her mouth was dry. What could she do?

He jammed a thumb behind him. "That lorry is trying to kill us. Jump on the low loader."

"What?"

"The low loader. The lorry in front of us."

Understanding now, Andy nodded. "How?"

"The window."

Andy stared. "Are you crazy?" She was not climbing out of the window of a moving car.

"Better to be a nutter than die." Spencer rolled down the window.

Andy's hair blew in her face, but she kept her hands firmly on the wheel. The gears sounded again. "He's coming!"

Spencer unbuckled his seatbelt. "Jump on the low loader and then roll to the verge."

What was a verge? Shaking her head, Andy peered behind her in the cracked rearview mirror. The driver gained speed behind her. "What are you talking about?"

"When I'm stressed, I can't think in American English." He held on to the window.

Smash! This time, the impact threw pieces of metal onto the road behind them.

Spencer glanced behind him as he clambered out the window. "The backseat is completely munched in. We have to go on the bonnet now, or we'll be tinned meat."

The bumper was still stuck on the flatbed.

Taking a deep breath, Andy thrust the car into neutral and slung off her seatbelt. She unrolled the window. Wind swirled around her.

Spencer already sat on the windowsill.

Being inside the car was dangerous with the madman ramming them. Clinging to the outside would be lethal. Sticking out her head first, Andy pulled herself through the window until she sat with her feet on the seat and her bum on the sill. Wind blew her long hair all over her face. She brushed it out of the way to see. Grasping where the windshield met the fiberglass, she brought a foot underneath her on the sill. The road whizzed underneath her. She was a breath away from oncoming cars. Using the handle inside, she lifted her other foot and placed it on the sill. Then she slid her right foot around to the hood followed by the left. She clung to the fiberglass hood and then turned to face the flatbed.

"Jump!" Spencer crouched on the hood.

Andy couldn't see the driver, but she could hear the engine roaring closer. She closed her eyes.

"Jump," Spencer yelled again. He leaped from the hood to the flatbed.

Opening her eyes, Andy held her breath. She let go with her hand and half jumped, half fell onto the moving flatbed in a roll.

Spencer caught her just before the truck made impact.

She jumped to the grass and rolled. The sky tumbled around her. Her elbows ached as they smashed into the grass. Nausea bubbled up in her stomach.

Spencer followed.

At last she stopped.

Metal and glass shattered. Debris flew onto the road. Drivers swerved. One honked his horn and pulled over.

Spencer shielded Andy from the flying glass.

He ducked her head underneath him.

When the truck passed, Andy poked up her head from Spencer's embrace. She wanted to identify the attacker before he zoomed away, but the glass was too dark.

The car crumpled into about a quarter of the size, spun, and landed three feet from Andy in the grass.

Holding her around her shoulders, Spencer glanced over her body. "Are you all right? Are you hurt anywhere?"

Trembling, Andy shook her head. At last she found her voice. "Who hit us? Why would they want to hurt us?" Her whole body felt like a giant knot.

"I don't know. But I am severely knackered." Panting and out of breath, Spencer rolled off of her. Standing, he wandered to the road and hailed the next car to stop.

The driver of the car slowed on the green grass and exited his cab. "I can't believe what just happened. Are you two all right? I saw the whole thing."

"Did you get his number plate?" Spencer asked.

The man shook his head.

She crossed to where the crumpled car landed. The car was beyond salvageable. The backseat was squished into the front, and the whole thing was less than three feet long. Andy toed the wreckage. "The car was small to begin with."

Spencer kicked a mangled tire. "Now you could call it a 'micro' mini car."

"I'm glad I got the rental insurance." Those hits were no accident. Who tried to kill them?

****

Once at the hotel, after the witness dropped them off, Andy flitted by the hotel staff.

A woman in a police uniform guarded the room still.

"Ah, a female bobby." Spencer's lips curled in a bit of snarl. "A proper challenge."

From around the corner of the hotel hallway, she gave a silent nod to Spencer.

He whistled as he slid his hands into his pockets of his silver suit.

Did he have to be so obvious? Running a hand down her face, Andy rolled her eyes, but she had to admit that it actually worked well to their advantage having a woman guard. She waited around the corner for Spencer to work his magic as he strode down the hall.

With a jovial smile, he paused by the door, striking up a conversation with the officer.

Instantly, he was a shy schoolboy propositioning a girl. He gripped his neck as if in an awkward situation and fiddled with his tie wrangling his neck. At first, Andy considered the policewoman a little dowdy with her hair wrapped in a bun and her smallish frame. But as the officer tilted her face upward to meet Spencer's, her eyes glowed and her lips parted in a dazzling smile. Although she couldn't hear what they were saying, Andy assumed he must've been flattering. Judging by her reaction, he was good. What a change to be working together with a man not constantly challenging her, like Christiaan.

Finally, they moved away from the door. The plan to persuade her to go the café for coffee worked. Spencer figured to detain her for no more than thirty minutes. Andy didn't need half that.

Once they rounded the corner out of sight, she gripped the handle. Locked. Of course, they don't want evidence tampered with. But she didn't want to tamper, she just wanted to examine it. From her discreet backpack, she extricated a small kit. Andy slid her lock pick into the handle, jiggling it. Thankfully they hadn't upgraded to the card system. Finally, she felt a pop. She slid the lock pick into her bag, scooted inside, and locked the door behind her.

Andy tiptoed to the bed. A suitcase in the corner contained all of her clothes, a few pairs of sunglasses, and sun visors. Golf shoes with small spikes and running shoes. Some Chemistry notes were in a backpack. Andy went to the ensuite bathroom. She heard a *plink*. Then another one. She left the bathroom for the window near the bed.

Spencer threw pebbles.

Andy opened the window to a crack. "What are you doing?" she hissed. He was supposed to keep her occupied for at least a half hour. She glanced at her watch. Only ten minutes passed.

"I want to come in, too."

"What happened with the cop?"

He shrugged. "She didn't think I was as charming as I thought. Besides, I didn't want to get left out of all the good stuff."

"Brother." Rolling her eyes, Andy opened the

window all the way. "Don't touch anything. You won't get any information that will help you with any other competitors here."

"You never know." He climbed over the sash.

Andy shook her head. The bed was neatly made, which meant the maid tidied before they knew this was all evidence. Who knew what was thrown away after her kidnapping? She sighed. Her room was just so normal. "I'm missing something."

Spencer leaned against the small writing table near the small TV stand.

"What's not here?" Andy spun in a slow circle, murmuring to herself. "This room is missing something. Christiaan said to search for something not there."

"Pardon?"

"Something is missing." Something just out of reach. Andy glanced around at all of Hin Cho's stuff. "Why would someone kidnap her?"

Spencer squinted with a shrug.

Andy slid out her phone and clicked a few pictures and video. She'd have to figure it out later. Opening the sash, she stepped into the grass below.

Spencer landed beside her. "Remember our bargain for my help? And now for the fulfillment of my contract for my services." He held her and brought her close. "You are the most amazing woman I have met Andy Baker. I—" He bent toward her.

A kiss?

He leaned in with his lips puckered.

Backing next to the exterior wall of the hotel, Andy gulped. With a thundering heart, she lowered her chin. "I'm sorry. I just can't."

Releasing her, Spencer straightened. "You love another, don't you?"

She looked up. His steel-gray eyes betrayed a bit of hurt. She bowed her head and studied the mulch beneath her feet.

"The waiter you hung around?"

Her head shot up. Andy had yet to discern her feelings for Christiaan.

Spencer narrowed his eyes. "He's not a waiter."

Andy met his gaze. "What tipped you off?"

He plucked off a leaf from a plant growing in the landscaping. "Probability and information. Let's start with probability, shall we? The man is constantly at your side. That amount of contact is improbable—statistically impossible—just to be chance. The meetings must be planned. Since men don't hang around women they find repulsive, therefore, conclusion: he loves you. And information I do know about you: you are not willing to get too involved with another man, therefore, conclusion: you love him, too."

Could his logic be sure? Her throat tightened at his words. The mulch reeked of an earthen smell. "I didn't mean to hurt you."

He waved a dismissive hand and stepped back. "Men like me don't get hurt. Disappointed, maybe. As I have no real heart, it's hard to skewer." Then he lowered his voice. "Okay, maybe I am hurt just a little."

"I'm sorry."

He batted the air. "Women are always apologizing. Stop it. If you love him and he loves you, why aren't you two a thing?"

Andy headed away from the hotel. She inhaled the verdant scent of sun on plants. "It's complicated."

He squinted his eyes. "You two have a few skeletons in the cupboard, do you?"

"You mean skeletons in the closet."

"Same thing." He shrugged.

"No. A cupboard is in the kitchen. Closet is in the bedroom."

"You don't use a wardrobe?"

"Only if we have so many clothes they won't all fit in the closet."

"Americans." He waved his hand back and forth in front of his face. "Back to you and the waiter. If you love each other, why aren't you together? You never answered my question."

She sighed. She'd love nothing more than to be with Christiaan. "Being apart is not my choice."

"The way he follows you like a German Pinscher, you'd think two were an item."

"Our relationship is complex." Christiaan's oaths bound him to chastity.

"Ah, you see, I'm a simple man. If I see something I want, I take it. I don't like complications." He stopped in the parking lot.

Andy faced him.

He grasped both her hands. "If you ever decide you don't want complications in your life, you are always welcome in my simple life." He kissed the tops of both her hands.

Andy's knees weakened. Such a sweet and tender gesture. "Thank you for understanding."

He dropped her hands. "Not at all. I'm quite relieved, to tell the truth." He tugged at his collar. "I wasn't sure I would measure up to that brute in bed."

"We haven't slept together." She hid her face

behind her hands. She wasn't sure what she felt—guilt for being so open, or embarrassment for having such little powers of persuasion over Christiaan.

"You haven't?"

Shaking her head, she dropped her hands. "Why are you so shocked?"

"I assumed." He dropped open his mouth.

"You know what happens when you assume…"

He gave her a crooked grin. "I know, but it's against all reason, against all…"

"Probability? See you don't know everything."

"You are right, which is why I am not a fortuneteller." He kissed her on her cheek.

Andy bit her lip. What was she doing waiting around for Christiaan? They would never be together. Why not just accept Spencer's offer?

****

As soon as Andy got back into town, she found Christiaan in an empty hall at the golf club.

He arched his brow. "You've been with him?"

Christiaan folded his bulky arms across his stacked chest. Andy had to admit, his muscles were a turn on. She glanced away. "We had a great time. We were nearly run off the road. The rental car is now the size of a soda can." If only she'd been able to see inside the truck cabin.

"See?" Christiaan stretched out his hands. "This is why you should return to the States."

Andy rolled her eyes. But the attack scared her. Who even knew she was in Scotland, and why would they try to kill her? Or maybe she was just paranoid. She sighed. The long day filling out insurance forms and the police report for the wreck exhausted her. "At least we got what we were searching for."

"Wimpy-Pants helped you find the room?" Christiaan blocked her with his body.

"He can be charming." Andy slid past him. Her tone took on a light, airy breeze.

"Now the biggest question is…"

"Who is Peter Spencer?" Who jumps off onto the back of flatbeds? In a suit. But she wouldn't share the tidbit with Christiaan. Spencer had more courage than even she suspected.

"An idiot."

Andy rolled her eyes. "Spencer acts like an MI5 agent."

"Until he opens his mouth. He's a *dàtóu xiā.*"

"What?" She sighed. Chinese. *Ugh.* Why must he always speak Chinese?

"A shrimp." Christiaan's lips flattened.

Andy jerked back. "What's that supposed to mean? He's not small."

"The phrase means he's an empty-headed shrimp. Shrimps have small brains."

"Will you stop hating on him?" Andy spun away. She couldn't take Christiaan's badgering. Shaking her head, she headed toward the foyer.

"Just FYI," he called. "He won fifty thousand pounds from Hin Cho's disappearance."

Andy's stomach dropped. *A motivation.* She faced him.

"That's a lot of lettuce." Christiaan tilted his head. "You need to talk to your friend."

A pit formed in her stomach. "Are we still searching the outbuildings?"

He nodded. "See you first thing in the morning."

He stepped past her.

Once alone in the hall, Andy sighed. Spencer wasn't a criminal, was he?

Chapter 16

The expansive green stretching in front of Blakely Manor soaked Christiaan's shoes in dew, and his footprints left tracks in the grass. Mists swirled around the trees. The outhouses loomed in the fog as large toads. Quiet blanketed the dawn. A shroud of mist wrapped the earth. The stillness of the morning comforted Christiaan. All was right in the world. He felt peace—perhaps because of Andy. He glanced at her profile. She focused on the ground before them, her hands stuffed into her sweatshirt. He shoved her with his shoulder. "Whatcha thinking?"

"Trying to figure out why anyone would kidnap Hin Cho." Andy glanced up.

"To win a large sum of money." His bet was on Spencer.

"The motive wasn't game fixing."

"Why not?" Game fixing could be a lucrative business.

"The pranks started during the women's competition. Why would they continue through the men's? If he kidnapped her to win, then why not return her after the games?"

Christiaan pondered her question. But he didn't utter his unspoken supposition that Hin Cho might be dead.

Andy shook her head. "They didn't keep her long

at Dornoch. Something else is going on. We are missing a piece of the puzzle."

"What about Mr. McGuffin?" Christiaan nodded. Talking with him earlier didn't relieve any of his qualms.

Andy brushed back her hair. "She was held at his house at his golf tournament. Of course, he loses the most if the games fold. He certainly wouldn't want to jeopardize what he's built here. We only investigate him as a last resort."

"But Sabrina says he's our suspect."

Andy frowned. She stopped on the grass and turned. "And you trust her above all else."

He faced her. Bitterness tainted her words. "I wish I could tell you everything, Andy."

"Why can't you? You seem to share a lot of secrets with Sabrina."

Andy leaned in, enforcing the question. Heat rose in his chest. "Why don't you like her?"

"Why do you assume I don't like her? You have funky chemistry with her. You don't have to explain anything." She stuck her nose in the air and crossed her arms.

"Oh, Andy, don't be childish."

"Why won't you tell me anything?"

An emotional dam broke in Christiaan. Too many emotions flooded him. He didn't know where to start. He faced away again, squinting at the haze off the green.

Andy sighed.

He owed her answers. Some honesty at least. Before the barn, Christiaan slumped on a pile of damp hay. "I will tell you part of the story." He patted the hay near him. "Sit."

With a frown still pasted on her lips, she sat. She kept her back rigid and her distance.

Rubbing his eyes, he sighed. "In my youth, we lived in South Africa. My great-grandparents emigrated from Europe before World War II. At first, people were welcoming, but when we didn't side with them on certain political issues, tension rose in the neighborhood. My parents tried to stay out of it. But we were constantly harassed by a group, the loudest and most aggressive group in Durbin. One night, they came when I was gone. I was fourteen and was out with friends." A lump the size of golf ball lodged in his throat. "They killed my parents, and I don't know what happened to my brother."

Andy clapped a hand over her mouth. "Your brother?"

He bowed his head. "I never found him. He was twelve."

"I'm so sorry."

He swallowed and studied the hay. He plucked at a strand and raked the roughness over his fingers. "I tracked the leader of the terrorist organization. After all these years, I finally discovered his name. He goes by Viper. But his organization is huge and well-funded."

"Not the man in black?"

He shook his head. "A different guy and a different organization. My personal mission is to find Viper. He's part of a terrorist organization. I use OverSight resources to track them, to predict their moves, and hopefully find them. I will root out the man and stop him. And I have to find my brother."

"You won't kill Viper?" She brushed hair out of

her face.

He just told her one of the biggest secrets of his heart. He tightened his jaw. "You're judging me?"

She shook her head. "I'm confused. This man terrorized people, killed your parents, and stole your brother. Why won't you kill him? Is it because of your Oaths?"

He flattened his lips. He hated explaining what he had done. "Listen, this sounds stupid when I say it aloud, but keeping the oaths means I'm still doing righteous work. If I break my vows, I won't have the power or authority to carry out this work. Besides, every time I break my oaths, something bad happens."

Her eyebrows rose. "Ah, so you're not perfect."

"I didn't say I was." He couldn't even tell her all the times he failed.

"Only with me."

She dropped the timbre of her voice. Christiaan leaned forward and grabbed her wrist. "I'm only perfect with a person who matters. And you mean so much to me." He drew her closer. Cupping her cheek in his palm, he slid his arm up her shoulder. He tilted her chin and leaned in. "I wish I could give you everything." He inhaled her breath.

"I wish you could, too."

Her expression tore emotion through him. He smiled. "I'd love to hear you beg."

Andy's hand flew through the air. "I will never beg!"

He ducked and caught her hand. "My reflexes are still faster." He kissed the back of her palm and tucked it into his lap.

"I don't understand. Didn't you say Blaine broke

up the Brotherhood?" While in the desert six months ago, he confessed his best friend might have sabotaged the Order. "Why still keep the oaths?"

Christiaan shook his head. "Blaine destroyed the Order both spiritually and physically. Blaine became a twisted, jealous, and inhuman traitor. He mocked the oaths and disregarded the sacred sanctuaries. In the end, I didn't recognize him. His death was a relief. He burned sanctuaries and ultimately killed Master Tso." The words tore out of him. What was it about Andy that made opening up so easy? Or was he just getting soft?

Andy touched him gently on the shoulder. Her touch enlivened him.

"I'm so sorry."

Ache throbbed behind his eyes. Master Tso was a second father to him—to both him and Blaine. "Master Tso only had one goal—to make the world a better place. He was always the last one to eat, the last one to leave a mission, the first one in, and the first to volunteer his services. He worked harder—trained harder—than any of us and pushed us to become better. Blaine wanted all the glory, but he didn't want to sacrifice."

Andy murmured something underneath her breath.

"What about you?"

Andy hesitated, picking at a piece of straw. "What about me?"

"You always play your cards close to your chest, too, you know." He poked her in the ribs. "I'm not the only one who keeps a tight grip on things."

She stared off into the white dawn. "People accuse me of being shallow, but I'm not shallow. After years of being an investigative journalist, I have to feel extremely safe before I'll open up." She inclined her head toward him. "You're not the only one with dark secrets. I just hide mine better." She flashed a tight-lipped smile.

"Secrets, eh?"

"Yes, and confessing this phrase doesn't mean I'll spill more." She tossed him a twig of hay.

"You sound like the guy you're hanging around." He tucked his hands behind his head and leaned back. The sharp scent of hay bit his nose. "What do you want more than anything else in this world?"

Andy drew breath until her chest rose. "My father. I want to know where he went and what he was doing. I hated leaving St. Louis, but walking away from my cover as Andrew Baker hurt the most. The pen name and the job were my last connection to my father. If I was exposing crime, I knew, wherever he was, he was proud of me. Now I've lost that connection. I've disappointed him. He was the one shining beacon of truth in my life. I trusted my father. He exposed lies and fought for justice. He was my hero. My greatest fear is to fail him. I have to keep fighting. For my father."

"Where's your mother?"

She cleared her throat. "Good question." She clasped her hands in her lap.

"Won't you say anything more?"

She shrugged. Her eyes glistened in the rising dawn. "I don't know anything more." Her voice caught. "My father said she left us when I was little."

"Did he say why?" What a sad story.

"No. The painful rejection might have been too much to talk about. She was awfully cruel, don't you think? What kind of mother leaves her baby?" She bowed her head into her slumped shoulders.

He'd never seen Andy so vulnerable.

"Maybe she had good reason."

"I dunno." Andy tossed away hay. "I can't forgive her. I harbor a rock in my heart for the pain she gave me and my dad."

"Do you know anything about her?"

"Only a name, Charlotte. Her maiden name was Travers."

"Have you tried searching for her or contacting her?" Christiaan had connections galore. Maybe he could find her.

"Once, when I was a teenager, I searched the Internet. I never found her. And for now, I'm fine if I don't make contact. My step-mom, Sandra, is the only mom I've really known, and I'm lucky that she's been supportive. Sadly, she'll never recover from losing her son. The hurt cuts too deep. She's a sensitive woman. She's living with her sister now in Ohio. After the Mafia showed up at our door, she changed her name."

So much had changed for Andy in the last six months. None of it was her fault. Christiaan brushed off hay. "No parent should bury their child. Time will help heal her pain. I'm glad your dad found someone nice to be with. Sorry she got mixed up with the mobsters."

Andy inhaled. "Although I think she suspected he was Andrew Baker. Maybe she was in denial."

"You wish you could go back to being Andrew Baker, don't you?" He'd seen how much she loved investigating. No one should take that away.

Her eyes brimmed with tears. "Doing nothing is failing my dad."

"I understand." He stood and offered his hand.

"Let's investigate, shall we?"

She headed to the tack and saddle barn.

He opened the food barn. Dirt, must, and hay hit his nose in full force. Animals lived here. He swept the barn with his phone flashlight.

Out of the darkness, a hulking man appeared.

When the man stepped out of the darkness, Christiaan noticed a scar slicing diagonally across his nose. Christiaan wound up for a wheelhouse kick to the chest. He'd fought this man before. He was one of Fabian's men from the Paris mansion.

As if anticipating his move, Fabian's man blocked the kick with his arms across his chest. Two leather gauntlets wrapped his forearms with curved, mini sickle-like blades protruding out of them.

Kicking those would shred his feet. With this horrifying realization, Christiaan changed the forward thrust of his momentum, kicking his attacker's knee instead.

The feint worked, briefly. The man staggered from the well-placed kick, but he rebounded with amazing agility, swiping upward with a lethal backhand. The blades on his gauntlets grazed the air in front of Christiaan's face.

He couldn't resist a joke at the man's expense. "Those blades are impressive. Did you have any difficulty getting those through airport security?"

The man's grimace didn't change. His focused concentration wrinkled his pink scar.

"I'll call you Blades." Christiaan plummeted a sidekick into Blades' ribs. Spinning, he dodged an incoming slice from another swipe of his arm. "You're cheating a bit, don't you agree?"

Christiaan's footing slipped, but he rolled as the man attacked again.

"Christiaan," Andy called out of his view.

He searched the darkness toward the sound of her voice. "Get back."

In the momentary distraction, Blades sliced through the air.

Christiaan crossed his arms to block an oncoming attack.

Blades' gauntlets tore into him.

Searing pain ripped through his forearms, and he staggered back.

Andy appeared behind a wooden support beam. She laid a solid kick into the attacker's chest.

Blades fell to the ground, scrambled to his feet, and ran out the barn door.

Christiaan surveyed his body. Blood pulsed from his wounds. The razor-sharp, hooked blades caused more than a few slices through his forearms. Panting, Christiaan collapsed into a pile of hay. "He was waiting for me. He knew I was coming. Did you tell anyone I was coming here?"

"Only Spencer."

"Of course." Christiaan huffed. He never trusted that guy.

She lifted him to his feet. "You can't really think Spencer—"

"He was one of Fabian's men. Fabian must still be mad about Paris. He knew I was coming, Andy. No one else knew. Except Spencer." Deep down in his heart, he knew Spencer covered his true identity. Who was Peter Spencer?

****

217

Forging on to the next outbuilding, Andy ducked inside. Spencer wouldn't betray them. His heart was pure. And yet…Spencer often surprised her.

Dismissing her thoughts, Andy nestled in the corner of the barn, with the musky scent of feed and animal, to clean and wrap Christiaan's wounds. Thankfully, she kept a well-stocked first aid kit in her backpack.

Christiaan held out his arm. "I heard something interesting you should know. Aiofa doesn't have anything on Peter Spencer."

"What do you mean?" She washed his wounds with alcohol wipes from her backpack.

Christiaan locked his jaw and held his breath. "He's not on the grid. No bank account, no credit cards, or no job. No P60."

"What's a P60?" She cut a length of gauze from a roll.

"End-of-year tax summary statement."

She bit off some tape to secure the gauze. She wrapped another length around his forearm and taped it on. Andy shook her head. "What does this mean for Peter Spencer? Not paying taxes doesn't mean he's a kidnapper."

"But it does mean he's flying under the radar. Sounds suspicious."

"Now what?" She finished with the bandages and repacked her backpack.

"Time to find out who this Spencer is and what he knows about Hin Cho."

"Fine." Andy clenched her jaw. Spencer was innocent.

"We'll try my way first."

"What's your way?" Andy hung her backpack over her shoulder.

"We kidnap and interrogate him with voice scramblers."

Andy stood and shook her head. "Are you kidding me?"

"I'm the one with the mandate to be here, legally."

Christiaan struggled to get up with the bandages around his arms.

Andy offered him a hand. "I like my way better."

He snatched it and stood. "What would that be?"

Andy gave him an arched eyebrow.

Christiaan cradled his arm. "You think he'd just give you information based on sex appeal alone?"

"I've gotten awesome results in the past." Sure most of those men were cads, men she'd never, ever want to be with, but she held up her neck high.

"I bet." With a glare, Christiaan wiped his mouth. "I'll tell you what. Let's use my way first. If it doesn't work, we try your way. We don't know who this guy is. He might be a kidnapper. Or worse."

"Only if you promise not to hurt him." Andy bit her lip. Would Spencer confess? Half of her wanted to know. The other half didn't want to hear the answer.

Chapter 17

Andy rolled her eyes while she undressed. While Christiaan left to find Spencer, she changed into black clothing in the upstairs servants' quarters.

She tugged the balaclava over her head. Christiaan insisted on using a mask. She preferred to use disguises. Using a mask was cheating. She picked up the voice scrambler with three settings labeled on the side: fast, normal, and slow. Andy exited the ensuite bathroom, with her voice scrambler in hand. "How do I—"

Already masked, Christiaan tied Spencer to a desk chair.

Poor Spencer. His jacket was gone. The sleeves of his partially unbuttoned white shirt were rolled up. Vials and a needle were on the floor near a case.

Christiaan removed a sack from his head.

Andy dropped her jaw. "Did you kidnap him?" She hissed to Christiaan.

He pushed her back into the bathroom before speaking. "Gah, don't talk without the scrambler. He'll recognize you."

"But you didn't have yours on." She returned to the bathroom.

"I don't need one." He situated the scrambler about her neck and slipped the box in the pocket of her black jeans. "We only met once. He wouldn't recognize my voice."

Andy picked up his black box and tucked it in his pocket. "You should still wear it. In case you meet him later." She adjusted the mike under his full-face mask. "Where did you find him?"

Christiaan rolled his eyes under the balaclava. "Outside your door. I just knocked him over the head. He didn't struggle or anything. Piece of cake."

Reaching in his pocket, she flipped his switch and smiled.

Back in the room, Christiaan injected him with a needle.

Spencer jerked. "Ow, why did you do that?" He glared.

Christiaan's mask and voice scrambler could only mask so much. Hard to hide his wide shoulders and his agility. Andy rolled her eyes. Spencer would know who they were. Andy at least disguised her body by slouching and moving with slow, contemplated speed.

"We want the truth." Christiaan's voice squeaked out at about five octaves higher than his normal register. "Not just a bunch of crap you are making up. What the—?" Christiaan glared at Andy.

She blinked innocently. Revenge at last. He couldn't change it. Not now. This whole interrogation he would sound like a chipmunk on speed. Andy grinned. A wide grin spread across Spencer's face, as if he'd had one too many drinks.

He arched an eyebrow. "I'm sorry. It's hard to take you seriously when you sound like you have puberphonia."

Christiaan whipped around to face him. "Puber-what?"

"A disorder when men talk like a child even after

puberty." He snickered again. "I'm sorry. I find it really hard to concentrate. Okay. There, now I'll be good." With forced sobriety, he sat up a little straighter, but wobbly. "What did you want to know again?"

Christiaan glared at Andy. "What are you hiding from the police?"

A lazy smile swept across Spencer's face. "Sweet Fanny Adams."

"What?" Maybe Christiaan had given him too much truth serum.

Spencer's neck lolled on his shoulders. "You are clearly not the police. I don't know who you are, but I only hide things which make me money. Now what do you want to know? And are these ropes really necessary?"

"Untie him." Andy's voice boomed five octaves lower.

"No." Shaking his head, Christiaan narrowed his eyes. "He's a weaselly one. I wouldn't be surprised if he slithered out of here."

Christiaan's chipmunk voice was determined. Andy giggled inside.

"Fine." Andy started. "Who are you? Why don't you have any tax records?"

A silly grin played on Spencer's lips. "Easy. Gamblers don't file taxes because it's seen as someone else's loss, not a gain. I split the winnings with the caddies who feed me information."

Andy exhaled. He was a gambler. Not anything vicious. Her muscles relaxed.

"Tell me everything you know about Hin Cho."

Christiaan's little girl voice sounded again. It was hardly intimidating.

Spencer grinned. "Good heavens, we went over this already. Chemist at UT. She left China, under deeply superstitious circumstances, and she's a damned good golfer, too. Too bad she's missing. I planned on making heaps of dosh off of her. If she's dead, her death would be a waste of talent."

"You think she's dead?" Andy caught her breath.

Spencer studied the beams in the ceiling. "No doubt she's lying in the gutter somewhere. Nobody understands ones' worth until she is gone."

"She better be alive and well." Her bass voice shook her rib cage.

Spencer raised his eyebrows. "A surprise of Easter morning proportions. Care to make a wager?"

Andy shook her head. Spencer babbled meaningless drivel. This was a waste of time.

"People want her for some reason." Christiaan's voice squeaked. "Tell me about her hobbies, who she saw, any boyfriends, or communications from others."

"How would I know?" Spencer shrugged.

"You know it all." Andy's voice scrambler reverberated to the beams.

Spencer winced. "Well, I do know a great deal but only what the caddies tell me and what other little tidbits reach my ears. I don't have a crystal ball, you know. I just use just information and probability."

"Well, then spill the information." Christiaan stepped closer.

"Why didn't you bet on Hin Cho?" Andy's voice boomed.

Spencer gulped. "I discovered Hin Cho is superstitious as all golfers are. She happens to always avoid courses with a seventy-four in them. When they

changed the T-box and added more holes for the Mens'
Open, she got all nervous. I knew she wouldn't win.
Because of conditional probability, I knew better than
to bet on her, and I switched my bet last minute."

"Seventy-four?" Christiaan stuttered.

"Excuse us for a moment." Andy held up her
pointer to pause the interrogation, such as it was.

"I'm not going anywhere." Spencer shrugged his
shoulders.

She motioned toward the washroom.

Christiaan followed and closed the door.

She peeled off the mask. "What does seventy-four
mean?" Her bass voice echoed off the tile.

"Will you take off that voice scrambler?"
Christiaan removed his and adjusted it. "There." He slid
it back on. "In Chinese, seventy-four sounds like
certainly will die."

In Austin, Hin Cho wouldn't even buy lunch with a
prince ending in seventy-four cents. Andy bit her lip. "I
don't think he kidnapped her. We're barking up the
wrong tree."

Christiaan's gaze landed on the pedestal sink.
"Then who?"

"Mr. McGuffin?"

Christiaan nodded. "Seems like Spencer's
motivations are explained here."

Andy readjusted her mask. "Let's go ask Spencer
more questions about her, China, and her chemistry
degree." She slipped on her voice scrambler but didn't
turn it on. "Do we have to keep him tied up?"

Christiaan sneered toward the door. "A sneak like
him? The only way he'll talk is if we make him
uncomfortable."

"Don't men dream of being tied up?" Andy arched her brow.

"Want me to get you a whip and leave you two alone?" Christiaan grasped the handle.

Andy blocked the door. "You think I like him?"

Christiaan folded his arms. "Listen, I don't care who you pick to lavish your attentions on, just as long as your flirtations don't interfere with the investigation." He cast his gaze toward the door. "I still don't trust him."

"Spencer is innocent. And nothing exists between him and me."

"I bet he wishes there were."

Andy blushed under her mask. True. Spencer begged for a kiss. But her heart didn't beat for him. "All he thinks about is the next game, the next in, the next...how to make money." Andy's voice scrambler box nearly fell from her pocket.

After catching it, he tucked it back in. "I don't trust the guy."

Andy shook her head. "I'm going back in there. Someone wants Hin Cho for a reason."

"Wait." Christiaan held the door closed. "We have to be united, especially in front of Spencer. If he suspects you're the weak one, he'll manipulate you."

Andy stepped back, as if he'd slapped her. "I'm the weak one? I'm not the one jumping to conclusions around here."

"I'm just saying, let's be a united front."

Andy sighed under the mask. "Fine."

"You want to ask the questions?"

"No."

"Then follow my lead."

She opened the door and activated her voice scrambler.

Spencer had been gazing at the ceiling.

"Ok, we want the truth. We are united on this." Christiaan's voice boomed loud.

Andy rolled her eyes.

Christiaan hit Andy behind her back.

"Tell us about Hin Cho's chemistry degree." Her voice came out in a little squeak. She glared. He must've messed with her controls when he touched her box.

Spencer glanced between them. "You guys mixing it up?"

"Just tell us about Hin Cho's chemistry degree." Andy tried in vain to sound tough. The squeaky voice sounded even higher-pitched on her.

"OverSight, I bet." Spencer squinted his eyes. "You're supposed to be great detectives and can read body language and understand people."

"Listen, you have information we need." Christiaan leaned nose to nose with Spencer. Christiaan grabbed Spencer's lapel and clenched a fist.

Spencer's eyes grew wide.

"We won't find out who kidnapped Hin Cho until we know more about her. So you can either talk, or you can get it beaten out of you."

Andy tugged on Christiaan's sleeve. "Bathroom."

Christiaan dropped Spencer's lapel.

Spencer exhaled.

Christiaan followed her into the washroom.

Andy closed the door behind him, removing her mask and her voice scrambler, and adjusted the setting. "No violence. Finesse over force, remember?"

Christiaan pointed toward the door. "The guy's just stalling."

"We need another tactic."

"What do you suggest?" He crossed his arms across his massive chest.

She dropped the mask and the scrambler on the edge of the pedestal sink. "I don't know. But I'm uncomfortable with this."

"This is how we do it in the real world."

"We need more honey and less punishment." She shook her head.

"You want to get information your way?"

She bit her lip and nodded. Though getting information her way would give her no pleasure.

Christiaan glared at the door. "I'd rather pound him good."

"Let me try my way."

Christiaan pointed toward the door. "The guy is a cad."

"Let's pretend I've had lots of experience dealing with cads."

"What are you planning to do? Straddle him and neck on him?" He jutted out his jaw.

She shrugged. "If I have to."

"I can't—" He shook his head.

"You can't what?"

Christiaan drew a breath. "I can't believe you'd rather kiss him than punch him."

"Oh, I want to punch him. I want information as much as you do. But I also want this to work. Hin Cho is my friend, and every day we don't find her is another day she's in harm's way." Andy's stomach turned with powerlessness. She needed the information from

Spencer—any way she could get it.

Christiaan slowly nodded.

She opened the bathroom door. Ropes lay all around an empty chair.

Picking up a length of rope, Christiaan swore and paced. "That little sneak! How will we learn anything from him?"

Spencer was gone. He must've hidden a knife up his sleeve.

Andy arched her brow and smirked. "Now it's my turn."

****

Thankfully, with the aid of the voice scramblers and masks, but mostly because of her excellent disguise skills, Andy bet Spencer didn't recognize her. She found him leaning over a glass of amber liquid in the bar area of the golf clubhouse.

He swept a hand through his disheveled hair. His eyes bugged out, and his collar crumpled over his collar bone. The silk lariat of his tie hung about his neck.

"Hey." Andy almost expected him to leer as he had up in the "interrogation" room in the attic. Instead he twitched, but when he saw her, he broke into a dazzling smile.

"You're a sight for sore eyes."

"We need to talk. Wanna grab a picnic later?"

"I'm free at about eighteen-hundred hours." Spencer plucked up his drink and knocked back a swallow. Dark circles ringed his eyes. "I really need a nap." He wiped his face with his sleeve.

Clearly, the drug still had an effect. "Right." A vine of guilt snaked its way up Andy's spine. "See you then. You want to arrange the food or shall I?"

He bobbed his head. "I'll make the necessary food preparations. I don't trust Americans to make the best wine pairings." He winked. "I'll leave you a note as to where to meet me."

She breathed a sigh of relief. He still trusted her. At least for now.

Later that evening, Andy, clad in a red-gingham dress with a white, short-sleeved sweater, exited the golf club. Her white, high heel wedges made navigating the grass tricky. She unfolded and folded her note from Spencer, then stuck it in her pocket.

Christiaan followed her and caught her by the arm. "I don't want you to interrogate Spencer by yourself."

"I won't be by myself. Your nagging voice will be in my head." She flicked on her comms unit.

Christiaan's gaze took in her dress. "He's no good."

A burst of anger heated her chest. "But since you and I are not dating, you can't say who I can see and in what condition I see him."

Christiaan's jaw dropped.

Andy stalked away into the dense forest where Spencer waited. She might have hurt Christiaan, but he deserved it. She wearied of waiting for him.

"Psst."

Andy thrust out her hands in a defensive mode.

"Psst," the sound came again.

She followed the sound.

Hiding in the heavy growth was Spencer. "Is he gone?"

"Who?"

"That hulking pounding machine you call a friend."

"Yes, I told him off." She glanced back to where she'd left him. Her chest still heaved from their argument.

He straightened as he stood. "Good. He is always following you around, you know."

"Oh?" How much did Spencer watch her? How much did he see? He looked so much better than when she last saw him. His nap really paid off.

He took her hand and led her through the brush. "I wonder if he has some connection to the police here or maybe Scotland Yard? Or that damnable OverSight?" He brushed a leaf off his tie.

Andy's heartbeat quickened. "I don't think so. Anyway, let's not talk about him. Let's talk about us."

Spencer scooped up her other hand and drew her into the cool of the shade. "I've been waiting." He pressed his lips across her knuckles.

A prickle of guilt sprung up inside. He anticipated this meeting with her, and she was about to use him. She had never felt guilty before an interrogation of this nature. "I've changed my mind. I want to thank you for helping me."

Arching an eyebrow, he brushed her hair out of her face.

Andy breathed in the pines, the cool musty smell of the shaded wood, and a deep musky perfume. He chose a great spot.

Spencer slid his arm around her waist. "I brought the picnic."

Behind him, a blanket spread on the soft, needled earth. A basket sat on top.

A pit opened in her stomach. After all these years, guilt now caught up with her? She mentally kicked herself. "Great, because I'm starved."

Lowering his chin, Spencer arched an eyebrow. "And what are you hungry for?"

She licked her lips. "Anything tempting me."

Squeezing her hand, he escorted her to the blanket.

Andy fought the twinge of guilt. She liked Spencer. His uncanniness attracted her. His smile melted her. He wasn't a horrible mark running illegal operations. He was a respectable gambler.

Kind of. Maybe?

Lingering before the edge of the blanket, he ran his hands down the sides of Andy's arm.

Goose bumps rose across her flesh.

"Are you chilly?" He dipped his chin and studied her.

"Just a bit in the shade."

"I'll warm you." He tilted her chin.

Flustered, her mind raced. She was supposed to do something, wasn't she? Instead, her heart pounded in her ears. She swallowed.

Spencer leaned in. He caressed her bottom lip with his.

Andy stepped into him, sliding her arms around his neck, and deepened the kiss. Her breath mingled with his. Where Christiaan tasted of passion and fury, Spencer's kisses tasted sweet and delicate.

"You don't have to enjoy it so much."

Andy forgot the comms link in her ear. Christiaan hovered near and watched. Just for his comment, she tilted her pelvis toward Spencer, walking him backward, and trapped him against a tree.

Spencer reciprocated and clutched her closer. His intensity increased.

The fact that Christiaan watched inspired her to really dig into her role. She ran her fingers through Spencer's hair and across the fine woven threads of the silvery suit on his shoulders. She ran her thigh up his leg. Her skin prickled. Warmth flooded her.

"Remember what the objective is. Don't go too far. Just get information."

Andy might've pushed too much. What started out as a joke on Christiaan turned increasingly serious.

Spencer broke from his embrace only to slip his hand into hers and lead her to the blanket. He sat and tugged her to the earth.

Andy's heart thundered in her chest. Spencer didn't really want her, did he? Surely, he played her as much as she played him.

Sliding up next to her, he settled near her on the blanket.

"Now would be a good time to ask him what he knows about Hin Cho's chemistry degree." Christiaan buzzed in her ear again.

She opened her mouth, but the words never left her lips.

Once on the blanket, Spencer softly brushed her hair out of her face, leaning into her for a lingering kiss.

His warmth melted all over her. Perhaps he was serious. The realization sent a jolt through her. If she wasn't careful, this would end badly. She wasn't sure who would hurt the most. She slowed her kissing just as Spencer ramped up.

At her hesitation, he halted. "What's wrong?"

"Nothing." Gasping for air, Andy straightened her misaligned skirt. "I didn't realize how much I would enjoy this."

"What are you saying?" Christiaan asked in her ear. "I know your tone, Andy. Now is not the time for honesty."

Andy ignored him.

"I'm enjoying this, too." Brushing his hand over her hip, Spencer leaned in for another serving.

Andy dished up a block instead.

His eyes lit up.

Andy gulped. "I don't want to hurt you."

"No, Andy, no!" Christiaan moaned in her ear.

"You stop because of the big oaf who follows you around?"

Andy froze. Christiaan only breathed in her ear.

The woods stilled, awaiting her reply.

Andy wasn't sure if she should lie or be honest. Matters of the heart had always challenged her, and although she'd never admitted out loud she and Christiaan were a thing, was love deeply burning in her heart? If so, the truth made Andy uncomfortable. How could her heart blow her cover? Andy exhaled. "You're right. He isn't who you think he is."

"Oh, Andy!" Christiaan groaned.

Andy gazed at the gauzy blanket. "He's—he's my stalker."

"Eh?" Both men asked at once.

Andy focused on the floral-printed blanket. "We had a relationship once upon a time, and now he follows me everywhere."

"Where are you going with this, Andy?" Christiaan asked.

She curled up in a little ball next to Spencer. "He scares me."

"Don't worry." Spencer placed an arm around her.

"I'll protect you."

Andy fiddled with his tie. "No, you can't save me from him. He's too clever—too skilled."

"You'd be surprised."

Spencer's tone deepened. Andy inwardly smiled.

"Hin Cho was another one of his old girlfriends."

"Oh? You don't say." His tone lightened again.

Andy kept talking into his chest. She couldn't lie to his face. "And he was searching for her and asked me to come and help him."

"He still has that kind of sway over you."

"He's very persuasive."

"Oh, please!" Christiaan said.

Still curled into Spencer's chest, Andy smiled a little bit, her face hidden from his view. "And if I don't find out what happened to her, I worry he'll hurt me."

"The violent type, eh?"

"You have no idea." Andy even managed to squeeze out a few tears. "Maybe if I help this fiend find this girl, he'll leave me alone."

"He's a dog, and you want to throw him off the scent?"

Andy sniffled and nodded.

"When I see you again…" Christiaan said. "You're in big trouble, girl, for going off script."

Andy ignored him and tilted her face upward to Spencer's instead. "What can I do? He thinks Hin Cho somehow left on her own accord."

Spencer brushed her lips with his. "Interesting theory."

Andy peaked her eyebrows as best as possible. "Yes, he's not right in his head."

"Certainly does seem to be one hoop short of a

croquet game."

"Careful," Christiaan said through the comms. "You are so dead for this, Andy."

"I just need to know more about Hin Cho. Why did she disappear?"

Spencer sat up suddenly. He stood with his hands on his hips. "Now you are a terrible liar."

Caught off balance, Andy nearly fell into the blanket. "What?" She scrambled to sit up, crossing her legs under her skirt.

"You can't lie to a liar." Spencer paced and rubbed his chin, pacing.

"Are you admitting to lying?"

"I admit nothing. I am accusing you." He stopped and pointed. "I've seen the way you two moon over each other. He's not your stalker any more than I am your grandfather."

Slumping her shoulders, Andy sighed, defeated.

"If you take that out," Christiaan hissed in her ear, "I'm coming in to bust this little party."

She removed her comms unit.

Spencer paced again. Needles and twigs crunched under his feet. "You're in this together, whatever it is. And you both were upstairs interrogating me."

"What?" She used to be able to control her emotions better.

"You pointed to the bloke and said, 'bathroom.' Only Americans use that term."

A blush burned on her face. *Caught.* "Listen. You're right. We need some information from you about Hin Cho. She really is my friend. I knew her in Texas before I came here. I promised her sister I'd take care of her. And he's helping me."

"That I do believe is the truth." He crouched, his eyes growing large and earnest. "Well, sadly, I don't know much about her. Just what I've heard from the caddies. They depend on my bribes. If you would've asked me nicely, I would've told you."

"You mean like this?" Andy moved to kneeling and kissed his chest through his white shirt.

With a sharp intake of breath, Spencer leaned back, embracing her. "This works, too. I might know some things."

"What do you know? Why did she leave China?" Andy loosened his tie and kissed his neck. His skin smelled differently than the sandalwood of Christiaan's. Spencer smelled of fresh linen.

He leaned against a tree. A breath escaped his lips. "She invented something the Chinese government really wanted."

"And what was that?"

His eyes rolled upward. "A way to heal precious gems."

"What do you mean?" *A clue!* A thrill of another kind caused flutters in her stomach. Andy kissed his collarbone and began to untie his necktie.

Spencer glanced down.

His nose breath tickled her forehead. She unbuttoned a button.

Spencer's breath increased. "I'm sorry. What did you ask?"

"I wanted to know more about the gems."

"Ah, yes. Um, it seems some gems have distinctive fissures, and she found a way to erase them through grinding up the gem and mixing the powder with some oil, rubbing in the mixture, and then baking the gems, like a cast iron, into a near-perfect seamless Balm of Gilead of sorts."

Andy faced him. "What are you talking about?"

"One can't even tell a fissure was even there, not even with a microscope. Her discovery was all over the news a few years back, then she disappeared and wound up the in the States. Are you going to kiss me some more?"

Andy sat back on her heels. "With her formula, no one could identify stolen gems."

"Correct. But not only that, a perfect gem will fetch a higher price than an imperfect one. Plus, healing a gem with a particular fissure would make selling them on the black market easier. Especially in Asia where emeralds are seen as part of the mystic arts." His eyes widened at the last part. "Kisses?"

Andy shot him a piercing look. "Perhaps the Chinese found out she was here and kidnapped her back. But then why kidnap her then hire someone to come find her?"

"What do you mean?" Spencer kissed her cheek.

"The Chinese government hired OverSight to find her. So, it's clearly not them."

Spencer's face paled. "Good Heavens! You're not OverSight, are you?"

"No." She was glad she didn't have to lie. "I promise. I am Hin Cho's friend."

"Ah, good." He sat back on his heels. "Who else would kidnap her?"

Andy couldn't shake a gut feeling. "Someone who has stolen gems."

Where was Christiaan? He threatened to break up this little meeting, and yet, he didn't? He possessed stolen gems, and now he knew how to heal them. Andy's heart beat faster but now for a different reason. She needed answers. "Excuse me. I have to go."

"But we're just getting started."

Andy had already left the copse. Christiaan had better confess what he wanted with emeralds and why he wanted to find Hin Cho. Was it possible he kidnapped her?

Chapter 18

Andy found Christiaan heading across the green toward the clubhouse. She called out, but he continued to stalk away. Finally, she ran across the scented grass and grabbed at his elbow. "Hey." She panted, out of breath. "We need to talk."

"Nope." He started to head away.

But she reined him back in. Then she noticed his comms unit smashed in his fingers. "I'm serious. Spencer just told me the reason Hin Cho left China. She knew how to heal emeralds. You are also searching for emeralds. What is going on?"

Christiaan glanced up toward some other competitors conversing near them. "Let's go somewhere private."

Andy held her ground. "Right now, you are number one on my suspect list. I'm not going anywhere with you."

"Me?"

A flash of genuine hurt crossed her face. But he was as good as she was at acting. "You dragged me to Europe to steal stolen emeralds. Then when you're assigned to find a kidnapped girl who can erase all traces of stolen emeralds, you disappear with more important things to do. You look really guilty."

Christiaan shook his head. "You don't understand."

Andy opened her arms. "Then help me

understand."

"Not here." He glanced side to side.

"I told you I'm not going anywhere with you."

His eyes flashed. "If I really wanted to hurt you, I could've done it a thousand times by now." He stepped closer.

"I don't trust you," Andy whispered. All this time she'd started to trust him. Now it was all shattered.

"You're right not to trust me. I could take you from here and make you disappear so fast, no one would know what happened. And who would ask after you?"

Fear raked her insides, penetrating her core. Christiaan was right. Who would search for her? Her step-mom Sandra? Spencer? Everywhere else she was known only by an alias. Emotion choked her throat. "Are you stealing emeralds and selling them for a profit? Or do you need them healed for another reason? I'm confused, Christiaan."

"I don't want—"

Directness was her only option. "Did you kidnap Hin Cho to heal the emeralds?" Afraid of the answer, she closed her eyes.

"No. But I might know who did."

Opening her eyes, she relaxed. "Will you please just tell me what's going on?"

"Do you trust me enough to go on a walk?" He pointed toward a small path beside the links.

The path led to the shore. Though away from competitors and the links, the walk was semi-private. To answer, she started on the path.

"Where shall I start?" he asked.

"At the beginning."

"The beginning is too far away. I'll start from

where the story gets interesting." Down a nearly deserted road, they passed pink limestone buildings and weathered rock fences.

At the edge of the road, they crossed the green in silence. The world fell behind them. When grass turned to sand, Andy removed her shoes, slinging them by their heels from her fingers. The sun tinged the sky with orange. The waves collapsed on the shore. They strolled along the beach. The rhythmic water relaxed Andy.

Christiaan drew a deep breath. "There were seven sanctuaries of the Order of Destroying Angels."

Andy stopped. Her feet sank into the cool sand. "Were? Not are?"

Christiaan faced her. "No. Blaine destroyed them all. There was one on each continent. Two in Asia."

"None in Antarctica?"

"Yeah, no." He kissed her on the nose.

She recoiled a bit.

He nodded. "The Order was disbanded and the sanctuaries shut down."

"Because of your dead friend Blaine."

He nodded and motioned for them to sit on a dune. "Blaine wanted to remake the sanctuaries in his image. He stole the powerful emeralds from the sanctuaries."

"The emeralds?"

"I have them all now." Christiaan nodded. "All but one: the Nero. I've been tracking it ever since Blaine stole them. The emeralds gave the sanctuaries power. But Blaine didn't know it and sold them on the black market."

Andy sat on the cool sand. Its grit tingled her fingers. Her throat tightened. She swallowed. "What kind of power?"

"This is where people get skeptical."

Brushing sand from her hands, Andy crossed her arms across her upright knees. "Martial arts have always been associated with the mystic arts, but this practical American will believe you."

Christiaan crouched near her, tossing pebbles into the surf. "The emeralds themselves came from all over the world. Each one possesses a power of their own. The last one I seek, an emerald the size of my palm, was handed down from the time of Nero."

"Nero." Was he taking her on another goose chase? Just how old was his Order? "In Ancient Rome?"

"Yes." He shifted and sat. His eyes reflected the pinkish sky. "He used the glass to gaze upon the events of the arena. He said the green calmed him. But the power went beyond that."

Andy's heart beat into her ears. "What was it?"

Christiaan dropped the pebbles and dusted his hands. "The emerald had power of its own. The gem didn't just calm Nero. He remained calm during the fight because the gem showed him the future. He already knew the outcome."

"How is that possible?" Andy sat forward, all her senses heightened.

"Emeralds are powerful even on their own, but these gems have sacred texts inscribed. When you gaze into them, those powers are transferred to the person. The inscription is what makes them powerful."

Andy leaned back and stared into the lapping waves. Was such a power even possible?

"I told you I believe in the unbelievable."

"Nero could see the future." Andy remembered some vague history lesson from Western Civilization.

She scooped up sand, letting the grains fall through her fingers. "In his speech to the senate, he spoke of removing all the ills of the previous regime. He spoke of ending secret courts. He ended the life of his mother for reasons unknown. He started a trail of bloodlust of potential enemies. History painted him as crazy."

"What laws would you make and what actions would you take if you knew your enemies' next move?"

"He knew they would betray him." Andy blinked. Goose bumps rose on her arms. She dropped her jaw. "What incredible power. And the emeralds you retrieved in Madrid?"

He picked up two stones about the same size of the gems and tossed them in his hands. "They are two sides of the same emerald, twin cut. They are Healing—one physical and the other mental. In case you were wondering why I can heal so fast. The body still needs time to recover, but not as long as without them."

Stunned, she checked his wounds. The bandages on his arms were gone. And he hadn't complained about his rib. This information was coming too fast. "Do the thieves know about their power?"

Shaking his head, Christiaan pocketed the stones. "If they know the true value, they don't care. The thieves sell the gems for large sums on the black market. Because they can easily be identified by their distinct fissures, they could fetch a higher price if resold on an open market, but they would have to be disguised by cutting or be healed with the formula. Emeralds are brittle and difficult to cut. Gem cutters are often left with shards of stone good only for small earrings. Why risk cutting them? With Hin Cho's formula, think of how much easier they could be sold if the fissures were healed. The unmarked emeralds would be perfect and unrecognizable. The gems would be more valuable, but healing the inscriptions would cause them to lose their power."

Andy tucked her head into her chest. "What kind of power do the others have?"

"Greater strength, agility, concentration, and speed. We would spend hours gazing into the emeralds to improve our physical and spiritual condition. I need all seven of them."

"What for?"

Christiaan tossed a handful of sand.

Andy guessed before he answered. "You want to restore the Seven Sanctuaries."

He nodded. His gaze remained on the horizon where the sea and sky met.

Andy let out a low breath. "And that requires you continue to live by your oaths."

He closed his eyes, leaning back on his elbows. Then he bowed his head in a single nod.

"Forever?" Andy gulped. She didn't have to see his reaction to know he would say yes. Last year, at death's door, he revealed he had sworn a vow of chastity. The confession hollowed her heart. Her nagging hunger for him persisted and grew. And nothing sated her thirst for him.

"Restoring the sanctuaries is the only way to avenge my parents and possibly find my brother," Christiaan continued. "The terrorist group is too big for one man. The organization can only be wiped out by a legion of warriors living in harmony and by living spotless lives—"

Andy gulped. "With semi-magical powers."

Christiaan frowned and glanced away. "I'm not asking you to believe me."

She touched his arm. "I do believe you. I just wish you didn't have to do it. I wish you could move on and let that part of your life go. And have me, instead." She leaned across him and gently kissed along his jaw line.

He moved toward her.

His cheek warmed hers. The prickle of his chin growth tickled her skin. His breath brushed over her. She closed her eyes. His lips caressed hers. His taste intoxicated her.

Drawing her close, he held her tight around her waist.

So much time had passed. Andy's mind buzzed with pleasure, but instead of sating her desire, his embrace intensified her lust and taunted her.

While the sun set, casting long shadows across the dunes and grass, he embraced her. Christiaan rolled to his back and drew her over him.

"Now if you didn't kidnap her, who wants the emeralds healed?" Andy brushed her nose along his stubbled cheek.

Christiaan kissed her forehead. "I know of a man searching for her."

"Who?"

A kiss separated the question from the answer. Finally, Christiaan responded. "Fabian."

"Who is Fabian?" Andy flushed with heat. She leaned forward for another kiss.

Shaking his head, Christiaan sat up. He held out his hand then wiped his face. "He's the French fence who sold them to Philipe. And I wager, the one who sent Blades. But now I wonder if he had a more nefarious purpose. We need to find Blades and ask him what he knows."

Andy sat back, still hungry for more. "He'll be looking for us."

****

Christiaan yearned to sit on the beach with Andy for as long as time lasted. But sunlight faded, and they had to find Hin Cho and return to real life. He stood and held out his hand.

Andy grabbed his hand. "We should apologize to Spencer."

He huffed. He had no desire to do any apologizing. "Why?"

She brushed off her bottom. "Because we've suspected him falsely."

"He's fine."

"No, he's really hurt. He's genuinely a good guy."

Christiaan huffed. "Oh, you know him well, then?"

"I am a good judge of character when people aren't lying."

Christiaan sighed and poked her in the ribs. "If I had told you I was from South Africa in the beginning in St. Louis, you would've been too suspicious and blown my cover. OverSight agents are supposed to sneak in, get the job done, and sneak out." He led her through the dunes to the path back to the road.

Andy shook her head. "Someone else must be after us." Her voice lowered, almost a whisper.

"What makes you say that?"

"The crashed car." Her eyebrows furrowed, and she bit her lip.

He clenched his stomach at the thought of her in danger. "Blades?"

"They were after me or Spencer. He jumped out the window. Are you sure he's not MI5?"

Dusk purpled the sky. The twilight swallowed her facial expressions. He paused on the green to study her. "They were after you?" A sinking feeling filled his gut. "Are you sure it wasn't an accident?"

"You can ask Spencer. He was with me."

Since she started hanging around Spencer, Andy had changed. Sighing, Christiaan shook his head. She seemed too wrapped up in Spencer. He needed to teach him a lesson. "I want to meet the guy."

"Spencer? You want me to introduce you to Spencer?" Andy let her jaw fall slightly agape, then nodded.

What did this *oke* have that he didn't have? Christiaan immediately repented of his thought. If he couldn't have Andy now, she might as well be happy with someone else, right?

Nope.

****

Standing in the hall at the clubhouse, Spencer frowned at the ape of a man in front of him. Andy asked him to meet Christiaan, her brute. He towered above Spencer and was nearly twice as wide in every body part. He was every bit as intimidating up close as he was far away. He was like an elephant in a glass menagerie shop.

"Stay away from Andy."

The brute spoke in nearly monosyllabic words. Did this man even have a neck? He was muscle from the tip of his head to the tip of his toes. "Wasn't this supposed to be a friendly meeting? That's what I was told." Spencer lightened his voice, keeping out all fear.

"You can't have Andy."

"Shouldn't she make the decision?" Spencer led him away from the few patrons who stared at their heated conversation.

Christiaan followed him to a side hallway.

Spencer rubbed his hands together. "I've an idea. Let's place a bet and whoever wins, gets to keep Andy." Christiaan had a confident air about him that exuded arrogance, but Spencer had his wits.

Christiaan arched an eyebrow. "You want to wager?"

"Choose a time and a sport." Spencer studied stats on all sports, cricket, croquet, and especially football. Not American Football, of course. "We can wager on which team or individual will win."

Christiaan thrust his chin forward to a poster hanging on the wall. "There."

Spencer swiveled to read the poster. "Highland games? Who do you bet will win?" He didn't know anyone competing, but he could find information on anyone.

"Me. You and I register, and the best man gets Andy."

Register? His knees nearly collapsed. The point wasn't to *play* the game but to *wager* on who would win—that was where his talents lay. Spencer slid the paper from the pin tacking it to the board. Tugging at his collar, he read the announcement. His face dripped with sweat. He dabbed it with a handkerchief and swallowed hard. "Quite a brutish sport. You mean, you and I both sign up for an event and whoever wins, wins Andy?"

"You game?" Christiaan towered closer.

"This isn't what I had in mind, exactly." Odds were more his thing. Probability and information were, too. Competition was not. "Sure you don't want to bet on someone else and leave off us both competing?"

Christiaan thrust up his chin. "This is between you and me."

Spencer drew his lips to a straight line. "All right. I'll wager. But I won't wager I'll win. That's not a fair bet as you are"—*gulp*—"by far my physical superior. However, I will wager this. I wager you won't win."

"If I win, you'll leave Andy alone?"

"Yes. But if you lose, to anyone, I have a chance." He jabbed a thumb at his own chest.

"All right. And I'll wager you won't finish."

"Finish?" Spencer stumbled back. How insulting!

"If you walk away from the games, then you walk away from Andy. Deal?"

"Deal." He shook Christiaan's outstretched hand.

"See you Saturday."

Spencer rubbed his forehead. What did he just get himself into?

Chapter 19

Scotland did not disappoint with its soggy morning on the verdant grass where the games were held. The weather turned chilly for summer. As to why they were taking a morning to do these games, Andy had no idea. She shook her head and hunched her shoulders. Male bonding? Hopefully, Spencer and Christiaan would become friends. Her life had been hectic trying to mediate between them.

Christiaan strode into the field, wearing a dark green kilt with the pouch hanging between his legs. His calves, stuffed into green socks, bulged from underneath the hem. He picked up something. His muscular biceps shone beside his white tank top. The drizzle glued the shirt to his ripped abs.

She had to admit, she never imagined that seeing a man in a skirt would excite her, but dang, kilts made her blood rush—if the man had the right physique. The older, hunched men shuffling with a cane did nothing for her, but Christiaan's trim waist and broad shoulders were made to wear a knee-length kilt. Attraction tugged at her. She tamped it down. "Why are we doing this again?" Although she didn't mind seeing Christiaan in traditional Scottish dress, Andy ground her teeth at this distraction. They were supposed to find Hin Cho.

"Just something I gotta prove." Christiaan slapped his hands together.

Andy crossed her arms. "To yourself or others?"

Spencer, in a blue velour workout suit, cantered across the green. He shook his head and then stretched his extremities on the wet grass.

"Is he competing, too?" She nodded toward Spencer. When he clasped his hands behind him and bent over, stretching out over his white trainers, Andy understood. She narrowed her eyes. "This isn't some manly competition, is it?"

When his gaze tracked Spencer, Christiaan's brows lowered. "Of course, it's a manly competition. We're throwing telephone poles around."

"Between the two of you." Shivering in her sweatshirt, Andy shook her head and kicked the dewy grass.

Christiaan's eyes reflected the dark gray clouds hanging overhead.

She huffed. "I should've known something was up when you invited me here in the morning. The games are mainly ego-fluffing feats of manly strength. Why is Spencer competing?"

Christiaan grinned wide. "You should ask him. You'd be interested in his response."

Spencer stretched his shoulders by pinning his arms across his chest. Then he jogged in place. When massive competitors passed near him, his eyes bugged out. His clingy velour jogging suit only accentuated his trim figure. His face broke into a smile, and he nodded toward Christiaan's kilt. "Ah, I see you've come to compete in the Scottish dance." He nodded to indicate a place across the field. "I believe the girls are on that platform."

Christiaan arched an eyebrow. "Never make fun of

a man in a kilt. Especially in Scotland." With a grunt, Christiaan joined a group of beefier contenders to warm up, making friends, and conversing easily. He was in his element here among high testosterone-filled knuckleheads.

Spencer rolled his eyes. "I just hope I don't get killed." He stared at a fifty-two-pound weight a competitor tossed over a bar and the shot put.

Slightly suspicious, Andy frowned. "What did you bet him?"

"That he would lose."

She dropped her jaw. "Are you crazy? Why did you egg him on?"

"He suggested it."

"I'll stop him." She took a step.

Grabbing her elbow, Spencer held her back. "Don't spoil the fun."

She sighed and rubbed her brow. "We have work to do. We shouldn't be wasting our time on this."

"This is much more interesting than golf."

True. Golf bored her to tears.

"Besides," Spencer lowered his voice. "I am expecting some remuneration if he loses."

Andy spun to face him. He made bets on whether Christiaan won? "You didn't."

He bowed slightly. "I am a gambler. Scots love to bet, and they hate to lose money."

"That's not all you bet." Andy cast him a sideways glance.

Spencer focused on the grass in front of him.

"Spencer. What were the stakes? With Christiaan."

Spencer shrugged and stood in a hamstring stretch, his heel to his bottom. "A friendly, zero-sum game."

She smirked. "Sounds awful. Christiaan said I would be interested in knowing what the stakes were."

"You'll know as soon as the games are over, and he loses."

A horn blew. Reluctantly, Andy left the field and found a spectator's bench to watch the show. Spencer's unusual question-dodging aroused her suspicions, but she couldn't for the life of her figure out why. Was Christiaan hoping to get more information from him? What did Spencer have that Christiaan wanted or vice versa?

Sitting in the stand, huddled under a golf umbrella, she donned a rain slicker. A chill went through her. What was she doing at these Highland games? Anxiety troubled her mind. Hairs rose on her arms. Uneasiness grew in her belly. Someone was watching her. She felt it.

Competitors slapped each other in friendly encouragement. Families gathered and ate local fare, speaking in a broad tongue Andy couldn't believe was English. Old men in kilts hunched over canes and argued. Plumb judges readied to record how straight the cabers fell.

Nothing was out of the ordinary. She brushed away the feeling as anxiety for her friend. For wanting answers and for being idle for a few moments. She didn't want to rest until she found Hin Cho or at least discovered what happened to her.

Spencer fared well in the hand to hand on a log over a pit of mud. He threw several bigger men into the pit. He managed to keep his head, his balance, and his velour suit unsoiled. When he climbed down the ladder with only a hint of mud on his face, he held up both his thumbs.

Music drew Andy's gaze.

Girls danced traditional dances on a platform near a copse of trees to the light sound of the bagpipes. When they made their delicate leaps into the air, their plaid kilts bounced. They held their hands upward toward the overcast sky.

Andy bobbed her head in time with the music.

They finished just before another light drizzle set in.

Again, an unease chilled the air.

Children played their own games on the lawn. Younger kids played a version of "What time is it, Mr. Fox?" Older teenage kids kicked a soccer ball around on the spectator grass.

Nothing out of the ordinary. The whole competition spread across three quarters of a clearing between two forests. But Andy couldn't relax. Was she nervous about Christiaan winning? Or being so far out in the open? She needed to focus. She huddled under her umbrella, wishing for sunshine and dry days. To her untrained eye, Christiaan was holding his own. In the caber toss, Christiaan got a full rotation, although it landed out of true.

A man ran from the trees.

Was this a rehearsed act, an impromptu surprise for the crowds, but then the audience screams were terror not delight? She recognized the man by the diagonal scar across the bridge of his nose and his massive build. Hooked blades protruded through leather gauntlets gracing his forearms.

He strode across the field, knocking anyone away who opposed him.

Andy stood in her seat, gaze glued to him.

The man forced his way to Christiaan.

"Look out!" Andy didn't realize she'd screamed until she felt pain in her throat from screeching so loudly. She opened her mouth again, but fear stole her breath.

Christiaan spun just in time to catch the gauntlet before it tore through his back. At first, Christiaan held his own against the man, but each slice of the gauntlet came closer to tearing flesh.

Andy rushed out of the seating to help. But there was little need.

The group of kilted men surrounded Blades, furious at the disruption.

"You pick on one of us, you pick on all of us, lad," one of the competitors said to Blades in a broad Scottish brogue. They were nearly the same size.

But Blades rallied even being outnumbered.

A shot putter grabbed him from behind while Christiaan settled a few hits into his chest.

But he took it, with glaring eyes. He broke the hold and landed in front of Christiaan.

Christiaan kicked and double kicked him into the crowd.

Another man grabbed him.

"Let him go, he's mine." Christiaan faced Blades.

Andy lost her view as the men formed a circle around the two competitors. But she heard the cheers rise above their heads. She would've loved to get her hands on Blades. At last, she broke through the crowd to find Blades on the ground, Christiaan readying his fists for the interrogation. Andy ran to him. "Where is Hin Cho?" She held his collar firm, but the man spat in her face. "What does Fabian want with her?"

"I'll never talk."

Christiaan stepped in. "After we're done, you'll wish we'd sent you to the police for interrogation."

Andy wasn't sure if Christiaan was bluffing or not.

But the man eyed Christiaan's twenty-inch biceps. "Fabian's only a fence. He doesn't want her. He already has a buyer."

Before Andy could ask what he meant, she was stopped. The police busted through the crowd and escorted him to the paddy wagon.

For all the authorities knew, he only disturbed the peace. He'd be out soon. What did Blades mean by a buyer? Andy had to act quickly.

****

"What do you think he meant?" Andy handed Christiaan a bag of ice for his bruises and bandaged the slices where Blades cut him. The Blakely Manor kitchen bustled with activity for lunch.

Spencer hit the wood table with a knife someone had used to cut cabbage.

"More importantly, *who* do you think he meant?" Andy pressed ice against Christiaan's knuckles.

Christiaan tenderly touched a bruised eye. "He has a point. Fabian doesn't steal. He's the fence. A broker."

"Someone knew what Hin Cho could do. But who?" Andy bit her nail.

The kitchen staff prepared the noonday meal.

Andy eyed them with suspicion. She stood suddenly. "Who's hungry? Let's go out to eat some local fare. I'm so hungry I could eat hummus."

Spencer, who had been quiet this whole time, arched an eyebrow and set down the knife. "I think you mean haggis."

"That, too." Andy shifted her weight.

Spencer stuffed his hands into his velour suit. "Nobody really eats that anymore, do they?"

Christiaan shrugged, eyeing Andy. "Don't forget your bag."

"I never go anywhere without it." Then Andy stopped. Light exploded in her mind. Revelation dawned. "I figured it out."

"What?" the two men asked in unison.

"She would never leave them." Andy dropped her mouth.

"What are you talking about?"

Andy hustled them out into the hall, away from listening ears. "Her clubs. What was missing from her room?" Energy prickled her senses. "She never went anywhere without them. If we find the golf clubs, we'll find her."

Spencer leaned against the table. "What do you mean?"

Andy inhaled sharply. "We need to find those clubs."

"Whoever has her clubs took her?" Christiaan leaned against the wall.

"Where do we start searching?" Spencer brushed his velour suit.

"Mr. McGuffin?" Christiaan bit his lip.

Andy clapped her hands. "Bingo." Mr. McGuffin wouldn't be easy to search. They had their work cut out.

Chapter 20

After lunch, Christiaan wrapped his knuckles and waited in Andy's room while she searched for more bandages.

Spencer lounged on her bed propped up on his elbow. "I still say, we need a rematch. I said if you walked, you lose. You didn't finish, so you lost. I win. I get Andy."

Christiaan shook his head. "The bet is off because our bladed friend showed up."

"The agreement still holds. You lost. You lose Andy."

Andy entered.

Christiaan coughed. Spencer would get them both into trouble. He hoped Andy didn't hear the conversation.

"What do I lose?" she asked.

Spencer ducked his head. "Nothing."

She threw the bandages at Christiaan. "I found a way to get into the McGuffin's personal quarters."

"Breaking in won't be easy." Spencer blinked. "He's a respected member of the community. He practically owns the town."

Ignoring Spencer, Christiaan faced Andy and finished bandaging a wound. "How do you propose we infiltrate his side of the mansion?"

"The closing social is held in his personal suites."

Andy spread wide her hands.

"Do we have invites?" Christiaan folded his arms across his chest.

Andy bobbed her head. "We can get them."

Christiaan tore open the new bandages. "Yes, but how do we investigate without getting caught?"

"I am going in disguise. The rest of you can be yourselves." Andy sauntered away with a smug smile. "Bye-bye, boys. I need to plan what to wear."

With mouth slightly agape, Christiaan stared after her. Did she have an extra sway to her hips? Visions of her costume appeared in his head. Something slinky and sexy.

Spencer stared, too. "You think she's special, don't you." He eyed Christiaan. "So do I."

Christiaan expanded his chest. "You know she's already spoken for."

Spencer raised himself to full height. "She didn't mention any prior attachment. She told me you were unavailable."

Unavailable? Christiaan scowled. "I know Andy. We're cut from the same cloth. We are two sides of the same coin."

Spencer paced with his hands behind his back. "I propose a different wager. Since the last one didn't actually get finished."

"Oh?"

He stopped and thrust out a finger. "We can't propose the first person who gets her in bed wins. Not only is that low and cheap, it's disrespectful to our friend."

Christiaan shook his head. "I would never consider such a thing—not with any girl, especially not Andy."

"Yes, but how else can we know which one of us knows Andy the best?"

Christiaan eyed him.

"How about, whoever recognizes her first in disguise and elicits a kiss, wins?" Spencer rubbed his hands together.

"Just a kiss?" Huffing, Christiaan arched a brow.

"Yes, just a kiss." Spencer widened his eyes. "Deal?" He proffered his hand to Christiaan.

"Deal. I can pick her out in a crowd." Christiaan shook his hand, adding an extra squeeze.

Spencer winced.

Christiaan's confidence strengthened. "Now for the stakes. We know the person wins gets full claim on Andy's attention, but what does the loser get to lose?"

Spencer's eyes narrowed. "Ah, yes, what would you like to lose?"

Ha! As if. Christiaan placed a hand on his chest. "Me? Nothing. But you on the other hand..."

"Money?"

Christiaan shook his head. "I want you to leave her alone. If you can't recognize her, you don't deserve her."

"Hm, interesting," Spencer mused. "If I win, I can pursue her. If I lose, I have to give up on her."

Christiaan nodded.

"All right. Agreed. And if you lose?" Spencer pointed to Christiaan.

"I won't lose."

"Let's just suppose you don't recognize her, either."

Christiaan huffed. "Won't happen."

Spencer crossed his legs. "All right, it won't

happen, but just in case it does, what should the stipulation be? Something has to be at stake, or it's not a fair bet. How about the emeralds in your red pouch?"

"No deal."

"You afraid you'll lose them?" Spencer raised his chest and chin.

How did he know about them in the first place? "They're not for betting."

Spencer blinked. "They would only be lost if you don't recognize her, which you most assuredly will."

Christiaan considered what weighed in his breast pocket. "All right. If I lose, the red purse and the rocks inside are yours." Turning his back to Spencer, he pulled out the red, silk envelope. He set them on the wooden table. "But I won't lose them. I'm sure of it."

****

The party throbbed in full swing at the McGuffin suites at his mansion in Dornoch. Though the late hour, the sun still beamed above the horizon, winking between the trees. The mansion blended in with the surrounds with its local stone. Inside McGuffin's private quarters had a medieval feel—coats of arms, armor hanging from the walls, and hardwood paneling. Christiaan entered. A thousand blinking eyes of candle flame lit the ballroom. Once he entered the great wooden double doors, he scanned the crowd for Blades.

Margret Prim spoke with a hunched elderly man with a puff of white curly hair. Jenkins and some of the other golfers celebrated the end of a tournament and victory. Several women in sleek, backless outfits paraded about the room in large hats.

Christiaan viewed all possible women. One debutante with long, dark hair could be her, but she stood too tall. Then he noticed her five-inch spike heels. The overhead lighting cast heavy shadows. Seeing clearly was difficult.

Another woman crossed the room and embraced a man. *Probably wasn't her.* Although her drumming up with a friend-cover on the spot wouldn't surprise Christiaan. Another woman hovered near a man Andy knew, Charles Stern. Weren't they supposed cousins? Christiaan squinted through the shadow and glare. The nose didn't seem right, but Andy brought latex.

Was the bet who could find Andy first? Or just recognize her? Christiaan couldn't remember, but he wasn't about to go charging up to Andy and kiss her, even if it meant securing the rocks.

He patted the red-silk encased stones in his breast pocket of his blazer and smiled.

Spencer approached him at the elbow. "Hello there, old chappy. Spot her yet?"

Christiaan guessed she was the woman with Charles Stern, but he wouldn't admit anything to Spencer.

"How much can she change her appearance?" Spencer's gaze darted from face to face. "Three-D printing is probably pretty effective."

Christiaan arched a brow. "I don't think she has access to three-D printing. She probably uses something less sophisticated, like homemade latex."

Spencer guffawed. "Are you ready to lose? I've just spotted her. Cherri-o, old chap!" He skipped around a few golfers and landed next to the woman in the red strapless pantsuit next to Charles Stern.

Christiaan maneuvered closer to catch the conversation.

"Great game." Spencer patted Stern on the back. "Is this your beautiful cousin I've heard so much about?" He grabbed the woman's hand and kissed first the fingers, then pulled her closer for a full-on smackeroo.

The woman fully embraced him for a few seconds, her hands combing through his hair. Then she smiled when he broke for air. "And Charles told me British men were so unaffectionate in public." The woman returned a coy smile.

Spencer bowed and returned to Christiaan.

A few breaths of silence passed between them.

"Wasn't her, was it?" Christiaan couldn't help but grin inside.

Spencer readjusted his tie and wiped the lipstick from his lips. "Nope." He cleared his throat. "Great kisser, nonetheless."

Christiaan rolled his eyes.

Spencer scanned the crowd again. "Have you any idea who she might be?"

"Of course I know who she is." Christiaan scanned the room in desperation. Which of these ladies was she?

"Then have you kissed her yet?"

Christiaan shook his head. "I don't want to ruin her cover."

"You have to kiss her."

Christiaan stuffed his hands into his tuxedo pockets.

"Go ahead then." Spencer urged him with a nudge on the elbow.

Christiaan inhaled and circled the room. He wasn't just concerned about finding Andy. He also sought Blades. Perhaps Blades wouldn't be among Mr.

McGuffin's guests. In fact, where was Mr. McGuffin?

The tall host wasn't conversing with anyone in the crowds—not the elderly Ms. Prim and the elderly man beside her—possibly her husband—and not in the circle of debutantes crowded near the most successful golfers.

Christiaan slipped down a vacant hallway and searched elsewhere. His kiss with Andy would have to wait. Tracking McGuffin was more important. He tiptoed out of the room, softly padding on the carpet. To his right was a room located off the main hallway with cameras outside of it. "Bingo."

At first, he casually passed by, observing from the sides of his eye. A light flickered under the door. With a flash, he headed outdoors. Outside the castle, he counted windows. The study should be about there. A light blinked from a leaded window.

From his pocket, he removed a metal grappling hook the size of his hand, with a thin, but sturdy, nylon paracord, and shot it up to the battlements on the castle walls with a handheld, dart-gun-like launcher.

He missed the first time. Rolling his eyes at himself, he reset it and fired again. This time, the grappling hook went through the embrasure and hooked on the merlon. He tugged to make sure the line was secure.

Without a harness, drawing only upon his upper-body strength, he climbed hand-over-hand up the stone wall, until he reached the window. With as much stealth as possible, he peeked into the iron-grated window.

Damn!

He swung out of the way, clutching the outside of the building. Mr. McGuffin was inside there now. With a little effort, he clung to the stones, tying himself into the rope. While holding his body aloft with the cable strapped only to his core, he swung his legs parallel to the ground. Using great control and body strength, he held to the hinges, peeking in the window, crossed with iron grates, and deeply set into the stone.

Mr. Mcguffin conversed with a man.

Gauntlets shone on his wrists. He clasped his hands in front of him.

Blades!

Christiaan retrieved an audio booster from his pocket and stuck it in his ear.

"What are you doing here?" McGuffin's voice rose. "Your very appearance incriminates me. Our deal is done. Concluded. I gave Fabian what he wanted. Why are you still here?"

"I have been arrested."

"Damn." He quieted Blades with a shush and glanced at the door. He fidgeted with a paperweight of the Tower of London.

Though his back was to Christiaan, Mr. McGuffin radiated nervous energy.

"They kept me on disrupting the peace." Blades arched his eyebrow. "We're really close to closing the deal."

McGuffin didn't immediately reply, and Christiaan couldn't see his expression.

"He found a buyer? What's the offer?"

"A group from Hong Kong called Unction." Blades grinned. "They offered twenty-five million euro. In five days."

Christiaan huffed. The price on his head was lower than Hin Cho's?

McGuffin sat back, finally at ease. "You have

taken her there? Why are you still here?"

Blades fiddled with the White Tower encased in a globe. "Complications came up."

McGuffin sat up. "Oh?"

"Someone is making our lives difficult."

McGuffin slammed a fist onto the leather top of his desk. "You don't need my permission to dispatch him. If it's the man you were sent to wipe out, take care of him."

Blades shook his head. "Actually, the man is not the problem. I could take him. A woman is giving us grief. Our plan is a little more complicated than just taking care of her."

Opening his mouth, Christiaan arched his eyebrow. Now Andy was more of a threat than he was?

"How many men do you need?" Mr. McGuffin tapped his fingers on his desk.

"At least seven."

Christiaan felt his stomach drop. Andy didn't stand a chance against seven men.

McGuffin waved a hand, granting permission and dismissal at the same instance.

Blades bowed and backed out of the room through a different entrance.

Finally, Christiaan had the evidence he needed. Now if he could just get inside and find hard proof— her golf clubs perhaps. He righted himself, trying to keep his balance and move slowly to avoid drawing attention to himself at the window.

When the door opened again, Mr. and Mrs. Prim entered. Mrs. Prim raised her chin. "We take game fixing seriously. We found the troublemakers in your employ."

Mr. McGuffin rocked back. "Am I now responsible for all my employees' actions?"

Mr. Prim puffed out his chest. "I am not accusing you, but you should tend to your staff."

Mr. McGuffin huffed. "I thank you for the warning. Now please rejoin the party, and I will contact my chief-of-staff to investigate this accusation."

The Prims shuffled out the door. Mr. Prim paused at the frame of the door, leaning against it and placed a hand against the frame.

"Are you ill, sir?" McGuffin asked.

Mr. Prim waved him away. "Thank you, no. Confrontations take a bit out of me, is all."

Mr. McGuffin waited until the old man shuffled out the door then sat at his desk. He picked up the phone. "Get me my solicitor's office please." He paused. "Nigel. I think you'd better get down here." He hung up the phone. Then he sat back.

His secretary entered the room. "Your company awaits you, Mr. McGuffin. You are to announce the Most Valued Player."

"Ah, yes, thank you." Mr. McGuffin slapped the armrests. "Before we go, do you remember the staff we placed here at the request of Mr. Fabian, our correspondent in France?"

"Yes." The secretary bobbed his head.

"See that they are all terminated." Mr. McGuffin held out a hand. "We have had complaints from the public. Do it quickly and quietly."

"Of course, sir." Another bob.

Mr. McGuffin rose from the desk and, with his keys, closed the door.

Now was Christiaan's chance. Hanging in front of

the casement, he attempted to break the lock inside. But the iron held. Frustrated, he extracted a mini blowtorch.

Then the door swung open.

He swore, dropping the torch. He glanced down. Bushes beneath him burst into flame. He swore again. Movement in the room caught his eye. A bolt of energy flushed through him. Would he get caught?

Instead of Mr. McGuffin, Mr. Prim creaked open the door. Only he wasn't shuffling. With a robust stride, he attained the library corner where he tugged a golf bag with the initials *HC*.

Christiaan dropped his jaw. Swinging from a rope two stories above the ground, he discovered who Andy Baker came as this evening. And she just discovered the clue he was hoping to find. How could they get McGuffin arrested and travel to Hong Kong on the next flight? But first, he needed to put out the fire.

Chapter 21

Tapping rapped at the window. Andy spun. Her wig moved with the rise of her eyebrows. All her old man makeup made her sweat even more.

A man dangled outside the window. Narrowing her gaze, she recognized the man's outline—Christiaan. She opened the diamond-leaded pane to let in Christiaan, swinging from a rope. She cocked her eyebrow, savoring this moment. "I believe I win." His line dropped from the battlements above. "What are you doing hanging around?" She helped him through the thick stone and casement window.

Christiaan grunted. "I need to stop a fire."

"What?"

He stumbled into the room and untied himself from the rope. "I dropped my blowtorch."

Holding on to the side of the casements, Andy glanced down. The whole shrubbery below raged in angry red flames, casting shadows of dancing light. "Why did you have a blowtorch?" Was he being like her—carrying lots of stuff around?

"No time to explain. How did you get in here?"

Andy thrust up her latex-covered chin. "I placed a thin magnet over the jamb, preventing the door from closing all the way. I found her golf clubs." In a corner wedged between two bookcases, Andy tugged out the bag.

Christiaan grabbed her elbows. "Hin Cho has been moved to Hong Kong. Fabian's men worked with McGuffin to kidnap her. They are ransoming her to the highest bidder. Unction is bidding. We have to find her before they complete the transaction."

"But what do they want? What does Unction even mean?" The information came too quickly, Andy couldn't process it all.

Christiaan inspected the clubs. "Anointed to do God's will."

"What do they want her for?"

Shrugging, Christiaan shook his head. "I'll answer questions later. I need to put out the fire." He ran out of the office.

Gulping, Andy called the fire department from Mr. McGuffin's phone.

Moments later, sirens blared outside. From her vantage out the window, she watched the scene below.

Christiaan removed his jacket and slapped at the flames beneath the window. The fire provided a fabulous distraction so she could find McGuffin.

People crowded around the flames. Some helped by pounding out flames with dinner jackets. Others just watched.

Smoke billowed into the window. Andy closed it. A noise sounded behind her.

With a grimace, Blades crept into the room. His scar across his nose shone pink and shiny in the lighting. His gauntlets hugged his forearms. Blood stained the blades.

Andy swallowed hard. "Mr. McGuffin sent you, didn't he?"

"You are difficult to get rid of."

Behind him, several other men blocked the door. Andy was out of options.

Then she remembered Christiaan's rope. She dashed to the window, threw open the sashes, and coughed in the smoke. She climbed up the rope to the rooftop, kicking her feet against the wall for support. Thankfully, she was wearing pants. Below her, an inferno blazed. Even at this height, the heat scorched her.

Blades started up behind her. But at least only one man at a time could climb.

At the top of the crenellations, she struggled to unhook the grappling hook, but Blades' weight made it impossible to dislodge. Instead, she dashed across the flat roof, searching for a way down from the ramparts. Once on the far side of the roof, she checked over her shoulder.

Seven men followed.

She broke into a run. At full speed, the latex loosened from the sides of her face. Her old man shoes were surprisingly comfortable to run in. However, the edge was fast approaching, and she had nowhere to go.

Then a man sprang from behind a chimney.

Andy lunged at him with a karate move, ready to fight.

"Andy, it's me, Spencer." He held her shoulders.

Andy had already grabbed his collar and was about to throw him in a judo move when she recognized his face. Then he did the oddest thing.

He kissed her.

"Spencer! What are you doing?" Andy opened her mouth.

"Getting you off of here." He tugged her hand.

"I mean the kiss."

"Oh, winning a bet."

Andy shook her head. How in the world did kissing her win a bet?

"Follow me."

She ran to another wing off to the left.

At the end, Spencer pointed to a rickety staircase, used to clean gutters and chimneys. He descended frontwards.

"How did you know I was up here?" Andy asked, out of breath. Her thighs burned from the taking the steep stairs one at a time.

"I saw you escape the window and climb to the roof while I fought the fire."

When they reached the ground, Spencer's tie had disappeared, and his shirt collar fell open. A smudge blemished his face. He was winded. And incredibly hot.

"I'll get the police." He nodded.

Andy didn't have time to ask questions. "I'll distract the men."

Spencer's eyes widened. "Where will you go?"

"I'll run until I can't run anymore, and then I'll fight."

Spencer just stood there.

Andy started running. "Go!" At the far side of the castle grounds, Andy faced the men. "Mr. McGuffin sent seven of you to fight me, eh?"

Flashing menacing teething, Blades lurched forward.

"I'll take that as a compliment." She ran out of the drive down the road.

The men trailed her.

The men couldn't all keep pace. If she kept

running, they could only come one at a time to meet her. She excelled at one on one.

As each approached, she readied for his attack. Nearly out of breath, she kicked the first one in the stomach. On the next, she did a Russian Sambo move and brought him down on his back. She jumped up and kicked him in the ribs.

Three and four she knocked into each other with a head butt to the stomach of the third who landed on the fourth. Five and six ran away.

Only Blades remained.

Wresting a knife from her fanny pack, she slashed the leather binding on his bound gauntlets. They fell from his forearms. With Blades nearly defenseless, Andy had all power over him. She jumped-kicked him in the face. "He should've sent eight men."

Blades, beat and stripped of his power, fell to his knees. Blood dripped from his nose.

A siren wailed in the distance.

Andy wiped her brow of a little sweat and faced the police cars as they careened into the street. A woman in a hot pink suit sat in the passenger seat of the first vehicle.

Spencer and Christiaan also leapt from the car.

Wearing a scorched tuxedo jacket and shirt, Christiaan surveyed the damage Andy had done to the men while Spencer helped Andy wrap her hands in an ice pack.

Margret, in her hot pink pantsuit, ordered the arrest of the men.

Clearly, she was in charge. "Margret Prim?" Andy dropped her jaw.

Margret approached her leaning against the

"bonnet" of the car. "You're the MI5 agent?"

"When you approached me with your suspicions about Mr. McGuffin, I believed you crazy. But it turns out you were right," Margret said. Once the men were all taken in the paddy wagon, she approached them again. "Thank you for your help, Miss Andy Baker. Mr. McGuffin is already in custody. MI6, our foreign relations arm of the Secret Intelligence Service, had warned us about him, but we didn't believe it."

Andy bit her lip. "But they've still got Hin Cho."

Mrs. Prim nodded. "But as MI5, I only deal with domestic cases. You're on your own for this one."

Smelling of burn and smoke, Christiaan kissed her on her temple. "They're taking her to Hong Kong. Don't worry. We'll bring her back."

"Be extra careful getting to Hong Kong from here. They'll be watching for you." Mrs. Prim glanced her over. "You need a ride back to the manor?"

Andy's old man shirt had come untucked, and half of her latex fell off during the fight, and she wasn't sure where her gray wig went. "I'm fine with walking."

"We'll be with her," Christiaan said.

Margret nodded her bobbed, shellacked head. "Well done, girl, well done." She winked at Spencer and Christiaan. "Make sure she returns home safe and put her to bed. Alone." Margret eyed both of them. "And let her sleep."

Christiaan nodded.

Spencer bowed.

Margret hopped into the police car.

When the scene was cleared, the three of them stood shoulder to shoulder, staring after the cars.

"The MI5 agent was Margret Prim." Blinking,

Andy studied the road where they left.

"I'm a little blown away myself." Spencer raised his eyebrows, shaking his head. "I considered her a rather proper British woman."

Christiaan stuffed his hands into his pockets.

Andy ribbed Spencer, playfully jabbing him. "I guessed the agent was you, Spencer."

"Me? MI5? Ridiculous. Perish the thought." Spencer linked arms with Andy. "However, I need to settle a score."

"What's this?" Andy avoided potholes in the road. Her feet ached from all the running in men's dress shoes.

Spencer elbowed Christiaan. "The rocks in your pocket, if you please. I kissed Andy on the rooftop. And I do believe it wins the bet."

Wordlessly, Christiaan opened his singed tux, drew out a red bag, and handed it to Spencer.

With his two forefingers, Spencer, grinning, pried open the top of the drawstrings and poured out the contents into his hands. "Why, they're just rocks." Two plain and ordinary pebbles filled his palm. "You cheat. I wagered for the emeralds."

"No. The words were, 'the rocks in your pockets.' I stashed the real emeralds in the safe deposit box at the hotel after the personal attacks by Blades. I thought it best to not carry them on my person. Those were a decoy. I see my paranoia worked, but not in the way I intended." Christiaan grinned and thrust out his chin. "The real emeralds are safe inside the real red envelope in town."

Balling his fists, Spencer squinted. "Why, you little—"

"Guys," Andy interrupted. "We've had a long night—a successful night—but I'm tired, and I want to get to bed. We have to leave early in the morning." She arrived at Blakely Manor before sunup. The mists rose from the grounds. The sky lightened to milky white dawn. After the arrest, the police searched Mr. McGuffin's manor, and guests milled about on the lawn, discussing the events of the night, shaking their heads, and expressing disbelief.

"Sure you don't want to come with us? To Hong Kong?" Andy asked Spencer.

He halted on the stone steps in front of the mansion. His shirt opened at the collar, and his rolled sleeves hit his elbows. "I'm a statistician, not an agent."

"Yes, but we could use someone with your talents."

With one foot on the bottom stair, Spencer stuffed his hands into his ash-smudged pants pockets. "Ah, but it would be a lot of responsibility. And hassle. And quite frankly, I don't care about the evils in the world. They can all sod themselves."

Christiaan coughed. "That's kind of a selfish attitude."

Spencer shrugged. "I am what I am—a simple man with simple tastes. I would hate to have anyone depend on me."

Andy shifted on the gravel. "The caddies do."

He nodded. "But they won't die as a result of a bad bet or a wrong turn." He sighed, shaking his head and loosening his tie. "No, I would probably ruin whatever it is you're trying to discover. I'm a rotten lout, and it wouldn't do me any good to change and be a better man. What would people think if I went around saving lives or some nonsense? No, I'm comfortable the way I am. I'm a gambler and a slithering snake among the grass. Go along, and have fun without me."

"Are you sure?" A pit formed in her stomach, thinking of the separation. Spencer had become dearer than she realized.

Christiaan stepped closer, placing a hand on her shoulder. "If the man says he can't go, then he can't go, Andy. No need to nag him about it."

With a half-smile, Spencer kept his gaze rooted on Andy. "Sadly, Andy, I cannot go with you. My success lies in knowledge and statistics to gain the upper hand to win, and as you are not a banker—" Here, he glanced at Christiaan. "I'd be hedging my bets to go. Besides, I'm not like you two, chasing after kidnappers and such. I don't have the stamina or moral courage to do so. I best return to my occupation." He took Andy's hand and then kissed it. "We had fun." With a final nod, he turned and bounded up the stairs. "Adieu."

"Cherri-o." Christiaan sighed. "He couldn't stomach coming with us."

Andy shouldered him. "You didn't want him to come anyway." With dawn creeping over the edge of the world, she hiked up the stairs to her room. How would she travel to Hong Kong without anyone detecting her?

Chapter 22

Christiaan figured Andy had no intention of sleeping as Margret Prim suggested. With the knowledge that Hin Cho was in Hong Kong, she would be anxious to go.

Before him, she bounded up the soft carpeted stairs. "We can leave on the next flight out of here."

Christiaan paused on the landing, holding the large, wooden corbel on the oaken hand railing. "We have to communicate our findings with OverSight and await further instructions."

"How long will that take?" She stood at the top of the stairs with her hand on her hips.

Christiaan shrugged, but he knew the truth. Operations could take days to plan. "We'll report our information. Boss will alert the Chinese government and let them handle the rest. Our mission wasn't extraction. It was detection. Our job is done." Once Andy was safely home, he hoped he could track down Unction and the Commander for Aiofa. Alone.

Andy stepped down a stair. "Are you suggesting we wash our hands and leave her to the fate of an extraction team?"

Her beautiful face crumpled. Christiaan's heart ached.

Andy thrust up her chin. "I don't trust OverSight. I'll bring her home myself."

"We have five days left to find the kidnappers before they deliver Hin Cho to Unction. OverSight has a trained team, and they can handle it."

"Not if we leave now for Hong Kong."

Christiaan stepped up a stair. "Fabian's men know who we are and will be searching for us. When Blades doesn't come back, they'll suspect we're coming for her. Fabian will be tracking every flight out of Edinburgh." Christiaan shook his head, slowly trudging up the stairs toward her. "They'll be expecting us."

"We can drive to London. They won't know to track flights out of Heathrow."

Shaking his head, he climbed another stair. "We'd need supplies and OverSight sanction. We can't just take off wherever we want." Travel was expensive and required paperwork. He continued up the stairs until he met her face to face.

She cocked a brow. "You can't. But I can."

The resolution in her face made him smile. This was the old Andy Baker he missed so much. The one he wished…what did he wish? Her lips crumpled into a beautiful, determined pout. He was close. Close enough to snatch up her shoulders and kiss her. Instead, he faced her with equal determination. "If you go, you're off the grid."

"So what does that mean?" She narrowed her gaze and placed a foot on a stair.

"You won't have money, hidden visas, or unmarked passports to travel the world. You'd be on your own." Last summer, they wandered the Chihuahuan desert without any money or supplies and nearly died. He didn't want to duplicate that trip.

Scowling, she stroked her chin. "That's a

problem."

He wasn't trying *not* to convince her. The realities were there.

"How do we get money?" she asked.

"You mean how do *you* get money?"

Just then, Spencer, whistling, bounded toward them, in a fresh suit. When he saw the two on the stairs, a smile lit his face. "Hullo! Still up? Aren't you tired from the night's adventures?"

Andy turned with a radiant smile. With a burning in his chest, Christiaan frowned.

"Spencer, do you have cash?" she asked.

"I have heaps of dosh." Spencer raised his eyebrows. "More than ten thousand quid." He patted his jacket pocket.

With a sinking in his gut, Christian raised his eyebrows. "You just carry it around on your person?" For a scrawny guy, Spencer was sure bold to carry so much cash.

He shrugged. "Gambling only pays in filthy lucre."

Andy lowered her chin and smiled sweetly. "Spencer, could you sponsor me on a trip to London and then to Hong Kong."

"I'd be happy to help as a financial backer. But I do warn you, I charge outrageous interest." He wagged his finger. "For you, however, I could make other payment options. Perhaps I'll come along and oversee my investment. At least partway."

Christiaan blew out an impatient sigh. "Spencer, will you excuse us for a few minutes while we discuss this?"

Spencer bowed and ducked into a doorway.

Christiaan faced Andy. "We don't need him."

Andy cocked her hip, meeting his gaze dead-on. "You might not. But I do."

Christiaan shook his head. "You want to owe him?" He scrutinized her expression of delight. "You want him to come with us."

"Us?" She leaned back and arched her brow. "Are you going, too?"

He rolled his eyes. "Of course." No way would he let those two gallivant around the world without him.

Andy jabbed a finger into his chest. "He's an asset, and I'm willing to use him, just like I've used every other asset in my life."

He knew better than to ask details about what those actions entailed. "The plan?"

"Rent a car and drive to London. Spencer can make all our transactions because he's unknown to Fabian."

Christiaan understood the logic of her reasoning, but still he resisted. "He can lend us the money and stay in London or no deal."

"He's not that bad. Once we get to London, he'll bail."

"Don't bet on it," he murmured under his breath. But Christiaan's resolve weakened. As much as he hated Spencer, Christiaan decided he was useful in this pinch.

Andy already backed away, her smile bent up in a tease.

"What shall I offer as collateral?"

He frowned, anger flashing in his eyes. "Better not be what he wants."

"Why not?"

Fuming, Christiaan slid her a somewhat dishonest smile. She wouldn't, would she?

****

Scowling, Christiaan exited the car rental shop later that morning. He clenched his teeth.

"I'm driving." Spencer flipped the keys. He waved them above his head.

"What?" No way was he letting him drive. Spencer might have paid for everything, but Christiaan would pay him back. Dishing out the cash didn't give him license to drive.

Spencer thrust up his chin and waved the paperwork. "I am listed as the only driver."

Christiaan frowned. "You've got to be kidding me. I don't sit in the passenger seat."

Spencer pointed the folded paper. "You'll get used to sitting on the passenger's side. It's on the same side as the drivers' side in America anyway."

When Christiaan saw the car, he nearly spit. "A tiny car? We have a ten-hour drive to London."

"This was the least conspicuous car I could get. What were you expecting? A Bugatti?" Spencer popped open the door.

Christiaan murmured a dig about Spencer's parents under his breath and squeezed into the passenger side.

Andy joined them in the parking lot.

Spencer ducked into the car. "Oh, actually, Andy said she called 'shotgun' and explained what that little phrase meant."

"The drive is only nine hundred kilometers." Andy grinned, opening the door for him to exit. "And I remember you saying you don't sit in the passenger seat anyway."

Exiting the car and folding back the front seat, Christiaan stuffed himself in the backseat, growling at

Spencer. He could nearly nibble on his knees.

Spencer pulled out of the drive, checking for cars at least four times and slowly taking the road.

Christiaan made faces behind Spencer's back.

At last, Spencer took the A26 heading south.

Ten hours was a long time in a car with someone he despised.

Spencer glanced at him in the rearview mirror. "You should probably sleep now while you're not driving. You might not have another opportunity for a while."

Christiaan stared at the passing countryside. "I can't sleep when someone else is driving."

"Today will be a long day. Might as well nap."

Spencer spoke to him as a child. Christiaan punched the back of Spencer's seat.

"What was that?" Spencer asked over his shoulder.

"Just getting comfortable here to take a nap."

Spencer glared in the rearview mirror.

Christiaan smiled innocently.

Because of Spencer's slow and cautious driving, the fields dragged by. This trip would take forever. Spencer talked about his childhood memories. Christiaan must've snoozed because the next thing he knew, awful sounds woke him. "What is that?" Christiaan sat up.

"Oh, I was starting to doze so we turned on the radio," Spencer answered cheerfully.

"Is that what you call music here?" Christiaan growled.

"Well, only people of culture and taste call it that, yes."

Christiaan sat back, tired of Spencer's barbs, and

watched the fields stretch over the hills. Little, white sheep dotted the pastures. Then a small village. Then another pasture. And lots of green. Christiaan sighed. This would be the longest ten hours of his life.

****

The outskirts of London didn't resemble the city Christiaan knew and loved. Row houses followed the roads instead of massive buildings, but still, home was home. But they didn't return to his apartment, driving instead straight to the airport.

"Sure you don't want to come with us?" Andy asked.

Spencer parked in the temporary parking across from the terminal and helped them unload their bags. Shaking his head, Spencer handed her an envelope of cash. "Too much security in an airport. I hate explaining why I carry such a large wad. Besides, I have to return the car."

Andy embraced him. "Thank you so much. I'm going to miss you." She picked up her bag. "I'll grab the tickets."

Christiaan nodded approval then faced Spencer. He wasn't so bad now that he was leaving. How nice it would be to not have his third wheel around.

Spencer coughed into a coiled hand. "Ah, well, I guess this is goodbye then? I've given Andy the dosh she'll need for plane tickets as well as any hotel, food, and necessities." He glanced around and stuffed his hands in his trouser pockets. "Where is she?"

"She went inside, I guess." But she should still be crossing the parking lot.

"Well, I guess you can give her my fond adieus."

Christiaan nodded, distracted by searching through

284

the cars for her. "Sure, I'll tell her bye for you."

Spencer stuck out his hand. "No hard feelings for kissing her?"

Christiaan shook his head. "No hard feelings for thinking you were the kidnapper?"

"None at all."

"You'd better go." Christiaan couldn't wait for him to leave.

"Yes." Yet, Spencer didn't leave.

"Quit stalling."

"I'm not stalling." Spencer scowled then bowed his head in a short curt nod. "Good night."

Spencer stalked up the stairs to the parking garage.

Christiaan finally relaxed. Where was Andy? Hauling luggage behind him, he marched in the direction where he last saw her. Through the glass of the sliding doors, Christiaan noticed two men had their arms wrapped around a woman. They dragged her out the doors and stuffed her in the backseat of a BMW waiting at the curb. Christiaan caught sight of the side of her face.

Andy!

Christiaan shoved a tired traveler out of the way before running after the BMW racing off with the door still open. Dropping the bags, Christiaan broke into a sprint.

The men in the backseat finally closed the door and sped ahead.

Christiaan swore and panted. He couldn't keep up.

Spencer caught up. "Who was that?" Spencer's mouth fell open. He dragged the luggage behind him.

"From the looks of it?" Christiaan hailed a taxi. "The Greek Mafia."

Spencer, out of breath from running with the bags, raised an eyebrow. "What is going on?"

Christiaan slapped him on the back. "Jump in." He threw the luggage in the back, slid across the seat, and shut the taxi door behind them. Weren't they after him?

Spencer was already in conversation with the driver. "Follow the car." He pointed to the BMW several car lengths ahead. "A cash bonus awaits you if you can catch them."

Christiaan gripped the headrest of the front seat, watching through the windshield.

Spencer peered around the driver's head. "What do they want with her?"

"They are after me." Although, now he wasn't so sure. Why target Andy? Their actions didn't make sense.

"Why?"

Instead of answering, Christiaan focused on closing the gap as the taxi driver weaved in between cars, gaining on the BMW. A few people honked. Three pedestrians scrambled out of the way. At last, the car stopped in a gnarl of traffic.

"I'll run." Christiaan thumped the headrest and propped open the door.

Spencer followed. "On foot?"

"I'll be faster."

"I'm coming." Spencer made a move toward the door.

"Pay the driver and take care of the bags." Shaking his head, Christiaan bounded off. When he glanced behind him, Spencer had tossed a fistful of notes before following, leaving the car door open.

"Close the door!" the taxi driver yelled.

"Sorry." Trailing the luggage behind him, Spencer ran back and slammed the door before following Christiaan through the traffic, the bags weighing him down.

Just then, Christiaan felt a pinprick on his neck. The mosquitoes must be coming out in full force at dusk. He reached up and instead of slapping away a mosquito, his hands extracted a small dart. Examining it, he already felt dizzy. *Oh, no.* They found him. Darkness gathered at the edges of his eyes, his legs felt light and useless and yet heavy at the same time. "Andy." He collapsed onto the pavement.

****

Andy was confused. No, she was pissed. Mostly because someone cheated and shot her with a mild sedative. A sore spot in the fleshy part of her shoulder testified to that. Huddled in the back of a BMW, she was squeezed between two burly, dark-headed men in blazers and oxford shirts, necks unbuttoned, sweating an odor Andy found vaguely familiar. But mostly, she was confused—maybe because of the sedative.

One clarifying thought worked its way through the fog: the men targeted her, not Christiaan.

Didn't Sabrina say many bounty hunters chased Christiaan? Who were these guys, and why were they kidnapping *her*? One of the guys wore a gold medallion. Like the man in the London bombing and somewhere else, but she couldn't remember where.

Christiaan mentioned something about the Godfather of the Night. Maybe they were luring in Christiaan. Andy hung her head. She was an easy target.

But Andy's brain broke down, resisting at first the

dark clouds forming in her eyes. But when she glanced in the rearview mirror to see Christiaan and Spencer running after her, she knew she was safe and let herself pass out.

Chapter 23

When she woke, she was in a room in an abandoned office building. Moisture had warped the walls. The stench of urine and mold swirled about her. She tried to cover her nose, but zip ties spiraled her wrists and ankles. A dim light shined on her. She tugged at her bound hands and feet. Animalistic heat bubbled inside. How dare they cheat and use drugs. What good were martial arts when your legs and arms felt like cooked spaghetti? Imagining her legs and arms as giant rolls of pasta, Andy laughed. What drug did they give her?

"You're awake."

A man sat in the corner just out of eyesight. She turned her head to see him. His scowl looked familiar. "What do you want?"

"To collect a debt."

Gritting her teeth, Andy wiggled feeling into her feet. "I don't owe you anything."

"You do not?" He arched a brow.

"I don't even know who you are." Again, she tested the strength of her bonds. Even at full strength, she couldn't break zip ties.

The man drew a deep breath. "I have been following you since Texas. One of my comrades died in London. From your car bomb."

Texas? Who would follow her from Texas? And

who died? Andy shook her head. Nothing made sense. "I didn't set off a car bomb."

"The car bomb was meant *for* you. But you didn't run after our man."

Andy gulped, but her throat was dry. "Why are you doing this?"

The door opened, and another man entered and spoke some unrecognizable language.

The burly man smelled familiar. What was the scent?

The man stepped close. A dark beard covered half his face. Neck hair sprang from his shirt collar. A gold necklace slipped from his open shirt. He leaned closer.

An icon relief of a saint shimmered gold in the dim light. Andy recognized the Greek St. Necktarios. She'd seen the medallion before in Austin. The food truck incident. She tightened her fists. Sure, he had more facial hair, but Nikki from Nikki's Gyros stood before her.

The scent he bore was the special *tzatziki* sauce. Nikki said they would enact revenge. The Greek Mafia. The Godfather of the Night.

They weren't following Christiaan. They were following her. The whole incident in London now had to be reexamined. The knife was meant for her. She chuckled softly to herself. They didn't even know who they were dealing with. She was lucky Christiaan ran after them. They wanted her dead. Dread clawed at her dry throat. "What do you want?" Nikki's breath reeked of onion when he leaned into her face.

"Who are you working for?"

"Right now? Technically, no one." Back then, she investigated for a friend, but they wouldn't believe her.

Andy inhaled to calm her trembling breath.

Another man joined him—a taller man with a grimace—followed by a third with huge hair.

Nikki slapped her across the face.

The sting across her cheek jarred Andy. "Working as a food blogger, I discovered your place. Your secret sauce is the best I've ever eaten. But when my friend ate there and got sick, I wanted to know what happened. I accidentally stumbled upon the heroin. In America, we tell the police about drugs, because honestly, I've had too many friends get strung out on that stuff, and it really messes them up. So, I wasn't targeting you." She struggled against her restraints. "Let me go."

A heartbeat passed while they stared. Finally, Nikki spoke. "You really think our sauce is the best you've ever eaten."

Andy sat back, mouth agape. Out of everything she said, he clung to that? "Yes."

He pressed his fingers against his hairy chest. "You really thought ours was special."

The second man slapped him across the chest with the back of his arm. "Shut up, you idiot."

She recognized him now. Gaspar.

Nikki shrugged. "No, it's just that, you know, you open a restaurant, and you never know if people are coming because it's good or if it's new."

The man with big hair furrowed his brows. "What are you blathering about?"

"Takkis, my mother's recipe was a big hit in America."

Takkis lowered his brows and stuck out his lips. "Quit talking. If she will not tell us who she and the man we captured are working for, we'll torture them until they confess."

They had Christiaan. "Where is he?" Andy's mind whirled. Would they discover who he was?

Takkis struck her across the cheek. "I'll ask the questions here."

Andy's head reeled, and her cheek burned. She glared. She didn't like the guy with the big hair, Takkis. His breath reeked of alcohol and garlic. Her bound hands and feet numbed. "I'm not working for anybody."

Takkis leaned in. "We'll see what your friend says when we tell him you told us everything."

The men left the room.

What kind of sick joke was this? Andy scowled so hard she thought she'd bust a blood vessel. Her whole body ached. What did they give her, and how long was she out? The small room had no windows. She guessed they were still somewhere in London.

Footfalls echoed in the hall. Andy strained to listen. The doorknob rattled. She clutched the sides of her chair. Weird because the men had the keys. Someone picked the lock. Perhaps Christiaan escaped. That man could get out of anywhere. When the door opened, Andy tried to pick out Christiaan's frame in the semi-darkness, but instead a slim man in a silver suit slipped inside.

"Why, hullo!"

"Spencer! What are you doing here?" Andy hissed, leaning forward as far as her bands would let her.

He placed a hand on his hip. "Well, now this is an odd greeting. You could at least say hello."

"Hello! Untie me. How did you find us?"

He glanced over his shoulder to the open door.

"Um, I think now's not the best time for stories. Why don't I try to get you out of here?" He patted his pockets. "I don't have anything with which to cut, and my mother always said I was all thumbs at untying knots."

"They're zip ties anyway. Just get my bag over there." She pointed with her head toward the corner.

"Oh, there you are!" His eyebrows shot up. He crossed to the room to where her black backpack lay on the chair. He raked his hand through the large pocket. "What am I looking for exactly?" He raised his head.

"A knife. A box cutter. Anything to cut these ropes."

"Will this do?" Spencer held some small sewing scissors.

Andy couldn't hide a hint of impatience. "That would take too long. Keep digging."

"What girls keep in their handbags is interesting, don't you think? Odds and ends. My mother's bag is mostly full of shopping receipts and doggie treats. Can't imagine her bag would do us much good in a situation like this."

Andy gritted her teeth. What was he blathering about? "Spencer, less talking and more doing."

"Right-o." He searched through the bag. "I'm not seeing any knives or anything."

"They must've taken out all the weapons." Finally, after what felt an eternity but was probably no more than forty-five seconds, Spencer produced something useful—a string hacksaw.

"What is this?" he asked, extracting the textured metal cord with loops at each end.

"That's perfect. Place that over the top of the ties

and yank it back and forth. It will cut the zip ties."

"I don't know how long it will take. All the men went into another room." He placed the cord on the tie over her wrist.

Andy jerked. The cord would tear through her flesh. "Maybe work on the part of the ties *between* my hands."

"Ah!" Spencer moved the long, textured wire over the ties wrapped around the chair armrests instead of directly over Andy's flesh. "Smart."

The textured wire snapped the ties rather quickly. Andy almost had a hand free.

Spencer set to work on the feet next. "I'm pretty good at this."

Andy kept her eye on the door, half expecting at any minute to see the men come through the door and catch them. If she were free, she might have a chance. The ties fell from her hands. She stretched and moved them. Blood tingled to her extremities.

With both hands free, she reclaimed the textured wire from Spencer and threaded it under the ties through the area between her ankle and the chair and with a vigorous, back-and-forth motion, cut through the plastic like butter.

With eyebrows up, Spencer kneeled back on his heels. "I say, you've used one of these before, haven't you?"

She'd cut off tree limbs and weakened lumber with that thing. Andy started on the other foot, sawing through with great haste.

Footfalls sounded in the hall.

When the last tie fell, she grabbed her bag and Spencer's hand and raced to the doorway, ready to attack whoever came through it. The door swung open, and Andy flew into action, only to stop herself.

Christiaan.

He glanced at Andy, then at her hand which still held Spencer's. "You got out, I see." He arched an eyebrow at Spencer.

"Spencer found us." Andy dropped Spencer's hand. Christiaan escaped on his own? How did he do that?

He glared at Spencer.

Spencer poked his head into the hall. "When they captured Christiaan and threw him in the trunk, I stealthily followed in a car. I hopped in the back of someone's sedan and told them my friends were kidnapped."

"Where are we?" Andy asked.

"In the valley of Ebbsfleet, about sixteen kilometers outside of London center. The Thames is just over there." He nodded his head. "Perhaps we could swim to safety."

Christiaan rolled his eyes. "Come on. We've got to go."

Spencer and Andy followed Christiaan through a maze of rooms until they reached a door.

"Why are the Greeks after you, Andy?" Christiaan glanced from the corner of his eye at Andy.

Pinching her face together, she shrugged. "I might have busted their heroin ring."

Christiaan sighed and rubbed his forehead. "But you promised no more investigating."

Her face burned with guilt. "This one was an accident."

Spencer tapped Andy on the shoulder. "Do you

think these were the same people who came after us in the truck?"

"Probably. They said they followed me since Texas."

Christiaan pointed toward an exterior door with sunlight gleaming around the edges. "We have to get out of here, now."

"Wait." Andy searched her bag. "They have my passport. We can't go to Hong Kong without it."

Eyes wide, Christiaan slapped his pocket. "They have my passport and my emeralds—the real emeralds. We can't leave without those."

"Oh, yes! I still have your phonies!" Spencer pulled the rocks in an identical red envelope out of his pocket.

Christiaan batted them away. "Nobody cares, Spencer."

Behind Andy, the door squeaked open.

At the far end of the hall, all three Greeks stood. Big Takkis swung a cricket bat. And Nikki and Gaspar, on either side, each held a gun.

Christiaan stepped forward. "Let us go. We have something very important to take care of."

"What could be so important?" Takkis, with the hair, shrugged and tapped his cricket bat against a palm.

"A friend was kidnapped." Christiaan stepped again. "We must find her and bring the kidnappers to justice."

The man swung menacingly close to Christiaan's face. "Justice is such a funny word. Everybody wants to give it, but nobody wants justice for themselves." He poked the bat into Christiaan's stomach.

Christiaan doubled over.

"Not again," Andy whispered.

Spencer glanced her way. "Does that happen every day for you?"

"Almost." Andy gave both Spencer and Christiaan a sideways glance. She hadn't started out that way. No one had threatened her life before. Being with Christiaan, it seemed to happen every day.

Despite being hit by the bat, Christiaan defied Takkis. His gaze never left his. "We need our passports. And my little red envelope."

"I'll tell you what." The man lowered his bat and leaned toward him. "You come with us to Argos in Greece and talk with the Big Boss, and you can ask him for your passports. Big Boss wants a small word with this young lady here. If not—" He picked up his bat again and swung it into his hand. "—we'll beat you to a pulp here."

"We should go with them," Spencer piped. "Sounds like a great adventure."

Christiaan glared. "You butted in here on your own, so I don't care about your opinion."

"We'll go." Andy gave Christiaan a somewhat steely stare, sure he was formulating a plan to fight these guys.

With his fists clenched ready for a fight, Christiaan shook his head.

Every muscle in his body tensed as if he were about to spring. But with two guns trained on him, he wouldn't get very far. She placed a hand on his forearm. "Back down, Christiaan," Andy whispered. She gulped.

Takkis' dark eyebrows rose. "Yes, Christiaan. You should listen to your girlfriend here."

Christiaan slowly relaxed.

Takkis smiled, spoke some words in Greek to the three men surrounding him, and tied them up again.

But Andy had her bag. And Spencer had one, too.

They led them down a dimly lit hallway in an old, partially abandoned building. Sunlight glared through the windows at the end of the halls.

Christiaan leaned toward Andy while the men checked out the doors. "Why are you giving up?"

"I'm not giving up," she spoke out of the side of her mouth. "I'm waiting for an opportunity."

"Like what?"

"You'll see."

Christiaan furrowed his brow.

He needed to learn to trust. Andy stepped into the sunlight.

Outside in the parking lot, the men argued in Greek.

"What are they talking about?" Christiaan whispered to Andy.

"Bickering over something about the car," Spencer whispered. "I studied some Greek in school."

Christiaan raised his eyebrows.

Spencer continued to translate. "They were only planning on picking up one. Now there are three of us. We don't fit in the car." The five-seater BMW sat in the parking lot.

Six of them. Christiaan smiled.

Finally, Tikkis finished arguing and tucked in his shirt and slicked back his hair. "We'll take the train."

Chapter 24

Christiaan stared out the window of the train heading from Ebbsfleet to Paris.

The Greeks conversed in a four-facing seating arrangement across the aisle.

After dipping below the English Channel in utter darkness, the train came up in a sunny France. The countryside flourished with green hills and were marked with small villages. The rails turned south at Amiens.

Christiaan snoozed with the train's gentle lulling sway. He shared a quad of seats with Andy on his right and Spencer across and to the right. Christiaan had the window seat. He felt almost as if he were flying, but not quite as smooth, and the scenery outside the window was much more interesting. He shook his head and chewed his fingernail. "I believed they were after me."

With a hint of a smile, Andy shrugged. "But that's because you're slightly egotistic."

"So the London bombing—?" He needed to reinterpret what happened.

"Even though you followed him, he threw the knife at me to lure me out to the car bomb."

Christiaan staved off his paranoia. Not everyone was out to get him. The man did say he wasn't trying to kill him. "Let's focus on the problem at hand."

Andy leaned forward. "The transaction with

Unction is Wednesday?"

"Yes." Christiaan nodded.

"That only gives us four more days." Andy sat back. She sneaked a furtive glance at the Greeks. "We need to steal back the passports and then hightail to Hong Kong. Paris has a direct flight. We have to get off the train in Paris. The next major airport is hours away."

The passports and Christiaan's emeralds bulged in a manila envelope on the train table. Escaping was one thing. Stealing and escaping another. Did Andy not expect to get caught? "What's the plan?"

"What do you think?" Andy elbowed Spencer.

Spencer gazed out the window and barely participated in this conversation. He shrugged. "This is between you two. Although I'll be interested in who wins. I have a little wager with myself. I'm sure I'll win the bet."

Christiaan scowled. Why was Spencer here anyway? He was taking up room and air. Maneuvering with two people was difficult. Three was a freaking party! Christiaan had to remember back to strategies with platoons instead of single evasive techniques. Escaping a train would not be easy. He sighed.

"I'm fresh out of ideas. We have so little to work with." Andy folded her hands over the table tray.

Christiaan sat back, exasperated. "We do have some resources."

"We do."

Christiaan raised his eyebrows. At last, she recognized his skills.

She stuck a thumb in Spencer's direction. "We got him. He's flush with cash."

That's not what Christiaan expected her to say. He slumped. Pursing his lips, he let out a small puff of air.

Spencer blushed deeply.

At least the pompous Englishman brought something to the table.

Spencer eyed the Greeks playing cards. "Okay, fine. So how do we get the passports?"

Christiaan bit his lip until it hurt. "Good question."

"I've got an idea." Andy leaned forward.

"I win."

Christiaan stared. What was he talking about?

Spencer grinned. "I bet Andy would come up with an idea first. I just collected fifty quid from myself."

"You are weird." Christiaan glared.

Spencer peaked his eyebrows. "I use information and probability."

"Okay, a plan." Andy rubbed her eyes.

Christiaan leaned forward.

"If we can get our hands on sleeping pills." Andy chewed on her lip. "I've knocked out many baddies in my day with those. Sometimes they sell them on board trains like this."

"I have sleeping pills." Spencer patted his leather case.

"Great! Why?" she asked.

He shrugged. "Intelligent people struggle to shut off their brains. Scientific fact."

Andy tapped her fingers on the small table. "Now how to administer it?"

Christiaan coughed. Intelligent people? He wouldn't count Spencer among that lot. "In coffee. The bitterness will hide the taste."

"When we boarded, I noticed a café two cars

back." Andy jabbed a thumb over her shoulder.

The train slowed. City replaced fields. "We better hurry. We're pulling into the *Gare du Nord*." Buildings lined the tracks. Christiaan knew this route well.

"How long before it takes effect?" Andy lifted her chin.

"Oh, I don't know. After I hit the pillow, I'm out." Spencer slapped his hands.

Christiaan frowned. "Your babbling told me nothing."

"I'll get the coffee." Andy rose from her seat.

"Better hurry." Christiaan held up her tray.

Before unlocking the hatch to the next car, Andy smiled at the Greeks. She couldn't escape on a train.

Spencer almost gave them away with his nervous over-the-shoulder glances every three-to-five seconds to where Andy went as he worked something out of his luggage under his feet. Christiaan used every restraint to keep from hitting him. Christiaan leaned near to him, stretching his legs. "Let me give you a little tip working on these kind of ops." He hid his conversation with Spencer in a yawn. "Calm down and act naturally."

"Oh, right." He dropped his bag and sat straight.

Shaking his head, Christiaan observed verdant hillsides. "You want us to get caught or something?"

"No, it's…I forgot to give her some cash so she'll be coming back."

Closing his eyes, Christiaan leaned back his head. *Amateurs.*

Andy fluttered through the passage. "I forgot cash."

Spencer dug into the pockets of his bag.

Andy grabbed the headrest. "At least I've already

ordered. They've started making coffee for us."

"Here, I'll just come with you." Spencer stood and shouldered his bag. "Together, we'll be faster."

"Order me a cup, too." Christiaan yawned. The lulling train rocked him to near sleep.

Andy and Spencer bustled through the hatch.

One of the Greeks raised an eyebrow.

"Ordering coffee." Christiaan pointed toward where Andy and Spencer left. "Want a cup?"

The men nodded and returned to their game.

Christiaan had no intention of allowing Spencer on a flight to Hong Kong from Paris. Once off the train, he would make sure Spencer stayed behind.

****

Andy returned with two cups of coffee and set them at the table before two of the men. They each nabbed a cup and nodded.

Spencer returned with two. He set one before Christiaan then the other in front of Takkis on the other side of the aisle. "Here." Spencer stood there, watching as the Greeks drank their cups.

From the corners of their eyes, they stared at Spencer, as he just stood there, watching.

Egad! What was he doing? "Do you have to be so weird?" Andy tugged on his sleeve and motioned for him to sit.

Spencer kept glancing at the Greeks.

Andy kicked him and warned him with her eyes.

"I might've made a mistake," Spencer murmured, wincing. Then he eyed Christiaan as he curled his hands around the steaming dark liquid.

"What do you mean?" Christiaan took a long drag on his white paper cup.

Spencer held his breath then exhaled. His expression suddenly changed to carelessness. "Nothing. Never mind. Can't do anything about it now."

Before she could ask what he meant, she heard the conductor announce they were fifteen minutes from the city.

Spencer bit his lip and eyed the Greeks.

Pretending to admire the city, Andy studied her captors. Then she nervously read her watch. Ten minutes ticked by. The lulling of the train would help, she prayed. More buildings sprang into view.

Maybe she should've slipped in more. She let Spencer do the dosing because he took the things. What if he underestimated how much they needed to knock them out? Each man weighed twice as much as he did.

At last, Gaspar's eyelids started to droop.

Nikki shook his head, as if to shake sleep from his eyes.

Christiaan gave a rather silly grin.

Andy shot him a questioning look but focused again on the captors.

At last.

Even while speaking, they started saying silly things to each other half in English and half in Greek.

Strapping on her backpack, Andy edged closer to the table where the passports sat in a folder with the emeralds under the hands of a nodding Nikki. All of them relaxed. Except the man farthest from them in the window seat. Takkis, the one with the big hair, carpet for a chest, and the thick gold necklace. He was still wide awake. Did he not drink his coffee? No, it was half empty.

When the train slowed at the *gare*, the intercom

announced their arrival.

Takkis elbowed the man next to him.

Other passengers stood to retrieve their baggage from the overhead shelves, creating a bit of commotion in the aisles.

The train stopped with the overhead bells and announcement of arrival.

Swaying, Andy reached across the aisle and slid the passports off the table, tucking them under her arm. "I got them. Let's go." She spun to encourage the guys to follow her.

But Christiaan slumped in his seat. He was out cold and drooled on his own shirt.

"Christiaan?" With a harrowing feeling in her stomach, Andy slugged his shoulder. No response. She turned to Spencer. "What did you do?"

The aisles filled with people.

They needed to jump off now.

Standing, Spencer motioned with his eyes to Takkis.

"Where do you think you are going?" He reached over his sleeping companion. Trapped by his tray table and Gaspar, he wasn't able to catch Andy as she easily side-stepped his swipe.

"You take Christiaan," she told Spencer. "I'll take care of this guy."

Gripping his fist, Takkis slammed up the foldable tray table.

Spencer hefted Christiaan and carried him fireman-style, with one arm over his shoulder out the door. He slung his bag over one shoulder and Christiaan's backpacks on the other.

Grabbing the overhead shelf, Andy hoisted herself

up and kicked Takkis square in the chest, slamming him against the window.

He was out cold, sleeping with the others.

Finally, Andy jumped off the train to the cement quay. People flooded all around her. Smells drifted up from the shops and bakeries below them.

On a bench on the quay, Spencer sat next to a prone Christiaan.

Christiaan snored with his head butted against the plexiglass advertisement.

"What did you do?" she asked.

Spencer shrugged. "I just couldn't remember which cups I spiked. Well, I remembered, but I was too late."

"You still let him drink it?" Andy wanted to shake him.

Spencer shook his head. "Once he started I couldn't do anything."

Andy threw up her hands. "What can we do now? We can't parade through Paris with a sleeping man."

"Personally, I'd just leave him." He shoved his hands into his suit pockets, scowling.

"We can't!" Tightness built around her chest. Andy needed Christiaan.

"Then try to wake him up."

"Christiaan, Christiaan." Andy slapped his face. She glanced around at the passersby.

People stared.

"He's not waking. What kind of sleeping aid do you take?"

"Temazepam."

Andy dropped her jaw. "That's one of the strongest sleeping meds on the market."

His eyes grew large. "I know. Trust me, I know."

"He could've had adverse reactions." How could Spencer be so insensitive? Andy half wondered if he did it on purpose.

"So might have the Greeks but you didn't care so much about them."

"That's different." She folded her arms.

"Oh?"

She brushed back her hair. "How much was in there?"

"The same amount as the other guys."

She gave them two pills each. Andy exhaled, gathering her patience. She didn't need a semi-conscious man to slow her down. "We have to get off the platform. Let's both carry him."

Tilting his head, Spencer glanced to his sides. "You don't think we'll look suspicious if two people carry a third around the city?"

She reached into her bag. "Here, put sunglasses over his eyes. Lean him over me, like he's giving me a huge bear hug."

Spencer hefted Christiaan over Andy's back.

He weighed a ton. She staggered and wrapped his arms around her neck like a mink stole and held him there.

Christiaan groaned.

"He's awake." She glanced behind her.

Spencer patted his back. "Not really. Just the diaphragm leaking air out his mouth. However, if you ever wanted to ask him something, now would be a great time."

Andy faltered under his weight. "Maybe later. Let's get him somewhere he can lie down."

Christiaan was quasi-awake. Enough to shuffle his

feet and kind of control a few movements.

Spencer bounced behind her. "I'll get the luggage."

"That's very kind of you." With Christiaan draped across her back, she grunted. The elevator was on the far end of the quay. Going downstairs was the quicker option. Andy stepped down.

Christiaan's teeth clinked together.

"Sorry," she said at each step. At last, she descended into the commercial part of the *gare*.

Spencer trailed behind her with the two backpacks and one leather valise—his own.

Andy had tucked the folder with the passports in her shirt, and it spilled out. She stopped to adjust. "This won't work."

"Oh?"

She deposited Christiaan on a bench near a patisserie. The sweet scents wafted up. Her stomach growled. "We need to take a rest here." She exhaled.

"Here as in Paris or here as in on this particular bench?" Spencer pointed toward the seating.

"Find us a flight to Hong Kong." She let Christiaan slump against her shoulder.

Spencer held up his phone. "I'll have to find a reliable connection." He stalked down the hall.

"I'll wait here." Andy sweated under Christiaan. His hand fell across her thigh.

He seemed to be completely out, but was he? Could she extract information from him now while he was in la-la land? She debated the moral ethics of asking him…for about five seconds. Andy leaned in. "What is it that you want most in this world?"

"Avenge my parents."

"More than love?"

"I do love."

"Who?" Her heartbeat pounded in her chest.

He wrinkled his face. "She doesn't love me."

"Who?"

Again his reply was too blurred to understand.

Spencer clacked up in his dress shoes. "Good news."

Andy sighed. "I need to hear some good news about now."

"I got three tickets on the first flight to Hong Kong." Spencer grinned from ear to ear.

"Great. Let's go." Andy readied to hoist Christiaan.

His smile fell. "Well, the flight doesn't leave until tomorrow afternoon, so we'll have to stay the night. I took the liberty of booking us a hotel room for the night."

Slumping, Andy sighed. She didn't want to lose the time. But what could be done? "Just as well. We should take Christiaan somewhere to sleep off the drug-induced coma you gave him."

This time, Spencer lifted one of Christiaan's arms. "We'll work together. He's a big man. Come now. You take that arm, and I'll take this one. We can kind of carry him to the waiting taxi."

Andy wrapped Christiaan's arm around her shoulder. Together, she shuffled out of the *gare* and into a waiting taxi. Once she checked in at the hotel, Andy helped Christiaan up the elevator to the door and landed him in bed. She rolled him to his side and left a glass of water in case he woke up thirsty.

Spencer brushed off his hands, removed his suit coat, laid it across a chair, and proceeded to roll up his sleeves. "I suppose you're hungry. I'm famished."

Wrestling Christiaan around the city required great exertion. Her knees trembled. "We can't leave him here. Can we order in room service?"

"We happen to be in the most romantic city in the world, and you want room service? That seems rather suggestive." Without his suit coat, Spencer transformed.

He shed not only his stuffy appearance, but his tone changed from the ditzy, careless gambler to a shrewd, analytical, and persuasive lover. He arched an eyebrow. His manner grew meaningful. Gone was all jest or playfulness. A flutter filtered through her. "You go out and order something and bring it back."

"Or we could both stay in." He crossed the room.

Andy folded her arms.

He hesitated. "Or we could both go out and enjoy ourselves."

"But—" She glanced toward Christiaan on the bed.

With a tug of her arm, he urged her to the door. "He'll be fine. We deserve a nice dinner and a break after all we've been through."

At the mention of food, Andy's stomach rumbled again. She stared at Christiaan drooling on the pillow. "We'll have to bring him something."

"Fair enough." Spencer leaned closer. His gray eyes beamed. "A small price to pay to spend the evening with you." He slid his gaze to Christiaan. "Without him."

Spencer's lips were almost within reach. She stood, her gaze locked on his for a few breaths. Her heart beat furiously. At last, she walked over and opened the door to the hall. Perhaps she could leave Christiaan for a few moments. Stepping out into the hall, she locked the door behind her. She stepped downstairs to the concierge desk where she left the key. "Why do you loath him so much?"

Spencer faced her. "Because he's managed to capture your affections, and I cannot understand why or how."

Andy's checks burned. She opened the door to the glistening cobblestone streets. Tonight would be an interesting evening. What did she want from Spencer?

Chapter 25

Christiaan woke to the darkness. Everything ached. What happened? Where was he? The last thing he remembered was the train.

The coffee.

He should've been awake, not sleeping.

Spencer.

The dirty rat slipped something into his coffee. He was totally going down for this. He tried to move, but his leaden limbs refused. Where was Andy?

Inching his chin forward on the bedspread, he managed to move his head to read the clock. Two a.m. Thumping and clunking echoed in the room next door and had been going on for a while and was probably the reason he awoke.

"Untie me, Andy!"

Spencer's voice. He recognized his high-pitched, whiney voice. What kind of sick game were they playing? He couldn't shake the mental image from his head.

"No way!"

Andy's voice.

A groan sounded.

Christiaan's stomach twisted. What happened next door? A vivid mental image appeared in his mind.

A lamp crashed. Then a picture fell from the wall.

She's an animal.

More groans.

Christiaan steeled his heart. Their relationship was over for him. Every daydream and hope he'd ever had about Andy needed to be erased. She was nothing to him now. How could she go for a man like Spencer? He was weak and…weak.

"Andy, Andy," Spencer called again, in clear agony.

The bed squeaked and broke under the strain.

Andy squealed.

Spencer groaned something.

Christiaan's heart ached. He stuffed it down, holding his breath against the pain. Women—they were all the same.

Then quiet fell.

Christiaan couldn't tell how much time had passed. He wouldn't turn his head to the clock. He was frozen, his eyes and ears alert to the horrible scene but not being able to move any muscles. The worst torture anyone could give him. An eternity passed with more than a few painful heartbeats. Then light from the hall spread across the bedspread.

Spencer dragged himself in, barely closing and locking the door behind him. His shirt clung to his chest, his tousled hair sticking out everywhere, his tie trailing behind him on the floor.

Christiaan glared at Spencer's back.

With key still in hand, Spencer fell face first onto his duvet.

Anger bubbled up inside Christiaan in the dark, wishing death threats upon Spencer. If he had use of his limbs, Spencer would've already been dead.

****

Two hours earlier
Twelve-thirty a.m.

Andy, stuffed to the gills, opened the door to the hotel. Whatever people said about French food, it was all true. She'd never eaten so well.

Spencer loosened his tie. He glowered. "I can't believe how disorganized this country is."

"Most people love Paris." Shaking her head, she slid her hand along the bannister up the stairs to her room.

His feet fell heavy on the tread. "I don't understand their transportation philosophy."

"You're just mad that we got fined by the subway police." She spoke over her shoulder. At the top, she faced him.

Spencer crossed his arms. "This has nothing to do with the rude controller. But I will say this: I won't be coming back to Paris in the future. In London, all the information you need is accessible and understandable. You pre-pay your Oyster card for the tube, and when it's depleted, you recharge it. How was I to know our metro tickets expired at midnight?"

"Thank you for dinner and a lovely evening." With a quick hug and kiss on Spencer's cheek, Andy backed to the door of her room. She didn't want an awkward ending to a nice day. After unlocking the door, she glanced down. Her hands were empty. She covered her mouth. "I forgot Christiaan's food. I ordered take-out for him and left it at the restaurant." She pivoted and headed back down the hall. "I'll run back and get it."

"I'll just let myself in, then, and wait for you there."

Andy barely heard his reply. Would the place still

be open? When she left, the wait staff folded tablecloths for closing. Would they be as unyielding as the subway police? Without taking the metro, she jogged. A few blocks' run down the street would take longer.

How could she be so thoughtless? Spencer was a distraction. As she stepped out into the light rain, she smelled Spencer's cologne clinging to her clothes from their embrace. How did she feel about him anyway? What about Christiaan?

Christiaan was more dedicated to his revenge. He even admitted as much in his drugged state. Would he ever make room in his heart for her? For him, work always came first. Could she let him go? Her heart constricted at the thought. She held such a strong connection with Christiaan. Their time in the Mexican desert where he confessed he loved her would never leave her. Letting him go was not an option. She wasn't ready for that yet.

So what was Spencer to her?

Amidst the drizzle, Andy crossed at the red light. A few cars splashed in the shallow puddles. Hurrying along the narrow sidewalk while skirting the tall buildings, Andy retraced her steps to the restaurant.

Spencer. Spencer. Spencer. Andy couldn't help but shake her head and smile at the thought of him. He was unpredictable and sometimes silly. But she couldn't help think he wasn't being truthful. Perhaps he was some rich lord in disguise or someone just playing the part of a petty gambler. Then sometimes, he just seemed too simple to be anything else.

Spencer was different from Christiaan. Christiaan acted on gut—emotion and instinct. Spencer calculated—predicted—and was often right. And

Spencer wanted her. Few things were more attractive than a man wanting you. He didn't have giant biceps or a mysterious past—just an honest, open appearance and a desire to love her.

Andy reached the restaurant and tugged at the doorknob, burnished with time. Locked. She knocked on the glass pane of the front door which had a sign which read, "*Fermé.*"

The maître d' spotted her. He raised his eyebrows and smiled. He disappeared beyond her view and returned with a little sack.

"Take away?" Andy didn't know enough French to communicate anything else.

"Take away," he responded with a heavy accent.

"*Merci.*" Wishing she could say more, she turned away. If only she were fluent like Spencer. She hugged the bag close to her chest. As it warmed her, she made the return trip to the hotel, dripping wet and with sore feet. Spencer popped in her mind again. Their evening at the small bistro—his features softened by the dimmed lighting, his hand holding hers across the table—warmed her heart. He ordered comfortably in French, so unusually confident.

Men speaking French? *Mmmmm.* No wonder people called it the language of love. He sounded so cultured and refined.

A car passed in front of her. She held the food closer. Sauce and meat aroma rose to her nose.

Christiaan. She was bringing back food to Christiaan. She loved him. They understood each other. They were a part of each other. They suffered so much together. But she could never have him. Physical pain tore her heart. Whatever they shared in the Mexican desert was ages ago, perhaps provoked because they were near to death, or it was a complete mirage. She sighed, waiting at a stoplight to cross. Or perhaps he no longer cared. Maybe he never cared. Andy was never sure about Christiaan.

Andy entered the hotel. The concierge wasn't at his desk. Spencer had picked up the key to her room and his. As she mounted the stairs, a TV roared in the back, a soccer match, or a *football* match as Spencer would say, played. But still, the lonely lobby made her feel uneasy for some reason. Mounting the stairs, she shook off the feeling. She paused in the hall between the two doors. Should she try and wake Christiaan so he could eat?

Spencer would be waiting in her room. She might miss an opportunity to be with him. She was curious what would happen. Not that she wanted their relationship to go far. She wasn't over Christiaan enough to let her heart go again. But she did find Spencer interesting and an intriguing conversation partner. What if she just peeked in on Christiaan? But then she didn't have the key.

Her room first, then. She held the handle. Wait, her room didn't have a fridge. Did the concierge have one behind the desk? Andy thundered downstairs. "Jean?" she called from the small front desk. She glanced at the clock. About two o'clock. Someone should be awake, right? Andy hoped he spoke English. "Jean," she called again toward the sound of the TV coming from a small cafe beyond the desk.

Then the TV roared with a goal.

Andy's ears prickled. No one reacted to the goal.

No groan.

No clap.

Nothing.

Andy's heart beat into her ears. *Calm down.* She was just overreacting. Swallowing, she peered in the small café through a doorway behind the desk. The room was empty. Perhaps Jean went for a smoke. She found a small fridge and parked Christiaan's take-out in there.

She glanced at the book on his desk. The room for Spencer and Christiaan was listed as the one she was staying in. *Interesting.* Spencer must've mixed up the rooms. Still uneasy, Andy mounted the stairs again. She couldn't calm her breathing. Her heart thundered as if she ran a marathon. With all senses on alert, she stepped lightly.

At her room, she opened the door slowly. All was dark inside except for a lit outline of the open window. A breeze freshened the air. Perhaps Spencer had fallen asleep.

Someone moved quickly beside her. The door slammed shut. Darkness swallowed the room.

Though an attacker moved stealthily, his clothes whispered each movement.

Despite the near total blackout, Andy blocked the attack. From the outline of his shadow, Andy guessed the attacker was a man, and he moved with great agility. The unmistakable outline of a knife caught her eye. Andy continued to block and strike the assailant. Where was Spencer?

When her eyes adjusted to the dark, she made out an outline of him tied to a chair. Andy push-kicked the attacker into the small ensuite bathroom, buying herself enough time to free Spencer.

She untied his gag. As her eyes adjusted to the dark, she noticed his swollen eye bled.

"The man ambushed me."

Apparently, his mouth was fine. But that was all he was able to say.

The man burst from the bathroom, swinging his knife at Andy.

She kicked him into a small nightstand and into the wall.

"Untie me, Andy," Spencer called.

Before the assailant could get up, she bent to release his hands. Two against one would be better odds. Even if one of them was Spencer.

The attacker returned before she could finish and struck Spencer across the face.

Spencer groaned.

"No way!" Andy dropped Spencer's bound hands and ran headlong into the attacker's chest.

He collapsed into the bed. The bedside table toppled over, and the headboard knocked into the wall. The attacker scrambled to his feet and pushed Andy into Spencer.

Spencer groaned again.

Andy retaliated with a frontal assault, backing the assailant into the wall. He was down for a bit. Now she focused on Spencer.

"Andy, Andy!" he called.

With jagged breath, she turned to check on how much time she had.

After regaining his footing, the assailant jabbed forward with the knife.

Standing and facing him, she joint locked his arm and kicked him in the face. Then again. And again.

With repeated groans, the man dropped his knife and clutched his face.

Andy swung him onto the bed. The frame crashed under the force of his weight and momentum. She lunged, smashing the standing lamp to the floor. She landed on top of him, elbow first.

The man groaned. He bucked her off, knocking the mattress and bedding off the frame and onto the carpet. The man scrambled free and headed toward the open balcony window.

Andy raced after him, only to see him disappear off the balcony onto a waiting truck bed.

Gone.

Andy hit the window sash in frustration. She couldn't report this attack to police. Reporting would take time they didn't have. They would probably miss their flight. Nothing was more important than getting to Hong Kong.

Spencer groaned again.

"I'm sorry," she whispered. She flipped on an intact desk lamp. "I didn't mean to knock you out." She found the man's knife and cut the zip ties off his hands.

He winced and embraced his shoulders. "Thank you. A friend of yours?" He nodded toward the window.

"I'm not sure who he is or what he wanted." Andy helped him sit up. "What happened?"

He thumbed his bleeding lip. "I unlocked the door and stepped inside. Before I turned on the light, he sprung. He got the better of me, I'm afraid. With both the darkness and the surprise, I was no match for his strength."

Admiration shone in his eyes. With intense

breathing, Andy backed away, trembling.

"But even under such conditions, you managed to subdue him."

"Black belt," Andy said, mostly under her breath, examining what was left of her room. She wasn't ready for any overtures of love. "Did he take anything? Ask for anything?"

"I heard him curse in French, but he could've been a hired thug. He didn't want me. He seemed to be waiting for you."

The attacker didn't want her either. "Hmm." Andy placed hands on her hips. The broken bed sagged in the corner. She straightened the overturned lamp. The picture fell off the wall. The nightstand was askew. Mattress sagged on the floor. "But I suggest we clean up and not report it to the authorities, or we'll never make our flight out tomorrow."

"True." Spencer rubbed his wrists. "I'll pay for any damages, but shall we keep this mum, hmm?"

Andy nodded. "Even from Christiaan?"

"He would be disappointed he couldn't disarm the attacker. And I don't want him to know I was so caught off guard, eh? The ego, you know."

His face blushed adorably. She chuckled. "All right. This will be our little secret."

With slumped shoulders, he motioned a thumb toward the next room. "I guess I'll go back to my room."

"Yeah." The night was spoiled.

Spencer untied his tie. His shirt hung half untucked and torn in a few places. His hair was out of its usual perfect style. "Not what I had planned for the evening."

Andy cracked a smile. "No, I bet."

"May I bestow one little kiss for saving my life?"

Andy's stomach flipped.

Spencer stepped closer. His tie hung in his hands.

But he still smelled of linen. Andy would always associate that scent with him.

Before she nodded, Spencer slid his arms around her, holding her tight. Leaning in, he closed his eyes to kiss her.

Andy stopped him with a knife-hand block to the kisser.

He opened his eyes. He wrinkled his brow.

"I can't." Her gut twisted. She didn't owe anything to Christiaan, and yet, she wasn't ready for anything new—not tonight anyway.

Spencer glanced over her head to the room next door where Christiaan slept.

"Not yet."

"So maybe?" He raised his eyebrows.

He looked so adorable. Andy couldn't resist. "Maybe."

Chapter 26

The next morning, Christiaan ruminated in a foul mood. He refused to speak to Spencer or Andy. With a fork, he opened his cooled takeaway box at the little café in the bottom of the hotel. He jabbed his fork into rubbery green beans.

Andy leaned against the café table. "Where did you go last night?" she asked Jean.

Jean wiped a glass with a towel. "I got a call asking me to come help move some boxes down the street. When I got to the corner, no one was around." He shrugged and answered a customer at the desk.

"Did you sleep okay last night?" Andy shifted in her seat at the café.

The sun beamed through the solarium windows. Other than Andy, him, and Spencer, no one else was in the little café. Christiaan grunted and forked the contents of his container into his mouth. A knife would be useful for the hardened chicken, but he had little appetite anyway. "Well enough. Although drug induced." He scowled at Spencer.

"He drugged you on accident," Andy said.

"I said I'm sorry, my dear chappy." Spencer read a Parisian newspaper. "The coffee with the sleeping meds was meant for the other brute."

Christiaan grunted and shoveled food into his mouth, barely tasting it. "How was last night?"

Andy glanced toward Spencer.

"Fine," he quickly answered.

"Anything happen?" Christiaan squinted.

Her face turned red. "No, nothing. Nothing happened"

"Nothing?" Food was as tasteless as straw in Christiaan's mouth. His stomach turned.

Andy shrugged. "I mean, we had dinner."

She sounded guilty.

"Yes, we ate." Spencer spoke over the paper.

Andy pointed to his meal. "And we brought you food."

"Uh, huh." They wouldn't even confess. Christiaan shook his head. Ache raked his chest. Breathing pained him.

With a smile, Andy clapped her hands. "Then we went to bed."

Spencer bobbed his head. "Yes, to bed. Me in our room. Andy in hers."

"That was it." Andy shrugged.

Spencer folded the newspaper and nodded. He clasped his hands around his crossed knee, staring into the windows. "That was it."

They lie. Spencer exhibited all the classic tells. Christiaan ground his teeth. "Fine. I'm going for a walk."

Andy glanced toward the clock over the café counter. "But our flight leaves—"

"I know when it leaves." He cut her off, refusing to be entrapped by her large brown eyes. He headed for the door. "I'll be back in time." He threaded his way through the café tables and chairs.

He needed fresh air to clear his mind, or to clear

Andy from his mind. The bull they dished out weighed too much on his heart. Having a relationship was one thing—lying about it was another. Why not just come out and say it? Was he being selfish? If he couldn't have her, nobody could?

He paced up the avenue. The sun sliced between the buildings, reaching the street. A few men avoided him by crossing the street. But he didn't care. Then he ran into someone. Or someone ran into him. "Pardon." He backed from the red-headed woman.

But she just stood there, unmoving.

He blinked. "Aiofa."

She stuffed her hands into the raincoat. "You didn't show in London."

Glancing up and down the street, he grabbed her elbow and ducked into an alley. "Something came up."

"I searched for you. You are a difficult man to track."

He didn't want to tell her he left the tracker back in Scotland, never intending to use it. He read a billboard behind her head. It advertised perfume. "I lost the tracker."

"Someone has the tracker here." Her eyebrows crumpled. She tilted her head. "Are you backing out of our deal?"

Who had the tracker here in London? "No, of course not. I might have a lead in Hong Kong, but no contact. He's meeting Fabian in a transaction."

"I'm coming with you." Grabbing him around his forearm, Aiofa arched a blonde eyebrow. "How will you find him among millions?"

He bit his lip. "We hadn't gotten that far."

She narrowed her lids. "We? Oh, you and the *girl*."

She flattened her lips to a straight line.

At the mention of Andy, Christiaan's stomach turned.

"Do you have contacts who know Fabian? Perhaps he would let us in on his little deal, long enough to apprehend the Commander."

Light blossomed in his mind. Andy didn't have to be the only one who planned and had back up. "I do know someone I met in Paris."

A grin parted her painted red lips. "And luckily we're in Paris."

Would she help? Was she still in town? Did he still have Mara's number?

****

Three hours before the flight left, at a sidewalk café, Christiaan tapped a teacup. Mara was late. Though they texted since she got her phone, he hoped she'd meet him quickly. He sent a vague text because of the sensitive nature of the meeting. Flipping over his phone, he checked the time. He couldn't miss the flight out of Charles de Gaulle.

Aiofa hung out of sight.

He specifically wanted to meet Mara on his own.

Mara strode up the sidewalk. Her hair hid her pink face.

Christiaan stood, offering her a spot at his table.

"I got your text." The wind swept away her hair from her pink face, and her eyes shone bright.

"Don't get the wrong idea about why I texted." He leaned back into his metal café chair.

Her face crumpled. "Then why are you here?" She threw out her hands.

"I need a number." He leaned forward. "Do you

have contact information for Fabian?" Caspian had given him his address in Paris and arranged the meeting. He'd strolled past Fabian's old place this morning, but no luck. All boarded up.

Mara froze. "Why do you need it?"

Christiaan fiddled with the edge of his glass. "I need to meet with him again. He has something I want."

She lowered her eyebrows. "What?"

He twirled a tea wrapper in his fingers. "A woman. He's auctioning a woman, and I want to stop it."

Faintly shaking her head, she narrowed her eyes. "He won't give her to you."

"I have a trade."

She arched a brow. "What do you have?"

"The emeralds." The thought of sacrificing the precious gems in exchange for Hin Cho tore at his heart, but he couldn't allow her to be sold to the highest bidder. Mara's cheeks grew a deeper shade of pink. Though young, she was pretty.

Mara guffawed. "He'll kill you for those."

Tossing up his hands, he dropped the wrapper. "I don't have anything else to give him." He'd run out of options. He didn't trust Andy. Or his heart was so bruised, he didn't know what to do. He wiped a hand down his face and sighed.

"Take me."

Her voice was timid, as if she'd just hatched the idea. Christiaan couldn't believe she said it. "What?"

Her gaze locked on his. "He'll trade whoever you need for me."

Why would she offer herself up like this? He shook his head. "I can't."

"I can take care of myself, or I will escape. Then

you can have your friend."

How did she know Hin Cho was a friend? "Mara, I can't—" He couldn't imagine her back in Fabian's hands. He was ruthless—conscienceless. "No."

She grabbed his hand. "Take me, if nothing more than a decoy."

Christiaan sat back. Using her as a decoy might be useful. Plus Aiofa was his trump card. And Spencer and Andy. They almost formed a smallish kind of army. "All right, you can come. But I'm not returning you to Fabian. You will help me get to him, but nothing else."

She nodded.

"I hope you travel light." They had to hurry to the airport. Time was nearly up.

****

Later that afternoon, Christiaan lined up to pass through security behind Andy and Spencer.

"Your tickets." Spencer handed him their paper boarding passes.

"Oh, nice. I got the window seat." Christiaan rolled his eyes. Once on the plane, he slid his hulking frame into the tiny spot. His knees pressed against the seat in front of him. He adjusted his legs to be more comfortable.

Spencer flashed his ticket. "And I was courteous enough to take the middle seat…"

"Giving Andy the aisle," Christiaan finished. "Nice."

Spencer snuggled down next to him, clicking the belt into place with a triumphant grin.

Andy slid next to Spencer.

Christiaan leaned forward, hoping to make eye contact with Andy.

Instead, she focused on her seatbelt and rearranged her bag under the seat in front of her.

Christiaan fell back, scrutinizing Spencer. What happened in her room last night? The Brit sure was cheery earlier this morning. With a souring stomach, Christiaan turned his attention outside the window. Workers loaded the cargo. Better not to ask. "Remind me to never let Spencer make reservations again," Christiaan murmured to himself. Why must Spencer come to Hong Kong? Sadly, without any resources, they needed him. If only they had left him in London.

Then Aiofa passed through the aisle.

He met her gaze over the sea of heads. Their eye contact didn't go unnoticed. Both Andy and Spencer faced him when she passed with her baggage.

"Why is she coming?" Andy asked across Spencer.

Christiaan couldn't help but feel a little smug as he settled in to read his inflight magazine. "She's backup."

Andy pressed closer to Spencer. "You bought her a ticket on the same flight?"

Christiaan shrugged. Actually, *she* bought the ticket. He secretly relished the hint of envy in Andy's voice. "Yes."

Spencer opened his mouth like a carp. "Well, I'm not paying for her to stay in Hong Kong."

"She's not staying with us. She'll be close by, if we need her." Christiaan prayed they didn't need her.

Mara passed.

Neither Spencer nor Andy knew her or noticed. Christiaan made eye contact but said nothing. Aiofa paid for her, too. Christiaan chewed his nail. Would they be enough against Fabian?

Chapter 27

After picking up a rental car at the airport, Andy stood before the small two-door in a parking garage. "Who will drive?" Driving on the crowded and chaotic streets of Hong Kong sounded like a nightmare.

Spencer coughed slightly into his hand, holding out the other. "Since I'm the only subject of Her Majesty's, I believe I should drive."

Christiaan grasped the key. "As the only one specifically trained in driving in tough situations, I should drive." Glaring at Spencer, he puffed out his chest.

"I'll drive." Andy stood between the two.

Simultaneously, both men turned. "No," they said in unison.

Andy crossed her arms. "Babies. Fine, fight it out. But we're wasting time."

Christiaan grinned at the suggestion. He cocked his head. "Yes, let's fight it out. The winner gets to keep the key."

"I'd trust a self-driving car before I'd trust you at the wheel." Spencer cast a wistful sideways glance.

Christiaan stepped closer, with a tight-lipped smile. "I'd trust a South African cab driver over you."

Andy crossed her arms. "While you two hurl insults, the clock is ticking."

"We need a driver used to the *correct* side of the

street." Spencer smiled.

Christiaan flexed his arms. "I can drive anywhere."

"Yes." Spencer spoke with understated British clarity. "Even on the sidewalks."

Andy rolled her eyes. "I'm hailing a cab." She stalked away.

"Wait, Andy." Christiaan turned toward Spencer. "I speak and read Chinese. Navigation will be easier for me."

Spencer's eyes brightened. "Ah, you volunteer to be my navigator? I accept."

"You misunderstood." In an aggressive move, Christiaan leaned closer, gritting his teeth. "We don't need you. I've got the key."

"Guys." Tapping a foot, Andy waved. "Let's find another option."

Christiaan faced her. "What do you suggest?"

"This." Andy pointed to a poster for the Airport Express. Would these two lunkheads get along long enough to find Hin Cho?

＊＊＊＊

Christiaan followed Andy and Spencer to the train depot. People buzzed around them in haste.

Andy stepped onto the Airport Express train. "The road didn't need one more car anyway."

Sidling next to her, Spencer smiled, grasping a rail overhead and leaning in. "And the Hong Kong public transport is the one of best in the world. British design, you know, even down to the Octopus card."

Christiaan glared, resting against the vertical pole, not even holding on as the train jostled and turned toward the Kowloon City. "I despise waiting for the convenience of other people's timetables."

"You sound very American." Then Spencer quickly glanced at Andy.

She raised an eyebrow.

"Not that I meant it as an insult. Americans are wonderful, independent freethinkers."

Christiaan thrust out his chin. "Why don't you tell her what you really think of Americans? You think they are consumerist, indulgent, and undisciplined. You Brits are all the same. A spoiled older brother who discovered his younger brother does everything better than they do."

Christiaan's phone buzzed. After flipping it over, he read a message from Mara:

Fabian said if you want to bargain for Hin Cho, meet us at this address. At this time.

"Fabian wants to meet." Christiaan clicked on the link.

Andy rubbed together her hands. "How did you get his contact information?"

Avoiding the question, Christiaan flipped his phone to show the designated destination, complete with pictures, address, and times.

Spencer peered at the screen. "A weird, live-action video game."

Andy scrolled through pictures of participants wearing black and florescent clothes. "With black lights."

Spencer shook his head. "Every part of this screams run away!"

"This is the only way to find Hin Cho." Christiaan flipped back his phone.

Holding the railing, Andy bit her lip. "We must meet Fabian face to face?"

"Or at least face to glowing mask." Christiaan texted a response to Mara.

"Glowing mask?" Andy swiped the phone again. "Do we bring our own costumes?"

Spencer retreated his chin. "We are supposed to wear our own attire and cover our faces."

Andy glowed with excitement. "Then we can beat this. We can plan for our own costumes, and we can outsmart Fabian. I'll just need to make one phone call."

"I'm glad you are feeling confident. I'm not feeling particularly so." With slumped shoulders, Spencer glanced out the window.

"That's because you're a putz." Christiaan grinned.

Spencer glared.

"Andy knows what she's doing." Christiaan continued. "Follow her lead, and we'll get our man."

Andy nodded. "First, let's get to our hotel and secure food."

The train whizzed them into the city beneath the pink, cherry blossom sky. The setting sun lit up the skyline with florescent colors. Lights twinkled on the water and the buildings.

Christiaan longed to ask Andy what happened in Paris.

****

The bustle and the energy of Hong Kong thrilled Andy. Lights flashed. The smell of salt and fish tainted the air. The humidity clung and curled her hair. "How are we ever going to find the hotel? Addresses are so bizarre." Andy searched the faces of the hundreds of passersby, thronging and moving as one.

"We'll find it." Christiaan nodded.

Andy arched a brow. "Isn't Cantonese different

than Mandarin?"

"Yes, I speak both." Christiaan dipped his chin. "The hotel is right there."

"Good." Andy thrust her chin toward their hotel. "We need to check in." From the pictures online, the rooms were tiny with a huge price tag. But then the amount was in Hong Kong dollars. Was that cheaper or more expensive than the US dollar? Spencer said the train ticket into town was less than a tenner. Whatever that meant.

Christiaan led the way through the doors. "This should be nice. It's owned by a Chinese tycoon who owns half of Hong Kong. In fact, he has offices upstairs."

After checking in and dropping off their stuff, Andy stood outside of her room. "Anybody hungry?"

"That would be the understatement of the year." Christiaan rubbed his tummy.

"I know of a good place." Spencer searched his phone.

"Can we take the metro?" If the guys got in yet another argument, she would lose her temper and leave them to eat alone.

"Let's splurge and get a cab." Spencer thumbed over his shoulder.

Christiaan thrust out his chin. "Go fetch one."

With a nod, Spencer bounded down the stairs.

With Spencer gone, Andy tugged Christiaan's shoulder. "Tell me what's bothering you."

Christiaan stepped closer to Andy. He drew his lips into a straight line. "Will you tell me what happened in Paris?"

Her face burned. "What happened in Paris?"

"Did you...you know?" He swallowed and glanced away.

"No? Did I what?" Andy shook. She clenched her jaw. He accused her?

His gaze returned to hers. "Did you...with Spencer?"

Andy rocked back. "Did you actually think I could...with Spencer?"

"I don't know what to think." He stared at the numbers on the hotel room door.

"And what about the redhead?" Andy retrieved the scarf from her backpack. "I found this in your room." She waved the smelly green scarf in front of his face.

Rolling his eyes, he batted it. "She embedded a tracker in this. I left it on purpose so she couldn't follow me. Now we know how she found us."

Andy dropped her hand. Words failed her. Heat washed over her. She was so sure Christiaan and Aiofa had something. Now Andy could only blame herself.

He arched a brow.

She turned to see what he smirked at.

"Seventy-four-seventy-four. Nice room number."

Andy turned his chin to meet him eye to eye. "Talk to me."

Christiaan slid his hands around her neck. He closed the gap between them and stepped into her. "I haven't been completely emotionally honest. I struggle to want you and not have you. But I have never wanted anyone as much as I want you. My raw and savage desire won't be subdued."

Andy's heart thundered. They were alone, just outside her hotel room. His breath feathered across her lips. A zing of desire went through her. Couldn't they just slip inside? Couldn't he let his guard down just once? His warmth was on her. Christiaan's lips tasted of restless hunger, of water rushing a broken dam, and desire let loose for a moment. His urgency pressed upon her. With a free hand, she unlocked the door behind her, tugging Christiaan inward, before being swallowed by the darkness.

****

Spencer ordered a cab and rounded the corner when Christiaan kissed Andy. Not just a simple friendly peck, either. Emotion he had never felt before burned before he had time to question what it was. Andy enjoyed it too much for him to think she could have any affection elsewhere.

Spencer stood stock still until they disappeared into the darkness of her room. With hot cheeks, he spun and headed back the hallway to the stairs. The exercise would help him work through what he just witnessed. He didn't want to process anything. In fact, he entered the waiting taxi without so much of a remembrance of what he saw, just a deep pain in his chest.

"Where to?" the driver asked.

"Dover's at Deep Water Bay. I have reservations." At least he could get some decent European food.

The driver nodded.

Spencer barely noticed the bright lights of Hong Kong, the traffic, or how much this ride would cost him. Neon lighting flashed and glared in his eyes, but he only saw his reflection on the dingy glass. Had Andy really gotten under his skin? Women came frequently into his life, but Andy was special.

Once out of the cityscape, the roads wound around tree-crowded hills. At last, the taxi pulled up to the

Dover, a four-star restaurant on the beach on Deep Water Bay. He paid the driver and slid out of the taxi, taking in the colonial building shining in the moonlight. He sighed, stepping into the building.

A man in a uniform opened the door.

Spencer crossed to the bar. He changed his mind about the food. He just wanted a drink, something that would make him forget about Andy and Christiaan. And what they were doing in the hotel room. He gulped. *Alone. Together.*

A woman in a gold dress, barely long enough to cover her thighs, propped her elbows up at the bar. Her sleek black hair parted over her soft, warm eyes and painted red lips.

Andy was forgotten.

Spencer sidled up into the seat next to her as she was alone and spoke to her in Cantonese. "They say the lights of Hong Kong cannot be compared to anything else, but you are brighter than them all."

Instead of being impressed, or surprised, she only smiled. "You are British?" she asked, in English. "But you speak Chinese well."

"Thank you," he said, returning to English. "Join me for a drink out on the beach?" Through an open window near the back of the restaurant, the water beckoned. This woman, or the drink, made him feel suddenly free. A weight lifted off his chest.

She glanced at her designer watch. A shy smile washed across her face. "I don't know if my father would allow. We are supposed to meet here for dinner."

"Your pop won't mind. Come." Spencer offered his hand and led her out on the veranda, then down to the pale pink sand, where he removed his shoes, leaving them on the deck. When she hesitated on the wood, he held out his hand. "You have to take off your shoes for the full effect."

"Hold my drink." She laughed as she removed her stilettos and joined him on the beach.

Leaving the drink on the veranda, and holding her hand, Spencer ran toward the water. The wind rushed all around him.

"Not in the water," she cried.

"Why not?" he asked. "Live a little."

She shrugged, allowing him to pull her into the water. The two of them splashed into the shallows. Spencer tore at his suit coat, throwing it behind him, as well as his tie, and unbuttoned his top buttons on his shirt. He splashed in the water. The tide assailed his calves. Her musical laughter intoxicated him.

Her hair hung in wet tendrils slicked to her face. Her smile beamed through the clinging hair.

Spencer paused. The world stilled. Even the ocean seemed to quiet.

She glanced up.

She was slender and youthful and yearned for him with those big eyes—he could just feel it. He stepped forward, slipping an arm around her waist and drew her closer.

Sea water soaked his clothing. The eddies swirled around his pants legs, tugging and pulling at him. He bent down and tenderly kissed her.

She kissed him back, holding his arms as they embraced.

He slipped his hands over her creamy skin and across her shoulders. Then he heard Chinese from the beach.

"My father." The woman's eyes widened.

Spencer, still tight in her embrace, glanced up to see a man in a suit with several men flanking him on both sides. *Uh, oh. Trouble.*

Chapter 28

Andy found Christiaan in the dark.

Christiaan's warm breath came quickly.

Andy closed her eyes, silently pleading someone would take this desire.

He led her to the small bed and sat next to her. His back rested against the headboard. "I'm so sorry," he whispered, running the tips of his fingers down her arm. "I can't. Even though I want you more than I have ever wanted anything."

Goose bumps pricked at his touch. "Except to avenge your parents."

"That's technically true."

"This situation is not fair. I can't lose you." Andy's pulse thundered in her chest at her admission. "I cried every morning for six months afraid I'd lost you." She studied his intense blue eyes. "Actually, what I fear the most is that one day I will wake up and feel nothing for you. Although my heart won't be broken anymore, I will be."

Christiaan bent and kissed her jawline.

His lips lingered there, then moved to her neck. His breath whispered across her collarbone. Goose bumps rose on her skin. Andy slid her head onto his lap. Temptation needled her.

Placing a pillow on his lap, Christiaan propped her head on his thighs. He ran a thumb across her lips. "I wish I could have you, too," Christiaan murmured. He caressed her hair away from her upward tilted face. He swallowed hard. "Somedays I wish I could forget my past and move on." His eyes pinched shut. "Terrible secrets lurk there. If you see them, you'll hate me."

She rose up on her elbow. "I could never hate you."

"Are you so sure?" His brows peaked. He brushed her lips with his. "Years ago, I was assigned to a Soviet woman's camp in Kazakhstan. We had orders to burn it to the ground. Women, young girls—relatives of Soviet spies."

Raising her head from her shoulder, she bit her lip. "Did you do it?"

He stared at the facing wall. "I let them. So yes."

Andy gulped a lump in her throat. "Was this the Order or before, with the mercenaries?"

"With the mercenaries. I was young, about eighteen, at the time." He bowed his head. "Do you hate me for what I did?"

Her breath caught in her chest. She couldn't imagine the scene. "Did they all die?"

He paused. "Not all of them. I heard a cry of a young girl. I broke down a door and found her and her mother. I got out the girl, but the mother"—his voice broke—"I couldn't save her."

"What happened to the girl?"

"I carried her to the hospital. Blaine was furious when I told him. He'd already started losing his humanity." He leaned back his head against the headboard. "Do you despise me?"

"For saving a little girl?"

"For killing people." Her heart ached.

Leaning forward on both elbows, she found his neck and kissed it. His scent intoxicated her.

He bent his head and swallowed her in an embrace. "I'm no hero." His words came between kisses.

Andy squeezed him. "No hero? If a man was tasked with a heinous act but still found enough humanity to save a soul? I'd call him a hero."

Touching his forehead to hers, he relaxed. "I have more secrets. But you'll have to wait."

"I understand." She brushed her cheek against his stubble. The intimate gesture warmed her. For now, this was all she would get.

No one else existed, no city, just the two of them quiet together listening, with more than their ears. Andy savored his closeness. But how long would this intimacy last?

****

Christiaan stirred. After years of sleep deprivation, he rarely needed more than a few hours.

Lights from Hong Kong shone in from the blinds, giving the room an unnatural glow, even in the dead of night.

Andy slept on his lap. Her lashes brushed against her cheek in peaceful sleep.

He didn't dare move his numb legs. So he leaned his head against the wall. He couldn't believe he'd told her about the fire in Kazakhstan last night. Had she really broken down his barriers? What kind of magic did she possess? Of course, he hadn't shared his worst crimes. Just one small sliver—a mere testing of the waters. So far, she hadn't rejected him. But what would happen when she heard the worst?

For so long, the only thing he cared about was

restoring the Order. It was his destiny—what he lived for. What he'd die for.

Andy shifted on his legs.

Where did Andy fit into all of his plans? He could not fail the Order. And what about the Commander? According to Aiofa, he was a ruthless, cunning man. What did he want? Christiaan couldn't let Hin Cho be taken by his organization. He'd rather see her in the hands of Fabian, but Christiaan had to juggle so many things. Many people depended on him. He swept a hand down his face. He wasn't quite sure what he was doing. Andy's nearness comforted him.

Andy opened her eyes.

He must've moved beneath her, waking her. "I can't do it alone." He wasn't sure what he was talking about. Life? The mission? His confrontation with Fabian and the Commander?

"I will be here to help you. I always will be here. And I have backup." She was not quite awake and not quite asleep. A smile spread across her lips.

He bent to kiss them, savoring the intimacy and the closeness. "You are both a blessing and a curse. You have incredible talents. You make me want you in ways that I cannot have you. But I cannot both have you near, and I cannot have you far away." What would he do with Andy?

****

All night Andy slept close to Christiaan, breathing him in and relishing his arms around her. Not once did she wonder where Spencer was or where he spent the night. In the morning, she searched his room. Not a trace of him remained and not even a hint he'd passed the night at the hotel.

Christiaan grinned and clapped his hands. "Oh, good. Maybe he finally decided to go back to England."

Andy scowled. "We need to find him."

Huffing, Christiaan raised his brows. "In this city? Good luck."

Stepping out to the busy street, Andy let the movement of the city exhilarate her and energize her. The scents of fried food, salt air, exhaust, and perfume assaulted her with each breath.

A dark sedan with tinted windows parked next to them. The men in suits left their car to enter a nearby building.

Pounding sounds hit the window in the rear seat.

Andy stepped closer.

The sound grew more frantic.

She cupped her hand around her eyes to view inside the tinted window of the sedan.

Spencer's large and wild gaze met hers. Stepping back from the black car, she yanked the door handle. "What?" She couldn't believe what she saw. Why was Spencer in the back of the sedan?

With his teeth, Spencer pried open the lever, but the door fell back on him.

Andy opened the door.

In soggy clothes on the back seat, Spencer was bound hand and foot.

His jacket and tie were missing, as were his shoes. His hair hung in damp strands across his forehead. A large, purplish goose egg grew on his forehead, a cut sliced his eyebrow, and a cloth gagged his mouth. On closer inspection, Andy noted his shirt ripped in several places. She removed the gag.

"What is going on?" Christiaan opened the door

wider. He chuckled and crossed his arms and leaned against the sedan. "What have you stumbled into?" With great relish, Christiaan ripped the duct tape off Spencer's hands.

"Yeow!" His eyes blazed at Christiaan. Then he inched his way across the seat, stopping only to rip off the tape from his ankles. "Ouch! Quickly, they might— ouch!—return at any moment. Owwie. You've got to get me out of here."

Christiaan leaned against the door. "Who is coming back?"

"I don't know. I heard the name, Chi She Hong."

Sighing, Christiaan wiped his face with his hands. "How did you get mixed up with one of the most powerful men in Hong Kong? We only left you alone for a night."

Spencer threw up his arms. "No time for the story. Get me out of here." He edged toward the door. "The men have already given me a bad night."

With his hands around Spencer's forearms, Christiaan lifted him out of the back.

Once upright and barefoot on the sidewalk, Spencer yelped. "There they are."

Wide men in black suits and sunglasses pointed to the open door and Spencer standing on the sidewalk.

Spencer ran first.

Andy, still confused as to why they were running, followed down the streets, heart beating.

Christiaan brought up the rear.

The suited men chased after them.

Spencer ducked in a busy street market near the meat freezer counter.

When all was clear, Christiaan stepped out. "All

right, you'd better tell us what you did to raise the ire of one of the most powerful gangs in Hong Kong."

A sheepish grin passed on Spencer's face. "I met a woman at a bar."

Christiaan rolled his eyes. "Oh no, you didn't."

Crossing his arms across his ripped shirt, Spencer straightened. "We didn't go too far. We just had a frolicking sea bath, but apparently her father didn't want me to even touch her and sent his goons after me."

Christiaan bought some pears from a merchant. He tossed one to Andy.

She bit into the sweet, tangy flesh. Juices dripped on her chin. When was the last time she ate?

Shaking his head, Christiaan took a bite. "You sure know how to pick them."

"I didn't know." Spencer shrugged.

Weaving through the crowded marketplace, Christiaan stood a good head and shoulders above everyone else. "That will just make our stay here even more difficult. Chi She Hong has men everywhere, owns ninety percent of the real estate, and has the governor in his pocket." He tossed him a pear.

Scowling, Spencer caught it. "I said I was sorry."

Christiaan stopped and faced him. "When will you learn to just have a nice drink by yourself?"

Passersby gawked at the trio.

Andy sighed. *Enough with the bickering!* Not wanting to create a scene, Andy stood between them. "Okay, boys, stop fighting."

Spencer arched a brow. "How did you spend your night?"

Andy shared glances with Christiaan but said nothing to confirm nor deny their nocturnal activities.

"Listen." Andy pulled Spencer by the arm. "We need to get back to the hotel and prepare for our rendezvous with Fabian and his men at the arcade. We don't know what we'll be in for, and we don't need the two of you fighting." She stood with her hands on her hips. "We need to buy costumes and get them all ready before four. We can't blow this." She had a tentative plan—an extremely tentative plan. She bit her lip. Would everything play out as she hoped?

****

Christiaan hated everything about the arcade. Only black lights shone, so anything not white or florescent faded into darkness. Loud music blared in his ears, disorienting him. Throngs of people dressed in black and white.

Andy spent the afternoon making costumes for them. All of them wore black. Each of them had a distinctive mark in glowing tape so they could tell each other apart, even in the dark—Andy's idea.

Bad things happened in the dark. He didn't want the others to get separated. Andy's mark was a T across her back and shoulders. Christiaan had two slants across his chest, and Spencer wanted a circle. "Is that meant to be a target?" Christiaan asked. "Or is that your lucky number?"

Spencer glanced down at his chest. "Circles are complete and whole."

Mara texted that Fabian texted.

They were to go to the four p.m. session.

Spencer picked up a colored pamphlet on the rules of the game. "It seems the game is a kind of laser tag you play against the 'computer'—a video game of different scenarios. Once you've taken out all the other targets, they open the door to the next room, those who haven't been shot by the computer will progress to the next level."

Andy arched an eyebrow. "We're going in with more than just us?"

"Sadly, yes. A group."

Andy bit her lip. "I hope my plan works."

Christiaan spread his hands across his costume. "I can't guarantee the safety of anyone who comes with us."

In the lobby of the converted warehouse several stories high, other players filled the room.

Christiaan checked their slot. Seventeen people had already signed up for their session. Maximum amount of people allowed was twenty. He didn't know how Fabian's men would get them out of here with all these people, but he asked Mara and Aiofa to track his phone.

Spencer forked over cash he exchanged. "I cannot believe how much money we had to pay to do this."

Christiaan rolled his eyes. "You'll get reimbursed."

Spencer shrugged. "I'm not worried about the money. Everything is a gamble anyway. Sometimes you make money, and sometimes you lose money."

Christiaan glanced around, then checked the time. "Where is Andy?" He was happy to change the subject. "The game's about to start."

"She had to visit the loo."

The lights dimmed and the music ramped. The door swung open to the first level. Christiaan's adrenaline thundered through him. Fog poured into the room along with a pungent smell. He still couldn't see Andy.

"She's over there." Spencer pointed to a girl with

her mask already on with Andy's mark across the back.

But she entered into the room before the boys.

Spencer nodded. "Good idea to split up. Care to wager? Who can knock out the most targets? I happen to be an expert shot."

Christiaan slid his mask over his face, lit up his target on his chest, and hefted his weapon. "You're on." He bowed to Spencer who had put on his mask and then dove into the chaos. He only had one chance to beat Spencer and rescue Hin Cho.

Chapter 29

Andy couldn't see anything through the fog or the crush of bodies immediately near her. She just had to get through the crowd, try not to get hit, and win. Despite the earplugs, the music pulsed in her ears. "Just stay to the shadows." Although the pulsing music drowned out any spoken words. Her two friends shot targets far from her—just what she wanted.

In the first room, twenty teenagers jumped off props, more interested in playing around than achieving the goal of hitting glowing aliens popping from windows and out of the shadows. This was not a place for people who were easily overwhelmed by stimulation. All the commotion actually energized her. She had a plan, and for now, hope swelled in her heart. She only had to stick to the shadows and watch.

Spencer and Christiaan stuck out—Spencer, because of his height and skinniness. The downward tape stripe elongated his lean legs. And Christiaan's broad shoulders and quick, skilled movements stood out for more than one reason.

Both annihilated their targets. They seemed to have a sort of bet as to who would kill the most aliens and were by far the most systematic and aggressive in taking out the targets. Both proved to be accurate shots.

Andy raised her eyebrows. For all his avoidance of guns, Christiaan accurately aimed, shot, and hit his alien opponents with precision. He adopted a tactical stance with his gun up near his face. He had been trained.

Spencer was no slouch, either. He must've had some training, as well. Neither was an amateur. Andy's eyes narrowed. They drew too much attention to themselves.

The contestants cleared the room and obtained the objective. A door opened on the far side. When Andy progressed with the crowd, she noticed a few of the teenagers had been tagged out. One could only be hit three times before forfeiture.

A Wild West scene decorated the next room. Silhouettes of old buildings sagged along wooden boardwalks. Aliens popped from saloon doors and through broken windows where *BEAR* was written instead of *BEER*.

Andy giggled. Some words were difficult to translate and spell.

In the second room, the teenagers took the threats more seriously than the first room, or maybe only the serious players remained. Somewhere in the jumble, she lost track of Spencer and Christiaan. Even without the marks on their costumes, Andy could've discerned their body types. They were gone. Were they shot three times already? Andy couldn't believe it. She searched through the crowd. They were not there. But a doorway off to the side shut.

Andy searched for someone else in the crowd, but she, too, was missing. Her gut turned. Her plan was set in motion.

****

Christiaan blinked his eyes and opened them. He

tried to move. Plastic binds held his hands behind him and his feet to chair legs. Still in his black costume mask, he blinked again. A bag over his head blocked his sight. How long had he been out?

In the chaos of the second room in the arcade, someone had pricked him with a drug that weakened his knees and dulled his senses. Even still, he managed to knock out one of his captors. He heard Chinese as they dragged him away.

"This man is heavy."

Was Spencer with him? Andy? His heart froze. "Andy?" he called.

A rifle butt smashed into his face. Incomprehensible Chinese assailed his ears.

"I'd guess you are not Andy." He shook his head to clear the ringing. Another hit slammed his head.

"You said you understood Chinese," Spencer called from a few feet away.

"I do."

"They had just told you to be quiet. Ow!"

After a few heartbeats, Christiaan blinked in the sudden light.

Spencer sat a few feet away, his head still covered.

Andy, with a bag over her head, was recognizable only by her marked black suit. Her T across her back was visible.

Next, the men removed Spencer's sack.

"A little fresh air does a man good." Spencer glared at his captors.

Why didn't they remove Andy's sack? Her head sagged to her chest, still out.

The men left them by a metal door at one end of a catwalk.

After the men disappeared by another exit, Christiaan surveyed his surroundings. Piles of boxed lightbulbs and broken boards lay in a corner. How could he alert someone? Christiaan rocked his chair until he fell over.

Footfalls sounded from behind. With a downward heel kick, the big man crunched into his stomach.

Christiaan groaned. While he had his eyes pinched together, a man returned the bag over his head and cinched it tighter around his neck. Heat from his own breath surrounded him. The scratchy burlap bag tickled his face and ears.

While still in the chair, he felt two men pick him off the floor. They placed him on a dolly and wheeled him away.

The temperature cooled. Instead of hot and humid, cool and wet air greeted him. Light seeped through the cracks in the burlap. Christiaan gulped and fought against his bindings, but a man butted him in the head with a rifle again.

Moaning, he straightened his head, a throb beating. Judging by the sounds, Christiaan guessed they carried him outside and across some steelwork—like a catwalk.

Next keys jangled, and a door squeaked open.

Next, he was wheeled into the shadows. And the temperature dropped. Wet chill bit at his exposed hands. Where were they? Dampness entered his lungs. He coughed at the smell of mildew.

Echoes of footsteps sounded down a hall. They stopped.

With muscles tensed, Christiaan listened. Dripping sounds echoed in a more cavernous room.

"Stairs," one of them said in Chinese.

They would have to take him off the dolly.

And that meant an opportunity.

He remembered his training from Master Tso in the temple. Grass mats had lain under his feet with the low-hanging ceiling and dim light of a few candles in the room.

The bearded Chinese man placed a silk ribbon over his eyes.

"What's this for?" Christiaan asked. Usually every method of training caused a great deal of discomfort. The silk ribbon must've been a trick.

Master Tso smiled. "The silk is a symbol of how our own prejudices can blind us. We are very comfortable in our prejudices, but they can hinder our progression. Now attack your enemy."

"How can I attack if I cannot see?" Christiaan asked.

"Your eyes can deceive you."

Christiaan listened intently, breathing in the smells around him and listening for footsteps. He smelled the man before he approached. Not an unpleasant smell, but he recognized the fellow by his use of lavender soap. Christiaan held up an arm to defend himself.

"You can mistakenly assume a bigger man can thwart you." Master Tso spoke in a soothing voice. "Your perception will prime you to fail. Use your other senses to detect and disarm."

Master Tso had taught him a valuable lesson.

Now, through drips, Christiaan heard the footsteps of other men swirling through the captives. Even blindfolded he could detect and disarm. With patience, he awaited his chance.

He felt someone close. Christiaan breathed,

focusing all his energy and waiting for the right moment. As soon as his hands were loosed, they were lethal. Though his wrists were behind him, he raised them over his head, sensing the breath and, therefore, the position of the man behind him. Christiaan grabbed his neck, crashing the man down on top of him.

Sounds of gunshots ricocheted around, but Christiaan knew the bullets hit close.

"That was a warning shot, Christiaan. There are several automatic rifles pointed right at your head."

He recognized Fabian's accent. He inhaled, steeling himself against the coming confrontation.

"If I had chosen to kill you, you would already be dead. But I need you for happier things. Please be respectful to my hired help. You know how it is to be a hired gun. They are here for the paycheck. I would not be happy about hiring more. We must keep down costs. So kindly do not kill them."

Christiaan couldn't see the ARs, but he smelled gun oil and fear. He wanted to make sure Andy was all right. Though he hadn't heard her speak, Christiaan knew she was close. Maybe Fabian had given her a higher dose. Whatever the reason, he had to make sure he stayed with Andy and Spencer.

"Though unpleasant, this method is for the best." Fabian voice came again.

A gun knocked him in the head, and everything went black again.

****

Christiaan opened his eyes. Darkness muted his vision. Pain pulsed in his head where he'd been hit. Heat surrounded his face. He was standing. He inhaled, trying to sense his surroundings.

"Leave on his mask."

Fabian's French accent was unmistakable. Christiaan blinked in the darkness. Someone held his arms from behind. "We've come to bargain for Hin Cho."

"And what do you have to bargain with?"

Fabian's voice oozed oily condescension. He hated the Frenchman. "The emeralds you sold to Philipe."

"Oh, I've already found them. Thank you."

Christiaan sagged. *Damn.* Bargaining chip number one, gone. "Then return the girl."

"The emeralds were mine in the first place. You stole them from my client. Besides, she's worth so much more than emeralds."

Shaking free the person who held him, Christiaan continued in the air of total control. "I have a better trade." A scent of dampness and years of wet met his nose. The ground was cement beneath his feet. A dull glow seeped into his burlap.

A hand pushed Christiaan in his chest.

At first, he resisted.

"Sit," Fabian said.

With hands still bound, Christiaan backed first to feel the chair against his legs before he sat. Then he waited. Snatches of Chinese conversation flitted around the room, but nothing Christiaan could sink his ears into. At last, a hand wrestled with the bag over his face, and it lifted off. A rush of fresh air greeted him.

Fabian's hair was longer on his neck, and his cheeks were covered in dark scruff. Deep wells circled his eyes. Bandages still wrapped his right hand.

Christiaan casted his gaze about the cement bunker. Thankfully, his two friends were nearby. No cell reception would get through this. His backup plan failed. He lowered his brows. It was not a bunker. He was in a water storage area, maybe?

Water pipes snaked around the damp floor beneath them and up the walls. Cool air bathed his face.

Nearby, Andy bent in her chair.

Spencer sat erect, his feet neatly folded beneath his chair.

Both still had bags over their faces.

What was Spencer thinking? Poor man. He should've stayed in England.

Fabian wore a corduroy blazer. Several armed mercenaries stood nearby.

So he wasn't lying. Automatic rifles pointed at Christiaan.

"Let's just see what we have here." He asked a mercenary to untie Andy's bag in Chinese.

"Me first." Spencer lifted his head.

Fabian arched an eyebrow. Then he stepped toward Spencer. With a flick of his injured hand, he directed the men to de-bag Spencer. Spencer still wore his black mask from the arcade.

They removed it, too.

"And who are you?" Fabian greeted him with a charming smile. He swept an assessing gaze over him. "You are just a worthless friend who got mixed up in this business, aren't you?"

Narrowing his eyes, Spencer glared. "Care to make a wager on that statement?"

Fabian raised his eyebrows. "Are you a gambling man? Oh, yes, you're Spencer."

He dropped his mouth. "You know me?"

Fabian only smiled. "I, too, have many

informational sources." Then he stepped in front of Andy. Her costume still covered every inch of her, bag covering her face and gloves on her hands tucked behind her back. This time, Fabian only nodded.

The mercs lifted the bag. They lifted the ski mask.

Christiaan dropped his jaw.

An Asian woman stared at them. Her eyes blazed.

Christiaan didn't know whether to sigh with relief or to be terrified. Or laugh.

Throwing out his hands, Fabian nearly jumped then spoke rapid French. "Who are you?" He finally switched to English. "And where is the girl who was with Christiaan?"

The Asian girl just stared at him with pure hatred in her eyes. She said something rather not nice in Chinese.

With anger flashing in his eyes, Fabian knocked out Christiaan again.

****

Christiaan awoke to a throbbing headache. "Where did everyone go?" He blinked and looked around the cement cavern.

The men's dark figures were lit up by something in their hands. A phone glowed. All of them stared at the device.

The woman's head slumped to her chest.

"Did you hear what they said a few minutes ago?" Spencer asked.

"No, I didn't catch it. I was still out." Spencer knew more about what the mercs searched for than he did. He ground his teeth. Christiaan liked being the one with all the knowledge.

Something important must've happened because

the guards disappeared, taking the source of light.

"Poor girl." Spencer nodded toward the unknown woman. "They knocked her out again. Aren't you going to ask me what happened?"

Christiaan pursed his lips. He hated being out of the loop. "Okay, what happened?"

"They must've been watching the security feed when we entered the arcade. They identified our costumes easily and dragged us up here."

"Yeah, so?"

Spencer kicked back his head and laughed. "Andy switched costumes. Our confused captors rewatched the video feed on a phone."

"When?" She was with them from the beginning.

"Must've been when she went to the loo." Spencer shook his head.

"How did you understand what they are saying?"

Spencer stopped laughing. "All by the subtext."

Christiaan smiled to himself. "So Andy is still out there." Hope rose in his heart.

Then she could come for them. What did Andy have planned?

Chapter 30

Christiaan thrust up his chin. His neck hurt from being slumped, and his head ached.

The outline of the woman who took Andy's place still sagged—unconscious—the poor woman. Was she part of Andy's scheme or just an innocent bystander roped into all of this? He wished he could ask her. "Andy has a plan."

"She's good."

"Yeah." *Wait.* What did he mean by that phrase? Christiaan tilted his head toward Spencer's shape. "I found her first."

"What's going on between you two?"

Water dripped in the silence. "Our relationship is...complicated."

"All relationships are. If you ever want to cast her off, send her my way, old chap."

Christiaan snorted. He faced forward again. "That's not happening." His voice echoed in the cavern.

Spencer cleared his throat. "Why do you want the emeralds?"

Christiaan inhaled. He didn't trust anyone, certainly not Spencer. "The reason is secret."

"Ah, we're about to die, but you still keep your secrets."

"I'm not good with male bonding." Christiaan rolled his eyes and shifted in his chair. The chair groaned under him. Too bad it wasn't wood because then he could smash it.

"So I see."

Memories stung his mind. Christiaan wasn't ready to face those dark times. "A friend betrayed me a few years ago. I'm a little suspicious of everybody."

"Except Andy."

"She's one of the few people I trust." Why did he respect Andy so much? She lied, cheated, and manipulated as much as he, but her heart was pure. She had no ulterior motives.

"One of a few?"

Christiaan nodded. "Very few." Only a handful of people made the list. No one Spencer knew. Christiaan found the incessant dripping of water annoying.

"Who was the guy?" Spencer's voice echoed in the darkness.

"Pardon?"

"Who was the guy who betrayed you? I'm assuming it was a guy since you are so bitter against male company."

Christiaan hadn't told many people about his betrayal. Could he trust Spencer? "His name was Blaine. Liam Blaine."

"What happened to him?"

Pain speared his chest. Blaine was his least favorite topic. "He died."

"Can I ask how he died?"

"No." He paused. Where was the damned water dripping from? He couldn't pinpoint the location and tried to not hear it. What would it hurt to tell Spencer? Christiaan's thoughts roiled. He hated talking about his past. So many people wouldn't understand. But

Spencer, untrustworthy as he was, seemed earnest. Christiaan inhaled and licked his lips. "We were assigned on a couple of missions. This was back when we were hired guns—assassins. Some of us saw some really bad stuff. Blaine, I think, caught the worst of the gore, because he was our squad leader. He always went first. He always came out last.

"We had clients, high-paying clients who ordered kills. We sneaked through jungles or crowded cities, take a shot, and retreat—never knowing who or why we killed. Sometimes we worked together. Often alone."

"That's a hard life."

"Our lives were not glamorous, for sure. Sometimes the fight turned ugly. Once we were ambushed in the jungles in the Thai mountains. They knew we were coming and were prepared."

"Somebody sold you out?"

Christian inhaled cool, damp air. "Or maybe our employers found a convenient way to silence us? I don't know, but that experience changed my life. I wanted out. I turned a new leaf. But something broke inside Blaine. Even after we left the business, he couldn't stop living there. He never could come home. We joined another group to atone for our bloody days, yet Blaine always twisted what was good and tried to make the organization into something different."

"Does Andy know you were an assassin?"

He told her bits in the dessert of Mexico when he thought them dead. But he didn't tell her everything. "Not really, and I'd like to keep it that way."

"You're afraid if she sees all the darkness inside you, she'll run away." He stated more than questioned.

A shot lanced through Christiaan's heart. He didn't

answer. He didn't have to. Spencer skewered him with the truth.

"Don't worry. Wild horses couldn't drag this secret out of me." He cleared his throat. "Not that I'm Mr. Lonely Hearts, but if she loves you, but only knows your good parts, then how do you know she really loves you?"

Spencer made a valid point. Christiaan nodded. A person who only knows the good about you couldn't love you. They have to see and accept the bad to truly love. She deserved someone better. He hung his head.

" 'The course of true love never did run smooth.' "

Christiaan raised his head. "Are you quoting Shakespeare?"

Spencer inhaled with a *whoosh* of air. "Oh, you know him? The Great Bard? The pride of Elizabethan England?"

"*Midsummer's Night's Dream,* Act 1, Scene 2."

"Bravo! I'm impressed. That's more than I would've given you credit for. How about, 'I pray you do not fall in love with me, For I am falser than vows made in wine.' "

"I don't know that one." His chest burned. Interesting that Spencer should choose that particular quote. Christiaan didn't need any more doubt in his relationship with Andy or his vows.

"You should tell her the whole truth."

Christiaan knew Spencer referred to Andy. "I'll tell her when the timing's right." Truth be told, Christiaan didn't ever want to tell Andy. That secret was buried deep inside.

"*As You Like It,* Act 3, Scene 5."

"Huh?" Christiaan shook his head, and he worked

his hands to loosen the plastic cords.

"The second Shakespeare quote reference. I know you will tell her. And I'm sure she will love you just the same. And the emeralds?"

Christiaan told Spencer so much, he might as well keep going. Spencer seemed to understand him for some reason. Understanding was a rare quality in people. "I am searching for a terrorist group who killed my family. The leader's name is Viper."

Lights flicked in the doorway.

Fabian and his men marched into the room.

Christiaan blinked against the brighter light. Fabian wasn't all that impressive in the semi-darkness of the underground water cistern. His slim figure seemed even smaller in the vast space. "I have a trade to offer you in exchange for Hin Cho." He would've traded himself if Fabian wanted him. He'd given Mara a tracker to trace his phone, but would it reach clear down here?

"What trade are you willing to offer me? I already have the emeralds." He held out the red envelope.

Christiaan was slightly hoping Mara had found him by now, but in this deep cement bunker, he doubted she could find his signal. "Somebody you want."

"Who?" Crossing the room, Fabian scowled.

"Mara."

Fabian paused, his black beady eyes growing large. Then his face returned to a sneer.

Maybe he really did care for her.

"I got a better offer."

Last bargaining chip—gone. His gut sank. Christiaan glared. "From Unction?"

Fabian frowned and shook his head, a hand resting over his heart. "My clientele list is strictly confidential."

"I wouldn't trust the Commander. He killed Philipe. He'll kill you, too."

Curling his lip, Fabian lifted the red envelope. "I don't listen to advice from prisoners. I will heal these emeralds. They will become completely mark free and unrecognizable to anyone. All fissures and marks will be erased."

Christiaan's heart ached. Healing the emeralds would erase all the power, and he'd never restore the seven sanctuaries.

Footsteps sounded as men dragged in Hin Cho. Her hair slipped from a loose hold behind her neck and brushed her crumpled and stained shirt. Her head hung to her chest, and bruises purpled her face. When she saw the woman's figure in Andy's clothes, her eyes grew large.

Recognition. Christiaan couldn't make the connection.

Fabian barked commands to move the prisoners facing him in French then sneered at Christiaan. "Our other buyers should be here shortly. I'm giving him both the woman who created the formula and the man who stole the emeralds. That was part of the deal, you know. The price on your head was far too great to pass up. You fell right into my trap."

The ten million euro bounty finally caught up with Christiaan. He wouldn't let Fabian cash him in. Christiaan worked on his binds. Plastic cut into his wrists as he twisted and wrangled his hands. No use. Even Spencer's bleeding and raw wrists hung behind him. At least the woman had her hands blood-free and... Unbound?

Christiaan's heart thundered in his chest. The woman was unbound. Where were Andy and her reinforcements? Christiaan wracked his brain for ideas. He had been in thousands of scenarios where he had been in more danger and in more difficult spots. He had to get to those emeralds.

With Fabian's back turned, he spoke to his minions about Hin Cho.

Christiaan wrestled once more against his bands. Staring at the men's backs with such determination, he wiped a dripping brow with his shoulder, and his body shook with pain. All his hopes and dreams for the future failed, right in front of his eyes. He dropped his head in defeat. The throbbing in his wrists beating with his heartbeat the cadence, "you failed, you failed, you failed."

He sensed movement and raised his head.

The chair where the woman in Andy's clothes sat was empty.

****

In front of a water tower dug into the side of the mountain on the outskirts of Kowloon, Andy stomped her feet along the gravel path leading to the sealed door. A breeze blew through the leafy trees filled with salted sea. The humid air clung to her face and hands exposed to the night air.

Her secret weapon deployed inside, she hoped. Now phase two.

After a phone call, she tucked away her phone. With thundering heart, she paced. Would they come? Timing had to be perfect. If she blew this, she would be in a world of hurt and so would Christiaan and Spencer. If she waited too long, her plan would fail.

Andy measured her breath. She watched the road. Twin headlights cut through the deeply wooded side of the mountain. Behind the car, other black sedans followed. A hundred yards from her, the cars parked on the paved road behind a concrete blockade.

"Now," she whispered to herself through wavering breath. She climbed up the mountain to the underground water cistern.

Men in suits hiked around the barrier up the gravel path. Words in Chinese floated on the cooler humid air.

"There she is," she hoped they said. How many times must she tell herself to branch out and learn a new language? Even Spencer knew French. At the rusting door, she paused.

Gun fire rang out from the crowd of men.

Oh, good. They did bring firepower. She'd need it in a few minutes. Andy reached for the locked door, but it shouldn't be a problem to open. The Chinese Mafia found her.

****

Was that a gunshot? Christiaan's whole body sprang on alert. The hairs on his arms rose. Had Fabian heard it? He was too busy seating Hin Cho. And the woman in Andy's costume must've been too chicken to stick around. He didn't see her anywhere.

Someone pounded at the door at the top of the stairs. Were these the guests Fabian expected?

****

After knocking with her fist on the metal, Andy stood outside the door. She faced the crowd. "Does anyone speak English?"

One particularly beefy guy nabbed her, held her hands behind her back, and spoke in near-perfect

English. "You must be American. All the other countries know how important it is to speak our language. Where is your British friend you promised us?"

Andy bowed as much as she could being utterly bound between two hulking Chinese guys. A third held her neck.

Another man stepped forward, a graying ponytail running down his side.

Andy bowed to the older man—the leader of the gang. He was shorter than Andy, but the pure power that came from his eyes—eyes with no light in them—gave her the shivers. His temples grayed. A few wrinkles feathered his eyes. He didn't look like someone who laughed often. Andy spoke quickly. "I know where the British man is."

His eyebrows constricted. "Where?"

Andy nodded with her head. "In there. He's waiting for you."

"Open the door," he must've said in Chinese.

His men unlocked the metal door and swung it open.

A rush of stale, dank air greeted her. The room was filled with men carrying rifles. They wore loose shirts and jeans. One skinny man in a suit leaned over Hin Cho.

He paused when the Chinese Mafia entered and dropped his jaw.

Andy smiled. Phase two was initiated.

Chapter 31

When he saw the men march through the door, Christiaan raised his eyebrows. He shouldn't have been surprised Andy would make a grand entrance. Bound, she was accompanied by several men. How did she manage to rope the Honorable She's men into her schemes? He recognized the Honorable She standing between two body guards near the steel door. Christiaan shook his head. Andy and her men.

"What is going on?" Fabian asked in Chinese. With widening eyes, his eyebrows lifted. He shuddered then bowed. "Honorable Chi She Hong. I did not recognize you at first. Forgive me. You must please let me continue my business. We are not breaking any laws."

"You are not authorized to be here." Chi She Hong moved to be in the midst of the armed men. "I own all the water rights in Hong Kong. You cannot conduct business here. You will have to leave. Now." He barked his commands.

His armed gunmen trained their rifles on Fabian's hired hands.

Again, Fabian bowed. "I am so sorry. We didn't know."

Chi She Hong squinted his eyes. "That's no excuse."

Fabian's shoulders slumped. "Please don't let this little incident taint our future business dealings."

"You are finished here, as well as our relationship." With a flick of a wrist, Chi She Hong directed his suited men to disarm Fabian's flunkies.

Crumpling the emeralds in his stubbed hand, Fabian scowled and hunched his shoulders. Ducking into the shadows away from the Chinese Mafia, he drew a knife from a blazer jacket.

Christiaan shifted. He needed to get out of here and fast so he could fight. He tugged on his wrists. He was still bound hand and foot to the chair. Gritting he teeth, he swore under his breath.

Chi She Hong turned to Spencer. "We are here for the British man who insulted my daughter."

Spencer sat straighter. "Insulted? I merely kissed her!"

Christiaan's heartbeat picked up. Spencer's hands hung free! When did that happen?

"That is insult enough!" Chi She Hong waved a hand for his men to attack Spencer.

When he felt a tug at his own wrists, Christiaan turned his head slightly

The woman in Andy's costume now worked on his binds.

Christiaan analyzed the situation for a few minutes as the woman worked on his zip cords. Just as he resolved on a plan of attack, he was stopped by a motion to his right.

Spencer jumped out of his chair and headed straight for the men in suits. "I barely touched your daughter." Even with guns pointed at his chest, he threw a punch at the nearest armed man.

Foolish move. But Spencer wasn't a bad fighter. His stance was a little off, and he couldn't kick very high, but all in all, he was clearing the room quite nicely. Christiaan underestimated him.

Fabian's men, too, jumped in, knocking out the armed men surrounding them.

Andy, bound between two men, felled one of the armed men with her body weight then head-butted the other.

The woman in Andy's clothes continued loosening his binds.

Before the ruckus was finished, Christiaan, using all his strength, popped off what remained. "Thank you," he whispered and rubbed his wrists where the plastic bit into his skin.

She bowed and disappeared into the shadows, her black clothes on inside out.

Christiaan battled his way toward Fabian.

Fabian's men contended with the Chinese Mafia.

Chi She Hong found Spencer, grasped him by the scruff of the neck, and hauled him toward the door.

Water rushed from somewhere—first a trickle, then a waterfall. The room smelled of musty concrete. The unknown girl must have turned on the water. Bold move, but a great one for getting people out of here. At last, Christiaan broke through the men surrounding Fabian. He tore the emeralds from his stubbed fingers. They spilled onto the wet concrete floor.

Christiaan's heart stopped. He stared at them on the cold cement. At least, they didn't break into a million pieces. He dove for the fallen jewels and picked them up. Relief washed over him.

Fabian grabbed Hin Cho and stuck a knife to her throat. "Drop the emeralds. Hands up." He stepped toward the door. "Everyone."

Swallowing hard, Christiaan stopped. He wouldn't push Fabian to hurt Hin Cho. He gently placed the emeralds onto the red envelope on the floor.

But the Mafia men still contended with Fabian's local thugs dressed in jeans and loose T-shirts.

Fabian snatched Hin Cho and nodded to his men. "This is where we stop and say *au revoir* and finish this another night. Gather up the emeralds." He held Hin Cho by the hair.

With her bound hands, she gathered the two, slipped them back into the red silk purse, tied it closed, and handed it to him.

With a flick of his wrist, he cut her throat. Deep red liquid ran from her neck. Flinging aside Hin Cho, Fabian snatched at the emeralds with his stubby fingers. His eyes lit up. A grimace replaced his sneer.

Christiaan caught Hin Cho. Life was more precious than the emeralds. Taking off his black shirt, he wrapped her bleeding neck.

She blinked. A faint smile crossed her lips, but her lips drained of color.

"You'll be okay." He meant to comfort her, but did he believe it?

****

With a tangle of men fighting before her, Andy crawled through a slick of water to her friend. Her heart throbbed in her chest. "Are you okay?" She picked up Hin Cho from the ground, settling her into her lap. Her whole body was damp and cold. "I got her," she said to Christiaan. "Go get the emeralds." She removed her jacket and placed it over Hin Cho.

Christiaan nodded and stood.

Shaking, Hin Cho's face turned waxen. "I'm so

sorry."

Anguish swallowed Andy. She hushed her over the din of men fighting. "No, no. Don't apologize. Listen, you need medical help." Taking care of an injured Hin Cho wasn't part of the plan, but helping her friend took priority over getting emeralds or saving Spencer.

"I'm not going to make it." Hin Cho's lips paled. Blood soaked through Christiaan's shirt.

"Don't speak." Andy helped her stand from the sopping floor, now inches deep in water. In the chaos, she carried her friend toward the door. Would Andy get to her to the hospital in time?

****

Christiaan tore through the tangle of men to Fabian, knocking him over and spilling the emeralds again. Christiaan snatched them up and slid them into his pocket.

Spencer and the Chinese Mafia fought.

Then Fabian stood with the empty red bag, his hand raised above his head. He pulled out a little device. "I hoped I wouldn't have to use this. Stop, or I will set off the bomb."

****

When the room quieted, Andy was about five meters to the door. The only sound was the rushing of water. What just happened? Supporting Hin Cho's head, she turned. Andy's shoulders ached with strain, and her arms shook with her weight.

Members of the Chinese Mafia scrambled past her to the lower steel door. Even the leader of the Chinese Mafia left with incredible stealth.

Fabian stood in the center of the chaos. "This is a detonator. If I activate it, we will all die. Now, I will be leaving, and the rest of you will stay here." Reaching into Christiaan's pocket, he snatched something red from him. The emeralds.

Holding Hin Cho under her neck and knees, Andy nearly cried. "At least let Hin Cho go. She needs medical help."

Shaking his head, Fabian backed toward the stairs to the upper exit, sloshing through the water covering the floor. "I don't need her anymore." He grinned. "I already have the emeralds and her secret formula. I couldn't care less if she died."

Andy's face burned. "You shouldn't have said that."

Out of the shadows flew Hin Chi, knocking Fabian to the ground. His device dropped into the six inches of water covering the floor.

Fabian scrambled on his hands and knees to retrieve his device.

Hin Chi grappled him to the ground.

"My sister is worth more than emeralds. How dare you find her life so worthless! She is worth a thousand of you." Hin Chi overcame him, holding him down with her legs on his back. Her hands pinned his arms.

He struggled to keep his head above the water.

Then with the same wire Andy gave her to cut the bonds, she wrapped his throat. A thin line of blood appeared where the wire cut into his skin.

Andy glanced away, hearing only the sound of his feet kicking the water.

"Stop."

Andy turned to see who stopped Fabian's death.

Christiaan stood over Hin Chi.

Her face contorted. "He deserves to die."

He shook his head. "But not like this. He lost. Let him go."

She gripped tighter, her expression intensifying. She held firm.

Andy held her breath. Hin Chi was protective of her sister. Seconds ticked by like minutes. Water continued to pour from the valve.

Fabian's face turned red, then purple.

Then slowly, Hin Chi relaxed her hands. The wire loosened from his throat.

He gasped for air.

Hin Chi grabbed his hands and bound them with the wire. "You live today, but someday, you will not be so lucky."

Andy held her friend. "We're free. We won." She pressed against the door she entered. The steel door was blocked from the outside. She gritted her teeth and shoved it again. Did the Chinese Mafia block it? The only other apparent exit was up the metal stairs.

Andy helped Hin Chi hold Hin Cho. After splashing through water, Andy hoisted her above the water to the upper entrance, high above them and up a series of stairs and metal workings. But when she reached the top, another group blocked them. This one dressed in black.

Chapter 32

Christiaan couldn't believe he saved this piece of scum. Better to bring Fabian home in a body bag than to let him live. He gulped. When had his thoughts gotten so dark? Everyone deserved a trial.

Fabian, wounded from the wire around his neck, was awash in water. Blood mingled with the flow around him.

Christiaan grabbed the emeralds, tucking them safely into his pants pocket, and hoisted Fabian out of the water.

Spencer waited behind a pillar.

Christiaan didn't hear anything but the splashing of water. He felt, rather than heard, the gunshot hit Fabian.

After jerking, Fabian's body went limp in his arms.

Christiaan didn't have time to analyze everything; he dropped Fabian's carcass and ducked behind a stone pillar. His heart thundered in his ears.

From the next pillar over, Spencer stage-whispered over the roar of the falling water. "Someone must be here."

"Using a suppressor, too. Someone who wanted Fabian dead."

Then suddenly the water slowed to a small trickle. The change in sound made the cavern echo.

Christiaan peeked around the stone pillar. He sucked in air at the sight of the newcomer.

The Commander stood at the top of the stairs with a whole host of black-clad flunkies. The Commander and his entourage thundered down the stairs and waded through the water, guns drawn. Several held Andy and the sisters.

Christiaan clenched his jaw. His stomach turned as if he'd swallowed a bomb.

"They have Andy and the girls." Spencer moved to gape at the newcomer.

"What is going on here?" A booming voice echoed across the cavernous space.

Christiaan stood stock still. Was he seeing a ghost? When he saw the Commander at *El Real*, he was far away. Now closer, he seemed familiar.

The Commander stood slightly shorter than Christiaan, but just as broad. His sleeves were rolled up to expose tanned and toned forearms with an eye-catching tattoo. Several wings curled around a seraph.

The mark of the Order of the Destroying Angels. Christiaan gathered himself enough to face the man. He straightened and breathed. Someone from his past? But who? He braced himself for whoever would be behind the mask.

Carrying an AK-47 around his neck, the Commander stepped over a few fallen Mafia men and Fabian's hired hands floating in the water.

Fabian's men bowed and kept their gazes low.

The men in black had bigger guns and were more numerous.

"I did not imagine chaos in our exchange, Fabian— oh, wait, he's dead. Who is his second?"

A man stepped from the fray, his plum corduroy jacket mussed and torn. "I'm sorry, sir. But we had some unexpected visitors…who brought more unexpected visitors, and well…"

"Enough." The Commander lifted his assault rifle and shot him. "And who do we have here?" The Commander turned toward Andy and the girls. He waved a hand. "Kill them. They are no use to me."

"Wait." Christiaan stepped from the pillar, unarmed, but he had the emeralds. The Commander came for the gems.

The Commander raised his chin. "At least, you have one of the people you promised me."

Christiaan opened his mouth.

Mara stepped from behind the men in black.

Oh, no, she'd been captured. But she wasn't bound. She walked freely among the men in black. Then the realization hit him. Bile rose to his throat. He faced Mara. "You work for Fabian, don't you?"

The Commander chuckled. "You have always been too trusting."

Christiaan finally understood. Everything came crashing down. The betrayal rocked his mind, clear to his core. "No, it couldn't be."

The man in black simply stared from behind his black mask.

Realization hit Christiaan like a thousand weights. Mara not only worked with him, she worked *for* him, executing his orders. He faced the Commander. "Is she one of your minions?" His stomach turned. Heat rose to his face. She betrayed him, after he saved her. "Mara, this can't be true."

Mara stared at something across the room.

The Commander erupted in a laugh. "She was working for me. I call her Lìjí—immediately. She has served me faithfully since I saved her life. I have taught her how to manipulate and to kill—all the things our master taught us. I embedded her in Fabian's household. Sadly, she lost track of the emeralds. Fabian sold them faster than she could steal them. She needed to redeem herself. But then you showed up at Fabian's. I thought perhaps it might be another errant knight from our order. How delighted I was when I discovered it was you—my brother-in-arms. She sent you to retrieve them. Sadly, we missed each other at the Opera House. I had to go to extreme lengths to regain the emeralds. And we lost you yet again. But she managed to keep you on the hook again and reel you in. I would've loved to have ended this quest earlier."

"Why him?" Christiaan stammered. Everything shattered. He couldn't trust his instincts. How could this woman betray him? He rescued her. He continuously had to re-examine his assumptions. Shattered trust over and over again hardened him.

"Thank you for bringing her to Hong Kong." The Commander's voice was with thick with irony.

A tight smile crossed Mara's lips. "I feared I'd lost you, but when you contacted me, I was back in play." Her voice was strong, not weak. Her eyes were bright, not dimmed. No longer the victim. "And thank you for truly rescuing those held by Fabian. I loved to see him pained."

"I trained her well, didn't I, Johannson?"

Christiaan jumped at his last name. Who was this guy? How did he know him? Christiaan examined the Commander. He had heard that voice before, but he dared not think…

The Commander removed his mask. His scalp was

burned in places. Mismatched grafted skin covered his bald head. Scars tore his face.

"Blaine?" Christiaan stepped back until he stumbled into a large concrete block. His whole paradigm shifted. Before him stood his best friend and arch enemy.

In the past, Blaine's hair was darker—almost coal black—but now his only hair was the stubble on his chin.

His gaze flitted to Christiaan. He wrinkled his forehead above his jet-black eyes. He scoffed, then shook his head.

Within seconds, Christiaan clasped his arms in a manly, meaningful embrace. The tension in Christiaan evaporated.

Blaine's men still held AK-47s.

Hin Cho still bled on the flooded floor, but even she lifted her gaze to the two men.

"I thought you dead." Christiaan couldn't believe his eyes. Blaine, his mentor—his savior—stood before him. "The flames, I saw you jump in."

A wide grin tore through the scars on Blaine's face. "I've been searching for you the world over. What are you going by these days?"

"Christiaan."

"Christiaan?" He chuckled, showing big white teeth. "The name suits you."

Christiaan inhaled. "What are you doing here? Tell me how you escaped the fire."

An eyebrow rose in Blaine's taut face. "You and I have been searching for the emeralds. Ironic, isn't it? The thing that broke us apart is the same thing that brought us back together."

He let out the throaty laugh Christiaan knew so well. Christiaan flexed his jaw. Blaine wasn't the youth of his memories. His eyes held no light.

"Tell me, have you changed your mind yet? Are you ready to join the New Order, Christiaan?"

"No, Blaine. I will not join you." Resolve hardened within him. All the memories crashed upon him. He flashed back to this same exact conversation years earlier in the South American Sanctuary. They had been fighting drug dealers. Blaine persuaded the Grand Master to allow a few of Blaine's friends to join the Order, friends who could not—would not—keep the oaths associated with the Order.

The Grand Master's lips drew into a straight line. He shook his head. Then he ordered Blaine to leave.

Blaine couldn't just leave. No, he had destroyed what he could not have.

A sneer twisted Blaine's features. Standing near a mainline, he smashed the butt of his automatic rifle into a pipe. Water gushed forth, spilling onto the inches of water already sloshing at their ankles. "After all these years of seeing the world descend into moral and materialistic chaos, don't you finally want to do something about it?"

Christiaan straightened. "I haven't changed my goals, Blaine." He almost murmured his response.

"The world has changed, Christiaan." Blaine's voice echoed over the water rushing from the pipes. "The oaths were thousands of years old, you see that. They no longer give you power. Without the emeralds, the Order is nothing. Help me reimagine the Order, bring it into light, and do away with archaic oaths and performances. We will have power to start a new regime with a new vision. We can irradiate materialism and go beyond what the Order restrained us to. With our new power, we can open it to anyone."

Christiaan lowered his chin. His heart pounded in his chest. "That was your vision, not mine. Your philosophy broke the Order all those years ago."

"You are not seriously continuing in the old ways?" Blaine straightened his neck.

Christiaan hefted the emeralds. "I'm restoring the Order. I have to."

"At one point, you and I had the same vision."

Christiaan set his jaw. "I never changed, Blaine. You changed."

Blaine shook his head. "The world no longer needs us as protectors. The world needs to be saved from itself."

Shaking his head, Christiaan puffed out his chest. "You're wrong. Most people in the world are still good. A few bad people and organizations exist, sure. But if you had your way, you'd destroy us all."

Blaine leveled his AK-47. "Give me the emeralds now, Christiaan."

A lump of fear swelled in Christiaan's throat. He gripped the emeralds tighter in his fist. "I won't let you remake the Order into something unrecognizable or uncontrollable. You want all the power but refuse checks and balances."

"You set artificial limitations on something that should be open to everyone." Blaine spoke through gritted teeth.

"Not everyone should wield such power. Power should be guarded and controlled—protected, even. Only trusted people should wield such power. The oaths protect the power so it won't be given to those unworthy or unproven."

Blaine snarled. "And here is where we come back to our original argument."

Christiaan backed away. "And you will never change my mind. Oaths prove our worthiness. You will never get the emeralds."

"Then I will have to kill you." His finger slid around the trigger.

"You can't kill me. You saved my life."

He raised an eyebrow. "Yes, you're right. I probably couldn't kill you. I've invested too much in you over the years. But what are your friends worth?"

Hin Cho quivered on the verge of bleeding out. Five men held Andy at gunpoint, and a red laser pointed at her chest from somewhere above him.

"I want the emeralds and the bleeding girl. Kill the other two girls and the coward." Blaine spoke over his shoulder.

Coward? Was he referring to Spencer hiding behind the stone pillar?

Mara nodded in response to Blaine's commands.

The men followed her.

She went slowly.

Blaine lowered his brow. "Mara, the girls and the coward, please."

Nausea swept over Christiaan. If only he could empty his stomach so he wouldn't feel weak. He gritted his teeth and clenched his fists. "You would know something about being a coward."

At the insult, Blaine blinked. "You call me a coward?"

"You set fire to the gulag in Akmola."

Mara halted. She faced Blaine.

Blaine sneered. "Who did you try to save again? Wives and children of Soviet spies. Traitors." He spat out the words.

"I saved a little girl."

Blaine's eyes widened. He glanced at Mara.

"Remember?" Christiaan's voice faltered at the memory. "I told you, only the little girl survived. She was burned all over, but I brought her to the hospital in Akmola. Everyone else was killed. By you. You set the fire."

"The city is now called Astana," Mara whispered, her eyes staring at a distant point. "The capital city."

Christiaan's gaze flew to Mara. The scars. She was about the right age. The incident was fifteen years ago. He waited by her bed until she was conscious, until the doctors were sure she would pull through. He remembered the smell of the antibiotic ointment they spread all over her.

Mara's gaze flicked to Christiaan. "What was the name of the little girl?"

Christiaan would never forget. "Ava."

Only her eyelids closed. "No one has called me by my name in many years." Then Mara splashed through the water toward Blaine. "You have twisted my memories. I had memories of a man, sitting by my bed for weeks, waiting for a recovery. I never saw his face. You were not that man." She shook a finger in his face.

Blaine shook his head. "But I found you."

"And fed me lies. For years, you told me he started the fires." She pointed at Christiaan. "I hated him for years. You painted him as the enemy." Her mouth dropped open. She doubled over. "You killed my mother." She winced. "You would've let me die."

"I saved you," Blaine stammered. He lowered the barrel of his gun.

Christiaan shook his head. "Are you still clinging to lies, Blaine?"

With urgent eyes, Blaine licked his lips. "Mara, he's trying to get to me through you. He's manipulating you. He set the fire." He pointed toward Christiaan. "We can talk about this later." He soothed his tone. "Kill the girls. We don't have time for this." Blaine stepped toward the sisters. "Or I'll kill them myself."

"What hospital did you take me to?" Mara stood between him and the victims.

Blaine's steps faltered.

Mara neared him, then she raised her chin. "If you saved me, what hospital did you take me to?"

"Andromed Astana." Blaine blinked.

Shaking her head, Mara scoffed. "That's a men's clinic. What other lies will you tell me?"

"The Presidential Hospital had just been built. I brought you there." Christiaan bowed his head, but the words echoed in the cavernous space. "I watched over you until I knew you would live. Then I sneaked away."

With a growl, Mara thrust herself at Blaine.

He swung a backhand and knocked her against the wall.

Light still burned in her eyes. Water lapped against her chest.

Andy stepped in her direction.

But the movement or the sound of the water drew Blaine's attention. He raised his gun again. "Don't move," Blaine commanded her. "Any of you."

Both women glared.

Christiaan faced Blaine. "You can't win, Blaine. Lies will destroy you."

His eyes narrowed. "I've already won. How do you expect to kill me? Your skills are no match for mine. We outnumber you. And you refuse to use firearms."

"I can kill you without a gun."

Blaine laughed, a brutal eruption deep within his chest. "Killing me didn't work last time, even with a gun." Blaine turned his head.

Christiaan could see the circle burnt into his skin on his neck, healed to a glistening white sheen.

"I'll never forget or forgive you for that."

Christiaan would never forget the smell of sizzling flesh under the barrel of Blaine's heated gun. Heated from overuse. Blaine's overuse. The vermilion bloodbath was fresh in Christiaan's memory, as were the screams and cries of agony fresh in his ears. "I left that scar as a reminder that I could've killed you."

Blaine sneered at him. "You should've finished me off. You're weak."

"No, I am the strong one." Christiaan couldn't kill the man who saved his life. Blaine's smile unnerved Christiaan.

"How does it feel to know that because you let me live, you've caused others to die?" He stepped closer, his voice a hoarse whisper.

Christiaan stared unflinchingly.

Stepping back, Blaine raised his chin. His eyes gleamed. "Because I lived, I have killed hundreds. You could've prevented those deaths by killing one man. Those deaths are all on your hands now because you wouldn't use a gun. You're pathetic."

With slumping shoulders, Christiaan felt his energy

falter. Was he right? He leaned against the stone pillar. Blaine was his mentor and his friend. He saved Christiaan's life. Even now, with scars marking the dissolution of years of friendship and sacrifice, Christiaan still listened to Blaine.

"He's manipulating you." Andy's voice echoed across the room.

New strength filled Christiaan. Andy was right. He shook his head, loosening the entrapment of Blaine's words. "You can't convince me I did wrong, Blaine. *You* chose to kill. You're responsible."

Blaine held out a hand. Tendons in his neck flexed. "Come with me, Christiaan. We can remake the Order. We don't have to fight. We only have to destroy all the emeralds."

Christiaan held his gaze. Resolve hardened in his chest. "No."

Blaine flattened his eyes to slits. "Oh? You're not in power here. I have all the power."

"But I have the emeralds." He slid them from his pocket. "If you want them, drop your gun and come and get them. But I warn you, you will pay with your life." Christiaan wasn't sure if he could best Blaine. Blaine had faster reflexes and more training than Christiaan. But Christiaan still had a conscience. But he might be able to buy time—time enough for the others to escape.

"I could drop you right now and take them. I don't want to kill you." Blaine retracted his gun, letting it fall to his side. "But I have no problem killing people you wish dead." With lightning speed, Blaine flipped up the barrel and trained it on Mara. "Mara betrayed you. She failed me. She deserves to die."

Horror raked Christiaan's heart. "You manipulated

her."

Blaine's eyes flashed. "She wasn't the only one to betray you."

A pit opened in Christiaan's stomach. Without flinching, he met Blaine's gaze. Who was he talking about?

Chapter 33

Christiaan couldn't hear any more betrayal. Already, his heart exploded with grief. He fell to the concrete pillar for support. A red light blazed on his chest from someone's laser sight focused on his chest.

Wading through the water, Blaine scoffed. "Haven't you guessed? Your friend, Hector, an explosives expert? He helped us get into the Opera House in Madrid. He concocted the plan to lure you to me."

The information rocked Christiaan. Heat and nausea rose within him. He stepped back into the water. Hector? He mourned Hector. With heavy heart, he alerted his parents. Tightness racked Christiaan's chest.

Blaine lowered his brows. "But for some reason, you didn't take the bait. I thought for sure if we roughed up your friend, you'd rush in to save him. What kept you? You're not becoming hardened, are you? You're still the noble one—the hero?"

Gulping for air, Christiaan replayed the scene. He would've run to Hector. But Andy held him back. He set his jaw. Andy saved his life. He kept his gaze unflinching on Blaine. "I'm no hero."

Blaine shrugged and lifted his gun again.

"Blaine, you don't have to do this." Christiaan held up his hands. Water streamed around his legs.

Blaine faced Christiaan. His scarred face twisted in

the scattered light. "You're right. I don't have to do this. You can give me the emeralds, and we can all walk away alive."

Christiaan stared. He shook his head.

"Then Mara will pay for your stubbornness. The emeralds or her?"

Christiaan's insides hollowed out. Pain racked him. "No." He swallowed around a lump in his throat. He stepped forward, the red laser still on his chest. He had to think of a compromise. Time ticked away. He couldn't lose either. "She has her own will. Let her choose." He weighed the emeralds in his hand in the red envelope. Everything he hoped for depended on what was in this pouch. Could he give away his mother and his father? His mouth was sandpaper dry. "If she comes with me, then I'll give you the emeralds." With pained tears behind his eyes, he held out the bag.

"So merciful." Blaine pulled Mara by the hair. He bent to her ear. "What do you say?"

She flinched and grabbed at her hair. Tears formed at the corners of her eyes.

Christiaan caught Mara's gaze. "Join us."

"Christiaan, you've touched my heart." With sagging shoulders, he lowered the gun. "Go to him, girl." He released her hair and pushed her toward Christiaan.

Grabbing her head, Mara arched an eyebrow and watched him as she traversed the water. Just as she reached Christiaan's outstretched hands, a shot rang out.

Mara's eyes widened. When her body collapsed under the wave, the water churned crimson.

Christiaan roared, grappled at her body, and held

her above the water. "Ava."

Mara's eyes opened. "Thank you for setting me free." She sagged in his grasp. Her eyes relaxed open.

Christiaan clutched her to his chest. Pain harrowed his soul. "Noooooo!"

Blaine motioned to one of his men.

He turned the water on full blast.

The water rushed, blocking out all other noise.

"This is where I get the emeralds, Christiaan." Blaine called over the water.

"Never!" He dragged Mara to a concrete block to keep her above the flood. Something rippled under the waves. Christiaan dove under the water. He studied the device in his hand. *Fabian's detonator.* He didn't know if it still worked or if it ever worked. But the device was his only chance to save his friends. Fueled by energy, he rushed toward Blaine.

Blaine raised his automatic rifle toward him. "You fool!"

Andy screamed.

Christiaan raised his hand above his head. "I have Fabian's device. If you, or any of your men, move, I'll plunge this button and blow up us all. Call off your men." Pain pinched his vocal cords from screaming, but he held his gaze firm on Blaine. His words echoed in the concrete room.

Blaine eyed him.

Grinding his teeth, Christiaan locked his gaze on Blaine. "I mean it. I might not use guns, but I have no issues with incendiary devices. I. Will. Kill. Us. All." The intensity in his voice scared even him. "Guns down," Christiaan shouted again. The water lapped at his waist. "Or I blow us all. How many of you feel like dying today?"

Blaine arched a brow. "This is rather dark for you, Christiaan. I can't believe you'd actually do it."

"I'd rather die than to see those emeralds in your hands, but if I'm going to die, then so will we all." Sweat prickled at his body and trickled down his back.

The water gushed from the broken pipe. Soon it would be chest high.

"If we settle this, it will be between you and me. Just like we've always done. You and me." Christiaan didn't flinch and wouldn't hesitate this time.

"I don't think so." Blaine pointed his rifle at Christiaan's chest.

"No." At the top of the stairs, Andy screamed.

A woman flew out of the shadows. The flash of red hair identified her. Wading through the water at lightning speed, Aiofa approached Blaine. "He's mine." She shot his chest. Blood tainted the water around him.

Blaine moved with the hit. He finally swung his gun around to the woman charging him.

Yet, she reached him first. She kicked the Commander in the face, sending him and his gun sprawling.

Christiaan waded through the water. Grabbing Aiofa, he half swam, half waded through the water to a pillar. He held both her shoulders. "Aiofa, stop. This goes way beyond Madrid. Please, let me take care of this."

Fury burned in her eyes. "We had a deal. You were to bring him to me."

"But that was before I knew who he was." Water dripped down his face.

"You know him?" She spat the words.

"I've known him more than half my life."

Her jaw tightened. "He killed Philipe."

"He's killed a lot of people." But years ago, Blaine saved his life—saved many lives. Splashing sounds distracted Christiaan.

Clutching his wound, Blaine ducked behind the pillar in a rush of water. A gunshot rang out.

Aiofa sagged into the water.

Christiaan roared. He checked her pulse. Faint but there.

Above him, Andy shot the man who shot Aiofa. In the confusion, Andy must've disarmed the men who held her.

But the fight wasn't over.

Water gushed from the pipes, filling the room, covering sounds, and creating waves. This whole area would be filled with water. The emergency lights around the doorways cast unholy shadows across the room. Guns and powder were useless except for those used by the people above them on the stairs, but Andy had him covered.

Christiaan searched through the quickly rising water for the detonator he'd lost while grabbing Aiofa.

Spencer threaded his way through the water. He lifted Aiofa, still bleeding, out of the water and floated her to safety behind a pillar.

With his hand over his side wound, Blaine moved slowly, fighting the effects of Aiofa's bullet. "Christiaan." His voice struggled over the rushing water. "This is about you and me now."

Spencer waded through over waist-high water to the concrete pillar and found an outcropping and leaned Aiofa against it, out of the water.

Water dripped from Christiaan's face. He spoke softly over the water rushing into the cement cavern. "Do you think you can get the women out of here?"

Spencer nodded. His black clothes dripped. He shook either from fear or from cold.

Christiaan tried to locate Blaine in the maze of pillars. The deeper water clouded the lights, making the room darker. "All right, then. I'll create a distraction." He clasped Spencer on his shoulder, handing him the emeralds in the red envelope. He nearly shouted over the rushing water. "Take Andy and the sisters to safety. Keep these emeralds as far away as possible. If I don't come back, make sure you get them to someone in the Order of Destroying Angels."

Spencer gave a wild-eyed stare.

"Go!" Now he saw his own blood. Though the shot went through Aiofa, it must've grazed him. He must not have felt it because of his adrenaline. Blood oozed from his side. A dark sickly mess mingled with the water, tingeing it pink. The water rose to chest high.

Finally, Spencer moved. He waded through the water and tripped but caught himself with his hand on a concrete pillar.

Christiaan shook his head. He trusted the fate of his Order on Spencer? His black costume dripped as he climbed the metal stairs to Andy and the sisters.

Above him, Andy tied up all the men in black.

Christiaan needed to stall for time and give Spencer enough time to get far away. He still couldn't see where Blaine hid. "How did you survive?" He wanted to pinpoint his location.

"That's what we are: survivors." Rushing water nearly drowned out the sound of Blaine's voice. "You left me there." Emergency light reflected off the water.

"No, Blaine. You don't remember. I went to get help. You've forgotten."

"All I remember is my friend left me."

Christiaan shook his head. He caught a sliver of Blaine's face. Christiaan didn't have anything. Not a knife, and not a club. The detonator was lost. "I would never leave you unless it meant saving your life."

"But you are alive. And you have the emeralds."

"Yes." He leaned against a pillar. Hopefully, they were traveling far from here in Spencer's pocket.

The water must've reached where it rushed out. A sudden silence fell over the cavern.

"The world is a terrible place, Christiaan."

At last, he caught a glimpse of Blaine. "Yes, but you and I see different enemies."

Leaning against a block of concrete, Blaine glared. "If you are not with us, then you are against us. I'm afraid you'll have to die."

Rising out of the water, Christiaan peeked at his wound again. Blood dribbled from his side. Now that he was aware of his shot, pain wracked through him. "You can't have the emeralds. They are far too powerful and should only be used in the right hands."

"And you say my hands are not right?"

"Your hands have blood on them. They are not clean."

Blaine let out a yell. "You can't rebuild the Order. There aren't enough pure people in the world. People are weak."

"You're wrong. Good people abound in this world. People are willing to sacrifice and to live according to a code. Andy is one of them. And Spencer." He couldn't believe he admitted that. The water lapped at his armpits. "Even Aifoa, Hin Cho, and her sister, as well." If he didn't survive this, at least the emeralds would live, and someone would be able to re-establish the Order.

"Give me the emeralds, then." Blaine called around the pillar. "And I'll save your people when I start my purge. You can't win in a hand-to-hand combat with me, Christiaan. You've never been able to."

The truth of Blaine's words stung Christiaan. His wound exhausted him. "I cannot give them to you. I don't have them." Hopefully, Spencer ran far, far away with the emeralds.

Nearly neck deep in water, Blaine rushed at him with his knife drawn. "You will have to die."

"I don't care. You will never get the emeralds." Blaine grappled with Christiaan.

The near neck-deep water impaired his movements, but Blaine fought better. The water was cold. Moving helped warm Christiaan. Blaine battered him—blocked his punches and attacks. At last, Blaine overpowered him, holding Christiaan in a stranglehold, about to cut his throat.

"Our friendship didn't have to be like this," Blaine whispered.

"I would rather die than to let you destroy the emeralds." Christiaan spit. His breath was running out. Darkness clouded the corners of his eyes. This was the end. He would die here.

Then something flew through the air and landed in the water in front of Blaine. A red envelope—the red envelope he gave Spencer not minutes before.

It sank below the water, out of sight.

Blaine's grasp loosened.

Gasping for air, Christiaan glanced up, holding his neck. He set his jaw. Spencer was an idiot!

Spencer smiled from above. "Here are the emeralds. Now, let him go. Do you really think I'm pure in heart, Christiaan, ol' boy? I'm flattered."

"Spencer, what are you doing?" Heat spread through him. He wanted to wrap his hands around Spencer's neck until he turned blue.

"Emeralds are not worth someone's life." Spencer cupped his mouth to shout the words.

Christiaan tightened his throat. "Those emeralds are worth more than everyone's life."

"Not yours."

Blaine released Christiaan, his face twisted in a smile at the rippling red bag just below the surface. He dove under the water.

Christiaan saw a chance. He slogged through the neck-high water as Blaine stuck his head under the water to reach for the packet. He knocked over Blaine, searching for the emeralds.

"Let him have them," Spencer called. "Come on. While you still have a chance."

Christiaan stopped. Water eddied around his neck.

Blaine scrambled under the water.

"Do you trust me?" Spencer lowered his head, then he cracked a smile. "Come. I'll wager you'll be glad you did."

Turmoil roiled within Christiaan. Trust was not something he gave easily. He bit his lip. Christiaan glanced one more time at Blaine searching for the emeralds. He gave them up for Mara and Hin Cho, so he could give them up for his own life. Emotional pain shook his chest. Allowing Blaine to win killed him.

Blaine's head broke through the water again. He howled, breathing before diving underneath the dark water.

The water continued to rise.

Setting his jaw, Christiaan climbed the stairs. Did he trust Spencer?

Chapter 34

Once outside, a chill infected Christiaan. He shivered. Dawn approached, but the wind whipped the wet clothes against him. Tension ached in his shoulders and temples. Outside, he took Aiofa from Spencer.

She hung lifelessly off his shoulders, dripping as well.

"We did it." Spencer elbowed him. "A few times, I didn't think we would make it."

Christiaan scowled. He stumbled on the dirt road. "We didn't make it. The emeralds will be in his hands." A pit formed at the bottom of his stomach. Defeat left bitter aftertaste in his mouth. He was so close.

After securing the sisters on the roadside of a concrete barrier blocking the dirt road up to the water cistern in the mountain, Andy stood.

Christiaan laid Aiofa against the base on the roadside next to the sisters. They needed an ambulance. Inhaling and crossing his arms, he leaned against the barrier facing the mountain. The emeralds were in Blaine's hands. Now what?

Stars twinkled above him. Lights from the city glowed on the horizon.

Next to him, Andy patted his hand. "At least we escaped with our lives."

Setting his jaw, he shook his head. "You don't understand. If he gets them, the Order will be over. And no one will be strong enough to stop him, or the likes of him, without the emeralds."

"You mean these emeralds?" Spencer slipped a red envelope from his jacket pocket and waved it in front of Christiaan's face.

"What?" Christiaan grabbed the envelope and dumped the contents into his hands. Green splashes of light winked in the night light. Could it be? Holding his breath, he blinked. Relief flooded his body. "You dunce. Where did you get these?"

"You gave them to me."

The tension in Christiaan's neck and shoulders relaxed. He almost wanted to hug Spencer, but not quite. Pointing to the mountain, he furrowed his brows. "Then what did you give Blaine?"

Shrugging, Spencer grinned. "The rocks I won in an unfair bet against a liar. Admit it, the plan was brilliant."

"I thought of it first." Christiaan couldn't bring himself to give Spencer a compliment, although the move was a stroke of genius. "We'd better get a move on. Once he discovers the fakes, he'll be after us."

"I also found this." Spencer held out Fabian's device. "I bet this isn't a real bomb detonator."

"Even if it were, I doubt it works after being dunked in the water." Christiaan cast him a sideways glance. "I used it as a bluff. Don't click it, just to be sure."

"I doubt that Fabian creature would think that far in advance. Here, I'll prove it. I bet it was a phony to begin with." Spencer pressed his thumb on the red button.

Christiaan heard Andy swear before he lost his

hearing to the fiery explosion behind them.

She dove, along with Spencer, for the cover behind the concrete wall. An inferno lit up the night sky.

Water blew upward and caught the light of the city in a radiant flash. Water poured down the mountainside, ripping out trees and causing a mudslide. Small chunks of concrete rained around him.

Christiaan glared at Spencer.

Andy punched Spencer's shoulder.

With wide eyes, Spencer gulped. Mud smeared his chin and cheekbones. "I lost that bet."

Shaking his head, Christiaan gritted his teeth. What a mess! How would they explain this to the officials? "I should've placed a wager then."

"I would've gladly paid out for that one." Spencer frowned.

In the distance, sirens screamed.

Andy nodded toward the wounded women. "Well, that was one way to get the ambulance out here quickly."

Christiaan studied the blown mountain. Trees lay on their sides, and a gaping hole exposed crumbling cement. Water gushed down the dirt road turning it into a river. Was Blaine still inside searching for the emeralds in the water, or did he escape? He never wanted to find out.

****

Andy, with the help of Spencer and Christiaan, nestled Aiofa and Hin Cho in the back of an ambulance.

Hin Chi rode with them and translated.

Andy waited until the women were safely away in the ambulance before she exhaled. She held the blanket around her damp shoulders. Her head throbbed. She had no idea what time it was. But the sun peeped above the horizon. Every bit of her body ached. She blinked dry eyes.

Christiaan slipped his hand into hers and led her away from the noise of the fire engines, and the police, wading in knee-deep mud and securing the mountain.

News crews reported the story to cameras in a language Andy didn't understand. Police questioned Spencer, who surrendered the detonator.

"Was all this hoopla worth securing the emeralds?" Andy asked.

The wreckage of the bomb devastated the area.

He dipped his head. "Of course."

"What will happen to Hin Cho? Will the Chinese authorities keep her here?"

He stopped and drew her near. "I don't know."

She studied his face—the scar in his eyebrow. "And us? What will happen to us?"

Wrapping his arms around her waist, he embraced her. Her clothes still clung to her body in the humidity. "That depends on you. I need help establishing the Order."

Would you take me with you? The words formed in her heart, but she never gave them breath. She didn't dare hope. The mud clung to her shoes under her feet.

"Would you help me avenge my parents?"

She lifted her head. "Me?" Her heartbeat kicked up a few notches. He wanted her to come?

"You can't get away from danger and adventure. This is your life. You know you need to be righting wrongs and fighting injustice, Andy. It is your calling. You can't go back to school. You have a gift."

If she got info from OverSight about her father, she

didn't need to go back to school. She swallowed hard. "But won't being with me be difficult? For both of us? Because of your oaths?" As much as she wanted him, she knew he wanted something else more.

Christiaan exhaled.

His breath tickled the hairs on her forehead.

"I'm willing to risk it, if you are."

Her heart beat in her throat. She could scarce draw breath. "I am."

He pulled her closer. "Then I'm not letting you out of my sight."

Andy tilted up her chin and met his lips in the sweetest embrace. His breath brushed her face. His warm hand cupped her chin. Despite the chill, warmth exploded through her.

"I see you two."

Andy broke and shot a scowl over her shoulder.

With a grin, Spencer hiked up the road to meet them. "The police want us to make a formal report at the station." He clapped his hands. "Chop. Chop."

Andy wanted the moment to last forever, but hand in hand with Christiaan, she followed Spencer down the mountain.

Chapter 35

At the police station in Kowloon, Christiaan shouldered his way past Spencer to explain to officials why the water tank blew up in Chinese. "The bomb was set up by a psychopath and set off by an idiot."

Spencer glared at Christiaan.

Christiaan glared at Spencer and finished explaining who all was there and why until ten in the morning.

Once outside and cleared of all wrong-doing, Christiaan sighed, strolling into the sun. Aiofa was mending well in the hospital. And Hin Cho and her sister were recovering, as well. "Well, nice to work with you, but Andy needs to get home."

Spencer bowed toward Andy. "A pleasure working with the beautiful and uncompromising Andy Baker." He swooped up her hand and kissed it. "Promise me you'll not change for anything."

Andy blushed.

"And as for you." Spencer turned to Christiaan and held out a hand.

Christiaan reluctantly took it.

"Always a pleasure to find someone of incomparable skill, talent, and the ability to annoy. I acknowledge we are equals."

Huffing, Christiaan still stood aloof, eyeing the outstretched hand. He grasped the proffered palm. He squeezed it—perhaps a little too hard. "No hard feelings?"

"No hard feelings." Spencer winced.

"Good." Christiaan squeezed, delighting in Spencer's squirm just a bit before releasing. "Until next time."

****

With bated breath, Andy snuggled next to Christiaan on the London Eye.

"So what's next?" He brushed aside hair and kissed her on the neck.

The Thames swirled below them as the pod rose higher above the fog. "I tried to get a degree to apply to the CIA. I wanted to become a master of disguise so I could find my father."

"But now, you're not so sure."

The gray skies hid the milky sun. She sighed. "Now, I don't know what I want."

He kissed her cheek. "Sabrina says you have a job at OverSight. No degree needed. You'd have access to resources to find your father." He paused. His blue eyes searched her face. "You want something else?"

Not having to get a degree did give her a shortcut to her goal. She inhaled. "I want to find my mother, too."

"Then join." He smirked. "And we can search for your parents and avenge mine."

"You're not scared anymore?"

He huffed. "Of what?"

"Of me?"

He barked out a laugh. "I will always be afraid of you, Andy Baker." London spread beneath them. "But I will never be afraid to be with you."

"Then we'll work together?"

He nodded. "Together."

Skeptical of his last offer and desertion, she arched a brow. "Shall we shake on it?"

"I'd prefer to kiss on it, instead." Christiaan leaned in for a kiss.

Andy blocked him. "You know. Spencer could still be MI5. He could be lying."

Christiaan gasped. "Gah, can you not accept reality?"

A flood of assurance filled her. "No, but I'm always right."

He grunted again. "I am a better judge of character than you are. Are you going to close your mouth, or do I have to close it for you?"

"I can totally take you." But before she could even react, his lips brushed hers. "I like this way of shutting up," she said between kisses.

"It must not be working. You're still talking."

He bent down and enveloped her mouth in the sweetest kiss. His lips tickled hers with undulating rhythm.

Chapter 36

Back in Christiaan's London flat, Sabrina handed Andy a folder.

"What's this?"

"Our agreement, remember?"

Andy slid the folder from Sabrina's genteel fingers and thanked her.

With realization, she felt her heartbeat thunder in her ears. This was information about her father. She slid her fingers under the tab and opened it. The file contained a picture of her dad—a much younger version, with more hair, less gray, and far fewer wrinkles.

His name caught her eye. Blazoned across the top of the file was Mikal Moworitz. Born in Ukraine.

Her stomach dropped. Andy's heartbeat quickened. Sweat pricked her body.

Men lie. Even her father.

Chapter 37

Dear Chris,

You don't mind if I call you that, do you? Since we are such good friends, and because you helped Her Majesty's Intelligence Service crack a particularly nasty case of human trafficking, game fixing, and kidnapping, I took the liberty of securing some sensitive information on a particular terrorist group whose leader's name is Viper. I enjoyed working with you and hope we can work together in the future.

Peter Spencer
MI6 Secret Intelligence Service
Vauxhill, London

With wide eyes, Christiaan clicked on the secured files. As the pages began to pop up on the screen, he felt his heart rate increase. His goal was closer than he hoped.

A word about the author…

Amey loves writing about different places because she grew up moving all around the United States. In her books, she explores the whole world. She is also the author of Baker's Dozen, a Romantic Suspense Mystery. The Swiss Mishap, a romantic comedy, won a Swoony for 2019's Best New Adult Contemporary Romance and won third place in the Book Buyer's Best Contest.

She lives with her husband and three children near Austin, TX. Follow her on BookBub, IG or Twitter @ameyzeigler and sign up for her newsletter at www.ameyzeigler.com

Other Titles by this Author
August Blues
Baker's Dozen
Summer of Sundaes
Swiss Mistletoe and Macarons
The Swiss Mishap
Wylder Bride

Thank you for purchasing
this publication of The Wild Rose Press, Inc.

For questions or more information
contact us at
info@thewildrosepress.com.

The Wild Rose Press, Inc.
www.thewildrosepress.com